A SELLSWORD'S VALOR

Book Four
of
The Seven Virtues
by
Jacob Peppers

This book is a work of fiction. Names, characters, places and incidents are either the product of the author's imagination or are used fictitiously. Any resemblance to actual persons, living or dead, or to actual events or locales is entirely coincidental.

A Sellsword's Valor
Book Four of the Seven Virtues

This book is licensed for your personal enjoyment only. This book may not be re-sold or given away to other people. If you would like to share this book with another person, please purchase an additional copy for each person you share it with. If you're reading this book and did not purchase it, or it was not purchased for your use only, then you should return to the retailer and purchase your own copy. Thank you for respecting the hard work of the author.

Copyright © 2018 Jacob Nathaniel Peppers. All rights reserved, including the right to reproduce this book, or portions thereof, in any form. No part of this text may be reproduced, transmitted, downloaded, decompiled, reverse engineered, or stored in or introduced into any information storage and retrieval system, in any form or by any means, whether electronic or mechanical without the express written permission of the author. The scanning, uploading, and distribution of this book via the Internet or via any other means without the permission of the publisher is illegal and punishable by law. Please purchase only authorized electronic editions, and do not participate in or encourage electronic piracy of copyrighted materials.

The publisher does not have any control over and does not assume any responsibility for author or third-party websites or their content.

Visit the author's website:
www.JacobPeppersAuthor.com

To mom,

What imagination I have,

I have because of you.

Sign up for the author's New Releases mailing list and get a copy of *The Silent Blade*, the prequel for The Seven Virtues, FREE for a Limited Time!

Go to JacobPeppersAuthor.com to get your free book!

CHAPTER ONE

Allia walked Baresh's Merchant's Street, weaving in and out of the bustle of people as they visited their favorite shops in search of some new trinket or bobble to waste their money on. She passed a shop where the owner shouted to passersby about his latest tonic, guaranteed to put hair on a man's chest while, at the same time, making a woman's body hair vanish. Allia thought it a foolish claim. After all, how would the potion know what did or didn't swing between the legs of the person who drank it? Nevertheless, the merchant had a crowd of at least a dozen people gathered around listening to his pitch in rapt attention.

If she hadn't been on the job, Allia would have most likely stopped and asked the man some pointed questions about his so-called tonic, but instead she only walked past, shaking her head in disgust.

The poor spent their time looking for money to support their families while, it seemed to her, the rich and wealthy searched for the next ridiculous thing to spend their coin on. The thought made her angry, and she almost turned around before grunting and forcing herself onward down the street. She glanced at the shops and vendors she passed so as not to arouse suspicion, but she never let her gaze stray far from her two marks.

Her mom, when she was sober enough to speak—less and less often of late—used to tell her that she had a nose for finding trouble and should only be thankful that the gods had given her the feet for getting out of it. These days though, the only words out of her mom's mouth were "Where's the wine?" or "Allie, you fool girl, pass your poor old mother her pipe." A pipe which was filled with tamarang, the same herb that was slowly killing her and hundreds of other addicts in the city.

Still, her mom was right about one thing; Allia *was* fast. She always had been. Something she'd had reason to be thankful for nearly every day in the years since her mother had lost her job at the clerk's office, and they'd ended up living on the street. Or at least, they would have if Allia, a girl of eight years at the time, hadn't taken matters into her own hands, stealing what they needed from those who had plenty to spare.

She didn't even look at it as a crime, not really. After all, she never stole from the poor or struggling, only the rich and well-off. If she didn't take the money, they'd only find some inane use for it anyway. Buying another shirt they didn't need or a dress they didn't want—who knows, maybe even a magic tonic to grow hair on their chest, though the gods alone knew why any man would want that, or why any woman would want it on her man, for that matter.

Not that Allia was an expert on men or relationships—though she could have been, if she'd wished it. She never really thought much about how she looked, but she'd heard enough to know that she was considered pretty by men—maybe even beautiful—and what virtue she had would have been gone long ago if not for the feet her mother talked about. It was a dangerous thing to live a life in the poor quarter as a young, pretty girl, but it wasn't as if she had a choice in the matter. Besides, as much as her looks might have been a burden, they also came in handy from time to time, particularly when she was on the job.

Allia realized she'd let herself become distracted by thoughts of her mother and glanced back up only to see that the couple she'd been following was gone, lost in the crowd that packed the streets. *Fool girl,* Allia scolded herself, though as was often the case it wasn't her voice she heard in the reprimand, but her mother's. Her mother rarely spoke now as the drug robbed her of her mind, but "fool girl" was one of the few phrases she remembered. *Lucky me.* She cursed and weaved her way through the crowd, her slight frame helping her to dodge around the people cluttering the streets and between the horse-drawn carts that slowly made their way down it.

She was just starting to accept that she'd lost the couple in truth when she picked them up again on the other side of the street, browsing the wares of a fat merchant's shop. Allia breathed a sigh of relief and made her way across the street, ignoring the angry shouts of one of the cart drivers as she darted in front of his horses. She paused at a tailor's shop, glancing inside at the dresses as if considering buying one, but she kept the couple in the corner of her vision. A well-dressed man in spectacles walked out of the shop, moving toward her, and she fought back an annoyed sigh.

"Hello there, little miss," he said, adjusting the spectacles on his nose. Allia had to fight back a frown at that. She'd had a hard life, had been forced to care for herself for years, and she wasn't fond of being called "little miss."

"Hello," she said, not bothering to look at him, hoping that he'd take the hint and go away.

He didn't though, and that was no surprise.

"A fine day we're having isn't it? Nice warm weather to make up for the cold spell we've been having lately."

Allia glanced up at the clear sky. The truth was, she hadn't been paying attention to the weather at all. She noticed when it was cold—the poor always did. Never enough blankets or enough clothes to keep the chill out, never enough wood to feed the fire ... but when the weather was fine, she always had other things to worry over. "Yes, I suppose it is."

The man grinned widely, leaning in close and following her eyes, which were once more on the shop's window, keeping track of the couple. "Oh yes," he said, "that's a fine dress. If you don't mind me saying so, you would look quite lovely in it, though, to be fair, a rare beauty such as yours would look lovely even in rags."

Allia harrumphed at that, a very unladylike sound that her mother had been trying to break her of. But, then, she'd been trying to break her mother of slowly killing herself smoking tamarang and that hadn't worked, so she'd keep her habits, thank you very much. And anyway, she *didn't* look lovely in rags; she'd worn enough in her time to know it. Still wore them, in fact, when she wasn't on the job and forced to wear the only fine dress she owned—an expense that had set her back for a week's work at least, but one that was necessary to avoid drawing the attention of the guards that regularly patrolled the streets.

"Would my lady like to try it on?"

Allia snorted this time—the only thing her mother hated more than the harrumph. *A lady now, am I?* She considered what this finely-dressed tailor might say if he saw the one room shack she and her mother called a home. Probably "lady" wouldn't be the first word that came to mind. Still, her craft, such as it was, was all about avoiding attention, so she really looked at the dress for the first time. "It is a very fine garment," she said, doing her best to mimic the bored, somehow whiny tones that seemed to be a way of speaking reserved solely for pampered noblewomen. "Still, I'm afraid I left my coin purse at the manse." *Manse,* she thought, and was only just able to hold her laughter back. "Perhaps I will come back for it another time." She hoped that would be the end of it, and the man would leave. Unfortunately, she wasn't that lucky.

"Ah," the tailor said, his jovial expression disappearing in an instant, "I see." Then he seemed to have an idea, and the smile he flashed her this time wasn't friendly, but slimy—a smile with certain expectations. She'd know well enough—she'd been given such smiles before, usually while the owner of that smile held some half-molded piece of bread or some stringy, rancid meat in front of her as if it were some fine delicacy.

"Well, if my young miss has forgotten her coin that is no great affair. A beauty such as yours deserves to wear a dress befitting its grace. I'm sure that, if you'd like to follow me inside," he said, leaning close enough that she could smell the sickly sweet odor of his breath, "we might come to some…mutually beneficial arrangement."

"Oh," she said, nodding and putting on her best innocent expression, "that is very kind, sir, very kind. Let me just ask my father and make sure it is alright with him—I'm sure he'll wish to thank you for your kindness." She looked around as if trying to find him. "Now, I wonder where he ran off to. He was here just a moment ago…"

The tailor squirmed, obviously uncomfortable. "Ah, well, please do tell your father I said hello, miss," he said, the lecherous look nowhere in evidence now, "and please forgive me, as I just realized there is a matter that requires my immediate attention."

"Oh, you're leaving?" Allia said in that same innocent voice, unable to help herself. "So soon?"

The tailor cleared his throat, nodding. "Sadly I must, my lady," he said, glancing around nervously as if he expected her fictitious father to materialize at any moment wielding a broadsword and screaming in rage like one of the barbarians from stories she'd heard as a child. "But I do hope you enjoy the day."

"You as well," Allia said, smiling, but the man was already disappearing into his shop once more. Snorting in satisfaction, she turned and ambled leisurely farther down the street, toward her marks. The woman wore a fine blue dress, the man rich sable trousers and a white, puffy shirt, but it was the bulging coin purse at his side that had first caught her attention and had held it for the last two hours. She shook her head once again in wonder at the thought that anyone would be so naïve as to keep his purse so visible for anyone's eyes to catch and anyone's hands to grab. Even the children of the poor district knew better than that, but the rich, as a whole, seemed preposterously terrible at protecting their coin. So much so that she sometimes wondered how they had any at all.

"You see, Mother," she muttered to herself as she made her way down the street, weaving around the crowd, "I'm not a criminal. I'm a teacher." Not that she would ever tell her mother as much in person, for her mother's anger was a fitfully sleeping beast, easily roused, and Allia had been left with more than one bruise for waking it.

Her good mood at the tailor's discomfort suddenly gone, Allia walked up to stand at the shop adjacent to where the woman was currently trying on a large, shining necklace, from which hung a jewel nearly as big as Allia's fist. The shop owner watched with a mixture of excitement and nervousness, licking his lips, his hands fidgeting anxiously as if to catch the precious necklace should the woman lose her hold on it.

A dangerous thought flashed into Allia's mind. The coin purse would be all well and good, no doubt its contents enough to provide food for her and her mother for at least a week—not that her mother did any more than peck at any meal. It sometimes seemed to Allia that the woman survived solely off of the smoke of the tamarang herb and whatever nutritional content she accidentally imbibed with her wine. The necklace though…such a prize as that would mean months, possibly as much as a year's worth of food and clothes, as well as the medicine her mother sometimes purchased for her aches and pains. Staring at the necklace, Allia thought there would even be plenty left over for them to stay at an inn, a place where they would never have to worry about the roof leaking or falling through when it rained or snowed.

Don't you even think it, Allie, she told herself, again in her mother's voice. *Just put it right out of your mind.* But the thought didn't *want* to be put out of her mind, and she stood there for several indecisive moments. *No,* she finally decided. It wasn't worth it. True, the guards would search for the woman responsible for stealing a man's coin purse, but they'd give it up as a lost cause soon enough. Baresh was a big city, after all, and there were many noblemen with many purses. The necklace though…that was a different story. Such an item as that would have a reward attached to it, and more than one enterprising young guard, looking to buy his way into his superiors' good graces or, more likely, into the good graces of his lady love, would be most interested in catching the person responsible.

Still, the necklace really was beautiful. Not that she'd ever consider wearing such a thing herself—might as well wear a sign saying "rob me." But she knew there were those in the poor district who would pay quite handsomely for such an item. Not its actual worth, of course—they *were* criminals after all—but enough that she and her mother would be well-fed for many months to come.

Don't Allie. Just don't. She eased her way up to the couple as the woman admired the necklace on her neck and the man admired a spot somewhere a few inches below that. Allia felt her face heat at the noblewoman's low-cut dress. It seemed that the man and woman both loved to put what wealth they had on display for all to see. Fools and ones that could do with a lesson. "If you don't mind me saying, my lady," Allia said, "that is quite a beautiful necklace. It looks radiant on you."

The couple and the shopkeeper turned to look at the new visitor in their midst. The woman smiled as if she expected as much. "Thank you, dear," she said, preening, "it really is quite fine."

"Yes, fine indeed," the man said in a distracted sort of way as his eyes roamed up and down Allia. "My wife is, of course, quite lovely. Though, I wonder how it would look on you yourself, madam."

Don't even think it, Allie. "Oh," Allia said, holding up a hand and not having to fake the blush that rose to her cheeks, "I couldn't."

"Oh, come now don't be so modest," the man said, winking at her before turning back to his wife. "May I see it, dear?"

The woman smiled, but Allia could see the annoyance lurking under the expression. "Of course," she said, taking the necklace off and handing it to her husband as if already bored with it.

The shopkeeper opened his mouth to object, but glanced at the noble couple, obviously wealthy by their dress and manner, and thought better of it.

"There you are," the man said, sliding the necklace over Allia's long blonde hair, his hand contriving, somehow, to brush her breast as he drew it back. "Quite lovely indeed."

And just like that, Allia's decision was made for her. She bowed her head slightly. "You are too kind, sir, truly."

The man smiled, winking once more. "You cannot imagine how kind I can be, lady."

His wife cleared her throat at that, but Allia was considering her options and barely paid it any attention. "Still," she said, starting to take the necklace off, "I really can't—" She stumbled then, bumping into the table the shopkeeper had set outside of his shop and sending several trinkets and bobbles—none as nice as the necklace—falling to the ground. "Oh gods, but I'm a clumsy fool," she said, "please forgive me."

The shopkeeper let out a yelp and dropped to his knees, hurriedly scooping up the items as if he thought at any moment some thief would materialize and run off with them. If only he knew the thief was already there. The nobleman smiled, putting a hand on her shoulder where he squeezed it in a possessive, insinuating way, "Never fear," he said, laughing. Then he, too, bent to pick up some of the merchant's goods as if to display his chivalry.

For her part, his wife rolled her eyes and looked around at the street as if searching for some distraction, and it was then that

Allia bent down enough to draw the slim knife secreted at her ankle.

While everyone's attention was elsewhere, her hand shot forward, little more than a blur, and cleanly sliced through the knot holding the man's coin purse to his trousers. The purse fell into her empty, waiting hand, and she disappeared into the crowd a moment later, none of them the wiser.

At least, that was how she thought it would happen.

Instead, the small knife didn't cut the knot in one smooth motion, only scored the leather. "You there," said the wife, who'd looked back at the worst possible time. "Are you trying to *steal* that?"

Allia's forehead broke into a sudden sweat, and she grabbed the man's purse with one hand where it was still attached to his waist and pulled it out as far as she could, sawing at the knotted thread with the small knife, her face flushed and feverish.

The husband, responding to his wife's tone, rose and turned to Allia only to see her finish cutting the purse free with an audible *rip.* "What?" the husband asked, a confused look on his face as he no doubt tried to understand how his charms had not worked on her.

The wife, though, was faster. "*Guards!*" she screamed. "Thief!"

Allia turned, her heart hammering a rapid beat in her chest, and pushed her way into the crowd, stumbling and nearly dropping the purse. She risked a quick glance behind her and saw that the wife and the shopkeeper were both screaming now, pointing their fingers at her, and several frowning guards were pushing the gathered people out of the way and coming toward her. The truth was, it wasn't the first time her hands had betrayed her in a critical moment, but she wasn't worried. Traitors her hands might be, but her feet were loyal and swift, and she used them then, breaking free of the crowd and sprinting down a nearby alley for all she was worth.

She ran faster and faster, putting on more and more speed until the angry shouts of the guards and the nobles soon dwindled behind her.

***

"—back here, you ungrateful bitch!"

A plate shattered on the wall less than a foot from Allia's head an instant before she threw the door to their house wide and stumbled into the street, slamming it shut behind her. An instant later, there was another crash, and Allia winced. *Look at the bright side,* she thought as she rubbed at her shoulder where the first of the three volleys had caught her, *she's out of plates now.*

She reminded herself to stop and buy some more as soon as she could. Otherwise, they'd be eating with their hands all because her mother hadn't wanted to understand that she was out of tamarang, going so far as to accuse Allia of *stealing* it. Not true, of course. Allia had her sins, but smoking the killing herb was not one of them and never would be.

She looked up and saw that the moon had risen in full now and darkness had fallen on the city. Allia frowned, troubled. Everyone in the poor quarter knew to avoid going out at night, especially alone. Those who did were either fools or criminals. She considered going back inside, but she could still hear her mother screaming through the door, so she decided against it. They might be out of plates, but there were other things she could throw—if she was able to think enough past the daze in her mind to realize it, of course.

An hour, two at the most, and her mother would be fast asleep. Not peacefully asleep, never that, for among all of its other side effects, tamarang was known to induce nightmares. Ones so vivid that, in the worst cases, people had clawed their eyes out in their sleep to avoid the terrible sights their dreams conjured.

She glanced uneasily around the street. It appeared empty, but that didn't mean much. Those who traveled the darkness of the poor district's streets waiting for their next victim were rarely kind enough to stand in plain view, as many careless fools had learned to their misfortune. *An easy enough thing to say,* she thought, *but, just now, Allie dear, you're one of those fools. And the gods know you have more reason than most to fear the night.*

And that was true enough. If the very real threat of being mugged, killed, or worse wasn't enough to send a shiver of fear up her back, there was always Hector. Hector, the leader of a small gang who had decided he wanted her and cared nothing for her own thoughts on the subject. Hector who, the last time she'd seen him—in a quick glance over her shoulder as she ran away from him and his men—had been bleeding from his broken nose. A nose *she* had broken when he had ignored her rebuffs and sought to take what he wanted without her consent.

Allia looked around once more, assuring herself that the street was empty, but the fact that she saw no one gave her little comfort. Her feet might be extraordinary, but her eyes were only average, and such men as might be waiting in the darkness were well-practiced at blending into the shadows.

Swallowing hard, her hands suddenly damp with sweat, she decided she would visit the Shelter. It was little more than a squat, ugly building that had once been the warehouse of some ambitious—and failing—merchant. He'd hoped to take advantage of the lower property prices the poor district offered by storing his goods in a large warehouse.

Of course, it had been only a matter of weeks before the entire place had been picked clean by thieves, no matter how many guards the man had hired. Since then, since long before Allia had been born, it had been the home of Nicoliander, an ex-priest of Salen's death cult who now used what little money he had or was given to offer a meal—a thin, tasteless broth, usually—and a safe place for the night to those who came to him.

Allia had been forced to make use of the place several times herself, often with her mother, and she considered the old priest a friend. Plus, there was the added benefit that the shelter was only fifteen minutes' walk away from where she now stood. *Fifteen minutes,* she thought, *you can do that, Allia. After all, what can happen in fifteen minutes?* The problem, of course, was that she knew the answer to that question all too well. Anything could happen in such a time. Anything at all.

She felt eyes on her as she walked, though whether real or imagined she did not know. *It's been a month since you broke his nose,* she told herself, *surely he's forgotten you by now.* She knew it was a lie even as she thought it. Men like Hector didn't forget a slight, no matter how small, but kept a tally of each debt owed, each revenge not yet taken, waiting for the moment to extract what they felt was their due.

Without realizing it, she'd started to walk faster, not jogging, not quite, but close. *Just relax,* she told herself, *everything's going to be fine. Ten more minutes, no more than that. Just take it easy and walk—don't run, never that, things that run are chased—but don't dally either. You'll be okay.*

The last felt like another lie, but she knew that if she could make it to the Shelter she *would* be okay. Even if Hector or his men knew she was there, they wouldn't come in. There were rumors—ones told often enough that most folks tended to believe them—that Nico was a practitioner of some dark, foul magic. Lies, of course, but even so, Hector wouldn't risk the anger of the entire district by causing trouble in Nico's shelter. It was one of the few places—possibly the only one—that was, by unspoken mutual accord, off-limits to any of the criminals.

A drunken, abusive father had shown up once to claim his young son when Allia had been but a girl; he had even gone so far as to strike Nico, leaving a bruise on the side of the old man's face that lasted for days. Still, bruised or not, the ex-priest had fared much better than the father himself, who'd been found dead in an alley the next day, a total of six knives sticking out of his corpse. It just so happened that there were six major crime gangs in the poor district. The message had been clear enough and since then, no one else had brought violence to Nico's door.

She would be safe there, protected. She walked for another few minutes before turning down an alley and breathing a great sigh of relief as she saw the shelter in the distance, the squat, ugly building, just then, the most beautiful thing she'd ever seen. The rapid beat of her heart in her chest was just beginning to slow when some of the shadows of the alleyway separated themselves from the walls, and five men materialized in front of her. One of them whistled appreciatively, a sound she recognized well enough, and she felt her skin go cold as someone lit a torch to reveal Hector's face.

Hector was hardly a man at all, only eighteen years old himself, but he was big for his age, standing a good head and shoulders over even most grown men. He towered over the four men of similar age that stood behind him. Hector's gang wasn't a real gang—at least, it wasn't one of the true powers in the city—but that was little comfort to Allia just then.

She turned, meaning to retrace her steps, but she found two more men standing at the mouth of the alleyway. Seven then. Real gang or not, seven would be more than enough to do whatever Hector had in mind.

"My, my," Hector said in a squeaky, nasally voice that was completely at odds with his normally deep tone, "well, looky here." His tone was amused and malicious at the same time. "When one of the boys told me they'd seen my lost kitten heading toward that old bastard's den, I thought surely they must be mistaken. After all, I says, she ain't been there in years now. Got to where she couldn't stomach the smell of all that patheticness at once, I figured."

"Patheticness isn't a word," Allia said, forcing what confidence she could into her voice, "and even if it were, I can hardly understand you for all the squeaking your nose is doing." She smiled viciously, "What happened? Did someone break it?"

One of the other boys sniggered at that, and the fake smile that had been on Hector's face vanished as his expression twisted with anger. "Shut the fuck up," he growled, and the boy did, swallowing hard. Hector turned back to her. "Oh, you've got a mouth on you, kitty cat. You always have. It's one of the things I've always loved about you. The nose though ... well, even good pets have to be punished when they get out of line, and you've got some punishment coming your way, Allie girl. You surely do."

Hector and the others started forward, and Allia backed away slowly, cursing herself for a fool. And had she actually been offended when the tailor had called her "little miss" earlier in the day? A woman, she'd thought herself, a woman grown. *Not a woman at all. Just another fool in a city full of them.* Her mother had always told her that her pride would be her downfall; usually such a lecture came at about the time when Allia told her she'd had enough wine or tamarang for the day. Allia hissed a curse that this, of all things, would be the one thing her mother's drug-addled mind would get right.

She shot a look behind her and saw the two shadowy forms of the boys moving closer to her, though she could barely make them out for the darkness of the alleyway. In another thirty seconds or so, they would all be on her, and she would have no more options. *Think, Allie,* she said to herself. *You have a mind so use it.* Then she realized something, and felt a faint glimmer of hope. If she could barely see those behind her, then they could barely see her, too. A slim chance, not much of one at all, not really, but if life in the poor district had taught her anything, it was that little was better than nothing every time.

Decided, she took a step or two toward Hector. "Hector, I'm sorry," she said in her most pitiful, terrified voice—it wasn't a particularly hard one to summon just then—"I really didn't mean to...to do what I did. Please, please don't hurt me."

There was some laughter from the gathered boys at that, and Hector opened his mouth to speak. "Now, kitty cat, the th—" but Allia didn't hear what else he said because she was already turning and running, sprinting on the right side of the alleyway toward the two waiting boys. Someone cried out in surprise, and she saw vague motion in the darkness ahead of her as the boys moved to intercept her darting form but, at the last minute, she pivoted and leapt to the left, slamming into the wall of the alleyway hard enough to elicit a gasp of pain as her shoulder struck. Then she was running again, darting past the two boys as one of them reached out, his hands missing her by inches.

Allia allowed herself a smile as she ran toward the mouth of the alleyway and, as always when she ran, she felt freer than she ever did. The wind was in her hair, not a real wind but the wind she made herself with her speed, and all the better for it. Her feet seemed to glide across the cobbled stone of the alleyway, barely touching it at all. It was, she thought, as close as a person might ever get to feeling the way birds must feel, knowing that at any time they could flap their wings and leave everything, leave their entire world behind.

She was grinning wider, exulting in the knowledge that she'd made it away once more, but as she was coming out of the alleyway opening, a shadow shot in front of her. She tried to dodge it but it was too late, and she let out a cry of pain and fear as she hit someone's arm and her feet flew out from under her. Her back struck the cobbled path hard enough to knock the wind from her, and she was still lying there, gasping for air, as Hector and the rest of his crew gathered around her, staring down at where she lay, their faces red and demonic in the torchlight.

"Oh, kitty cat," Hector said, shaking his head slowly, "you've got away from me too many times before. You didn't really think I'd let you do it again, did you?"

"Hector...please," she gasped, the fear all too real this time, "I don't..." She made to rise, but his thick hand lashed out and struck her in the face.

She screamed in pain and terror and collapsed back onto the ground, still struggling to get a breath, one of her hands going to her face and feeling the blood leaking from the corner of her mouth.

"I told you you'd pay for what you did, bitch," he said, but what was scarier than the words themselves was the smile he still wore, the smile that never touched his eyes. "Nowhere left for you to run a—" His words turned to a choked gargle and warm blood splattered across Allia's face. She recoiled with a cry and stared in frozen shock as Hector's head slowly slipped from his neck, carried to the cobbles on a river of blood. The torch he'd been holding fell to the ground in a shower of sparks, the orange, ruddy light illuminating the blood pooled on the cobbles, making it appear almost black. She meant to scream, *wanted* to scream, but the only sound that came out of her throat was a dry, rasping croak.

The men gathered around her, though, didn't seem to have the same problem. They shouted in surprised anger, a chorus of it, but another that stood above her—Alec, Allia thought his name was—hadn't even managed to turn before his head, too, came flying from his shoulders, rolling to a stop only inches away from Hector's. Allia managed the scream this time, her voice joining in the chorus of them that now filled the alleyway. She scooted across the ground, backing away unnoticed, the men who, moments before, had been intending her violence now preoccupied with scanning the alleyway in search of the killer.

Allia, too, was staring with wide, terrified eyes, and thought she saw a vague, shadowy outline of someone standing at the opposite end of the alleyway. The remaining men had apparently noticed it also as they'd turned and started toward the figure at a run.

The man, if it was a man, didn't seem daunted in the least by their approach, standing there in an almost casual way. Then there was a blur of *something*—it was too fast for Allia to make out exactly what—and two more of Hector's men collapsed to the ground mid-stride, flashes of dark blood splattering against the alley walls as they did.

What is it? Allia thought. *Gods what is it? Nothing's that fast.* She was on her feet before she realized she'd moved and then she turned and was running, the shouts and agonized wails of Hector's men fading behind her as terror lent strength and speed to her legs, and she ran faster than she had ever run before. Her heart hammered in her chest, her breath came in great, whooping gasps, and she realized distractedly that the sounds of the fight—no, that wasn't right, not a fight at all but a massacre—had abruptly cut off.

She turned the corner of the alleyway, then screamed as a figure stood waiting for her. She skidded to a halt, stumbling and almost falling. "Excuse me, sir, I didn't—" Her voice broke as she really took in the figure standing in front of her by the lights of the unevenly-spaced street lanterns. The figure was short, a few inches shorter than her, and it wore a dark, hooded cloak that covered most of its face. By some trick of the light, the part that showed, its chin, mostly, looked impossibly stretched and thin.

Allia gasped as she noted the strangest, scariest thing about the man standing before her. The thick cloak it wore did much to disguise its form, though she could still tell that it was thin, terribly so. What the cloak *didn't* manage to hide, however, were the long arms that protruded from its sleeves, so pale as to be almost white, with deep scars seeming to cover every surface of skin. Something was *wrong* about those arms, and it took Allia's mind several panicked moments to realize what it was; when she finally did her breath caught in her throat. Despite the fact that the man—if a man it was—was standing straight, its left arm was impossibly long, ending at a slim, tapered hand that hung halfway down its calves.

The creature held a long blade in its right hand, angled up and behind it, pointed at the dark sky. The blade was at least five feet long and thinner than any Allia had ever seen. The steel was coated in blood that dripped from it, and in the preternatural silence, Allia was able to make out each *plop* of blood that dripped onto the cobblestones of the city street.

For a moment, neither of them moved. Allia was frozen in shock and terror, and the creature remained unnaturally still, as if it were some gruesome statue erected in the middle of the street by some demented sculptor. Looking closer at it—unable to make her eyes do anything else—Allia thought she could see the muscles and tendons beneath the creature's chalk-pale skin twisting and writhing like dozens of snakes. She swallowed hard, fighting down the urge to vomit, and turned to run. She called on all of the speed she could muster as she took the corner back down the alleyway she'd come from, depending on her swiftness to get her out of this trouble as it had so many times before.

She'd only taken a few steps down the alleyway when something flashed by her in a blur, and she saw what she thought was the creature, its impossibly long, slender arms extended out behind it, and then she let out a cry of surprise and terror as it came to an abrupt halt only feet in front of her. *It can't be*, she thought, her mind panicked and wild. *It's impossible.* There had to be two that was all. One in front of her, one still in the street.

Decided, she turned and ran back toward the mouth of the alleyway. She'd only made it two steps when there was a flash of something at her side, so swift that she could feel the wind of it, and in another moment the creature was standing at the entrance to the alley. Its hood had been thrown back by its movement, and Allia was unable to repress a whimper as she saw that the creature's eyes shone a bright, ghostly amber in the light of the still burning torch. They weren't human eyes at all and resembled nothing so much as the sharp, somehow haunting eyes of a cat.

"What...what are you?" she gasped, her fear and exhaustion making each word a struggle.

The creature didn't respond, only cocked its head to the side on a neck that seemed somehow too thin and too stretched like the rest of it. "Well," a voice said from behind her, and Allia spun to see a man approaching, "that, I'm afraid, would take a little bit of explaining."

Allia found herself backing up against the alley wall, trying to keep her eyes on both figures at once. "Oh, there's no need for all that," the man said, his voice cool and calm, "you'll break that pretty neck of yours, bending it so much." He held up a hand, gesturing. There was a gust of wind and abruptly the creature was standing beside him, its hood once more covering its face.

"There," the man said, "that's better."

"W-who are you?"

The man smiled, but there was nothing pleasant about it. Hector had smiled in much the same way when he'd looked down at her lying in the alley and told her she would be punished. At least, that was, until his head had flown from his shoulders. Allia was surprised to find tears gathering in her eyes, not because of Hector or his men but because of the sudden, shocking violence that had descended on the alleyway.

"You may call me High Clerk Evane," the thin man said, walking forward and coming to stop only a few feet from Allia herself.

"What...what do you want from me?"

"Oh, we'll get to that," the man said. He took a moment, looking her up and down. "I have heard about this Oleander thief. A woman, it is said, of great beauty, one whose words glide along a man's ear like honey, whose unparalleled allure is matched only by her equally impressive swiftness." He chuckled. "Some even theorize that the woman has the blood of some animal—a deer or antelope, perhaps—running in her veins, claiming that it is the only possible explanation for such uncanny speed." He shrugged helplessly. "Fools, of course, but then even fools manage to be right every once in a while, and I must admit that your beauty is truly a thing to be admired."

A new kind of fear wormed its way into Allia at the man's words, at the way he was looking at her—like a man considering purchasing livestock. She took a slow, deep breath, forcing her building panic back down. She was no terrified child to be sent scurrying into her bed. She was a woman grown, and she would act like it. "If you've got...*that* in mind, you'll have to kill me first."

The man chuckled again, the sound grating to Allia's ears. "Ah, but you are a sweet thing. Have no fear, young one, I've no intention of using you for 'that.' No," he said, stepping closer, "my interests in you are quite...different."

Allia let him draw nearer until he was right in front of her, his hand reaching out and caressing her face. "Still," he said, "even a man such as myself can find himself tempted—"

His words turned to a scream of surprise as Allia's palm flashed out, striking him in the nose. The cartilage gave way with a loud *pop* and blood gushed from the wound. The man stumbled backward, but before he could regain his composure, Allia's knee flew out, hitting him hard between the legs. The stranger let out a sound that was halfway between a squeal and a shout, but Allia was already turning, sprinting back toward the alley's entrance.

"*Get her!*" the man screeched, and before Allia had made it to the street, the creature appeared in front of her once more. Its arm lashed out, a blur that was impossible to follow, and Allia felt rather than saw, the handle of its sword strike her in the head. The next thing she knew she was lying on her back in the alleyway, starbursts dancing before her eyes.

"Bitch," the thin man said, coming to stand over her, the creature beside him. "I heard she was fast," he said, one hand cradling his broken nose, "but gods, I hadn't imagined that."

Allia tried to speak, to beg the man to leave her alone, but her thoughts were muddled and unclear, and she couldn't make the words come. Darkness gathered in the corners of her vision, and the last thing she heard before it overcame her was the man grunting, "Take her."

CHAPTER TWO

Odel took the rag from his back pocket and wiped it across his brow as he stared into the blazing forge. The fire was burning in earnest now, and sweat traced tiny rivulets down his thick arms and face. But he didn't mind. He and the fire were well-known to one another—not friends, of course, for no one could ever be friends with a thing whose existence depended on destruction, but acquaintances at the least. For thirty years they had spoken to one another nearly every day, and though there was no friendship, there was perhaps at least some mutual respect.

He reached for the long metal tongs lying on his worktable, then turned and glanced at the boy, Andiel, grunting in disapproval. "Work those bellows like you mean it, boy," he growled, "the metal won't answer to anything less than your best."

The boy worked the bellows faster, rolling his eyes. Odel frowned. It had been ten years since he'd trained his last apprentice. Ten years, but not long enough. Not nearly. Ten years of bliss, only him and the metal and the fire. He still couldn't believe he'd been fool enough to take on another apprentice. If the lad's mother hadn't shown up begging, claiming that her son had fallen in with a bad crowd and needed a good trade to keep him busy, Odell would *still* be enjoying his time alone, watching the metal take shape with a satisfaction that never seemed to wane.

Studying the boy, the way he held the handles of the bellows in dainty hands, his nose upturned as if to keep his face away from the heat of the flames, Odel had a hard time imagining him getting into any trouble. At least, not the kind of trouble he'd gotten into when he was younger, back alley fights and bar room brawls. When the boy showed up for work that morning—late, as always—Odel had been certain he'd smelled some sort of perfumed scent on him. As far as he was concerned, the only trouble the lad's mother had to worry about was the boy deciding to wear face paint, maybe starting to go by "Andrea" instead of "Andiel." And what sort of name was "Andiel" for the son of a clerk anyway?

Odel sighed and started toward the forge. "Harder, lad," he said, not bothering to turn and not really needing to. Six months the boy had been helping him, if help it could be called, and he knew well enough that Andiel would slack off in his efforts as soon as Odel's back was turned. Odel paused at the fire, glancing at the length of metal within it, the steel glowing a bright orange with the heat. Then grunting with satisfaction, he clamped it with the tongs and drew it out. He stepped to the nearby basin of water and slid the glowing metal inside. The water hissed and steam billowed around him, carrying with it the smell of fire and metal, and he breathed it in.

There was peace in the forge, satisfaction of coaxing a shape from the metal, of working it and hammering it until it was straight and true, but it wasn't a satisfaction he could make the boy understand. It was in the making of something from nothing, of realizing a thing's potential. He hadn't much understood it himself when he'd been the boy's age. His own master had tried to tell him, but Odel had been young and stupid, his thoughts on chasing skirts and fighting. Now though, he realized that neither of those things offered anywhere close to the satisfaction he felt here, in this sanctuary of heat and steam and sweat.

Still, fighting had been a distracting enough pastime, and Odel had always been bigger, stronger than others. It meant that there were few bar room brawls or back alley scuffles that he didn't win. Sure, he'd have a few more bruises and aches, but the other man—or men, as his stupidity and courage had known few bounds in his youth—would be lying unconscious in the street. At least, later, when he was sober and the urge to fight was no longer in him, he'd hoped that they'd only been unconscious, but the truth was that his had always been a strength few could match, and he'd held nothing back in those brawls. For all he knew, there were some corpses lying in their graves with his fists to thank, another brick to stack on the shame that he carried on his back wherever he went. Great strength or not, that load was a heavy one, and it was only in his refuge, among the fire and the smoke, that he could set it down. At least for a time. For the thing about fighting was, win or lose, it left its mark on a man. Knife scars from blades he'd never seen coming, an ear that was little more than a fat lump of flesh on the side of his head, and a gap in his teeth that whistled if he breathed the wrong way.

Still, between fighting and chasing skirts, Odel would take fighting any day. When he'd been young, he'd had a fair enough idea of what he would do with those skirts, those women, once he finally caught them, but age had brought some degree of wisdom, and he now understood that those women weren't running at all, not really. They were only biding their time as the men pursued, waiting to lay a trap and ensnare them. At least in a fight, a man understood the dangers he faced, knew that his opponent's anger was the twin to his own, his emotions the same. It was a dirty, bloody business, but it was an honest one, and he had been one of the best at it, a man whose fists were legendary in Baresh. As for his dealings with women, well, the worst beating he ever took in a fight didn't hold a flame to those, and that was a fact.

Sighing, he drew the steaming blade out of the quenching tub and laid it flat on the worktable, giving the metal time to cool before he would heat it once more. It wasn't that he didn't liked women—he did, had liked many in his time, and had the scars to prove it. But love? No. Never that. He loved the forge, loved the smell and the feel of the heat and the fire, loved the sweat of an honest day's work and the way it felt when he stepped out and the night air cooled it against his skin. That was freedom for him, and it was enough—at least it always had been. It was only that he was a battered old warrior, weary beyond his fifty years, and though much of the size and strength of his youth remained, the will to use it had withered.

He took the filthy rag from the back pocket of his trousers and wiped the sweat from his face again, "That's enough for now, boy," he said. "Go on and grab yourself somethin' to eat, if you'd like. Just come back tomorrow, and we'll get to it. With all the orders the castle's been puttin' in, the work'll be steady for months to come." He glanced at the massive blade lying on the table, then at the finished swords lying in a bundle beside it and shook his head. Lengths of steel six feet long with a weight greater than any man he'd known—himself included—would ever want to swing in battle.

He looked back at the boy in time to see him roll his eyes at the prospect of the work to come and decided that though some words might fall on deaf ears, they needed to be said anyway. "I don't want to catch you rollin' your eyes again, lad. Not about the work. There's plenty of clerks and merchants you can go apprentice to, if you want to get fat at some desk, let your hands grow soft like a woman's. It's a privilege to work the metal, to shape it, and you'd do well to understand that."

The boy nodded, properly chastised. "Sorry, sir."

Not a bad lad, not really. Just spoiled and that was alright—the world would break him of it soon enough. It always did. "It's alright, boy. You're young yet, but you won't always be. Right now, I reckon you think you've got a thousand different opportunities, standing at paths reaching to the hundreds, any one you could walk down if and when you chose, and you'd be right, mostly. Thing is, as you get older, the paths grow over with weeds and bushes and soon you can't go down them at all. Remember that, lad. Choose your path before one is chosen for you. That's the best advice I can give you."

The boy nodded again. "Yes sir. I was wondering…could I take the rest of the day off?" His face colored slightly, "There's a dance being held at *The Tilting Cup* tonight, and a girl there…well," he said, hesitant, "a girl will be there who is a friend of mine."

Odel grunted. A boy his age didn't have girls who were friends, only girls he was after and that was alright. Odel could tell him a thing or two, share some of his own wisdom on that subject as well, but why bother? The years between his and the boy's age weren't so many that he'd forgotten what seemed more important than everything else at the time. "Your mother okay with it?"

The boy smiled, seeing hope. "Yes sir I asked her before I came."

Odel nodded. "Alright then, but I want you here bright and early in the mornin'. There's plenty of work to be done and not enough hands to do it."

The lad beamed. "Yes sir, thank you. Thank you." He turned and started toward the door, pausing when Odel called out to him.

"Boy?"

"Yes sir?"

"I want you here on time, understand? If you can't make it on time, don't bother comin'. I got no patience for a worker can't show up on time."

"Yes sir." The boy nodded, serious and meaning it, at least then. But Odel knew well enough that a boy of that age was capable of meaning a thing passionately one moment and then forgetting it the next. There were plenty enough pregnant single women in the city who could attest to as much.

Still, he smiled and waved at the boy. "Go on then, off with you." The youth didn't need any more encouragement. He turned and disappeared out of the shop door almost too quickly to see.

Odel stared after him for a minute, wondering if it was too late for him to find a wife, maybe have some kids. They'd be a trial sure, but he thought they'd be good, too. He'd forged enough blades in his time, shaped and made them, he thought it would be a joy to help mold a human being. *And just who are you kidding, old man?*

Shaking his head ruefully, he turned back to the work and slid the next impossibly long length of steel into the forge, grunting with the strain of the heavy metal. The gods alone knew who would be wielding these things. Unless maybe they'd discovered some giants somewhere, but he didn't think it likely.

He'd only been at it for a little over an hour when he heard a knock coming from the other section of the shop, the area—separate from the forge itself—where he displayed his finished goods. He grunted, tossing the hammer on the worktable and glanced back toward the shop front with a frown. He'd learned over years of working with the public of Baresh that you could tell a lot about a man by his knock and this one was imperious, no doubt belonging to an equally imperious, self-important person. It was a knock he'd become familiar with in recent weeks.

Sighing, he removed the leather apron he wore and wiped his hands on the rag. He walked to the store-front past rows of the over-large swords he'd been commissioned to forge, past the counter where the boy often stood and took orders—when, that was, he could be troubled to do anything. He didn't bother to hide the frown on his face as he unlatched the door and swung it open.

A thin man stood in the doorway, an impatient twist to his features, his hands on his hips as if he intended to punish the man who had invented doors and thereby stolen a few moments of his precious time. "The shop's not open yet, clerk," the blacksmith growled, staring down at the man who was at least a head and a half shorter than Odel no matter how he might strut and lift his nose. "Not for another two hours or more." He glanced meaningfully at the sun, only just now rising over the horizon, then back to the thin man. "The only reason I'm here this early at all is because I'm working on the job you commissioned me for. It's a lot of swords and not a lot of time you gave me to do it in, and with the strange specifications it's taking even longer than it normally would. Each interruption like this is only going to increase your master's wait."

The clerk sniffed, "My master, the king, does not *wait*, blacksmith, and you will call me High Clerk Evane, in future."

Odel snorted. Another woman's name, that. He wondered why the man's parents hadn't gone all out, named him Mary or Elizabeth, maybe. "Threats and pronouncements won't smith your metal for you, *clerk*. Words are only that, with no shape or substance, and no blade has ever been sharpened by the use of them." He raised a bushy eyebrow at the man as he leaned forward, his thick bulk and height towering over the small clerk. "Not sharpened by them, but dulled often enough, I think." He sighed, telling himself to control his temper. "Anyway, words won't get your blades made in time, only I will, and I won't be able to do that if I'm constantly being interrupted."

The thin man frowned for a moment then gave a slight shrug, a smile appearing on his face. It made his mouth look strange and alien, as if the man weren't exactly sure how to do it and whatever muscles it required were weak from disuse. "Never mind the swords," he said, waving a hand dismissively, "I've come on another, more important matter."

"That so?" Odel said, only now taking the time to look behind the clerk at what he'd first taken as a castle guard who had no doubt been brought along to convince him of the seriousness of the situation. He couldn't see much of the man or his face as he wore a hooded cloak, but he could see enough to know that the shape underneath that cloak was big. No, not big. Huge. Odel had always been the biggest man in the bar or the alley or, if he was being honest with himself, the whorehouse, but this man was a giant, standing at least as tall over him as he stood over the clerk. And where Odel's shoulders and arms were thick with slabs of muscle from years spent in the forge, this man seemed bigger than him by far.

"Who's your friend?" he said, trying to see under the stranger's hood. But he lowered his head further, and Odel noted great heaps of muscle, so large they seemed unnatural shifting beneath the thick cloak the man wore.

"Oh, him?" the clerk asked, glancing back at the man behind him, that strange smile still in place. "Never mind him," he said, winking at Odel, "he's not much of a talker, my companion. Still, he has his uses."

Odel grunted, "I imagine so. I guess he could pull a plow smooth enough, if the ox gave out. Now, are we done here?"

"Done?" the clerk asked, amusement dancing in his eyes. "Oh, Odel, we are barely getting started. Now, aren't you going to invite us in? I have an interesting prospect to discuss with you, and I believe we will want our privacy."

Odel frowned, hesitating. For some reason, he found he didn't want the two men to follow him into his shop. It wasn't just the fact that the little bastard was annoying (which he was); it was more than that. There was something about the man's companion that he didn't like. Looking at him, even covered as he was, Odel had the same feeling he got when he sometimes saw a dead mongrel lying in the street. A slight twisting of revulsion, not threatening to spill out his guts, not quite, but letting him know that they were still there and that they had their limits.

It wasn't that the man was bigger than him; at least, he didn't believe it was only that. There was something *wrong* about the silent stranger. Something that felt unnatural, and his mind and heart told him in no uncertain terms not to let the two men into his shop, not under any circumstances.

But old or not, Odel wasn't weak or feeble. He'd never let his fear get the better of him, and he wasn't going to start now. "Come on in then," he said, swinging the door wide and stepping to the side. "Whatever it is, let's get it out of the way, so I can get back to work."

The clerk moved past him, taking in the shop with a mild look of distaste, like a king visiting a poor tavern. *Probably looks too much like a place where a man actually works,* Odel thought. After a moment, the stranger followed his companion inside, and as he passed, Odel caught of a whiff of something foul. Odel grimaced, running an arm across his nose.

He eased the door closed and watched as the light of the sun thinned and finally cut off all together. *No way through but through,* he told himself, turning. "Alright then, clerk," he said, determined not to let the uneasiness that was growing in him show, "what is it you feel is important enough to take me away from my duties?"

The clerk rubbed at his chin thoughtfully, as if he hadn't heard a word the blacksmith said. "Odel, Odel. I knew your name, of course, even knew you were a blacksmith and a man who was ridiculously big, almost grotesquely so—no offense, of course."

Not yet, Odel thought, *but you're getting close.* The old Odel would have already grabbed the thin man by his collar and thrown him against the wall if for no other reason but to feel his own strength and be comforted by it. "Of course not," Odel said, "and don't worry, you'll be the first to know if I get offended."

The clerk gave a laugh. "And just the sort of thing I would expect a man known as Stone Fist to say. Why, imagine my surprise when I discovered that one of the blacksmiths whose services I had sought was actually none other than the legendary street brawler. Tell me," he said, leaning in conspiratorially, "is it true that you once fought a whole gang of men—ten or more the stories say—and beat them all? They say that several of them never walked right again and another two didn't have the wits left to remember their own names."

Odel sighed. They were old times, times from a past that he'd rather forget. When he'd been young, he'd loved fire the same as he did now, only then it was the fire that burned within him, a rage and anger that could never be quenched. "Eight," he muttered.

"What's that?" the clerk said, turning his ear toward the blacksmith as if to hear him better.

Odel rubbed a thick-fingered hand across his stubbled chin. "There were eight of them. Nine of us fools altogether, and none of us any better off for it. Anyway, that was a long time ago, and I was a different man then."

The clerk shook his head. "Oh, surely not so very long ago, Odel—or should I say Stone Fist," he said with a grin. "As for being a different man ..." He hesitated, glancing Odel up and down, studying him. Odel knew well enough what the man would see. A big man, taller and wider than most you were likely to meet. A man with a thick chest and thick arms and a thick head too, though the clerk might not notice that as quickly. Still, he only had to take a closer look to see the scars and the bulbous, misshapen ear to know the truth of it. "I admit that I never had the pleasure of seeing you while you were in your prime—I was just a child then, perhaps not even born—but you still look to me like the type who could send men scurrying for their mother's skirts." He laughed at that, a shrill, unpleasant sound, and Odell frowned.

"I was a fool then. Still am in many ways, but I thank the gods that fighting isn't one of them. You see, it isn't just the scars and the wounds that take a little piece of a man every time. They aren't even the biggest part."

The clerk grinned. "You speak of morality then? Is this the wisdom of Stone Fist or the wisdom of a blacksmith?"

Odel shrugged, tired of remembering and tired of the clerk. "Take it as you like. Now, what do you want of me?"

The thin man gave him a wink. "Oh, I think you know. I have a certain individual who would be very interested in making use of a talent such as yours."

Odel narrowed his eyes. "If this friend of yours has some smithing he needs done, you send him on by. But if it's got anything to do with my past, you tell him to forget it. The past is behind me, and that's where I intend to leave it."

The clerk shook his head slowly, making a tsking sound. "Oh, I'm afraid that won't do, Odel. Not at all. I must insist that you hear my employer out. It would be the wisest thing—the safest thing—for everyone involved, I assure you."

Odel met the man's eyes, his own stare cold and hard. "Are you threatening me, clerk? I tell you what, I *insist* that you and your friend here," he said, nodding his head to the cloaked man, "get the fuck out of my shop. The king will have his blades, but you tell him to send someone else along the next time. I'm apt to be less patient if I find you at my door again. Do you understand?"

The thin man sighed theatrically. "Oh, I understand well enough, Odel. I think it's you who doesn't truly grasp the situation. You are strong; one of the strongest, but you must be what, fifty years old now? Fifty at least? I would have loved to have seen you in your prime, old man, truly I would have. But time has done to you what it does to us all, I'm afraid. You are not the man you once were." He glanced meaningfully at his silent companion, the hulking giant having not so much as moved since he came into the shop. "You see, now there are others who have taken the place of the strongest man. There are other legends now, and yours is one that will soon be lost and forgotten. Unless, of course, you take my friend's offer. I think that, if that were the case, you might very well find yourself a hero to the common folk once more."

Odel studied the man for a second, hearing the threat for what it was. When he'd been a child, his father had told him the best way to train a dog. The stick and the sugar, he'd called it. You always started with the sugar, giving the dog a reason to be good, but you kept the stick handy, just in case, for no matter how good of a pup, it would always mess up, would always act up from time to time, and in moments like that the sugar was of little use. Then it was the stick that answered, and the stick that taught. The clerk had shown him the sugar, or at least thought he had.

The truth was, Odel hadn't cared much about what people thought of him—legend or not—when he'd been young, and he cared even less now. As for the stick, well, the big bastard was standing as still as a statue a few feet away from him, and although his head was tilted down, the hood of his cloak obscuring his face, Odel got the distinct impression that the man was studying him. Instead of answering, Odel walked back to the door and swung it open, glad to see the sunlight once more, realizing that for the first time in his life, the darkness of the shop felt stifling. Then he turned back to the two men. "I think it's time you both left. I'll make your swords, and I'll finish the job. Who knows, maybe if you have another few like this fella here, you might even find some people that are able to swing them. But I'm done with fighting, done with hurting and being hurt. I'll thank ya to leave and take your other offer with you."

The clerk sighed again. "There's nothing I can say to talk you into this?"

Odel didn't answer, only stared at the thin man who finally nodded. "Alright," the clerk said, raising his hands as if conceding, "alright. You've convinced me, Odel. I see that you are not at all interested in my friend's offer, and that you're not the type of man who can be talked into doing anything he doesn't want to do. I guess my friend and I will be leaving now."

Odel nodded, making sure not to let the relief show on his face. It had gotten strange there, for a moment, with the quiet one's smell, with his *wrongness*, but it was alright. Would be alright. *Got a little bit of fight left in you after all, old man.* "Well," he said, "sorry I couldn't be more help."

"So am I," the clerk said, "so am I." He motioned with his hand and started for the open doorway, his hulking shadow following after him, the giant's shoulders scrunched forward in a duck that Odel knew well enough. He thought that, probably, the tallest people had to be the stupidest. They spent enough time knocking their heads on things, anyway.

The clerk walked to the doorway, and Odel was getting ready to close it behind them—had already started to ease the door shut behind the giant, in fact—when the thin man's hand shot out, pausing the door in its frame. "There's just one more thing," he said, his face full of regret as he turned back to look at Odel.

"Oh?" Odel said.

"Yes," the man said, "you see, my master really doesn't like to be told no." He motioned to his companion and suddenly the giant leapt forward, grabbing Odel by the apron he wore and pulling him up. Odel, shocked by the suddenness of the thing, stared down, amazed to find his feet not touching the ground. He was just starting to get over his surprise when the giant shifted and, the next thing he knew, Odel was flying through the air. He struck the desk with a crack and a splintering of wood, and he groaned, shaking his head to clear it before turning back to look at where the clerk and the stranger still stood in the doorway.

"I would have preferred," the clerk said, shaking his head sadly, "if you had gone of your own free will, but you will go either way. Such a legend as yourself, a man known for his strength...why, there are many uses my master will find for you." He crouched down, meeting Odel's eyes. "And do not worry, Stone Fist. You will get your strength returned to you, and more. My master has his ways."

Dazed, Odel ran a hand along his head where it had struck the desk and saw it come back red with blood. *Get up old man*, he told himself, *get up. This isn't going to be the kind of fight you can run away from.* Grunting with the effort and ignoring the dull throb in his head, he grabbed hold of the cracked desk and pulled himself to his feet. "I don't know what in the fuck you've got planned," he growled, "but if it's a fight you're after, you got it."

The thin man sighed. "Oh, Stone Fist, this will not be a fight. Not nearly that." He motioned to the big stranger and the thing—for Odel found himself thinking of it not as a man at all but as some unnatural creature—started forward.

"Alright then," Odel said, watching it come. "Alright." He raised fists that hadn't been raised in anger in nearly thirty years and found that it felt good to do so. It felt right. He was worried, sure, and he felt uneasy about this thing that towered before him, but mostly he felt relief. He'd heard a story once, a children's tale, really, about a frog and an alligator. He didn't remember all of it, just that the frog had helped the alligator with something and, by way of thanks, the alligator had told the frog he'd carry him on his back across the river. Only, before they made it to the other side, the alligator turned that long snout and ate the frog. There had been no malice in it, no anger. The alligator had only done what it was made to do, what was in its nature. Now, squaring off against this man, not knowing whether he'd win or lose, knowing only that the two of them would be matched against one another, Odel felt better, *lighter* than he had in a long time. Finally, he was doing what was in his nature.

The giant didn't speak, only stomped forward, its walk strange and ungainly, and Odel, alive with the thrill of the fight, rushed to meet it. He landed two hard, fast punches on the creature's stomach before it could react. Two punches that would have been enough to end a fight with almost any man, and send most to a healer or make them piss blood for a week—they hadn't called him Stone Fist for nothing. But the creature didn't so much as flinch, and Odel took a step back, shaking his hands where a sharp pain had gone through his knuckles. He told himself that it had been a long time, that the callouses that had once served as padding were no longer there, but that wasn't all of it. Hitting the thing had been like hitting steel, and he hissed as he flexed his hands and felt fresh waves of agony lance through them.

The creature moved forward again, swinging one of its massive arms in an awkward, flailing way, and Odel turned, putting both of his forearms in front of him to block. His left was slightly forward from his right and took the brunt of the brutal, terrible impact, and Odel screamed in surprised pain as the bone cracked, and he was thrown back to strike the wall.

He kept his feet, barely, his left arm hanging useless at his side, feeling as if it was full of shards of glass. "Son of a bitch..." he gasped, "what...what *are* you?"

"You'll have to forgive my friend," the clerk said, "as I believe I've said, he's really not much of a talker. It's not one of his...*strengths*, shall we say? Still, he has other things to recommend him. As for what he is...suffice to say, blacksmith, that he is better. The way that you, too, will be better before long. I would say that you'll thank me for it, but then, I suspect you won't be able. Everett here was once quite a talker but the...let's call it training that my master had him undergo, seemed to rob him of that."

Odel gasped, raising his good arm as the creature drew closer, "Nobody's that strong. Nobody."

The creature said nothing as it stalked forward and that, perhaps, was the worst thing of all, that eerie silence in which Odel could hear little else but the harsh, pained sounds of his own breathing. There was a sharp ache in his side that let him know one of his ribs was cracked at best and broken at worst, but he straightened as best he could, bringing himself to his full height. When the creature drew close enough, Odel rushed forward, swinging his arm wide, aiming a fist at the cloaked figure's head, but the creature reached up almost casually, catching Odel's fist.

The blacksmith struggled with all of his considerable strength to tear his arm free, but even legends can find themselves outmatched. He grunted in pain, fighting back the scream that threatened to come out, as the creature gave his fist a squeeze, and the bones of his hand and fingers shattered.

He gave one last ditch effort, jerking his body away with a growl and was rewarded by the creature staggering a step forward—but instead of loosening the thing's grip, it only grew tighter instead. Odel screamed again, some distant part of his mind thinking that he'd never imagined he could scream so loudly or so terribly. Then the creature's hood, knocked around in the struggle, fell backward, and he surprised himself. It turned out, even legends screamed and in the end, their screams sounded much like those of other men.

CHAPTER THREE

You're going to be late, Co said. *You know that, don't you?*

Aaron sighed heavily. He stood on the balcony near his room in the castle, staring out at the city spread beneath him. The walls of Perennia had taken some damage in the battle against Belgarin's army, but the work crews were well on their way to bringing the walls back to their former state. At least, almost. It had been a month since the battle, yet neither rain nor the washing rags of men and women assigned to the task had been able to fully clean the blood stains off the white stones. They were still at it down there; he could see many of them scattered about the walls, washing and scrubbing for all they were worth.

Aaron could have told them, had they asked, that it was pointless. He'd been in enough fights, seen enough death, to know that blood never really came out, not completely. It was one stain that would linger, always. In the stones, seeping into them, on the blades of those who'd spilled it and, most of all, on their hands. On his hands. He saw it there, even now, never mind the fact that he'd washed them dozens of times since the battle. Since he and the other Ghosts had stood their ground at the gate, butchering and killing and dying and reveling in all of it. Blood stained, that was all, and a man could feel its tacky warmth even if he couldn't see it. Some things never really left, and he thought that that was alright, was as it should be.

Aaron, they'll be waiting.

"I know," he said. Beyond the city walls, the fields spread out, green and vibrant in the morning light. The corpses had been cleared away—it had taken weeks to do it—but aside from the trampled grass, a man could have been forgiven for not realizing a battle had been fought on that ground at all. Nature, it seemed, was better at forgetting the deaths of men than the things they built, than they were themselves. There was a lesson there, he thought, but he'd learned enough lessons lately and had little patience for more. "He'll be back, Co," he said. "I don't know what happened, but he'll be back and never mind what the others say."

I believe you, Aaron, the Virtue responded, though you'll forgive me if I wish I didn't.

Aaron grunted. "Nothing to forgive, firefly. I can't blame you for wanting to believe the best—we all do, after all. The difference is that you're not fool enough to convince yourself of it just because it's what you want."

I don't know if that's a good thing. They say that ignorance is bliss.

Aaron snorted. "Ignorance will get a man dead quicker than a sword to the gut, firefly. Well, as quickly anyway. Not knowing its coming doesn't stop the blade from finding its mark."

As you say. Still. The meeting?

"Fine," Aaron sighed, "though I think I know well enough what they'll say. Anyway, I don't exactly love the idea of having to watch the damned castle guards drop to their knees when I pass like somebody struck them dumb with a mace—and don't think I haven't been tempted to."

But you're a hero, Aaron, she said, her voice heavy with amusement, *the man-god who managed to hold off an army of thousands with no more than one hundred men. I'm fairly sure, if we looked close enough, we'd find some shrines dedicated to you in the city.*

"Go fuck yourself, lightning bug." He cast one final look over the walls of the city before turning and reluctantly heading into the castle.

He came to the end of the hallway on which his and Adina's room was located and, sure enough, the two guards there dropped to one knee. They brought their fists to their chests in salute, lowered their heads as if he was a god with light shining out of his ass and they feared being blinded. "Oh, get up, damn you, before I kick you over."

The two guards rose and grinned at each other as if it were a privilege to be threatened by him. The damned fools. Aaron sighed and walked on, making his way to the queen's audience chamber and weathering the worshipful stares of the serving men and women he passed in the castle's hallways. *If these meetings keep up like they are*, he thought, *I'm going to just start sleeping in the audience chamber. If not to save myself a trip, at least to save one of these fools' lives, as I'm growing low on patience.*

The audience chamber? Co asked as if seriously considering, *not a terrible idea, I suppose. Though, I wonder if Adina would mind the cold bed. Still, I suppose that there are plenty of men within the castle who would be more than happy—*

Aaron frowned. "Leave it, firefly."

In a few minutes, he was at the queen's audience chamber, and he nodded to the guards. As the two men went about opening the doors, Aaron took a slow, deep breath and tried to gather what little patience he had left. He had a feeling he would need it.

When the doors were open, Aaron stepped past the two guards and into the queen's audience chamber. The same people who had been gathered at all of the meetings of late were waiting for him. Queen Isabelle sat on her throne, nodding her head to him as he entered. At the left table sat Adina, flanked by Leomin and Gryle, the chamberlain, holding his hands clasped tightly on the table's surface as if afraid to move lest he break something with his newfound strength. From what Aaron had heard, the man had reason enough to be cautious—it seemed that every castle servant or guard he spoke to had some story about the chamberlain breaking some priceless chair or vase.

Captain Festa also sat at the table. The captain was dressed in an assortment of thick shirts and coats so that he looked like a homeless man who was doing his best not to freeze. Despite this, Aaron noted the man's red nose and constant sniffling. Captain Brandon Gant sat at the end of the table, his back straight, and he winked as Aaron came inside.

On the other side of the room sat General Yallek, the commander of the forces from Avarest and representative of the city's ruling council. The general wore his military uniform, the picture of a commanding officer. He nodded once to Aaron as the sellsword entered. Sitting beside Yallek was Hale, one of the two most powerful crime bosses in the Downs. The big man was reclined in his chair, his feet propped up on the table as if he wasn't in a castle but some tavern or brothel. He waved the thick, meaty fingers of one hand at Aaron in an almost dainty gesture, and Aaron nodded back.

Beside Hale sat Grinner, the older man rolling his eyes as if disappointed in Aaron's lateness. The thickly muscled bodyguard who was his constant shadow and, if the past was any indication, quite a bit more than that, stood behind the crime lord. His thick muscular arms folded around his chest as he surveyed each person in the room, a challenge in his eyes.

Gods help us, Aaron thought as he made his way toward an empty space by his Adina and the others, it's a wonder we haven't killed each other already. "Sorry for being late," he said as he took his seat.

"It's no problem, lad," Hale said, "no doubt you were out doing something heroic and didn't have time to stop in and see us little folk." He laughed, a loud, full belly laugh that was not reciprocated by anyone in the room. "Tell me, boy, are we goin' to be hearin' some new legend when we leave here?"

"Gods forbid," Aaron muttered.

"I think maybe it is a problem," Grinner said, the older man running a finger over his eyebrows. "It does not speak well of you, Aaron Envelar, that you cannot even show up on time for a meeting. It isn't as if you did not know about it in advance."

Oh, I knew alright, Aaron thought, I've been dreading it for a week. He opened his mouth to speak, but Isabelle beat him to it. "I'm sure that General Envelar has perfectly good reasons for his tardiness, and I do not believe it is productive to waste our time discussing them now."

"Of course you're right, Your Highness," Grinner said, bowing his head to the queen, "as you say, there are more important things to discuss."

Hale bellowed laughter at the other crime lord's obvious attempts at winning the queen's favor. Grinner's face turned a deep shade of red; Aaron expected him to order his bodyguard to attack the other crime lord, and was shocked when the older man only sat silently.

Well, Aaron thought, if we can't all be friends, perhaps we can keep ourselves from killing each other. At least for a little while.

"Yes...well," the queen went on, "I have gathered you all here to discuss what our plans for defense will be, going forward."

"Defense?" General Yallek asked in his soft voice. "Forgive me, Queen, but in order to mount a defense, there must first be an attack, and I see no indication that one is imminent. Belgarin's armies have retreated, and for a month's time we have received nothing but silence from Baresh. It is my belief—as well as that of the Ruling Council—that the royal prince has decided to give up his plans of conquest and be satisfied with those kingdoms he has already taken."

Sure, Aaron thought, and maybe all the tigers in the world have decided to give up meat. Why not? And even if Belgarin had given up his dreams of conquest—a very unlikely possibility in Aaron's mind—then they still had Boyce Kevlane to worry about. The ancient wizard had failed to sabotage Perennia's defense, but Aaron drew little comfort from that. The man was out there, somewhere, and wherever he was, Aaron had no doubt that his mind was bent on the city's destruction.

Still, the majority of those gathered here did not know about Boyce Kevlane or his machinations, and Aaron did not think it wise to tell them. The alliance—such as it was—was tenuous enough without trying to convince them that a man they believed to be nothing more than a character in a children's tale wasn't just real, but a threat even worse than Belgarin's army. So he only sat in silence, giving them all a chance to speak.

"We need not wonder at all about what Belgarin is planning," Captain Gant said, rubbing his gray, stubbly beard in a nervous gesture Aaron had come to know well, "as we have sent spies to Baresh. In a few months' time..."

"In a few months' time, I'll be fatter than I already am on castle food, and grown soft from silk clothes and soft beds. Sorry, Silent," he said, shaking his head, "but a few months is too long when we might not get any answer at all. For all we know, the men that were sent might be shacked up in some brothel, drinking their fill and sticking their wicks in anything they can afford. Sure, it was one thing when Belgarin was trying to take over the entire kingdom, but the bastard has either turned coward or decided that a man's ass can only sit on so many thrones at once. Whatever the reason, he's tucked tail and ran, and that's fine as far as I'm concerned. Meanwhile, I've got men and women back in the Downs that rely on me, and if I stay gone much longer it'll all go to shit." He snorted. "Probably already has."

Grinner rolled his eyes, running a hand through his white ponytail. "Hale's assessment is crass, and though I despise the thought of agreeing with anything he might say, I must admit that he is right. Although I have most enjoyed my stay and am thankful for the gracious hospitality that has been extended to me and my men," he said, pausing to bow his head low to the queen, "I must confess that while I am here there are certain...interests of mine in Avarest that are being neglected."

Hale bellowed a laugh. "Interests, is it?" He snorted. "You ask me, the only interest you got is in that thick muscled fella behind you there and how tight his trousers are. That and maybe tryin' to get yourself your own throne to sit on. I'd watch this one, Highness. You ain't careful, he'll plop right down in your lap."

Grinner's face turned a deep crimson. "How dare you? I have only the best interests of everyone involved in the fore front of my mind. Not that an ignorant buffoon like you would understand."

"Buffoon, is it?" Hale said, and then they were arguing in earnest, the two most powerful men of the Downs shouting back and forth like children fighting over a favorite toy.

Aaron rubbed at his aching temples. He glanced at Adina and saw his own worries reflected in her troubled gaze. "Gentlemen, please," Isabelle said in a tone of exasperation, and both crime lords quieted as they turned to face the queen. "I do not doubt either of your valor and courage, for you both showed up and helped to save us in our time of need." She glanced at General Yallek, the representative of Avarest. "Surely though," she said, "you must understand that the danger is still very real. My brother is not known for mercy or half-measures. His army will march again, and we will need to present a unified front when it does, or we will all be destroyed. General Yallek, is there not something I can do to convince you to stay?"

The general shook his head slowly. "Forgive me, my queen, but there is not. In the end, the army's disposition is not my decision to make but the Council's, and I received word from them only yesterday. I am to remain in Perennia for one month's time and, if Belgarin still does not rouse his army to battle, I am to return to the city."

"A month is it?" Hale asked, rubbing a meaty hand over his chin. "Aye, that'll do me fine. The lads'll survive another month without me. Besides," he said grinning, "there might just be one or two whores in this city I haven't seen to yet, and I wouldn't want 'em feeling left out. One more month then me and the boys will head back ourselves." With that, he grabbed a wine glass from the table and downed it in one long gulp.

Grinner glanced at the big man with disgust then turned back to the queen. "I am sorry, Your Majesty, but my men and I will also be leaving at the end of a month's time."

Isabelle's expression was troubled, but she said nothing, looking to Adina as if for help. The princess swallowed hard. "Gentlemen, my sister was not wrong when she spoke of my brother. He has little mercy in him and even less patience. He will not give up on his dream of ruling Telrear so easily. Please, I beg you, listen to reason. If he comes upon our armies separately, we will be butchered like those he has conquered before us. Only together can we have some hope of victory."

"Victory, is it?" Hale said. "Lass, you're a pretty enough thing, I'll grant you, but victory to me is countin' my coins and drinkin' ale. That," he said, winking at her, "and maybe havin' a roll with a pretty thing like yourself, that is. And anyhow, if you want troops so bad, why not go to your own kingdom, find 'em there?"

Adina ran a hand through her long hair. "Is there not some way I can talk you out of this? General," she said, turning to Yallek, "you strike me as a wise man. Surely you must understand the danger Belgarin and his army pose to Avarest."

The general nodded slowly, a regretful expression on his face. "I do, Princess, but as I said, the choice is not mine to make. Without some plan in place, without some surety that Belgarin still intends to continue his campaign, I must bow to the will of the council."

The room lapsed into a troubled silence then, each of them thinking their own dark thoughts. Aaron's were darker than most, for he knew well what they faced. Not just Belgarin's army, one that outnumbered their own—even including the troops from Avarest. There was also something worse, an ancient evil that had bent the whole of its will toward destroying the world of man. Had they seen what he'd seen, had they only understood what Boyce Kevlane was capable of, then this conversation wouldn't be necessary. And it wasn't just the man himself—a man who could shake off being thrown from a castle balcony in a matter of weeks—that worried him.

For a month, they'd had peace. No war, no assassinations, yet that too was worrying, for the creature would never give up its quest for destruction and death. If they didn't see it, it was only because it was hidden away preparing some new evil . What's more, Aaron felt something building, had felt it for weeks now. He'd woken up in the morning on more than one occasion in a cold sweat from dreams he could barely remember. Always, in the dreams, he was someone different. Upon waking, all that was left of the dreams were broken fragments, but he remembered that he had been being chased. By whom or by what he didn't know, but that feeling of being pursued never entirely left him even in his waking hours. Something was wrong, something was coming, and he knew it with a certainty that he could not explain or even understand.

He knew it in the same way that some men were said to be able to smell a storm before it arrived, to know of it even when the sky was clear and the sun was shining. While their allies argued and fought, Boyce Kevlane was hidden away somewhere, plotting and preparing some new threat...but there was no way to convince them of this. They'd have only laughed at him, if he'd tried. You couldn't tell a man about the things he'd seen the ancient wizard do and expect him to believe you. You would have to show him.

Aaron's eyes widened in realization. That's it, he thought, we have to show them that the threat is real.

Aaron, Co said, her voice nervous, I think I see the direction of your thoughts, and can I just say that I think it is a horrible idea.

Maybe it is, firefly, he thought back, but it's also the only one. "Two months," he said aloud, surprised to find that he'd risen out of his chair and was now standing, meeting the eyes of those gathered.

All eyes in the audience chamber turned to look at him, and he saw a myriad of expressions in them. Confusion, mostly, but in Adina and Leomin's face he saw not confusion but concern. "What's that, General Envelar?" the queen asked.

Aaron met Adina's eyes for a moment, saw that she was shaking her head slowly at him, then turned to the other side of the room where General Yallek, Hale, and Grinner watched him expectantly. "Give us two months. You'll have your proof by then—proof enough for the council. Who knows, maybe even proof enough that you two'll agree on it," he said, glancing at the two crime bosses.

Hale grunted, "May as well hope that we all grow wings, Silent; then we can fly up in the sky, spend our days drinking ale, reclining on clouds with naked goddesses sitting on our laps."

"Crude as always, but I agree," Grinner said. "And anyway, two months changes nothing, Silent. The chances of your spies returning with any information worth having—returning at all for that matter—are slim to none, and every minute I'm away, my interests are put at unnecessary risk."

Hale nodded slowly, a regretful look on his face. "I'm afraid I've got to agree with the old bastard, Silent. Sayin' two months doesn't change anything—we're still in the same situation we were in before."

"But it does," Aaron said, glancing at Adina once more. "In two months' time, you'll have your proof of the danger. I can guarantee it."

"Guarantees now, is it?" Hale asked. The heavily muscled crime lord picked at his teeth for a minute and sighed. "Had a whore once guarantee me she was clean and, being drunk, I was ready enough to take her word on it. Didn't stop a rash from croppin' up on my fruits a week later though. Boils too, so far as that goes." He grunted. "You wouldn't believe what the healers charge to fix such a thing, and I don't mind tellin' you it wasn't a pleasant experience."

Grinner frowned at the man, sliding his chair further down the table before turning back to Aaron. "Guarantees are only words, with no more weight than wind. They are easy enough to say,

Aaron Envelar, but saying a thing does not make it true and empty promises won't have your spies back in time with proof that Belgarin's still up to his mischief."

"No," Aaron agreed, "they won't. But I guarantee it just the same."

Grinner sighed. "And how, I wonder, might you guarantee such a thing?"

"Aaron," Adina said, "don't. There's got to be another way."

"You know there's not," he said, meeting her eyes. Then he turned back to the others, "I'll go to Baresh myself. I'll find the proof you all need and come back with it in two months' time—you have my word."

Grinner frowned, considering. "The word of Aaron Envelar. Well, that just might change things. Two months, you say?"

"Two months."

"And if you die?"

Aaron gave the man a humorless grin. "I'm sure you'll find a way to go on without me."

The old man gave him an almost hungry smile. "Yes," he said, nodding slowly to himself, "that could work."

"Words," Hale said, yawning heavily. "Gods, but I miss the days when a problem could be solved by beating the shit out of it. All this thinking's gonna have me in the grave before my time. Speakin' of that," he continued, turning to Aaron, a mischievous glint in his eye, "seems to me you swore to kill me not so long ago."

Aaron smiled. "There's still time."

The big man guffawed at that then broke into loud, boisterous laughter, slamming his fist on the table. When he'd gotten control of himself, he rubbed a thick finger across his eyes. "'Still time,' he says. Gods, but you really should have come and worked for me, lad. We'd have had a grand time."

"Maybe," Aaron agreed, "but, then, I prefer working alone." He paused, glancing around at all of the people gathered in the audience hall. "Or, at least, I did. Things change."

"So they do," the big man said, nodding, "so they do." He rubbed at his chin for a moment, thinking, then finally grunted, "Ah, fuck it, why not? You've got your two months. Either you come back with proof, and me and my boys get to be in one of the biggest scraps this world's ever seen, or you end up dead. Seems to me that I come out ahead either way."

Aaron nodded. Not exactly the vote of confidence he would have liked, but it was the one he'd expected. "And you, General?" he said, turning to Yallek.

The general studied him for several moments then gave a single, stiff nod. "Very well. I wonder if it is courage or stupidity that will have you walk into the lion's den, but either way I will write to the council and tell them of your plan. You will have your two months."

"Courage or stupidity," Aaron echoed. "In my experience, General, they're pretty much the same thing."

"General Envelar," Queen Isabelle said, her voice troubled as she spared a glance at Adina's worried expression, "are you sure about this?"

Sure? No, he wasn't sure. But then, the only sure things in life were the grave and the pain a man would endure before he got there. He would have even preferred sitting around the castle, drinking ale and getting fat, listening to the damned fool guards whisper about him every time he walked by than walk into a kingdom full of his enemies. But, then, it was a close thing either way. Not that the queen needed to hear that—not that any of them did. "I'm sure," he said with as much certainty as he could muster.

She studied him for a moment more as if to give him an opportunity to back out. Then, finally, she nodded once. "Very well," she said, "if it is your wish, then that is what we will do."

Gods no it's not, I'd rather get blind drunk and juggle knives than go back to Baresh. "It is."

"When will you leave?" the queen asked.

Aaron spared another glance at Adina. "Tonight. I'll be nearly a month traveling back and forth to Baresh, and that only leaves me a month to get the proof we need. There's no time to waste."

The queen nodded. "As you say."

The conversation went on from there about more mundane matters, mostly revolving around Isabelle's concerns about the petty crimes that had been committed in the city since Hale and Grinner's men had taken up residence behind its walls. She asked the two crime lords to ensure that the men and women they commanded were on their best behavior, and the two agreed, Hale smiling a small smile. Aaron could have told her that if no one had been killed then they were behaving themselves, at least as much as lifetime criminals were able, but he wasn't really paying attention. His thoughts were on the journey ahead, and the days to come. Going back to Baresh would almost certainly mean his death. Sure, he'd managed to survive things no man had a right to, but he had to think that there was a limit on the amount of luck any man could expect. If that was the case, he'd spent his and then some already. The God of Luck was a fickle god and sooner or later every man was dealt his final hand. This, he thought, might very well be his.

Then why do it? Co asked.

Because I don't have any choice, firefly. If the army leaves, we're fucked and you know it. This is the only option.

You've hurt her, you know.

Aaron glanced over to where Adina was still studying him, her expression somewhere between anger and sadness. I know, he said, but if the choice is between her living and being pissed off at me, or her dying, then it's really no choice at all.

The meeting went on for another half hour or so until the queen called an end to it. They all rose, and Aaron had started to Adina, wanting to talk to her, to apologize, but he'd only made it a few steps when he heard his name called. He turned to see Hale walking up, the thickly-muscled man striding forward and offering his hand. Aaron glanced at it in surprise, then took it. The crime lord laughed, "Gods, boy, but if you ask me, you've got a death wish. You sure you know what you're doing?"

"Hale," Aaron said, "I haven't known what I was doing for years."

The big man snorted. "Aye. Well, I always thought you were a crazy damned fool. Guess this just goes to show I was right."

"Guess so."

"Well," the crime lord said, still smiling as he slapped Aaron on the back hard enough to make his teeth knock together, "I'll leave you to it. And don't go gettin' greedy and killin' the whole damned army, Silent—leave some for the rest of us. There's some of us don't feel normal, if we ain't got to wash the blood off our hands at night."

Aaron gave the man a half-grin. "I'll try to restrain myself."

"You do that," the man said, "you do that." Then he turned and noted Grinner and his bodyguard leaving the audience chamber. "Son of a bitch always has to be first," Hale said, shaking his head. "Guess maybe they've got some catchin' up to do, if you know what I mean."

"I think I do."

The crime boss nodded, hesitating as if he wanted to say something more. "Anyhow, try not to let 'em kill ya if you can help it, boy. I'd hate for it to happen when I wasn't there to see it."

"I'll do my best."

Hale nodded again before turning and walking out of the audience chamber, bellowing for Grinner as he did. Aaron watched him go, shaking his head slowly. It was a damned miracle the two men hadn't killed each other yet. Hale seemed to make a game of poking and prodding all of Grinner's sensitive spots and for a man who spent his time among some of the world's worst criminals, Grinner had a lot of them.

"You ask me," Captain Gant said, coming to stand beside him, "it's a stupid thing you're doing."

Aaron turned to the older man. "You've known me for a while now, Brandon. Have I ever given you the impression that I'm a genius?"

The captain grunted, "No. No, I don't guess you have. Still, though, I have a hard time figuring out how you'll survive such a foolhardy thing. That said, I thought you were dead for sure when you and those crazy bastards of yours charged into Belgarin's army at the gate." He paused, meeting Aaron's eyes. "A man can't count on luck though, can he? I figure there's a good chance that this won't be like last time."

"Shit, Brandon," Aaron said, "the most recent story I heard about the fight at the gate, there were only five of us, and we killed a thousand men by ourselves. Next thing you know, we'll have grown wings and horns and engulfed Belgarin's army with fire we breathed from our mouths. The last time wasn't even like the last time."

"Yeah," the captain said, "well." He offered his hand. "I wish you luck. Anythin' you need, you just ask, you understand?"

Like a brain, maybe? Co said, but Aaron did his best to ignore her as he took the captain's hand.

"I appreciate that, Brandon."

The captain nodded, looking at Aaron as if he never expected to see him again which, Aaron supposed, he didn't. "Alright then." And he, too, turned and walked out of the audience chamber.

"Were you even going to talk to me?"

Aaron saw Adina standing beside him, her jaw set in anger. "Of course I was," he said. "How was I to know that I'd have everybody in the city wanting to line up to shake my hand?"

"Yeah," Adina said, "well, they probably think it's their last chance, considering that you'll most likely be dead in a month." Her voice broke on the last word, and Aaron reached up and cupped her face in his hand.

"It's not as bad as all that, Adina," he said. "Baresh is a big city, and I'm sure that Belgarin will have plenty of other things to worry about than me sneaking into it."

"Maybe," she said, her tone angry, "and what of Boyce Kevlane? Do you think he'll be too busy to hunt for you too, Aaron?"

He hesitated then sighed. "No, no I don't think he will. But I've beaten him before, Adina. There's always a chance I can do it again."

"Sure," Adina said, "always assuming he happens to attack you on a castle balcony again. But somehow I find that fairly unlikely, don't you?"

Aaron winced. "Fairly, yeah."

"If my father had lived," she said, grabbing his hands tightly in hers, "I would have been married off to some noble, a bargaining chip to increase the strength and standing of our house. It was how my mother and father were married, after all. I wouldn't have loved him, at least not at first, but perhaps over time I would have come to. Anyway, my father died, and I fell in love with a sellsword. I suppose I can't blame anyone but myself."

"It won't always be like this, Adina," he said, not sure it was true even as he said it. "Sooner or later, the fighting will be over."

Adina sighed, shaking her head sadly. "The fighting's never over, Aaron. As long as there are men and women on this earth, there will be fighting. You know that as well as I do."

He did, but saying so wouldn't help matters. "Well. My fighting then. Once we know that your brother and Boyce Kevlane are no longer a threat, then it can be over. There can be an ending to it. A beginning for us."

"Sure," she said, "something to look forward to, if you somehow manage to survive your latest suicidal quest of traveling into Baresh alone."

"Oh, he will not be alone, Princess," a new voice said, and they both turned to see Leomin walking towards them. "Although I have quite enjoyed my stay in Isalla thus far, mine is a mind that seeks its inspiration in the seeing of new places, the hearing of new sounds. My feet are ever searching for—"

"Some married woman's bed to climb in," Aaron finished, scowling. "And what are you talking about new places? You've been to Baresh. You were there along with the rest of us."

"Ah yes," Leomin said, "the me of months ago visited Baresh, and he enjoyed several aspects of it, I'll freely admit. The me of now, though, has never seen the fabled city and would very much like to feast eyes on it for the first time…again."

Aaron rubbed at his temples where a headache was beginning to form, where one always seemed to form when he spoke to the Parnen. "The me of you then is the me of you now." He paused, scowling. "Gods, but I've no idea what I just said. The shit's contagious."

Leomin grinned widely, showing his bright white teeth, "I have never understood you better than I do now. As for the old me, why, I haven't been him in months, Mr. Envelar.

"Call me Aaron, you bastard," Aaron said. "It's a privilege I allow to people who I'm considering murdering. Anyway, is it that you want to see Baresh again for the first time or whatever the fuck that means? Or, more likely, has some husband learned that you and his wife have been playing snuff the candle while he's out, and decided that one less Parnen in the world might not be such a bad thing?"

Leomin cleared his throat awkwardly. "I'm sure I don't know what you're talking about, Aaron. Though—completely unrelated to what we've been discussing—I must admit that I've found that the men of Isalla can be quite…possessive of their women. And if such a man were searching for me—not that I'm saying Gerald is…" He frowned thoughtfully, "At least, I believe his name is Gerald. I couldn't tell for sure what the dear lady shouted, as I was busy climbing out the window and trying to get dressed at the same time..." Suddenly, his eyes went wide as he realized what he'd said. "That is, hypothetically, I was climbing out the window. Anyway, if such a man were searching for me, I'm sure it would be only to have a conversation. After all, violence is so very rarely the answer, and it is very unbecoming. Probably one of the reasons his wife has sought her pleasure elsewhere, in fact." He cleared his throat. "If she has."

"What are you worried about anyway, Leomin?" Aaron said. "You could just wave your fingers at the man, talk some of your normal nonsense, and the next thing you knew, he'd be folding back the blankets for you himself."

Leomin placed a hand to his chest. "Mr. Envelar, you wound me. I would never use Aliandra in such a way. The Virtues are magical beings of great power and prestige and to use one in such a way would be a...sort of defilement. It would be crass and rude, the equivalent of dressing a cow in a woman's fine silk dress."

Aaron grinned. "Aliandra tell you that, did she?"

Leomin cleared his throat. "I...that is ..." He glanced at Adina for help and saw that despite her fear and anger, Adina was grinning too, then he looked back to Aaron. "I'm sure I don't know what you mean. Anyway, it is a poor way to use such power."

"Huh," Aaron said, nodding slowly, "good enough to use to get into a woman's bed, just not for the husband who normally shares it with her."

Leomin looked around as if hoping someone would rescue him from his predicament but everyone save the three of them had already left the audience chamber. He sighed heavily. "I do believe I remember telling you once before, Aaron, that having been bonded with Aliandra for so long, I cannot completely control the usage of the power. In fact, you could say that I do not use the power at all, but that it uses me. Yes," he said, nodding with more confidence, "that's it. I am merely a vessel."

"Yeah," Aaron said, "and a damned horny one from what I'm told." The Parnen could drive a man insane, but Aaron had known him for a while now, and he knew that Leomin could be a handy man to have around. "Fine, Leomin," he said, "you can come. But I need to make sure that you understand the kind of danger we're going to be walking into."

"That," Leomin said, casting a quick look over his shoulder as if he expected someone to be creeping up behind him, "is the funny thing about danger, Mr. Envelar. It is the only thing I know of that a man can walk out of to walk into. And some dangers, I find, are more well...shall we say, dangerous than others."

"Meaning jealous husbands."

Leomin frowned. "And fathers. Really, if a woman has seen two decades of life, I think it quite suffocating to treat her as if she's still..." He cut off, sighing, then straightened himself, brushing an invisible speck of dirt from his tunic. "It would be my honor and pleasure to accompany you, sir."

"Fine," Aaron said, "just so long as we're back in nine months or so."

The Parnen frowned. "Nine? I will admit that I was slightly distracted during the meeting—you see, there's this woman that goes by ..." His brow furrowed in thought and finally he waved a hand dismissively. "Anyway, she works at one of the inns near the castle. A truly fine establishment, at least I seem to remember as much. Though," he continued, rubbing a hand thoughtfully along his chin, "I suppose I didn't really pay much attention..."

"You don't even remember her name?" Adina said.

The Parnen froze for a moment, like a deer seeing a wolf, then he visibly gathered his confidence and smiled smugly. "Ah, Princess, I do not know how to explain it to you. You see, when two people find themselves sharing such a connection as she and I shared, there is little need for such mundane concerns as names."

"Yeah," Aaron said, "a need for clean sheets though, no doubt."

"Putting the matter aside for a moment," Leomin said uncomfortably, "I had felt quite certain that those gathered here today had agreed on a two month time frame for our journey to Baresh."

"They did," Aaron said, nodding, "but I thought in nine months we should come back regardless, see if maybe there's been an unusually high birth rate of dark skinned Parnen babies. I suspect that, if so, some of those women whose bedrooms you have frequented might be very interested in meeting with you again."

Leomin's shoulders hunched as if he was a turtle trying to slide his head under his shell, "Alas," he said, glancing around as if half-expecting to see an army of pregnant women marching toward him, one hand on their belly the other raised over their head in a fist, "we are all as the gods made us and it is given to men of certain dispositions to wander and women of...certain...err...conditions to wonder. It is a truth that is beyond us all, Mr. Envelar."

"As interesting as all of this is," Adina said, frowning at the Parnen before turning to look at Aaron, "I still think it's a mistake. If May were here, she'd tell you as much."

Aaron was thankful the club owner wasn't there, just for that reason. With her and Adina together, he figured he would have been in just about as much danger as he would be if Belgarin found him sneaking into his city. She'd been invited to the meeting, of course, but had explained to Aaron the day before that she wasn't feeling well. He'd taken the opportunity to express his surprise considering that, from what he'd heard, she'd been spending most of her time lying around in bed with a certain first mate, no doubt getting plenty of rest. She hadn't found the joke as funny as she might have, though, and he was glad that the already irate club owner hadn't been here for this meeting. "We don't have any choice, Adina," he said, "We have to do something. If the armies leave...well, you know what happens."

"I know that," she said, "but that doesn't mean it has to be you." Leomin started to raise a finger, and Adina spun on him. "Or you, Leomin," she snapped, "Of course, I don't want anything to happen to either of you."

The Parnen meekly lowered his hand, his eyes studying the ground.

"And what if I were to say that I was going to come with you?" Adina said, her eyes filled with challenge.

Aaron shrugged. "Then you would, that's all. Although I've got to tell you, Adina, it doesn't seem like a good idea. I need you here keeping track of what's going on and making sure that these fools don't kill each other before I get back. And if not that, then you should really go to Cardayum for a time. You are their new ruler, after all, and you have only been there once since your brother's death. Besides, the mountain city is more defensible than Perennia and—"

The princess's expression grew dark, cold, "So I'm to hide away in some castle while you risk your life, is that it, Aaron Envelar?"

Aaron saw the trap but didn't know a way around it. "I...that is...I'm a sellsword, Adina. You're a princess. If you don't like it, I suppose you could ask Leomin's gods. Maybe they have the answers. All I know is that if we don't keep this army together, the entire country is going to drown in blood."

She sighed, some of the fight going out of her. "You'll come back."

It wasn't a question, but Aaron answered it anyway, "Yes." *If I can.*

She opened her mouth as if to say more then glanced meaningfully at Leomin.

"Yes, Princess?" the Parnen said, not getting the hint.

Aaron grunted. "I think we should go to our room. It would be better to talk there, away from prying eyes and ears."

"Yes, of course," Leomin said, nodding, "that is a most wise decision, Mr. Envelar, within the confines of said room, I am sure that we might—"

"We, Leomin," he said, pointing at Adina and himself, "Why don't you go and get some supplies?"

"Oh. Aaah," the Parnen said, smiling, "Why, I would be happy to, Aaron. I know of a horse merchant not far from here who has some of the finest beasts I have ever seen." He nodded slowly. "A bit of a grumpy man, I must admit, though he is not given to idle chatter, and that is something I respect greatly in a person. His daughter though...why, she is most hospitable, a very kind, giving soul. Would you like for me to tell you the story of our first meeting? It was truly—"

"No," Aaron and Adina both said at the same time, and the Parnen winced.

"Very well," he said with what dignity he could summon, "though I must observe that it is a shame that not everyone enjoys a good story. And speaking of good stories, I should tell you about this woman I met—Anna or no, wait, was it Amy...it was something like that I'm sure of it. Abby, perhaps? Wait, it'll come to me..."

The man was still speaking as Aaron led Adina from the audience chamber, his voice carrying on a monologue to an empty room as the doors closed behind them.

CHAPTER FOUR

"Son of a bitch," Sergeant Wendell muttered, tossing his cards onto the table in disgust. "Really figured you were bluffin' there."

"I never bluff," the gray-haired swordmaster said, smiling and raking the coins toward his increasingly large stack and beginning to organize them. The bastard had so many that it was taking some doing. Wendell frowned at his own quickly diminishing pile of coins. Not enough to be called a pile, not really.

"That a fact?" Wendell said sourly, staring at his own coins. Not a pile at all. He wasn't sure what you called an amount of coins you could fit in the palm of our hand, but he thought maybe "pittance" would work. "Seems to me," he said, looking back at the swordmaster and his smug smile, "that you took some of my coin from me not two hands ago on a bluff."

"Well," Darrell said, grinning, "you've caught me. Still, Sergeant, something I've learned is that in cards, as in battle, misdirection is one of the best strategies a man can use."

Wendell shook his head. "My momma used to tell me I was a fool, and by the gods I think she was right. What other reason would bring me out here to meet you at this tavern week after week to give you all my gold? And I had plans for this here. There's a new girl over at *The Serving Wench*, goes by the name of Stretching Sallia, if you can believe it. Folks say she can do things to a man that'll leave him screamin' and beggin' for more at the same time."

The swordmaster sighed. "Brothels. Friend Wendell, if you don't mind me saying so, I think there are, perhaps, wiser things to do with your coin."

Wendell scowled, "Like give it to you, I suppose."

Darrell laughed at that, and despite himself Wendell found himself grinning as well. "Another hand?" the swordmaster asked.

Wendell grunted, rubbing at an ache in his arm from where one of the practice swords had struck him during training earlier in the day. Wood or not, those damned things hurt. He'd spent the morning and early afternoon getting beat on then he'd come here only to get beat on again. Except, this beating wouldn't end with bruises and shouts of pain but instead empty pockets and a lonely night. Stretching Sallia would have to wait for some other time. *Unless*, he thought, a flash of excitement running through him, *I double up. It could happen—the man isn't a mind reader, after all.* He leaned forward and waved his hand, "Deal 'em, you old bastard." He watched the swordmaster shuffle and glanced again at the small pile of coins on his side of the table. *Gods, I really am a fool.*

They'd been playing for a short time—and Wendell's remaining coins were so few that they were destined for extinction unless the two that were left got together and started poppin' out little coin babies—when the door to the tavern opened, and the swordmaster looked over Wendell's shoulder, smiling widely. "Ah, a princess enters a tavern. There's a joke there somewhere."

"Oh, you ain't gettin' me to look that easy," Wendell said, keeping his gaze steady, "I turn around, and the next thing I know I'm missin' some coins."

The swordmaster raised his eyebrow at him and glanced meaningfully at the two left on his side of the table. "I think you'd notice."

"Smug bastard," Wendell muttered. He glanced at his cards. "Well, those two are gettin' ready to have a couple of friends," he said, pushing the two coins into the middle of the table. "It's on you."

The swordmaster considered and was reaching for his coins when a woman spoke from beside the table. "Darrell."

Darrell rose and bowed. "Princess, it is very good to see you."

Wendell cursed and stumbled out of his own chair, nearly knocking it over as he bowed low. "You could have told me, you old snake," he said.

"And here, I thought I had."

Wendell only frowned, but Adina laughed. "Oh, please, no need for all of this fuss on my account." She glanced around at the crowded tavern and saw several people watching curiously. "Sergeant," she said, "there really isn't any need to fall to both knees. I'm not a god, after all. Besides, we're drawing more attention than I'd like."

Wendell's face heated. "Sorry about that," he said, standing once more, "I ain't had much cause to be around royalty, as such. Gods be good, my mom was always too embarrassed to even take me to market with her. Overreacted, if you ask me. You set a horse's tail on fire *one time* and all of a sudden nobody trusts you."

Darrell cleared his throat as he drew out a chair for the princess. *Damnit, I should have thought of that,* Wendell thought. He considered pulling the chair out further, but as the princess was already sitting in it, he didn't think it'd do any good, so instead he followed the swordmaster's lead and sat himself. "A horse's tail on fire, you say?" Darrell asked, grinning.

Wendell grunted, not wanting to talk about it. "Weren't much of a tail no ways. Just a stringy, shriveled thing, hairless and all. 'Course," he said, considering, "that might've been the fire done for that last bit. Anyhow, I ain't sure it was the burnin' tail itself so much that put my mother off bringin' me with her, as it was the merchant's stall that took a bit of a beatin'. That horse wasn't a big fan of the fire, you understand. Fella blew the whole thing all out of proportion."

Darrell blinked. "A merchant's stall was damaged?"

Wendell cleared his throat. "Err...that is, stalls. Couple of 'em...maybe a few more...anyhow who keeps track of such things as that?"

"I imagine the merchants," Adina laughed.

"Yeah, they did too, the bastards. I had to do chores for years to pay 'em back. Anyhow," Wendell said, deciding it was time to change the subject, "you don't mind me askin', Princess, what's got you out here? The ale tastes like dog piss." He glanced at Darrell. "And the company ain't nothin' to speak of."

The princess's smile faded at that, and she turned to Darrell. "As to that, I've been looking everywhere for you. I didn't think I was ever going to find you until one of the soldiers told me you and Sergeant Wendell met at this tavern every week."

"Bastard probably laughed when he said it," Wendell muttered.

"I apologize for the trouble, Princess," the swordmaster said. "How can I help you?"

Adina winced. "Can we talk somewhere a little more private? It's about Aaron."

"Of course," Darrell said, rising. Adina also stood, and Darrell pulled her chair back. *Damnit again,* Wendell thought.

"This way, princess," Darrell said, grabbing his winnings—*bastards gonna have to get bigger pockets,* Wendell thought—then the swordmaster turned back to look at him. "I apologize for cutting our game short, Sergeant. I will seek you out soon. You may keep your two coins, if you'd like."

Wendell snorted as he watched them walk away. Of course he was keeping his coins. The bastard was just lucky the princess had walked in when she did. It had been obvious the man was gonna call, and there was no way he had Wendell beaten. No way. He glanced back once more to make sure they were gone then leaned forward, grabbing the swordmaster's cards from where he'd laid them on the table. "Son of a *bitch,*" he said. Sighing, he took his two remaining coins and put them in his pocket then rose.

He considered buying another ale but suddenly found that he didn't feel much like being in the tavern. Dark was still an hour or two away, but he found that he was tired. Maybe a good night's sleep would be all he needed. And was all he could afford at any rate. He turned and headed out the door, and happened to see Adina and Darrell disappear around a corner.

The way they'd walked wasn't in the direction of his room. "Well, that's alright," he muttered to himself, "a walk in the fresh air will do me some good." Decided, he set off in the direction Adina and Darrell had taken. He made it to the alley they'd gone down and a quick glance showed them about halfway down its length. *Well,* he thought, *a walk is all fine and good, but there's nothing quite like taking in the sights and sounds of the city. That'll be just the thing.* And if he just happened to overhear someone's conversation? Well, that wasn't his fault, was it? He propped his back up against the front of a tailor's shop on one side of the alley and relaxed. He started to whistle a tune but decided against it. Not that he was hiding from anyone. After all, he was just a man out to see the city—what cause did he have for hiding?

The two voices were low and hushed, and Wendell could only make out snatches of the conversation. "going to Baresh ..." the princess was saying, but her voice grew more distant.

Wendell cocked his head, but still almost all of the words were too quiet to make out. He grunted, suddenly dissatisfied with the view. If you'd seen one main city street, you'd seen them all, so far as he was concerned. The real character of a city wasn't in its main street, but in its alleyways, away from the hustle and bustle of visitors. He glanced down the alleyway and saw that Adina and Darrell were walking toward the opposite end of the alley, and he followed them, keeping a quiet, respectful distance. Wasn't his fault they just happened to be walking the same direction as him, but he didn't want to make a lot of noise and disturb them. Based on their postures, they were talking about something serious and, whatever that something was, it had to do with the general.

"...not such a bad idea..." Darrell was saying, and Wendell drew closer still. Finally, they turned down an alleyway, and Wendell decided to walk a little faster—good for the heart and lungs, was exercise. He made it to the end of the alley and glanced around the corner to make sure once more that he didn't stumble into them and disturb them, and saw that they had stopped on the street right around the corner.

Well, he thought, *don't want to bother 'em none. Probably, I'll just relax here for a moment.* And that was exactly what he did, propping his back against the wall once more.

"Of *course* it's a bad idea," Adina was saying. "Don't you understand, Darrell? He could be *killed.*"

"We do not know how many traitors are still in the castle, Princess," the swordmaster said. "For all we know, Aaron will be safer in Baresh than he will be here. At least there, he'll know who his enemies *are*. Besides, he's right—we can't afford to lose the armies. If the people of Avarest leave, we will have lost a significant portion of our strength in the coming battle."

"*Our,* you say," Adina said, "but is that what you mean, Darrell? Tell me, truly, where does your loyalty lie? Is it with Aaron or is it with the Tenders?"

There was a hesitation then as the swordmaster considered the question. "Can it not be both?"

"No," Adina said, "no, I don't believe it can. I think you know as well as I that Tianya will not be happy with Aaron's decision to go. After all, we don't know where Boyce Kevlane is. If she had her way, Aaron would be locked in a padded room for the rest of his life—Leomin too, I suspect. No, Darrell, there is no middle ground here. I need to know the truth. If it comes between Tianya and the Tenders or Aaron, who do you choose?"

The swordmaster sighed, and there was something defeated about it. "You're right, of course. Tianya won't be happy when she hears of it. She has tried to get me to speak with Aaron again about leaving the country, but I've told tell her that it's no use. That boy's never run from a fight in his life, and I don't expect he'll start to do so now."

"You didn't answer my question."

Another hesitation, and when Darrell spoke his voice was low but full of certainty. "Aaron was—*is*—like a son to me, Adina. I pray that it doesn't come to that, but if it does, I will choose Aaron. Always."

"Thank you, Darrell," Adina said, and Wendell could hear the tears of relief in her voice, "thank you. Will you go with him then? Will you keep him safe?"

"Yes," Darrell said. "Tianya will not be pleased, but if it is within my power, I will keep any harm from coming to him."

If it is within my power. Wendell had seen the man slaughter several men in the space of a few heartbeats. Well, he'd sort of seen it—he'd been being choked to death at the time. And General Envelar was no slouch himself. Why, people told stories about him in the city like he was some living legend, and Wendell had seen what he did on the battlefield. The man and the Ghosts with him took on thousands of soldiers by themselves, and Wendell thought that the general must have killed at least two or three dozen people alone. He pitied the fool that would try to do either man harm, and he snorted at the thought of it. Then he clapped a hand over his mouth, realizing what he'd done. *Shit.*

"Wha—?" the princess began, but Darrell only sighed.

"You can come out now, Sergeant."

Wendell winced and reluctantly walked around the corner. "Right," he said, clearing his throat, "so when are we leaving?"

CHAPTER FIVE

Aaron was in the room he and Adina shared, packing a traveling bag for his journey when a knock came at the door. He opened it expecting it to be Adina, and was surprised to find May standing in the doorway, her hands on her hips. "May," he said, "I thought you'd be with Thom. What brings you here?" Though judging by the angry scowl on her face he thought he knew well enough.

"You're a fool."

Aaron sighed and swung the door open. "Come on in, May." He motioned to one of the two chairs at the small sitting table. "Have a seat. If you're going to yell at me, we might as well both be comfortable."

She walked past him into the room, glancing meaningfully at the pack sitting on the bed before looking back at him. "You honestly intend to go through with this madness."

Aaron reluctantly closed the door and turned back to look at the club owner. "Yes."

She shook her head angrily. "Silent, I've seen you survive some things no one has a right to walk away from. Do you remember when Hale asked you to join his crew and you refused?"

Of course I remember, he thought, *I've still got the scars.* "Yes."

"When he sent those assassins after you, you somehow managed to survive. Then when Grinner's men took your mother's necklace, you rushed off like a fool and took on Grinner's entire criminal empire. Do you remember that?"

More memories. More scars. "I remember."

"Even when you tried to save Prince Eladen and ended up being chased by pretty much every coin hungry criminal in the city—which is *every* criminal in the city. Do you remember that?"

Aaron nodded slowly, "You know I do, May. But that's not fair. I didn't know it was Prince Eladen I was rescuing. Or...failing to rescue."

"Just shut up and listen," she snapped. "*Now*, as I understand it, you intend to travel to a city ruled by a man who would no doubt pay more coin than exists in all of the Downs to have your head on a pike. Not to mention that you'll be putting yourself at the mercy of a pissed off mage that's been alive for thousands of years and, as far as I've heard, is pretty much a damned immortal."

"We don't know where Boyce Kevlane is," Aaron said. "The man changes faces more than a noblewoman changes shoes, May. Shit, if you weren't so pissed off, I wouldn't know for sure that *you* weren't him. Don't you understand? That bastard could be anybody."

"And *if* you somehow survive this," she went on as if he hadn't spoken, "a thing that seems damned near impossible to me, then when does it end?"

Aaron frowned. "What?"

"I asked you," she said, "that if you are somehow victorious, what will happen next? Will you then challenge the gods themselves? Or maybe jump in the ocean, see if you can't find some sharks to wrestle?"

Aaron sighed. "That's ridiculous, May. It's not like I have a death wish."

"Isn't it?"

Aaron felt the anger rising in him. Thanks to his bond with Co, it was always there, lurking beneath the surface of his thoughts. "No," he said, "this has to be done, May. You know that as well as I do. Just as you know what happens if Belgarin attacks and we don't have the troops from Avarest."

"Yes," she said, "I do know, and I understand that it has to be done. I can even understand why you think you have to be the one to go—after all, it's the only thing that I can think of that would have made Hale and Grinner stay. Either way it comes out, they'll be satisfied."

"If you know all of that," Aaron shouted, his anger getting the better of him, "then why are you giving me all this shit?"

"I'm giving you all of this *shit,* as you call it," she said, her voice calm, "because despite the fact that you understand the importance of your mission's success, despite the fact that you know that without you returning with proof that Belgarin intends us harm, we are defeated before the battle even begins, you decided—without talking to anyone *else,* I might add—to go alone. You didn't even consider asking for help."

Aaron frowned at that, his anger dampened somewhat by the truth of her words. He'd grown accustomed over the years as an orphan and then a sellsword to not asking for anyone's help, to solving problems on his own.

"You are not alone anymore, Silent," May said as if reading his thoughts. She sighed then and laid a hand on his shoulder. "You'll never be alone again."

Aaron nodded slowly. "But, May, it won't be safe to—"

"Never mind what's safe and what isn't," she interrupted. "We're not children to be protected, Aaron, nor are we some pampered nobles to be coddled and assured while our homes burn down around us. We are your *friends,* the gods help us. And besides, in case you've forgotten, we've got just as much riding on the success of this mission as you do. It's not as if Belgarin or Boyce Kevlane will stop if they kill you. This is about everyone's lives, Aaron. Not just yours."

Aaron frowned, considering.

She's right, you know, Co said in a satisfied voice.

I know she is damnit. "I'm sorry, May. You're right—I should have asked."

May stared at him for a moment then nodded in apparent satisfaction. "Perhaps not a total fool, after all. Now, when do you leave?"

"Tonight," Aaron said. "The sooner the better, as we'll lose a month in travel, at least."

"And I've heard that Leomin is coming along."

"He is."

She grunted again. "I'm not sure whether that makes me feel better or worse. Still, the man knows how to talk himself out of just about anything. And what of this other one you told me of, this Tianya?"

I don't think she'll be happy about it," Aaron said, shrugging, "but what can she do?"

May frowned, "I wouldn't dismiss her so quickly, Aaron. Such a woman like that will be used to giving orders and having them followed. She won't appreciate being ignored."

"Sounds like somebody else I know."

She snorted and started for the door. "Just be safe and make sure that you all make it back in one piece."

"All of us? I told you, May, it's just me and Leomin."

She smiled. "Oh, I don't know about that. I guess we'll see." She winked then, and was out the door before Aaron could ask her what she'd meant.

"Damnit," he muttered, "I don't have a good feeling about this."

CHAPTER SIX

High Clerk Evane was scared. The realization had come slowly as it was not an emotion he was accustomed to, but he'd had some time to consider it since receiving his master's summons the day before. He'd finally come to know that sinking, fragile feeling in his stomach for what it was. Fear.

Up until a few weeks ago when the man, Caldwell, had come to him with his offer, Evane had led a double life. During the day, his existence had been normal enough. Normal and boring. He'd served as a clerk in the merchant's guild. A safe, secure position that, though it would never make him rich, had made him enough money, to afford a decent house and clothes. His parents, had they still been alive, might even have been proud, might even have celebrated his achievement, his demonstration of responsibility. Not that such things mattered.

He'd learned long ago that it was better not to be noticed at all. Better to be a quiet, awkward clerk, the man who ate his lunches by himself and spoke only when necessary. The man who never went out to taverns with his fellow clerks, and was never seen with a young woman on his arm. They thought him harmless enough, if a little strange, and that was alright. That was just fine.

The Clerk Evane of the daytime was a skittish, nervous man, a man who spent his days in boring drudgery, checking and balancing accounts, taking payments from customers when payments came due, and, all in all, keeping to himself. Just another boring soul in a city full of them.

He was invisible, not worth attention, and that was just the way he liked it. For while Evane's colleagues knew him as a shy clerk, it was no more than a mask he wore. He'd learned to wear the mask at an early age, the first time his mother had caught him with some dog he'd found in the street. The mongrel was wounded and had only three working legs, which made it easier as it couldn't run or fight back when the blade went in, searching. He didn't know what he was searching for at the time, only that each carving cut he made into the howling beast's flesh drew him a little closer to it, that each hot sluice of blood over his hands brought him nearer to that indefinable reward toward which he worked.

He was eight years old at the time, and the dog was not his first, though it was the first time with an animal quite so large. He wasn't ready when the tortured beast found some last burst of strength and tore away from his bloody attentions, darting up the cellar steps, howling and screaming in pain, leaving a bloody trail behind it that his mother would later force him to clean up.

He chased after the wounded animal, but three legs or not, it made good its escape, though not before his mother—come home early from the market, saw the dog pass her by with its bloody, torn flesh. In his haste to capture the animal—his experiment, he called it as he called all before it—Evane had forgotten to put down the knife he'd used, and he rushed out the front door only to freeze at the sight of his mother standing there.

She took in the bloody clothes he wore—clothes he'd intended to change long before she got back from the market—and noted the short, cruel knife he held, the blade bloody and matted with fur. For a moment, she looked at him as if seeing a stranger; that was the first time he understood what it meant to do the things he did, that the hunger somehow set him apart from other children, other people. Then, her face seemed to regain some of its normal expression, and she nodded slowly. "Put down the knife, Evi," she said, "and help your mother with this." He took one of the baskets she'd been carrying and helped her inside, his hands leaving bloody prints on the wicker basket. She made him go bathe in the river and scrub himself clean, and he had, thinking that would be the end of it.

It wasn't though. When his father got home from a day—and most of a night—spent drinking, he came into Evane's room. He did not speak, only jerked his son out of his bed and commenced beating him with his fists until Evane couldn't even make out his own cries for the dizziness that overcame him. It was a week before he could walk without a vicious pain tearing through his body. A week spent lying in his bed while his mother spoon fed him thin broth—real food having proved too much to keep down—and told him in apologetic but justified tones that he had to learn, he had to learn his lesson. And he *did* learn a lesson, though not the one they wanted.

He learned that it was better to keep that part of himself, the hole inside of him that could only be filled with the blood, the suffering of others, secret. It was a lesson he learned well and when he was fifteen and a burglar broke into their home, killing his mother and father, the guards who came to investigate saw nothing but a frightened, crying boy with blood on his hands from where he'd tried to rouse his dead mother and father.

The guards saw nothing of the smile that hid beneath that tortured expression, heard none of the laughter that bubbled just beneath the surface of his cries; and that was as it should be, for that was his day-time self, the mask he wore to show to the world. But at night, when the sun was down and the shadows hid the truth of things behind a veil of darkness, only then did he take the mask off, only then could he really and truly *breathe*.

It was a good enough life, he supposed, if a bit stifling. As the years passed, he found that his needs grew more pronounced. Once, small animals had done the job but that had passed quickly enough. Only a few years after his parents' "murder" he began to experiment with people—there was no shortage of experiments available in the poor district. Men with no wives and no children, no one to miss them when they were gone. Women, alone in the world, who sold their bodies to feed their flesh. They weren't as strong as the men, but they were less trusting, more suspicious and so presented their own challenges when he chose one for his experiments.

There was a time when one or two a year had been enough, but his hunger, his *need* had grown, and now he found himself prowling the streets at night in search of prey at least once a month if not more. It wouldn't be long, he knew, before people began to take notice.

And even more troubling, he'd found his daytime mask seemed to grow tighter and tighter even as his nighttime need grew more prominent. He found himself looking at those people at work or those customers who came in to make payments on their loans, found himself imagining them screaming, imagining how their blood would feel on his hands.

Such thoughts were dangerous, he knew, but the Evane of the night had always been stronger than the Evane of the day. Now, he was growing increasingly worried, sure that one day or another he would not be able to silence the voice inside of him. Sooner or later, the mask would slip off, and they would all know the truth, would come to understand that they were sheep and a wolf stalked among them, picking out one of their flock as their backs were turned. Once discovered, he knew his life would end at the blow of some headsman's axe, and he'd been seriously considering leaving the city when the man, Caldwell, had approached him.

He'd approached him in the darkness while Evane had been following a young woman of the night. She was nineteen, twenty at the most. Old enough to have that used up, hopeless look that so many of her kind seemed to have, but not so old as to be as suspicious as many of her counterparts. Oh, she was old enough to have heard the stories, old enough to know the dangers for women such as her, but she was not quite old enough, he thought, to believe it.

Evane was following her through the streets of the poor quarter, always sure to keep his distance. She'd be heading home, he knew, as he'd followed her on other nights. Home, to where no one waited for her, no family or friends, not even a cat or a dog to keep her company. He was reveling in anticipation of the night's fun when a figure stepped out of the alleyway in front of him, blocking his path.

The man wasn't much bigger than Evane himself, and his blood was up, ready for violence and the relief it would bring. Still, he did not make a move on the man, did not draw the crude, short blade he kept in the pocket of his trousers. *This,* he thought, *is no sheep.* A wolf, after all, knows another wolf when he sees it. "Hello, Clerk Evane," the man said, and those words sent a shiver of fear running through Evane's heart, such a feeling as he had not felt in a very long time.

The man knew him, knew his name and his profession both, neither of which was supposed to happen. He'd taken great pains, always, to disguise his identity, going by different names, even staining his normally light blonde hair with soot to make it appear black in the darkness. He shifted his stance, ready to run or fight—he wasn't sure which—but the man only smiled, his face looking somehow twisted and wrong in the moonlight. He turned to glance at the departing woman who was oblivious of how close she'd come to being the night's experiment, leaving his back to Evane, apparently unconcerned by what the clerk might do.

Finally, the woman disappeared around a corner. One more turn, Evane knew, and she would reach the small shack she considered her home. When she was gone, the man turned back around, eyeing Evane in the moonlight. "Not a bad choice, I suppose, if a man is in the market for such things. I suspect she'd scream loud enough. Bleed too."

"What do you want?" Evane asked, his voice sounding strange and alien to his own ears. It wasn't the voice of the daytime Evane, quiet and subservient, nor was it the voice of the nighttime Evane that was confident and sure and always seemed on the verge of laughter. Instead, it was an odd mix of the two.

The man's grin widened. "My name is Caldwell. And I've got a job offer for you..."

The man brought the promise of not having to hide his true self any longer, of being able to glut himself on the pain and suffering of others, maybe even enough to fill the hole inside him once and for all. And, of course, Evane had said yes.

So far, he'd seen only a fraction of what the man had promised him, but it was enough. He'd been sent out nearly every day of the last month in search of men and women who showed exceptional abilities. Men and women who were known for their speed or their strength, their cruelty or their anger, some quality that set them apart from normal people. He spent his days, when not working, running other errands for Caldwell and his true master, King Belgarin himself. Otherwise, he was sitting in taverns, talking to the patrons there to hear any rumors about people who had somehow set themselves apart—never a hard thing that, as ale and liquor had a way of loosening people's lips.

Evane did not know what Caldwell and the king did with these people when they were taken, knew only that they were to be used in experiments. Ones, perhaps, like those he himself performed. Now, though, he had received the king's summons to the castle, a thing that had never happened. He was excited and scared at the same time. He'd once asked Caldwell if he could see the experiments himself, but the man had made it clear that Evane was reaching beyond his bounds and that he should only concern himself with his own role in things.

Evane had agreed, partly because he was satisfied. Watching the fear, the terror in those he chose as they were taken held a satisfaction all its own. And, of course, there were sometimes others among those who were taken who by necessity, had to be killed. Mostly, though, he hadn't asked again because of Caldwell himself.

There was something wrong with the king's advisor, something *off.* The man hid it well, when he wanted to, but as another who did not share any true similarities with the ignorant sheep that filled the city, Evane recognized that wrongness. He did not understand it or know what it meant, but he saw hints of it from time to time. He had decided that whatever set the advisor apart, whatever madness—for madness it was, he had no doubt— he held within him, Evane would rather not see it. Even a wolf, after all, knew when to bow its head to another, knew when it was time to put away the teeth and claws and lay down on the ground digging its muzzle into the dirt. After all, there was always a bigger wolf.

Evane thought that today might be the day he learned the truth of the "experiments", the first time that he met his true master, the king himself. No wonder, then, that he was nervous. If Caldwell was a bigger wolf, then what was the king? Not a wolf at all, surely. A lion, perhaps. Still, nervous or not, he couldn't help the thrill of excitement that ran through him at the prospect of seeing the true nature of his work, and he found his steps growing faster and faster as he made his way through the castle, following the directions he'd been given.

The guard at the dungeon entrance frowned as he approached, and Evane felt a new wave of fear wash over him at the man's attention. He'd spent his entire life—his *daytime* life, anyway—

doing his best to avoid the attention of such men. What if he'd been wrong? What if he'd somehow confused Caldwell's directions, or if the man himself had given Evane false information intentionally, setting him up? *No,* he told himself, *you are a wolf, not a sheep to scatter at the first sign of trouble. Do not be a fool.* "State your business here, stranger," the guard said, and Evane couldn't help but notice that one of the man's hands had drifted toward the sword at his side.

Evane swallowed hard, drawing himself up as tall as he might and meeting the guard's eyes. "My name is High Clerk Evane, servant of His Majesty, Belgarin, and I have come as summoned to attend him." He heard the breathless whine in his voice and hated himself for it. Yet as foolish as it was, he couldn't dismiss the notion that the guard would, at any moment, draw the sword at his side and either take Evane into custody or cut him down where he stood. The guard studied him for a moment, and Evane felt his hands begin to sweat.

After what felt like an eternity, the guard finally bowed his head, "Pleasure to meet you, High Clerk. The king's advisor told me you'd be stopping by. Follow me, and I'll show you to where he waits."

With that, he turned and unlocked the dungeon door. Evane followed him as he started down the hallway, unable to suppress the grin that came to his face.

The dungeons were dark, the only light that of the sputtering torches placed at uneven intervals along the wall, bathing the hard-packed dirt floor, the cells, and their occupants in a ruddy orange glow. Evane had thought that the dungeons would be alive with the sounds of prisoners screaming and shouting for their release, begging for another chance or another trial, but he was surprised to find that the prisoners didn't scream at all. Some few stood at the front of their cells, staring fearfully at a door at the far end of the hall. As the king's advisor approached, they shrank away and into the corners of their cells.

As they made their way further down the hall, Evane realized that he *could* hear screaming, after all. It was muffled, and he realized that it was coming from behind the door. He looked around at the prisoners who watched them with subdued expressions. "I would have thought they'd be more…active."

The advisor paused, turning. "The prisoners, do you mean? Yes, well, they were, once upon a time. But my master has been desperate for new subjects on which to perform his...experiments, and, at times, he has culled those he needed from the dungeons themselves." He smiled, and there was a dark hunger in the expression. "I suspect some of them are worried that they may be next."

Evane nodded slowly at that, glancing at the prisoner in the cell to the left of them who watched them with wide, fearful eyes, sucking on his thumb like a child. "And are they?"

Caldwell grunted. "They are poor specimens, these. Malnourished and weak from deprivation. Still..." He paused, shrugging. "Perhaps. After all, the work must continue, and a desperate carpenter must use what wood as comes to hand."

With that, the robed advisor lifted a torch from its bracket on the wall, turned and started down the hall once more. Evane followed him, troubled by something he couldn't quite define. *It's those damned screams, for one,* he thought. It was, he found, very different when you were the cause of such screams, of such pain and terror. There was a feeling of power that came along with the causing of such things, a feeling of invincibility; but to hear them, to know that someone besides yourself was the creator of them...he decided that he did not like it. After all, one man sounded much like another when he screamed himself breathless. It could have been anyone behind that door, screaming. It could have been himself.

Finally, they came to the door, and Caldwell opened it, motioning Evane inside. The screams were louder now, more real, and Evane found himself hesitating. He could see little more than darkness ahead in the poor, flickering light cast by the torch the advisor held. There could have been anything inside there, anything at all, and he licked his lips nervously, a habit the daytime Evane had acquired years before but one that had never—until now, at least—followed him when his mask was off. "Well, come now," Caldwell said, amusement in his tone. "After all, you asked to see this, did you not, *High Clerk?* You wished to understand more of the work we do and now is your chance. Or have you changed your mind?"

There was something in the man's voice Evane didn't like, and he swallowed. "O-of course not, sir," he said.

"Then go on," Caldwell said, "the master waits for us both, and he is not a patient man, Evane. Not patient at all."

A sudden, powerful urge to turn and run came over Evane, but he fought it down. He'd seen some of Caldwell's men in action, had seen them demonstrate impossible strength and speed that beggared the imagination. A man could not run from such things as that. Wiping the sweat from his forehead, he stepped through the door and into a hallway. The screams—not so muffled as they had been—were coming from up ahead. Evane's feet seemed to grow heavier and heavier with each step, but he kept walking forward, knowing that he didn't really have any choice.

When they reached the door at the end of the long, dirt hallway, Evane reached for the latch to open it, but Caldwell spoke. "I wouldn't do that, were I you," he said. "Our master does not like to be interrupted during his work. We will wait until he is finished and then we will go in."

Evane nodded slowly, turning to look at the advisor, the man's face seeming somehow demonic in the torchlight. "How will we know?"

Caldwell spread his mouth into a grin. "The screams will stop."

Evane swallowed hard at that but managed a nod. "Of course."

They stood there in silence for several minutes, shivers of dread running up Evane's spine at each fresh, tortured scream. He looked around the hallway, searching for something to distract him from that terrible sound, and noted that unlike the dungeons proper, the earth here looked recently dug. He mentioned as much to the advisor, and the man smiled. "Yes, my master found it prudent to create a new space for his...work."

"It...it must have taken forever to dig out so much extra space," Evane said.

"Oh, not so long," the advisor said, smiling, "my master has some tools at his disposal that few men do."

Evane found that he had nothing to say, didn't think he could have managed to get the words past the growing lump in his throat even if he had. He nodded, and once more they lapsed into silence. After about fifteen minutes, the screams abruptly cut off, and Caldwell gestured to the door. "You may go in."

Evane reached a tentative hand out and pulled the door open. Inside, the hallway opened up into a large, hollowed-out cavern. Torches were interspersed along the walls, and in the center of the cavern sat a large stone table upon which lay a bloody figure. As he watched, two of the large, hulking forms of the men who sometimes accompanied him on his missions moved forward and removed manacles that had been fastened to the figure's wrists and ankles. They lifted him up, carrying him away, and Evane saw the man's body sag in their grip, lifeless. He stared with a mixture of fascination and horror as they dragged the corpse to a corner of the room and threw it on top of a pile of other such corpses.

"Unfortunately," Caldwell said beside him, and Evane jumped, letting out a squeak of fear. He turned to see the advisor smiling regretfully, "Not all experiments are successes. When dealing with such forces as my master employs, sometimes there are...failures."

"But there are...so many," Evane said, finding himself once more studying the mound of corpses heaped in the corner of the room.

"Yes," Caldwell said, a note of what sounded like admiration in his voice as he followed Evane's gaze, "our master does not believe in half measures and, as I believe I have said, he is not a patient man."

Suddenly, Evane was sure that he didn't want to be here. He didn't want to be in this room with this man, with that heap of bloody corpses, their faces—or what remained of them—twisted from last moments spent in agony, their eyes glazed over with death. Had he truly thought himself a wolf? He was realizing with a growing sense of dread that he was no wolf at all, not really. He was only another sheep. One that had perhaps risen above his counterparts but no more than that.

"Oh, do not look so afraid, High Clerk," Caldwell said, "Yours is the privilege of looking on a great work."

"Y-yes sir," he managed, his voice coming out in little more than a croak.

Caldwell opened his mouth to speak but closed it again as a door opened in the side of the cavern and a man stepped through it. He wore a robe, and the sleeves had been rolled up to display hands and forearms coated in blood. His face, too, was splattered with it, but Evane could see enough of it to recognize King Belgarin. The king was wiping his hands on a crimson-stained rag.

"*Bow before your master,*" Caldwell hissed, and Evane dropped to his knees, bowing low to the ground.

"Rise," came a voice, and Caldwell pulled Evane to his feet. "Caldwell," the man said, tossing the rag on the floor. "And this must be the man you told me about."

"Yes, master," the advisor said, bowing low, and Evane felt the weight of the robed man's gaze as it fell upon him.

He started to speak, thinking that he should say *something*, when an agonized, breathless moan came from one of the bodies in the corner, and he turned, staring.

"Never mind them, boy," Belgarin said, "they are failures, one and all. There have been many of such, lately. Too many." He turned to gaze at Caldwell.

When the advisor spoke, Evane was shocked to hear fear in his voice, "Master, forgive me, but efforts to procure the specimens you need have been somewhat difficult. Given more time—"

"*Enough!*" the robed man roared with rage, and Evane noticed Caldwell recoil even as he did himself. "I ask for the best, and you bring me old men and old women, the weak and decrepit, long past their prime. Either that or children too young to be of any use. It seems that I am destined to work with worthless men. First, that fool Aster gets himself killed, *losing* one of *my* Virtues, then *you*, Caldwell, managed to fail so spectacularly that Belgarin's army lost thousands of its troops to Ellemont's own before you allowed that fool Belgarin to *retreat*."

Evane stared, his mind a jumble of confused thoughts. The man spoke of Belgarin as if he were someone else, and the Virtues...Evane had heard the stories, of course, everyone had. Myths and legends told to children.

Caldwell, though, did not seem confused. Only terrified. Gone was the confident, sinister figure which had traveled into the dungeons with Evane. "Master, please. One more chance, I beg you. I will not fail you again."

The man seemed to consider the advisor and, as he did, the two large, robed figures stepped toward Caldwell. They were nearly on him when the king raised his hand. "Stop," he said, and the two figures froze as if statues. "You have failed me twice,

Caldwell. Should you fail again, it will be the last time. Do you understand?"

"O-of course, Master," the advisor stammered.

"Very well," Belgarin said. "Now rise and tell me of this one that you have brought to me."

"His name is Evane Baleck, My Lord. He works as a clerk in the merchant's guild, but has, for some time, spent his nights engaging in the torturing and killing of innocents. There is no compassion in him, Lord, and he will make a fitting specimen."

"W-wait," Evane said, his skin going cold as he turned to the advisor, "p-please, you don't mean—"

"Oh, relax, boy," the robed man said, "it is not so bad as that."

Evane fell to his knees. "My king, I have served you faithfully, and I wi—"

"I am not your *king*, mortal," the robed man hissed, and as he did his face twisted and shifted, muscles and bone writhing beneath his skin like snakes. After another moment, he didn't look like Belgarin at all but a man that Evane had never seen before. "I am your *god*. And it is you," he said, and Evane noticed with a shock that even his voice had changed, "who I have to thank for bringing me these worthless specimens." He gestured at the heap of bodies in the corner, and when he turned back to look at the High Clerk, he was smiling a too-wide grin.

Evane recoiled, stumbling onto his back, unable to repress the scream that came out of his throat. "P-p-please," he stammered, "Master, I will do better, I swear it. Only, give me a chance to redeem myself. I will—"

"Oh, you will have a chance to redeem yourself, of that I can assure you." He motioned to one of the two robed, hulking men, and the figure started toward Evane.

Screaming, the High Clerk stumbled to his feet and ran for the door. He'd only just managed to grasp the handle when one thick, massive hand landed on his shoulder, and another grabbed his wrist. The grip was impossibly tight, and he could not pull away. Abruptly, the figure gave his wrist a twist, and a loud *crack* split the air. Evane screamed as white-hot agony lanced through his body. He fought, struggling against his captor, but he might as well have been a child for all the good it did him. The creature holding him pivoted and suddenly Evane was flying through the air.

He hit the hard-packed dirt floor of the cavern with jarring force and rolled to a stop a few feet away from the robed man. The man stepped forward and stared down at him as the clerk moaned in pain, cradling his shattered wrist. "Do not worry so, Evane," he said, smiling in what was almost a comforting way, "there will be pain, great and terrible pain beyond anything you have ever experienced, beyond anything you thought you *could* experience. But then, when it is done, you will be better than you are now. Stronger and faster, and *then* you will redeem yourself."

Evane barely took heed of the man's words, his agony too great to allow him to concentrate. His hand and wrist felt as if they had been filled with broken, jagged glass that seemed to cut into him with every movement. He was not too far gone, though, to notice when one of the cloaked figures lifted him up off the floor as if he weighed nothing.

The figure started toward the stone platform in the center of the room, and as they drew closer, Evane saw that it was coated in fresh and old blood, trails of it running down the sides. He saw, too, what looked like bits of skin and flesh littering its surface, and he screamed, struggling against the thing's grip. The creature holding him didn't even seem to notice and, in another moment, Evane was slammed onto the table. He fought, thrashing, knowing what was coming, but the creature grabbed his ankle in a vice-like grip and snapped the steel manacle around it. He proceeded to secure Evane's other ankle the same way, as well as his wrists.

The creature leaned over him then, its robed face still covered in shadow, and Evane did the only thing left to him. He jerked his head up and slammed it into the creature's face as hard as he could. The creature's head barely moved, but the hood was knocked back, and Evane gasped at the disfigured, twisted features that it revealed.

The thing's—for whatever it was it was no man—nose was bloody from where he'd struck it, but it smiled, the expression strange and unnatural on its face, as if it had never smiled before and didn't really understand what it meant. Something struck Evane then, and he realized with a shock that he recognized this man, or, at least, the man who it had been. "*O-Odel?*" he rasped, his voice hoarse and desperate, "please, you have to let me out of here. I didn't want to do it, they made me, you must—"

"There is really no point in talking to him," the robed man said as he came up to stand beside the grotesque figure. "You see, High Clerk, the working of the Art in such a way may grant a man remarkable gifts, but as any true practitioner of the Art knows, there is always a cost. The man standing before you could lift a horse over his head with no more thought than you would give to lifting a glass of ale. He could batter a hole into the wall of a house or a castle as easily as you might open the door, yet there is little of that which is human left in him, I'm afraid. Certainly, there is no compassion or empathy and that is just as well, for the tasks he will perform for me might only be made worse by such trivialities."

"P-please," Evane sobbed, "please, don't do this."

The robed man smiled reassuringly, patting Evane gently on the head even as his other hand withdrew a wicked looking blade from the inside of his robe. He leaned so close that Evane could feel the warmth of his breath on his cheek. "It is not so bad, High Clerk. Come," he said, grinning and bringing the knife closer, "let me show you."

***

Caldwell stood in the room and waited as his master went about his task. As he worked, Boyce Kevlane muttered words that Caldwell could not make out, and that he would just as soon not know. He was no god, after all, only the god's servant, and that was not such a bad thing. As long, at least, as one stayed in the god's favor. Nearly two hours had passed before his master had finished his first working, and he motioned for the hulking figure that had one time been a blacksmith to take Evane—long since passed out from pain—away. The creature removed the manacles from the High Clerk's body, lifted him easily, and carried him into the adjoining room where he would be caged with the others who were waiting for his master's attentions.

Boyce Kevlane turned to Caldwell then, his arms and robe, even his face, covered in blood. "You have pleased me, Caldwell," he said, smiling. "This one, I think, will take to the working well. That is good, for I had begun to think you had outlived your usefulness. The specimens that your men have delivered to me of late have been of poor, low quality. Such weak mortals as that cannot survive the changing, do you understand?"

Caldwell swallowed hard. His master might seem pleased enough just now, but his temper could rise from nowhere, striking as swiftly and unexpectedly as a snake hidden in the grass. Just as unexpectedly, but much more deadly, and Caldwell saw the trap before him. "I understand, Master," he said, bowing his head, "only, the ones Evane and the others bring to you are the best that the city has to offer."

"The best?" his master said, his voice low and deadly.

Caldwell opened his mouth to speak, knowing that his life hung by a thread then he paused, rethinking his words. "Master, if you wish for me to travel to some of the neighboring villages, to any city, to find you what you need, I will do so."

Boyce Kevlane studied him then, and Caldwell saw his life and his death dancing in the man's gaze. Finally, he spoke. "No. No, Caldwell. I want you here. It is important, at least for now, for those of the city to still believe that Belgarin is king, and your presence helps to maintain that fiction. Already, some of my agents have told me of rumors in the city about people disappearing in the night, about creatures taking them. So far, none of those rumors have been connected back to me, and you are to keep it that way."

Caldwell resisted the urge to frown. "Agents, master?"

"Oh yes," Belgarin said. He smiled, but there was no humor in it, "Yours are not the only ears I have, Caldwell, nor the only hands. You would do well to remember that. No, you will have to find what I need here, in Baresh."

Caldwell felt a shiver of fear run through him, but he knew that he had to speak. "Master, the city is not full of warriors as it was during the tournament. Most of those who live here are simple people—merchants, nobles, beggars and prostitutes. People who, I'm afraid, would not be worthy of your attention."

Kevlane's eyes narrowed only a fraction but Caldwell, whose life depended on reading his master's moods, dropped to his hands and knees, bowing before him. "Please, Master. I only wish to serve you, but I cannot lie to you, either."

The robed man considered him for a moment then a slow smile that was somehow terrifying eased onto his face. "A tournament, did you say?"

"Yes, Master," Caldwell said, rising once more. "The council member, Claudius, held a tournament when he took over the city after Prince Eladen's death."

Kevlane was nodding before he was finished. "Very well. Arrange it then, Caldwell. I wish for a tournament to be held in the city as soon as possible."

"Of course, master. And...the prize?"

Kevlane waved a dismissive hand, "Make it whatever you feel is necessary to draw in as many warriors as possible. A hundred gold pieces, a thousand, it makes little difference. After all, they will not have time to spend it, I think."

Caldwell shared his master's grin. "Of course, Master."

"You may go now." Kevlane glanced at the door to the adjoining room through which moans of horror and pain could be heard, "I will continue my work."

"Yes, Master," Caldwell said, bowing low and starting for the door, relieved to be living for another day.

"And Caldwell?"

He paused, turning. "Master?"

"If you fail me in this, it *will* be the last time."

CHAPTER SEVEN

By the time Aaron finished with his preparations, the sun was low in the sky, and he made his way to the queen's stable. Queen Isabelle had also had much to say on her thoughts of him going, telling him she believed it to be an unnecessary risk, but when she'd seen that he would not be swayed, she'd finally acquiesced, offering him one of her finest horses for the journey. Not that Aaron would have known the difference between a fine horse and an average one—four legs, a face, ill-tempered, they all seemed the same to him.

The stableboy was waiting outside the queen's stables, standing just in front of the two wide doors. His eyes grew large as he saw Aaron approaching, and he fell to one knee, bowing low and bringing his fist to his thin chest in salute. "General Envelar, sir," he said, his voice high and squeaking with anxiety, "it's an hon-honor to meet you, sir."

Aaron barely managed to repress a groan. If they weren't telling him how stupid he was, they were busy bowing and scraping like he was some fat-assed king smelling of flowers and chicken grease. "Get up, lad," he said, "I'm nobody worth bowing to. Anyway, I'd be real careful who you fall on your knees for, boy. Once you start kneeling, it gets harder and harder to stand up again."

"Yes sir," the lad said, shooting to his feet as if Aaron had bared his sword and threatened him with his life. The boy looked up at him, and Aaron saw to his dismay that, if anything, the adoration in his eyes had only grown stronger.

He sighed heavily, glancing around. "Where is everybody anyway? I can't imagine the queen's stables go unguarded."

The boy squirmed, obviously uncomfortable, "Shift change, General, sir. The new guard should be here any minute."

Aaron grunted at that. He'd have to have a word with Brandon or one of the other soldiers before he departed. Leaving the queen's personal stables unguarded, even for a moment, was beyond foolish. "The queen said that she'd have a horse waiting?"

"Yes, My Lord," the boy said, bowing his head in a quick bob, "Thunder, he's called, My Lord, and if you don't mind me sayin', he's the best horse in Perennia. Maybe even all of Isalla."

Aaron nodded. "Show me."

The boy bowed again. Poor kid would have whiplash if Aaron hung around for much longer. "This way, My Lord," he said, and Aaron followed after him. The stables were dark inside, the only light the wan illumination provided by the setting sun, and Aaron found himself squinting into the darkness at the vague shapes of horses standing in their stalls.

"Is it always so damned dark in here?"

"No, My Lord," the kid said, and Aaron thought he heard nervousness in his voice. Most likely, it was from being in the presence of Aaron Envelar, leader of the Ghosts, who—according to the latest stories—had killed a thousand men with his bare hands, all while banging their wives and striking heroic poses. "This here's Thunder."

The kid stopped abruptly in front of a stall, and Aaron nearly ran into him. Then he turned and studied the horse. The light was poor, but there was enough to see that the beast had a black coat, and he was able to make out its muscles shifting beneath its skin as it stomped one foot. "Thunder, is it?"

A fine horse, Co said. *Still, the boy is nervous.*

Yeah, he is, Aaron thought sourly, *what else is a youth supposed to be when he's in the presence of a hero?*

You really need to let that go, the Virtue said. *You cannot keep people from being grateful. You saved their lives, after all.*

The army saved their lives, Aaron thought back. *I was just one man among thousands.*

A man who killed more than any other ten men combined. But, then, she said, her tone smug, *who's counting?*

Aaron sighed, reaching out to pat the horse on its muzzle. *A man shouldn't be celebrated for being good at killing, firefly. Paid, maybe, but not celebrated.* His hand had only just touched the horse's snout when it suddenly let out a snort, twisted its head, snapped forward as it tried to take a bite out of Aaron's hand. Aaron jerked his arm back, managing to get it out of the way just in time. "Well," he said, "fucker's got all his teeth, anyway."

Aaron was still looking at the horse when he realized the boy hadn't responded. Frowning, he spun in time to see the stable doors closing shut behind him. "Son of a bitch," he growled. He ran for the door, tried to push against it, but the boy had locked it from the outside, and the stout wood would not budge.

Feeling the presence of someone behind him, Aaron turned, sidestepping away from the doors so that whoever it was wouldn't be able to see his outline in the light that filtered through the cracks. He drew his sword and peered into the darkness, but he could make out nothing but the vague shapes of the stalls and the horses within them. He concentrated on listening, searching for any sound that might give away a man or woman sharing the stables with him, but he could hear nothing over the sound of the horses.

"You can put the sword away," came a woman's voice from somewhere further in the darkness, "you won't be needing it."

It took Aaron a moment to recognize the voice, and when he did his frown deepened. "Shit, I should have known. Tianya. As for the sword, I think I'll keep it out for now, thanks."

"I don't mean you any harm, Aaron Envelar," she said, "far from it, in fact. I only wished to speak with you."

Aaron grunted. "I guess maybe you don't get out a lot, Tianya, but people looking to have a conversation generally offer to buy one another drinks in a tavern, or maybe just ask to meet with them. What they *don't* do, is ambush a man in the darkness. I'm guessing you're the one behind the guards not being here, then? The reason why the boy was acting like he was about to piss himself?"

"Don't hold it against him," she said, her tone amused, "Ian is a good boy, and he does his job well. He was not easy to convince, but then, I have had more experience in such things than most."

"That I don't doubt," Aaron said.

"As for the guards," Tianya went on as if he hadn't spoken, "they were much easier. And, of course, I must apologize, Aaron. As you know, due to my particular gift, I cannot abide much light or noise. A tavern would be enough, I'm afraid, to drive me quite irrevocably insane."

"And I generally can't abide being locked in against my will—I'd say ask the last guy that did it to me, but then, he's not saying much of anything lately."

"I understand that you are upset," Tianya said, "and I apologize."

"Upset?" Aaron said. The anger that always loomed so close to the surface threatened to turn into a blaze, but he pushed it back down with a will. "Not yet, but I promise you'll know when it happens."

The leader of the Tenders sighed at that. "Please understand, Aaron, that even such a trip as this into the city has its own perils for me, and it will take me days, possibly weeks, to recover. I do not say this for sympathy, only to make you understand that I have not come lightly."

Aaron frowned. "That was your choice, lady, not mine. Now, why don't you just tell me what you want, so I can get about my night, and you can go back to your cave? I've got things I need to be doing."

"It is precisely because of those *'things'* as you call them, that I have come, General Envelar. I have come to ask you, to *beg* you. Please, reconsider. What you do now is beyond foolish. You will be leaving yourself—and the Virtues—open to not just Belgarin and the danger he poses, but also to Boyce Kevlane, who is much worse."

"Lady, Adina couldn't talk me out of this. Shit, the queen herself couldn't. If neither of them were able to convince me to stay, what chance do you think you have? I don't even *like* you."

"I do not ask you to like me," Tianya said, "that is not my concern. I ask you to think of yourself, of the danger you're putting yourself in. And not *just* yourself, understand, but every living, breathing person in this world. That includes the queen *and* your princess."

Aaron snorted. "If I've got that kind of power, maybe they ought to make some shrines to me, after all."

"This is no *joke*, Aaron Envelar," Tianya snapped, her composure finally breaking. "You know as well as I what Boyce Kevlane is capable of. You have seen it with your own eyes. You know, too, what it is that he seeks."

"After the last time I saw him," Aaron said dismissively, "I suspect he's seeking someone to pull my knife out of his back." He sounded casual, unworried, but that couldn't have been further from the truth. Aaron knew the danger the ancient wizard posed, knew that, if given the opportunity, the man would kill Aaron and everyone he cared about.

"A *knife*," Tianya said, her patience gone, "you speak to me of a *knife*? Such a thing is little more than a trifle to the enemy. He is out there, Aaron, he and those who serve him, and he will not stop until he has gathered the Seven. Once he's done so, there will be nothing and *no one* that can stop him. He will bring the world to its knees, and the people you care about will suffer for your foolishness."

Aaron frowned. "Are we done?"

"There is still time to avoid this folly," Tianya said, her voice desperate now. "Come with me. Let me and my men protect you. That much is within my power. As dangerous as he is, Boyce Kevlane is only one man. He cannot be everywhere at once. We can hide you, keep you safe."

"Yeah?" Aaron said. "And maybe if I'm good, you'll let me out of my cage for play time, is that it? A leash around my neck, three meals a day and a coffin to die in, is that what you're offering me, Tianya?"

"You damn *fool*," she spat. "I'm offering you the chance to *live* to ensure that those you care about live as well. I'm offering you a chance of saving the world instead of damning it."

"I thought I told you before, Tianya," Aaron said, "the world's been damned for a long time." He walked back to the door and knocked loudly. "*Ian*," he yelled, "open this door, lad."

He heard the boy working the latch from the other side, and Tianya spoke once more. "Last chance, Aaron. Come with me, now.

If you choose to continue this folly, I cannot guarantee your safety."

Aaron glanced back at the woman there in the darkness, her vague outline suddenly blazing magenta as his bond with Co did its work. "Safety is a thing that can never be guaranteed, Tianya. I'm surprised the years haven't taught you that. And a man never wins a fight by running from it."

The door opened then, and Aaron stepped out of the stables, noting that night had come in full while he'd spoken with the leader of the Tenders. He turned to the boy who stared at him with terrified eyes, as if expecting to be killed outright for his deception, and suddenly Aaron felt very, very tired. "Bring the horse."

***

Gryle stood with his hands spread out at his sides, sweat running down his forehead, his jaw set in concentration. "Come on then," he said, his gaze level and steady, his fingers fidgeting in anticipation.

The woman reached down into her basket—in his darker moments, it seemed to him that it was an unending basket—and retrieved something from it. Her hand moved in a deceptively gentle way as she tossed the thing she'd withdrawn toward him. Gryle moved a step forward, thrusting his hand above his head, and snatched the egg out of the air. He had a brief feeling of victory before it shattered it in his grip and yolk splattered his hand, oozing into his hair and on his robe to mix with the remnants of the dozens of other failed attempts that had come before it.

Gryle let out a sound of dismay as he stared down at his once fine tunic and pants, clothes fashioned by Queen Isabelle's own tailor. "Ma'am, forgive me," he said, holding his hands out and away from him as if they had been infected with some terrible plague, "but...is this truly necessary?"

"Probably not," Beth said, the old woman grinning widely, "but I enjoy it."

The boy, Michael, laughed from where he sat on the grass of the castle courtyard, watching. "You can do it, Gryle!" he yelled. "I believe in you!"

Why? Gryle thought, but he resisted the urge to ask. He was no hero like Aaron, not clever like Leomin or determined and passionate like the princess. He was grossly overweight, he knew, and a displeasure to be around, yet for some reason the boy had taken to him, following him around as if he were some knight from the story books. At best, he thought, he was the bumbling squire that followed after the knight, cleaning his sword and washing his clothes. The thing was he didn't *mind* being the bumbling squire. Most of the time, he even liked it. After all, *somebody* had to make sure that the knight was fed and his horse was well-groomed. *Someone* had to sharpen his sword for him. Not that Gryle had ever sharpened a sword, of course, as staying as far away from them and other instruments of war and death had been one of his life's main goals. A goal that he had been succeeding at as well. That was, at least, until recent months.

If Michael's attentions weren't awkward enough, Gryle found that the boy's grandmother's were far worse. Beth had—for reasons he couldn't imagine or explain—decided that she would take on the role of being his teacher, showing him how to use his new strength. Which meant that, so far, she'd spent the last several mornings throwing eggs at him. At night, Gryle sat in his room, considering his ruined wardrobe—a wardrobe that he'd been incredibly excited to wear when one of the queen's servants delivered it—and found himself wishing that he could somehow give the Virtue away. On such nights, he would sit and mourn for his clothes, grieve for his hair that seemed to smell of egg yolk no matter how many times he washed it. He didn't weep though. Not quite.

"Ma'am," he said, as he wiped his hands daintily in the grass, "I appreciate what you're trying to do, truly. But I am no warrior. I am a chamberlain, that's all."

The old woman smiled. "No, you are not a warrior, Gryle. Not yet. Right now, you're an egg juggler and a piss poor one at that." Suddenly, there was another egg soaring through the air directly at Gryle's face. He let out a yelp, throwing his hand up to catch the egg, but he missed and it struck him in the forehead, splattering yolk and pieces of shell on his face.

Gryle spluttered and gagged, wiping the slimy yolk away with his hand. Finally, he sighed heavily, turning back to the old woman, "Ma'am, don't you understand? This is pointless."

Beth cackled. "You missed a little something, chamberlain. Just there." She waved her hand, indicating the entirety of him, and he sighed again. "And you're wrong, you know. It's not pointless. Me putting some noble's silk dress on these old bones and going to a ball with the intentions of finding some rich lord to pamper and coddle me, *that* would be pointless. This, chamberlain, is necessary. Or do you want to walk around for the rest of your life with your hands in your pockets for fear of breaking something or some*one*?"

"You know I don't."

"Besides," Beth said, "I've got a feelin' we'll be needin' that strength of yours in the days to come and better you learn now than when someone's slingin' a sword at you."

A cold shiver of fear ran up Gryle's spine at the thought that he might find himself in a battle, but he was aware of the boy's eyes on him. He was no hero, had not been born with courage and charisma, with cleverness or skill, but the boy watched him anyway, an expectant expression on his face. Gryle was no hero. But, for the boy, he would try. "Very well," he said, bracing himself, "let's go again."

***

As he led the horse through the city streets, Aaron found himself replaying Tianya's words in his mind. It wasn't that he was worried that she was right—he knew she wasn't. A lifetime living in the Downs had taught him that hiding and running only worked for so long. Sooner or later, some battles had to be fought, whether you wanted to or not. Besides, running and hiding wasn't a plan; it was what you did when the plan failed. Every moment a man spent cowering and running for his life, his enemies grew stronger, so that when the battle finally *did* come, he would find that all of that running and hiding had made him good at nothing but running and hiding.

You know Tianya is going to be a problem, don't you? Co asked.

"Going to be?" Aaron muttered, "She already is a problem." He still couldn't believe the woman had locked him in the stables to speak with him. He didn't hold it against the stable boy—a woman like Tianya would do what she had to if it got her what she wanted. The boy had never really stood a chance. Aaron had tried to tell him as much when he'd left, but the boy had still watched him with wide, frightened eyes as if Aaron was some vengeful god come to punish him.

He was angry, sure, but not at the boy. He was angry at Tianya, true, but mostly he was angry at himself. Angry that he'd been taken in so easily, stumbling stupidly into an ambush as if he was one of the dozens of rich merchants or nobles who visited the Downs thinking to find himself a good time, and leaving with empty pockets. If, that was, he left at all.

You can't always look over your shoulder, Co said, *you can't catch everything.*

I have to, firefly, he said. *I don't get the luxury of making excuses for myself. If I don't catch everything, somebody dies.* The horse drew its muzzle close, no doubt meaning to try another bite, and Aaron slapped it away. "You know," he said, thinking of the dangers he would face in Baresh, "it's going to be a very long couple of months, or a very short couple of days. "

***

Aaron walked through the city trying, his best to ignore the stares and whispers that accompanied him as he did. It seemed that the whole of Perennia had heard about the fight at the gate though he was grateful that at least none were so bold as to come forward and speak to him. When he finally made it to the gate itself, he was surprised to find dozens of soldiers lined up, as well as several figures on horses, and he felt a sinking feeling in his stomach as he recognized them.

Bastion walked up to him from the crowd of soldiers, bringing his fist to his chest in salute. "General."

"Bastion," Aaron said, nodding at him. The giant youth had taken some injuries in the fighting with Belgarin's troops, but he seemed to have shaken them off well. Aaron motioned to the troops crowding the gate. "What's going on here?"

"It's the Ghosts, sir."

Aaron frowned. "Which?"

"All of us, sir. We heard the news that you're going to Baresh, and we've come to accompany you."

Aaron sighed. "Do they understand that it's a suicide mission?"

Bastion shrugged. "We want to go with you, sir. You are our leader, and we are your men."

Aaron stared at the youth, at the earnest, serious expression on his face. Then he grunted, clapping the man on the shoulder and stepping forward. As he did, the men moved to encircle him and listen as they had so many times during their training in the forest outside of Perennia. "I thank you for coming," Aaron said, looking around and meeting each man's gaze in turn, "all of you. But I cannot bring you with me—not this time."

He saw several frowns at that, but the men did not speak, waiting to hear what he would say. He sighed, heavily. "And what the fuck, anyway? What is it? Do you all have a death wish?"

"We could say the same to you, sir!" someone shouted from the back, and there was scattered laughter at that.

"That's fair enough," Aaron said, studying the men. *So few*, he thought. *So very few are left.* "But you have done your duties, and where I go, numbers will only hurt, not help." There were some more troubled looks at that, and some of the men whispered to each other. Aaron raised his hand. "If it helps you any, boys, I don't mean to fight anyone at all, and I'll be back before you know it. Now, go home. Go to your families and your loved ones. If anything happens, I'm counting on you all to protect the city and its people. For now, rest. The gods know you've earned it, all of you."

"*And what of you, sir?*" another shouted.

Aaron smiled. "There'll be time enough for me to rest later." *When I'm dead, most likely,* he thought, but he kept the smile and tried to make it as genuine as he could. "Now, go home. That's an order."

The men glanced at each other and, finally, began to disperse, making their separate ways back into the city. When they were gone, Aaron was able to better see the gate and the figures waiting at it, and he sighed heavily again, walking his horse toward them.

"What is this, some sort of reunion?"

Wendell grinned wide, and Darrell shrugged. "Something like that, lad."

Aaron glanced to the side where Adina and Leomin sat watching. The princess met his eyes, challenging. "You mean to go with me," he said to Darrell.

The old swordmaster nodded. "I do. You were right to tell the Ghosts to relax and get some rest. In a task such as this, the fewer the better."

Aaron looked at the man wryly. "That was my thought exactly."

Darrell only grinned, saying nothing, and Aaron turned to look at Wendell, the man not even trying to hide his smile. "Sergeant."

"General," the man said, his grin widening. "Nice weather we're havin', isn't it?"

"Good enough as any other to die in, I suppose," Aaron said. He leaned close to the sergeant, speaking quietly so that Adina could not hear. "You do understand that the mission we go on is almost certain death, don't you?"

Wendell shrugged. "Sir, I've been dealin' with certain death just about all my life. My mother told me, when I was a man grown, that she never thought I'd make it as far as I did, bein' such a fool as I was. I suppose I've become accustomed to it. Besides," he said, straightening his back and saluting, "someone's got to be around to change the general's bedding and kiss his owies, make them feel all better."

Aaron couldn't help the smile that rose to his face. "Is it because of how ugly you are that you want to commit suicide? Because believe me, Sergeant, there are whores in the world who would ply their trade even with one such as you. Just so long as it was dark, and you had the coin, of course."

Wendell laughed at that, but did not speak, and Aaron turned to Adina. "This is your doing, I take it?"

"You can be mad if you want, *General*," the princess said, "but you're being a fool already. At least with Darrell, Wendell, and Leomin along, you'll have some chance of making it out alive."

Aaron stepped in close, taking her hand in his. "I'm not mad," he said, "it was a smart decision, asking them to go. I should have thought of it myself. And I *will* be back, Adina."

"An easy thing to say," she said, meeting his eyes.

"Adina," he said, speaking low. "It'll be okay."

"Of course, it will," Leomin said, walking up to them. "We only travel to the heart of our enemy's strength, to a city with thousands of men who would see us dead, if they could. I doubt that it is so very different from a normal day for our sellsword companion."

Aaron frowned at the Parnen. "Thanks for that, Leomin." He turned back to Adina. "I *will* return. The gods themselves couldn't keep me away."

She nodded, and he could see the tears in her eyes, "Be careful, Aaron. And come back." Then she leaned in and kissed him and, for a moment, it was only the two of them. For a few seconds, he was able to forget about all of his worries, all of his concerns, about the three men standing, waiting for him. His thoughts were only on her, on the feel of her lips against his. Then she pulled away and favored him with a pained smile. "I'll see you when you get back."

"Alright," Aaron said, and he watched as she led her horse back into the city.

"Sir?" Wendell said from behind him. "If you aim to go, we'd best be on our way. The general will be needing his nap soon, and I reckon you'll want to get as much traveling done tonight as we can."

Aaron watched until Adina disappeared in the distance then he turned back, favoring the sergeant with a smile before meeting Darrell's gaze. "Tianya won't like that you're coming with me. You know that, don't you?"

Darrell shrugged. "Tianya has her beliefs, and I have my own. Just because our goal is the same does not mean that we agree on the way to get there."

"You're sure, then?"

The swordmaster smiled, "Lad, there is no place that I'd rather be."

Aaron swung up into the saddle of his horse. "Then you're a fool." He glanced around at the three men and nodded. "Alright. Let's go."

CHAPTER EIGHT

The tavern's cellar was dark and scary. Caleb didn't like it. It had a funny smell also, one that reminded him of old things, of cobwebs and spiders. He *hated* spiders. Rats, too. He wasn't a clever boy—his mother always told him so—but even he knew that spiders and rats were nasty, dirty things. When he'd been younger, there'd been rats in his bedroom. When he slept, they'd sometimes come out and bite him. He'd scream, and his mother would come in to the room, angry because he was scared and loud. *Gods,* she'd say, *but you are a stupid, worthless boy.*

But the rats, Mommy, he'd cry, rubbing at the most recent bite marks on his toes or fingers—the rats liked those parts the most—*they bit me.* He'd try to explain in his halting words that every time he fell asleep, some part of him would come out from under his thin blanket, would hang over the too-small bed, and then they'd bite him. The thing was Caleb had never been good with words. Never much good at thinking, either. Other people always seemed to know just what to say or do, but not him, and he had never been able to make his mom understand.

"They're just rats, stupid boy," she'd say. "*If they bite you when your hands or feet hang off the bed then don't let your hands or feet hang off the bed.*" She'd sigh then, complaining that the gods had seen fit to punish her with a stupid, dim-witted child, saying that she was forced to waste her life, to spend her days on her back letting any filthy man who had the coin have his way just so she could support her worthless, idiot son. Caleb had felt bad about that, and his crying had always turned to regret about all that his mother was forced to deal with.

He tried to be smart, he really did, but it was as if there was always a fog over his thoughts. Things that took most people only a few moments to understand or figure out were always harder for Caleb. It was, to him, as if their thoughts were organized about them, on shelves maybe. Caleb *liked* shelves, even had one in his little room that held all his precious things, a stone he'd found that sort of looked like a face, a copper coin, his very own, and a few other objects. He always felt as if people could just reach out and grab the thought they needed as easily as he sometimes grabbed the face stone from his shelf.

But Caleb's mind had no shelf. He thought it was sort of like he was carrying his thoughts around in a bucket, the way he'd toted water from the well so that his mother could take a bath. His mother had been in a hurry sometimes, to clean off what she called "the day's stink" and she'd yell at him to "hurry for the god's sake, you idiot boy." And he'd try to hurry, but sometimes he'd hurried *too* much, filling the bucket up too high for him to carry, and it would drop and spill. He thought maybe that's what had happened with his thoughts, when he was a baby. He'd been carrying the bucket, but he'd dropped it, and now they were scattered everywhere, and it took him a while to find them sometimes because of the fog that never left his mind.

They're only rats, stupid boy. Caleb was thirteen years and four months old now, at least he thought he was—he kept track by marking each month down on a paper he kept special for the purpose in his room but sometimes he forgot to mark—and he hadn't seen his mother in several years. She told him that she had found a husband and a new family, and that their small house wasn't big enough for him and her new family. Caleb understood; it was a small house. But he went by there sometimes, and he never saw his mother or her new family, wasn't sure that they lived there at all. He didn't remember much about her anymore, wasn't sure exactly how her face looked or what she smelled like. But he remembered some. *They're only rats, stupid boy.*

And she was right, he knew. Rats were little, and if they were mean, you could stomp on them with your foot. But he still hated them, so as he pulled the ale cask out from where it sat against the wall of the basement, his eyes roamed the shadows, searching for any sign of the little creatures.

The cask was heavy, and he strained, grunting with the effort as he pulled it free and started the slow, painstaking task of dragging it toward the stairs. He'd just reached the bottom step and was about to start up when a shadow appeared in the open doorway at the top of the stairs, blocking out almost all of what little light made it into the cellar from the common room of the inn.

"What is taking you so long, boy?" Alder growled. Alder was the innkeeper—that meant he was the boss.—and just then he didn't look happy. He crossed his arms over his protruding stomach, a frown on his face. "Gods, but I was a fool to take you in when your mother asked. *Free work,* she said, and I, being the fool that I am, believed her."

"Sorry, boss Alder," Caleb panted as he dragged the cask up one step, but he really wasn't thinking much about the innkeeper at all. He was thinking about the rats. The darkness kept Caleb from being able to see the floor of the cellar. For all he knew, it could be *crawling* with rats. Rats on top of rats, and they could be, even now, moving toward him. Groaning in anticipation of the feel of their sharp little teeth on his skin, he jerked the cask up another step.

The innkeeper shook his head in disgust. "Just hurry it up, idiot. Customers don't come to an inn for the conversation; they come for the ale. If I see even one person walk out because you took too long gettin' that damned cask up these damned steps, I swear by all the gods you'll regret it, boy. Your mother, bitch that she is, might have fooled me into takin' you, claimin' that I owed her. Maybe I even did, but there's a limit to how much a man can put up with, lad. You remember that."

"Y-yes...yes sir, Mr. Alder, sir," Caleb gasped. His arms were shaking now, but he forced the cask up another step.

Alder grunted and spat before turning and stalking away. Caleb was glad to see him go because now the light was back, and a quick glance at the cellar floor showed no sign of rats *or* spiders. But knowing that didn't make the cask any lighter, and by the time Caleb made it to the top of the steps he was gasping for breath and covered in sweat.

"It's about damned time," Alder said from his place behind the counter. "Now get that ale over here behind the bar before I take a switch to you."

Caleb felt like he could barely stand, but he grabbed the cask and, shaking with the effort, began dragging it toward the bar. Alder had taken the switch to him a few times before, mostly when he was too slow or too stupid and messed something up, and he didn't want it to happen again.

"Look at that idiot go," a man at the bar called, laughing. "Well, hurry up then, boy. There's men here that need a drink."

Caleb risked a glance up to see several men sitting at the bar, grinning as they watched him. The man who'd spoken bared his teeth in a wide smile, and Caleb saw that they were black, the way his mom's had sometimes been when she smoked her pipe. She'd said that tamarang was the only thing that helped her deal with having a witless moron for a son. Caleb always thought it stank, but he'd never told her so.

The man scratched at a black scab on his neck with dirty fingers. Caleb thought to ask him why it was black but decided against it. Alder was in a hurry and, besides, he'd told Caleb not to talk to the customers, said that men would just as soon find a different tavern to drink at, if they had to listen to some idiot boy's nonsense, so instead he hauled the cask another step.

He was nearly at the bar when the man with the scab kicked his foot out, and Caleb tripped. He tried to hold onto the cask, tried to regain his balance, but he couldn't. He fell onto his back, the cask following him and striking him in the head hard enough to bring tears to his eyes, before landing heavily on the tavern's floor.

There was the sound of wood cracking and, suddenly, ale was pouring out onto the ground. Gasping, Caleb rushed to his feet and tried to haul the cask upright once more, but it was no use. The crack was so big that all the ale had poured out of it before he was finally able to get the cask right side up once more. Terrified, he bent down and began scooping up what ale he could in two hands and trying to put it back in the cask.

"*Idiot boy!*" Alder roared, but Caleb didn't turn to the tavern keep, thinking that if he could get enough of the ale back, maybe Alder wouldn't be mad.

The men at the bar and at the nearby tables were roaring with laughter, but Caleb's attention was only on the ale, only on scooping it up and putting it back as fast as he could. Suddenly, the man with the black scab's foot kicked out again, striking Caleb in the side, and he fell over, landing in the spreading puddle of ale. His clothes were immediately soaked through, and he found himself coughing as the sharp, bitter smell of the ale coated his nostrils.

He was trying to rise again when something struck him in the side of the head, and he cried out, falling over on his back. He looked up, moaning with pain, and saw the thick innkeeper standing over him, the switch in his hand. "You stupid boy," he growled, and then the switch was coming down again and again, and Caleb screamed.

The men around the tables and bar laughed louder still, but Caleb could hardly hear them past his screams, could hardly see them past the tears of pain and shame that were gathering in his eyes. "Get out of here!" Alder bellowed. "And don't come back until tomorrow—you can sleep on the fucking street for all I care! Maybe if I'm lucky someone will kill you and save me the trouble."

Caleb stumbled to his feet and lurched toward the door as fast as he could but not fast enough to avoid another strike of the switch that hit him in the back of the head and sent him stumbling into a table. One of the men at the table laughed as he pushed Caleb away. He nearly fell again, but managed to keep his feet this time, and in another moment, he was outside, muffled laughter coming from the closed door behind him.

He looked around the city and realized with a rising fear that it was night. The tavern was in the worst district of the city and the worst part of that district. A place where, his mother had always told him, only a stupid little boy who was even slower witted than him would think to go out at night. He didn't remember much, but he remembered the memory vividly. He remembered her walking him to the door of their house after she'd claimed he'd stolen the last of her wine. He hadn't, had tried to tell her so, but she wasn't convinced, and she dragged him toward it, her fingers digging into his shoulder, her scent heavy with the sharp, acrid scent of the tamarang she smoked. She opened the door to their small home, only a crack, as if even under the effects of the drug she didn't dare open it any further, and pointed out into the darkness, shoving his face toward the opening.

"*Do you see that, idiot boy?*"

"*It's night-time, momma.*"

She cackled at that. "*That's right, fool child, its night time. And do you know what happens to little boys who go wandering out into the city at night?*"

"*They...they get lost?*"

She slapped him, and he cried out as much from the surprise as the pain of it. She knelt down then, her eyes on level with his own, and he thought that she might hug him—she did, sometimes, when the drug was in her system, usually after an unexpected slap such as the one he'd just gotten. She didn't hug him though, didn't whisper that she was sorry, that it wasn't his fault he'd been born an idiot, as she sometimes did. Instead, she grabbed his face in her hands, squeezing his cheeks so that her nails dug into them painfully. "*Oh, yes boy, they get lost, and that's the least of the things that happen to them. Maybe better to say that they come up missing. Either way, their families never see them again and that's a fact. Maybe not such a bad thing for their mothers, but bad for the little boys, I can promise you that.*"

"*What happens to them, Momma?*" he asked, his voice breathy and panicky, not just with pain, but with fear.

"*Oh, many things,*" she said, releasing him and rising, suddenly looking bored. She shrugged. "*The lucky ones are killed and that's the end of it, the end of them, but there aren't many lucky ones. The others...things are done to those little boys that you cannot even imagine before they're finally allowed to die.*"

He'd studied her face with wide, frightened eyes, and even now, thinking of it, he found himself growing afraid all over again. "*I won't go out there, momma,*" he'd said, "*not in the night. Not ever. I promise.*"

She leaned close again then, her breath soured and smoky. "*And you won't have to go out,*" she said, "*because if you ever steal my wine again, boy, I'll throw you out there myself, and the kiddie fiddlers can have their way with you. Do you understand?*"

"*But I didn't, Momma. I swear I didn't,*" he said, wanting, *needing* her to understand, the thought of being thrust out into that darkness where anyone, any*thing*, could be waiting terrified him. She slapped him again, almost casually, before going back to her pipe, and she said nothing more about it, at least that night.

In the nights and years that followed, she would threaten him with it, sometimes, when he was stupid and did something wrong, and he always lived in fear that she would follow through on her promise. She never did, though, and he had managed to stay safely away from the darkness. At least until now.

Caleb found that he was moaning, a slow, desperate sound, and he couldn't seem to make himself stop. He stared down the street and at the openings of the alleyways, and it seemed to him as if they grew darker even as he watched, their shadows lengthening, stretching out as if they would pull him into the waiting night.

He decided then that the switch was better, was a thousand *times* better than being out at night alone. He turned to go back into the tavern, actually had his hand on the door, when suddenly it flew open, and he stumbled backward, tripping and falling on his backside with a startled yelp. He looked up to see the man with the black scab staring down at him, a wide grin on his face. "Well, if it isn't the idiot." He snorted. "Look at this here, lads. Looky what I found."

Caleb scooted away, heedless of the dirt that was getting on his only good pair of trousers, as three more men came out behind the scabbed man. "S-s-sorry, s-sirs," Caleb said, barely able to get the words out past the stutter that often took over when he grew nervous or afraid.

The scabbed man threw back his head and roared in laughter. "Well," he said, studying Caleb, "I'll say this for that bastard, Alder, he knows how to train a dog, anyway. What are you goin' to do, boy? Sit there all night in the road until your master lets you back in?"

Caleb glanced from one man to the other as they laughed. "I-I-I… s-sir," he said, straining, his face turning red with the effort of getting the words out, "I…w-want to go…b-b-back. B-back inside."

"Oh?" the man said, grinning. "Back inside, is it?" He shook his head, "Nah, not for you, lad. Not tonight. You see, you cost us our drinks now, didn't you? Because of you, the ale we were gonna buy is soakin' into the floor of this shitty little tavern even now. I think that you owe us for that don't you?"

"O-owe you, sir?"

The scabbed man grinned. "That's right. Now, boys," he said, turning to look at the others, "what do you think this idiot here can do to pay us back for all the trouble he caused us?"

A thin man with a bent nose and crooked, black teeth, drew a cruel-looking knife from his waist, a hungry look in his eyes. "I think I'll start by cutting his little stuttering tongue out, Darrin. Can I?"

The scabbed man rubbed a hand thoughtfully over his chin, seeming to consider, then he glanced back at Caleb. "That seems fair to me."

The thin man with the bent nose started forward, and Caleb screamed, jerking to his feet and running toward the nearest alley. He heard the men laughing behind him, but he ran as fast as he could, ignoring the aches and pains that the switch had caused as he sprinted deeper into the darkness.

He wasn't sure how long he'd been running—he'd never been good at keeping track of time. His mother had always told him it was his idiot mind that wasn't able to remember things. What he *was* sure of though, was that there was a sharp, biting pain in his chest, and he felt like he couldn't draw a breath. Still, he ran on, terrified of the men and terrified of the darkness both. He stumbled and fell more than once, but he only lurched to his feet and ran on. He might have very well kept going until he'd made it out of the city altogether, but he'd no sooner turned down another alleyway than he heard a scream from the other end and froze in place, his heart hammering in his chest.

At the far end of the alley, he could see what looked like three men standing over the prone form of another. The night was quiet, the only sound that of the men, and Caleb's gasping, whooping breaths. He did his best to steady them, scared that the men would hear him and decide to beat him up instead, but they didn't seem to notice him and that was good because try as he might, he couldn't seem to get his feet to move.

"You ought not have cheated us and run out that way, Castor."

"*I didn't...cheat,*" the man on the ground gasped. "*I just...knew.*"

The standing man snorted. "Just knew, is it? What are you then, some sort of mind reader, is that it? If that's all, then why'd you run?"

"Wasn't...running...from you," the prone man gasped, and even in the poor moonlight, Caleb could see what looked like blood coming out of his mouth. "The...man...in the cloak."

The three men looked at each other, confused. "What man in a cloak? The fuck are you goin' on about, Castor?"

"The...king," the man said, and it was obvious that each word was agony, "he isn't...it's...obvious if...if you *know*."

"Alright, I'm tired of listenin' to his bullshit. Somebody shut him up."

One of the other two men stepped forward, drawing a long blade. The wounded man tried to rise, but he seemed as if he could barely move the way Caleb sometimes felt after he'd done something wrong, and Alder punished him with the switch. He'd only managed to lift himself up to his hands and knees when the man jammed the blade into his side. Castor screamed. His attacker growled, giving the blade a jerk, and the wounded man's cries abruptly grew silent.

"Check him for our coin," The leader of the three said, "and be quick about it."

Caleb watched as they rifled through the man's pockets, too shocked to think to hide or run, and it was only dumb luck that saved him as the men turned and left the alley the other way. When they were gone, he waited several minutes, his heart hammering an unsteady beat in his chest. Then, slowly, he started forward, sure that at any moment they'd come back and see him, would hurt him the same way they'd hurt the man. They didn't though, and soon he was kneeling beside the man who did not move.

"Oh, m-mister," he said, "t-they must have hurt you r-really bad." He felt warmth on his knees and looked down to see that he knelt in a spreading pool of blood. "P-please, mister," he said, shaking the man, "you have to wake up. You ha—" He cut off, falling backward with a scream as a bright light shot out of the man's body. It floated in the air above Caleb, a blue orb trailing smoky tendrils of all the various shades of blue that somehow made it look as if it was in constant motion and, not knowing what else to do, Caleb screamed again.

"I really wouldn't do that, if I were you," came a voice, "there are some places where such screams will bring help, but this is not one of them. To those who live here, such screams are like the sounds of a wounded animal, the promise of an easy kill."

Caleb cut off, gasping. He spun, looking for the owner of the voice, thinking the men must have come back after all, but there was no one there. He turned back to see that the blue orb was still floating in the air and he moaned, his arms breaking out in gooseflesh. He snapped his eyes shut, as he sometimes did when he'd had a bad dream, and shook his head. "No, you're not really there. C-can't be. Stupid, Caleb. *Stupid*," he said, hitting himself in the head in a futile attempt to make his brain work.

"Of course I'm really here," the voice said, "you've *seen* me, after all, haven't you? There's nothing worse than a man who refuses to believe the things he is seeing only because they do not fit with the reality he wish for himself."

Caleb opened his eyes and saw that the orb was in the same place. "W-w-what...are you?"

"What am I?" the orb responded, swaying back and forth in the air. "That is a question not easily answered. Say, perhaps, that I am the success of a great failure. Perhaps the greatest failure of all time. I am the remnant of men attempting the impossible in an effort to fend off a reality that they found probable."

Caleb blinked, rubbing his head where he was beginning to get a headache the way he sometimes did when he thought too hard. "I...I don't understand."

"We can talk about it later," the orb said dismissively. "For now, you may call me Palendesh. And what do people call you?"

Caleb rose warily to his feet, keeping his eyes on the orb, not daring to even blink. "I...people call me idiot, mostly. Or stupid boy, sometimes. Other times, they call me words that I don't understand."

The orb stopped its swaying, and Caleb felt as if it were watching him. His stupid mind, again. Of course, the thing couldn't watch him—it didn't have any eyes. Though, it didn't have a mouth either, but it was talking... He rubbed at his head again as the orb spoke; "No, that will not do, not at all. Tell me, what is your name?"

"C-Caleb," he managed. "I...I think I need to lie down."

"Very well, Caleb," the orb responded, "but not here."

"But what about the man?" he said. "I...I think he's hurt."

The orb bobbed up and down as if agreeing. "Do not worry for him, Caleb, for he is as hurt as he will ever be. Besides, the man was a poor choice, a gambler and a lecher and worse. Still, I suppose I cannot fault myself too much. Needs must and all that. Now, I do believe it's time we left."

"W-why?" Caleb asked, terrified that the creature was some demon—his mother had told him stories of such things when he'd been a child.

"Why?" the orb said, hovering closer to him, and Caleb winced as if expecting a blow. "Because you, dear Caleb, are currently standing over a man who is very d—*hurt,* and you just so happen to be covered in blood. It is unlikely that any guards should come—I calculate the odds at no greater than eleven percent—but intelligence is taking risks only when they are necessary and this one, at least, is not."

"I-I'm sorry," Caleb said, because he couldn't think of what else to say.

"This is not a time for apologies, dear Caleb," the orb said, "*this is a time for haste.*" Caleb started toward the orb then paused to glance once more back at the man. "D-do you think he'll be okay?"

The orb hesitated, then finally spoke. "He will be as okay as any of us, in the end, dear Caleb."

"C-Castor," Caleb said, "they s-said his name was Castor."

"And so it was," the orb agreed, "though I called him 'prison,' as I do all men. Another in a long line of them and one that I am not sorry in the slightest to leave."

"Prison?" Caleb said, "Like, the place the guards send you if you're bad and don't get bath water for your mom or have her pipe waiting when she gets home?"

"Ah...something like that, dear Caleb."

"Am...am I a prison?"

The orb floated closer until it was only inches from his face, and Caleb could feel some sort of heat on his skin. "Yes, Caleb, you are. All men are prisons, their prisoners thought and reason, their jailers cruelty and willful ignorance. Still, prison though you might be, you appear as if you may yet be an agreeable one. Now, let us leave this place and quickly. The night draws ever onward to its conclusion, its only *possible* conclusion, but we need not share it, not yet. The wheel has been spun, the die has been cast, and the pieces begin their plodding movements across the board. Soon, very soon now, the final confrontation will be at hand, and we dear Caleb, will take our own place on the board, among the other pieces. But not yet, not now, for there are things we must learn first, the both of us. And so many, many things to do."

Caleb gave one more glance at the man, Castor. "I'm sorry, C-Castor," he said, "I hope you get better." Then he turned and followed after the orb. "All that you s-said," he managed, "I'm sorry, but I'm stupid. Dim-witted. I don't understand what you meant."

"You are neither stupid nor dim-witted, Caleb," the orb said in a slightly scolding tone, "or, at least, no more so than all the rest. No, they are dumber still, for in their madness they see reason, and in their posturing they claim logic. As for not understanding," it continued, beginning to float down the alley, "do not fret. You will understand in time. You will understand *much* in time."

CHAPTER NINE

The attack came fast, but Adina managed to get her sword up in time, blocking the blade with her own and stopping it. Their blades locked and, for a moment, she and her opponent were at an impasse, each pushing against the other. But no matter how hard she tried, he was the stronger, and in a sudden burst of power he pushed her sword wide. She grunted, pivoting in an effort to get her blade back around, but when she turned she found the tip of a sword at her throat. "*Damn,*" she hissed, but she backed away, nodding her head in acknowledgment.

Captain Brandon Gant smiled, letting his blade fall to his side. "You really are getting better, Princess. Much. There are many soldiers in the army who would be hard pressed to stand against you, let alone win. Your father's swordmaster did well in teaching you."

"Not well enough," she muttered, taking the opportunity to catch her breath. "What could I have done? I'm just not as strong as you, Brandon."

The older man smiled. "Perhaps not, Princess, but then you will not be as strong as most of those you face." He held up his hand. "That is no attack on your person, I assure you, only a statement of fact. Women are, in general, not as strong as men, that's all. The gods saw fit to make it so, do not ask me why. Still, they also saw fit to grant women their own gifts."

"If the next thing out of your mouth is something about cooking or cleaning," Adina said, arching an eyebrow underneath her helmet, "then you might be surprised how much strength a woman can summon, when she has a need."

The grizzled captain laughed at that. "No, no, princess, I wouldn't dream of it. What I meant to say is that while men may be stronger, it is often women who are faster. Your lighter weight means that you can turn quicker, can already be gone when your opponent's strike falls. You are smaller—this means you're weaker, yes, but it also means you make a more difficult target. Your opponent might be a rock, armed and armored, built for strength, but you are the wind, swift on your feet, always forcing him to try to catch up. And in a battle between the wind and the stones, Princess, the wind wins every time. You need only look at the mountains, at the wounds thousands of years of wind have left them, to know the truth of it."

Adina nodded slowly. "Speed then. Not strength."

"Yes," the captain said, "you are fast, so *be* fast. Strength means little, if your opponent never lands a blow. Your gift is speed, so use it. And when you're done," he said, favoring her with a grin that made his face appear almost boyish, "Perhaps you might cook us all a good meal."

Adina found that she was smiling despite herself. "Cook your own damn meal," she said, lifting her sword. "Now, come on, old man. Let's go again."

"Old man, is it?" a voice said behind her. "'Damn,' is it? Are these truly the words of a princess that I'm hearing? I'm beginning to think that Silent is rubbing off on you, for better or worse. Next I know you'll be stalking around grumbling and waving your sword at anyone who comes too close."

Adina turned to see May standing a short distance away, the club owner smiling widely, her hair seeming to blaze in the early morning sun. "May," she said, "what are you doing here?"

The club owner laughed pleasantly. "I might ask you the same question. Is it typical, I wonder, for princesses to spend their time practicing fighting instead of learning to play the harp or to sew? To stand around sweating in shirt and trousers and armor rather than swooning in silk dresses and shoes so fine they'd break if you so much as thought about running in them?"

A Sellsword's Valor

"Music and quilts won't help us in what's coming," Adina said, "and I never could stomach heels. They make me feel as if I'm some strange bird walking around with my chest puffed out."

May raised a delicate eyebrow. "Not that it needs any puffing, I'm sure."

"*May,*" Adina said, scandalized.

The club owner grinned. "Oh, I'm sure you've heard worse than that since meeting our mutual friend and sellsword. Or, perhaps," she said, winking, "*better* than that, depending on the circumstances."

Adina felt her face flush with heat, and did her best to keep her voice calm despite her embarrassment. "What can I help you with, May?"

"I was wondering if we could talk. It seems," she said, glancing Adina up and down, "that there are some few things we might talk about."

Adina glanced back at Captain Gant who raised his own helmet and wiped an arm across his sweaty forehead as if relieved. "That's more than alright with me, Princess. I'm an old man now, and an old man needs to take a rest. All this swinging swords around and walking around in armor, and I can just about hear my bones creaking, begging for a break."

Adina laughed at that. "I remember you saying much the same when I was a child in my father's castle. How old were you then, I wonder? Mid-twenties, perhaps? Twenty four or so?"

Brandon smiled widely. "Sounds about right, Princess, but a really *old* twenty four. Anyway, you take your time and have your talk. When you come back, I'll probably be passed out on the ground, but I'll make sure to find someone who doesn't mind getting his ass kicked by a princess. In fact," he said, rubbing a hand over the gray, bristling hair on his chin, "considering our conversation, I think I've got just the lad for the job."

"Fine," Adina said, grinning, "but see if he can't be slightly less sexist than his captain, won't you? I'd really hate to have to educate two fools at once."

The captain winked. "I'll try, Princess, but it is an army, and they are soldiers."

Adina shook her head ruefully then turned to May. She pulled her helmet off, grateful for the opportunity to take a break from the hot and sweaty metal. She gave her damp hair a shake, "Alright, what is it?"

The club owner whistled. "Damn, but if I looked like you, Princess, I'd rule the world, and make no mistake. I'd be careful, maybe try to look a little uglier, if you can. The gods know I can go up a set of steep stairs and look like a sick, gasping cow by the end of them. You keep on like you are, you'll have hundreds of soldiers lined up to practice with a princess, but they'll have their minds less on using the sword in their hand than the one in their trousers."

"*May*," Adina scolded again, her face heating. The red haired woman only grinned, and Adina cleared her throat. "Anyway, there's something you wished to speak to me about?"

May nodded, her smile slowly fading. "Walk with me, Princess."

They made their way away from the inner courtyard of the castle toward a bench sitting beside a large fountain. Seeing the water cascading down it made Adina realize just how thirsty she truly was, and she wondered amusedly what Gryle would think if he were to come to check on her and see his princess slopping water out of a fountain like a pig at a trough.

"Sword practice in the morning," May said, her tone quiet as if she was speaking to herself, "archery in the early afternoon, and horsemanship training late into the evening. If you don't mind my saying so, Princess, it seems to me that that's an awful lot of training."

"It is," Adina said, feeling defensive, "and what's wrong with that?"

"Oh nothing," the club owner said, "nothing at all. Except, a man—or a woman—generally practices a thing when he or *she* intends to do it. Men train in arms and combat, noblewomen try on dresses and shoes—at least *some* noblewomen do," she said, glancing at Adina's dirty and sweat covered clothes askance, "priests wear their robes and say their prayers, and they all do it in preparation for a battle of one sort or another." She stopped and met Adina's gaze. "Tell me, princess, what battle is it that you're preparing for?" She held up a hand as if to forestall a comment. "And don't tell me that all of this," she said, gesturing expansively at the courtyard and Adina's training clothes, "is for Belgarin and his army. We don't even know if he *is* going to attack, no matter what Aaron says, and besides, there seems to be a certain sense of urgency about you that wasn't there before."

Adina considered the woman. May might sometimes come off as a simple, kind-hearted matronly figure—if somewhat lewd when the opportunity arose—but she was much more than that. May not only ran the most successful club in the Downs and was a rival who was respected and feared even by Grinner and Hale, the district's two most powerful crime lords, but she had also been the leader of an underground rebellion against Belgarin long before Avarest ever considered taking a stance in the war. She was intelligent, resourceful, courageous, and—if some of the stories Aaron had told her were true—merciless and uncompromising when necessary.

"I warn you, May," Adina said, gathering her courage and meeting the club owner's gaze, "I will not be stopped in what I am doing. I am no pitiful wife to sit at home weeping while she prays for her husband's safe return, nor am I some child to hide under the bed and be comforted and lied to while the adults fight and die outside her bedroom. I am a princess born, a daughter of the late King Marcus, and I will fight, will *die,* if necessary, to protect Telrear and its people."

The club owner studied her for a moment then finally nodded. "I had hoped you'd say as much. You are your father's daughter, Princess, and that's the truth. And if your sword arm is half as strong as your heart then your brother should be the one hiding under his bed, if he knows what's good for him."

Adina smiled at that, surprised that the club owner hadn't tried to talk her down. "So you don't intend to stop me?"

May laughed. "Stop you? Princess, to stop you, I'd first have to know what it is that you're doing—I would like to know, by the way—and besides, that's not why I came. Not at all. I didn't come to stop you, Princess. I came to help you."

Adina frowned, "Help me?"

May nodded, and they made their way to the bench and sat. "Whatever it is you're intending to do," May said, "I'd like to help. Particularly if it gets me away from the castle for a little while. I swear by the gods, if I have to listen to Hale's posturing and boasting or Grinner's grumbling for one more day, I'll kill them both and do Belgarin's work for him."

Adina laughed but thinking of what she intended to do she quickly sobered. "What I plan...it's dangerous, May. It's necessary, I think, and worth the risk, but there *is* risk."

May met her eyes. "Now who is treating who like a scared child, Princess? Why don't you just tell me what it is you've got planned, and I'll tell you my thoughts on it."

Adina sighed, nodding slowly. "Very well. You've heard, of course, that my kingdom was taken from me by a rebellion among my nobles?"

"So I've heard."

Adina hesitated, then finally spoke. "The coup was perpetrated by the commander of my armies as well as several high members of the castle staff and a few nobles. Had they not approached Gryle to ask for his aid, I would have been killed then, for it was only due to his warning that I was able to escape the city in time. The people know nothing of it, of course. They were told that I died in a riding accident when my horse went wild and trampled me. By my reckoning, there were only a handful of people involved in the coup, but all the *right* people, men and women who were close enough to the throne to add veracity to the fiction that I was dead." She paused before she spoke again and when she did she was surprised by the anger in her own voice. "Their leader was General Ridell, the commander of my armies and a man who I had always considered a close friend."

"Approaching the leader of the armies...it does sound well within your brother Belgarin's usual methodology."

"Yes," Adina said, her eyes cold and hard, "it does. You cannot imagine what it's like, May, to know that all my people—people whom I love—think that I am dead. You cannot comprehend what it's like to sit here while I know they are forced to endure the rule of that *pretender*. That *traitor* sits on my throne while I hide in my sister's kingdom."

"To be fair, Princess," May said, "you've had just a few things going on to occupy you. And anyway, you still haven't told me what you plan."

Adina turned to May, and there was no doubt or uncertainty in her eyes, not now. "I intend to take my kingdom back, May."

"And how will you do such a thing?" May asked. "Will you order your late brother Ellemont's troops to attack your own city? Your own kingdom? For as I understand it, your brother gave over rule of his kingdom to you upon his death."

"No," Adina said, shaking her head adamantly, "innocent people would die in the fighting, and the people of Galia have suffered enough. Besides, the troops are needed here in case Belgarin's armies attack from the east, and Galia is several weeks' travel in the wrong direction. No," she said again, "this has to be done a different way. I aim to go myself."

"But not alone though, surely," May said, frowning. "I've known you for some time, Princess, and I'd like to think you're smarter than Aaron to go rushing off on your own trying to get yourself killed."

"I'm not going alone, May," Adina said, "I've already spoken to Gryle about it."

May arched an eyebrow. "The chamberlain? I'm not questioning his loyalty, Adina—the gods know that man would light himself on fire, if you asked him to. But do you really think that's a good idea? The man's more nervous than a priestess in a whorehouse. Now, I'll grant you that with the Virtue of Strength he's strong, incredibly so, but last I checked, the man couldn't so much as sit in a chair without breaking it."

"Maybe it's not a good idea," Adina admitted, "but do you really think I could stop him from coming, even if I wanted to?"

"No," May said, sighing, "no, I don't. Still, I love Gryle as much as anyone, but the man's not exactly a fighter. And anyway, what do you plan on doing once you're in the city? Seems to me that what you believed then still holds true now—the best that can be said is that if you step up and declare yourself, you won't have to worry about Belgarin or Boyce Kevlane anymore." She leaned in, "Because you'll be dead, you see."

Adina sighed, running a hand through her long hair. "I'm not committing suicide, May, and I wouldn't go if I didn't think there was a real chance of accomplishing something. As I told you, there are those in the city and the castle who plotted against me, but there are more still who would rally behind me, if only they knew I am alive. Or, at least," she said, her expression growing troubled, "I believe they would."

"People such as who?"

"Captain Oliver, for one," Adina said, "Ridell's second in command. He served under my father. He'll back my claim; I'm almost sure of it. And the troops in the army have little love for General Ridell, a man who has always spent far too much time wining and dining rich noblewomen instead of strengthening his command. If they're shown the truth, I'm almost certain that they'll turn on Ridell and the others."

May frowned. "That's a lot of 'ifs' and 'almosts' for a princess who will be recognized on sight, and a chamberlain who is more likely to faint than fight, if it comes to it. And how do you plan on speaking to this Captain Oliver without Ridell or one of the others noticing, anyway? It seems to me that he'll be around the general mostly, or at the castle, and it doesn't strike me as particularly clever to strut into the castle asking after the captain."

"As for the castle, I know it better than anyone, save perhaps Gryle himself. And say what you will about him, Gryle knows every single person in the castle by name, knows their stories and their pasts, as he made it a point to speak with and interview everyone all the way down to the lowliest scullery maid before allowing them to work in the castle."

"What about these traitors?" May said. "Interviewed them, did he?"

Adina shook her head, clearly frustrated. "I'm going, May, with or without your help. You know as well as I do that even with Ellemont's troops, even with Avarest's, Belgarin's army is still greater than our own, never mind Boyce Kevlane and whatever evil he is up to."

"I know you are, Princess," May said, "and I'm going with you. I only wanted to make sure that you had thought through the dangers, that's all."

Adina nodded and let out a tired sigh of her own as she leaned back against the bench. "I'm sorry, May. I don't mean to snap at you. I'm just frustrated, that's all. Aaron and the others have been gone nearly two weeks, and all I've been doing is sitting on my hands and worrying myself half to death. I'm tired of waiting and hoping for things to happen. It's time that I did my part, and the troops that Galia can provide would be a great help in the coming battle."

"It's alright, Princess," May said, patting her hand, "I've had much worse than that, I assure you. And I understand. I've never been much for sitting around and waiting for a man to fix my problems myself. Still, speaking of Silent, how do you think he'll feel about all this?"

Adina shrugged. "I don't know, May. Aaron means..." She felt her face heat but didn't look away from the club owner's eyes. "He means much to me. But I won't cower and do nothing while people suffer. I *can't*. Besides, if we're lucky we can be to Galia and back before he and the others return."

May studied the woman's steady gaze for several seconds then finally nodded. "Alright, Princess. I agree with you. As for Silent, he'd no doubt have some grim pronouncement to make about the whole thing but then that man would have a grim pronouncement to make about breakfast, so that's as may be. Still, when do you plan on leaving?"

Adina shrugged. "Another day or two, no more than that. The sooner we go, the sooner we can get it done, one way or the other."

May nodded. "Okay, but I wonder if you wouldn't let me look around. You're right that bringing an army to Galia would be a bad thing, but surely a group of three or four travelers wouldn't arouse any suspicion, and it would give us some help we'll most likely need."

Adina considered that. "Alright," she said reluctantly, "but the gods only know who would sign up for such a mission."

"Oh, not only the gods," May said, smiling, "I've an idea about a couple of people who might be interested in just such a thing."

CHAPTER TEN

Aaron frowned. *Gods, but this really is a fool idea.* He and the others stood on a hill, the reins of their horses in their hands. In the distance, he could make out the walls of Baresh. The sun had only just risen and by its light he could see men and women—farmers mostly, from their look—entering through the city gates.

Yes, Co agreed.

Aaron thought that she would say something more, but she remained silent, so he glanced at Leomin. "No tricks this time, okay? It won't do us any good if you give away our position to anybody that might be in the area."

"As you say, Mr. Envelar," Leomin said, nodding his head.

Aaron should have felt relieved, but he didn't. For one, the Parnen had a habit of saying one thing and doing another and, more importantly, he felt a strange foreboding when he stared at Baresh; his stomach twisted into knots for reasons he couldn't explain.

Perhaps it has something to do with the fact that you plan to walk into an enemy city and do everything short of handing yourself over to a man who would love to kill you, Co supplied.

I don't think so, he thought back, deciding not to acknowledge her sarcastic tone. He'd faced death before—as a sellsword, such a thing was pretty much in the job description—but this was different, somehow. He stared back at the city and, once again, that sense of impending doom rose in him.

Tell me you don't feel that.

I'm sure I don't—The Virtue cut off, hesitating. *It...it can't be. Can it?*

What can't be what, damnit?

What you feel is fear, *Aaron,* she said, her voice subdued and worried.

"Damnit, I told you that's not it."

"I'm sorry, Mr. Envelar," Leomin said. "What was that?"

"Not you," Aaron said, his eyes never leaving the distant city.

"I wouldn't worry 'bout it much, fella," Wendell said. "The general's got a habit of talkin' to himself sometimes. Never says anythin' interesting, anyway."

Aaron was barely listening, too busy staring at the city. His bond with Co had been growing stronger with each day that passed, the anger along with it but, so far at least, he had been able to keep that last in check. Still, stronger or not, he had never seen or felt anything like what he now discerned coming from the city. It wasn't a smell, but if it were, it would have been the sickly sweet scent of meat lying in a hot sun. It wasn't something he could see, either. Nevertheless, he could *feel* it, could feel dark shadows surrounding the city, shadows that shifted and curled about the distant walls and buildings like living, breathing things. *I don't like this,* he thought.

Nor I, Aaron, the Virtue said, and there was no mockery or amusement in her voice now. *I have never seen anything like this, not in all my years. The good news is that it means that our bond is more powerful than any I have ever had before. The bad news ....*

The bad news, he finished for her, *is that there is something evil at work in the city, something that has its entire population on edge.*

Yes.

Aaron sighed. It wouldn't make dealing with the guards any easier and as soon as he had the thought, he realized that they were still going in. That *he* was going to lead them there. Into that city of fear and darkness. After all, what choice did they really have?

"Is everything alright, Aaron?" Darrell asked, and Aaron forced his gaze away from the city to the swordmaster crouched beside him.

"I don't think so, Darrell. There is something wrong with the city—the people there are afraid. So afraid that I can feel it even from here."

The older man's eyes widened, "Do you mean...the Virtue?"

Aaron grunted, "Yeah."

They all turned to look back at the city, as if they might see some proof of whatever evil was taking place behind its walls, but there was nothing.

"Well," said Wendell finally, breaking the uncomfortable silence, "what do you reckon we should do, General?"

"We go in," Aaron said, "it's the only real option we have. Whatever it is, let's pray it has nothing to do with us. We came here for a reason, and the reason hasn't changed. That said..." He paused, turning to look at the others. "If any of you wants to turn back, I won't fault you for it. I don't know what's happening in Baresh, but whatever it is, I get the feeling it's dangerous."

The three men met his eyes, and Wendell grunted. "Of course we're goin', sir. Now how about we stop yackin' about it and get this thing done?" Crouched on the balls of his feet like the rest of them, he motioned to his legs. "We sit here like this much more, I won't be able to walk, let alone fight."

"If it comes to a fight," Aaron said, "we're dead already." He took a moment to consider as they watched him, waiting for him to tell them how it would be. "Alright," he said finally, "this is how we're going to do it..."

**

Aaron stood in line, waiting for his turn at the gate. They'd decided to go in separately as they would be less likely to draw attention or be remembered that way, and he had insisted that he be the first one to attempt entry through the gate. Wendell had argued at that, claiming that he should be first in case anything went wrong, but Aaron had held firm and finally the man had relented. *The fool wanted the first chance at getting his head separated from his shoulders.*

Yes, Co said in an amused voice, *what a fool he is. Surely, no one would volunteer for such a thing. At least, no one except a fool, that is.*

This is different, firefly, he said, *I'm the general.*

Forgive me, she said, *I had forgotten that generals always fight at the front of the battle, risking their lives before the soldiers themselves.*

"Damnit, this is *different*," Aaron said again, and a thin, older man leading a cow by a rope leash glanced back at him suspiciously. "Hi," Aaron said, "sometimes I talk to myself. Sorry." The man frowned and grunted what might have been taken as a greeting before turning back around.

He thinks you're crazy, Co said.

I know that, firefly, Aaron snapped back, *I can feel it just like you. And anyway, the bastard's probably right.*

No argument here, not on that, at least. I still stand by my opinion that it's stupid for you to try the gate first. Wendell could have done it just as well, probably better, and Leomin certainly could do it better—that man's got a silver tongue just like Aliandra did. And I hope you don't take this the wrong way, Aaron, but you're not particularly good with people.

Or floating balls of light with superiority complexes, he added, and though she didn't respond, he could feel her sulking, and that was alright. He didn't feel like talking just now, didn't feel like justifying his decision. He'd given Wendell reasons for him going first, of course: if he was somehow captured, Wendell, who knew more woodcraft than the others put together, had a better chance of escaping than any of them. As for Leomin, the only thing the Parnen knew about swords seemed to be how to make another man want to stab him with one. Besides, the swordmaster had not been involved in their escape from the city and therefore wouldn't be as good a test. It was better for Aaron to try. That way, they would know—and quickly, he didn't doubt—whether or not the guards at the gate were looking for men matching their descriptions.

These were the reasons he had given, and they had worked. The problem, of course, was that they weren't the real ones. The real reason was that Aaron felt responsible for the men with him. If not for him, they would have been back at Perennia safe or, at least, as safe as any man could be in such times. *Gods, I'm becoming soft,* he thought.

No, Co said, *you are becoming human, Aaron. Not such a bad thing, really.*

Aaron grunted but chose not to reply to that. His bond with the Virtue had grown so strong that it was difficult to separate the effects Co had on him with his own personal feelings—impossible really. The compassion and the rage both, always there, a part of him now. Still, at least he'd felt nothing so terrible, so all-consuming as the rage that had led him and the other Ghosts to slaughter the men at the gate, the rage that had driven them away from a perfectly good, defensible position and into a waiting army of thousands of soldiers. A foolish thing, that, and it would have been a deadly one had Ellemont not shown up in time, had he not sacrificed himself to save them.

If you hadn't done what you did, Aaron, the entire city would have fallen.

Aaron didn't answer, but he forced the shame that had begun rising in him down, burying it. There would be enough time for that later, if they survived. Now though, he had other things to worry about. Such as the guard who eyed him warily as he stepped forward, doing what he could to mimic the slightly beaten down, weary step of the farmers.

"Whoa there," the guard said as if Aaron had been galloping full speed on a horse instead of shuffling toward the gate.

"Hello, sir," he said, nodding.

The guard studied him. "And what brings you to Baresh?"

"The war, sir," he said, taking the tack that he and the others had agreed upon. "I had a farm—a small one, nothing fancy, but it was burned in the fighting outside Perennia. I've come to Baresh hoping to find work."

The guard looked around. "No family with you then, farmer? No wife or little kiddies running about?"

Most guards would have been satisfied with that answer but not this one, it seemed. The man was good at his job. The bastard. "No sir," Aaron said, thinking on the fly, and he did his best to look exhausted and sad. The first, at least, wasn't too much of a stretch. Not at all. "Had a wife, but she died. In the fighting."

"Died, did she?" the man asked, nodding slowly. "Sorry to hear that one, friend. Those bastards in Perennia. There's no end to what they'll do."

Aaron was as much surprised by the compassion in the man's expression as the sincerity in his voice. "Thank you," he said, bobbing his head in a slight bow, "I appreciate that. The gods know I'm lost without her."

The man grunted. "Well, come on in then, and I'll pray that the gods grant you a better turn here than they have so far."

"Thanks," Aaron said, "but I doubt it. The gods never do." He started past the guard. He thought he was going to make it, was nearly inside the gate, when the guard shouted at him.

Wincing, Aaron turned, putting on a depressed expression once more. "Sir?"

The man nodded at the bundle on Aaron's back. "What's a farmer need with a sword, anyway?"

Aaron did his best to school his features as he glanced over his shoulder and bit back a curse. They'd bundled the sword as best they could in a horse blanket, along with a few other things—a cooking pot they'd used at the campfire, a change of his clothes—but the tip of the sharp metal had slipped out, and there was no mistaking it, no point in lying. His mind raced, and he grunted to buy himself time. "Well, sir," he said, "since the wife passed, I thought maybe it'd be better to go armed. Farmers die like anybody else, after all, and an unarmed one dies easier than most."

The man studied him for several seconds, meeting his gaze, and Aaron resisted the urge to reach for the handle of his sword. He would kill the man if he had to, but he didn't wish it. Doing so would certainly draw the attention of the other three guards at the gate. They'd signal for more help, and soon there'd be an entire city up in arms, and Aaron's mission would fail before it even truly began. Besides, he found himself thinking of the very real compassion he'd seen in the guard's eyes when he'd heard of Aaron's dead wife. Aaron's wife wasn't dead, of course—he didn't have one and it would take some miracle to let him live long enough to ever get one—but the guard didn't know that. He'd seen only a man in pain, a man who the war had touched and taken from as wars always did, and he had done the only thing he could do in the face of such pain—he had acknowledged it.

The guard took several steps toward him until he was standing very close, and it was all Aaron could do to keep his eager hands from reaching for the blade at his back. Then, the guard surprised him by clapping him on the shoulder, "I understand," he said, nodding slowly, "I truly do. The war hurts us all, farmer, good and evil alike. We can only pray that King Belgarin is able to quell this rebellion soon, so that we can go back to what lives it leaves us. And you're right," he said, nodding to the sword, "these are troubled times, and a man must do what he can to protect what's his. A word of warning though, farmer. There are strange goings on in the city just now. Perhaps it would be better if you found another city or town to search for work. Vasek is north, only half a day's walk would bring you there. Nice people—simple but nice. I grew up there, if you'd believe it."

Aaron hesitated. Why did the man have to be so damned agreeable? If Aaron refused to take his advice, it would look suspicious, but he couldn't very well travel to Vasek and become a gods-cursed farmer in truth. Then, without even realizing he was doing it, the power of the bond rose up in him, and suddenly he was inside the guard's mind, feeling his thoughts.

The man was anxious about the things going on in the city, about people *disappearing.* At the same time, he was excited about the shift changing in two hours so that he could go home and be with his new wife. *Of course he'd have a wife. The bastard.* Neither of these was the worst though; the worst was the sympathy he felt for the man standing in front of him, a farmer who'd lost his wife in the war. He was considering, not for the first time, doing something different with his life and damn what his father thought. There were more important things than hurting people and scowling at citizens. A baker, maybe. He'd always loved bread and...

Aaron severed the link with the man, shaking his head at the flood of information and feelings. *A baker,* he thought, *gods help me.* "Thing is," Aaron said, deciding on an excuse he thought would resonate with the guard, "I would, sir, truly, and I appreciate the advice. But my wife's father would never let me hear the end of it. You see, we never have gotten along...he always believed farming was a poor man's job. Actually wanted me to be a town guard, if you can believe it."

Aaron sighed heavily. "Maybe I should have listened to him. If I had, maybe my wife would still be alive. He blames me for her death, and I can't argue it. I've come to Baresh because I've heard there are a lot of opportunities here. I enjoyed farming, working with my hands, but I always thought to do something else, to *be* something else." He shook his head at his own foolishness for the guard's benefit. "A chandler, if you can believe it. After my wife...well, I packed up everything I owned—everything the soldiers left—and came to Baresh. Thought I'd make a go of it. But maybe you're right," he sighed, "and maybe my wife's father is right too. I just don't know anymore."

Laying it on a bit thick, aren't we? Co asked, but Aaron wasn't listening. He was focused on the guard, watching his eyes widen slightly.

"*No,*" the man said, and Aaron tensed as the guard leaned forward and grabbed him by the shoulders, "no, he's not right, and I was wrong to suggest it. Look, the city is dangerous, just now—I wasn't lying to you about that—but if you stay smart, stay indoors when night comes then you should be fine. All the ones taken were taken during the night." He nodded to himself, "Yes, it'll be fine. You go and live your dream, farmer," he said, patting Aaron on the back once more, "at least some of us can." He smiled. "Or should I say, chandler?"

Aaron smiled back. "The gods be kind to you, sir," he said, and he started toward the gate once more, but paused as the guard grabbed his arm.

"Here," the guard said, withdrawing several coins from his pocket and forcing them into Aaron's hands, "it isn't much—the next time you talk to your wife's father, let him know that being a guard isn't all it's cracked up to be—but maybe it'll be a start to getting your own shop."

Aaron stared dumbly down at the coins in his hands for several seconds. Finally, he managed to look back up at the guard and saw that the man was smiling. "Sir," he said, "if you don't mind me sayin' so, maybe you might think of taking your own advice. If things in Baresh are as bad as you say, maybe you should get out of the city while you can and take your wi—anyone you care about with you. After all, is there any dream you have yourself? The war will go on for as long as it will, and I suspect a lot more people will die before it's over. Why not take your family—if you have one—and find a life somewhere else, away from all the killing?"

The guard considered that, and he nodded slowly. Then he smiled wider than Aaron had yet seen, and before Aaron realized what he was doing, the man had wrapped his arms around him in a hug. Aaron froze for a moment, unsure, then he reluctantly patted the man on the back. "You're right," the guard said, his face that of a child who has just been given a treat, "I'm going to do just that. Good luck, farmer."

Aaron smiled. "Good luck, guard."

He stood, stunned, as the guard walked over to one of the other men on duty and proceeded to take off his sword and hand it to him. In a moment, he was disappearing through the gate at a near-jog. *What. The. Fuck?* Aaron thought.

That was amazing, Aaron, Co said, her voice filled with joy, *you might have just saved that man's life.*

Or killed him, Aaron thought as he watched the confused looking guard toting the scabbarded sword into the gatehouse. *Really should have told him to keep that sword.* Shaking his head in wonder, Aaron walked through the gate and made his way into the city.

Baresh was much the way he remembered it, though not as crowded. And those he passed wore very different expressions than the excited, happy faces he'd seen crowding the streets in the days leading up to and during the tournament. They looked at him warily, several going so far as to scowl in his direction. Aaron glanced behind him to make sure that he'd rewrapped the sword at his back but after a moment he realized that they were looking at everyone who entered the gate in the same way.

It's as if they think that everyone who enters is going to cause trouble, Co said. *Perhaps it has something to do with what the guard was saying.*

Aaron frowned. And what had the man meant by all of that anyway? "Those who are taken are taken at night," he'd said. Taken where? Once more, the feeling of doom rushing toward him was back and stronger than ever, now that he was inside the city walls. *Then they're fools,* he thought, *whatever the trouble is, it's already here. We need to be very careful here, firefly. Very careful.*

As opposed to getting into a life or death fight with the first person that says something you don't like? That will be a change. It had been meant to be a joke, but there'd been no amusement in her tone, and Aaron knew that whatever he felt, she felt it too.

"Well," he muttered, "whatever's happening, it has nothing to do with us. If everything goes according to plan, we'll be in and out of here before it matters."

He set off down the street toward the tavern Darrell had told them of, the place where they had all agreed to meet. *And how often have your plans worked out in the past, I wonder?* Co asked.

Aaron grunted, and an older woman that was passing him in the street frowned and hurried past. *Never,* he thought, *but a man can hope.*

***

Aaron stood in the street, staring at the tavern the swordmaster had told them about. Darrell had said it was out of the way, a place the city guard never went, and he thought that was probably true enough. The tavern was deep in the poor district, a squat, ugly building that reminded him of some of the places his job as a sellsword had forced him to frequent in the Downs. Not a place for nobles or rich merchants out to have a good time—there were always such places, he knew, had been several in the Downs. Such places usually appeared nicer on the outside but were just as rotten on the inside as the other, more obvious ones—a whore in face paint and a fancy dress is, after all, still a whore.

This tavern, though, made no attempts at disguising what it was—a den for criminals. And judging by the two thugs standing outside the doors, eyeing and haranguing anyone that approached, its owner had some understanding of the dangers such a place might attract. *Well,* Aaron thought, looking at the building with its crooked door, noting that one of the windows had been broken with what looked like a large rock—or possibly a head, there was always that—*the place is a shit heap, but at least it's honest.*

If you say so, Co answered dubiously, *but it looks filthy. If I had hands, I'd want to wash them just from looking at it.*

Good thing for us both that you don't then, Aaron responded as he made his way across the street toward the tavern.

One of the thugs stepped forward, sneering as he drew close. "And just who the fuck are you and what the fuck do you want?"

Aaron studied the speaker. A small man, a head shorter than Aaron himself, and thin at the shoulders. Aaron could make out a crude, rusty blade slipped into the man's belt. He'd dealt with the thug's kind before. Small men with big tempers, always looking for a fight where there wasn't one, doing their level best to get offended by anything that was said. Normally, he had little patience for such men, but the last thing he needed was to cause a scene. "My name's Aaron," he said, "and I was thinking I'd like a drink."

"Oh yeah?" the man said. "A drink is it?" He puffed out what little chest he had, looking Aaron up and down like he'd taken shits that were more impressive. "And what if I told you you ain't gonna get one?"

Aaron sighed. "Well, then I guess I'd find a different tavern. I wonder, though, if the man who hired you would be thrilled to know that you're turning away customers."

The man's pinched face twisted into an angry expression, and he jerked the blade from his belt, nearly fumbling it in his haste before pointing it at Aaron. "You threatening me, boy? I'll cut your fucking heart out and make you watch while I eat it, you understand me?"

Aaron rubbed at his temples, telling himself to keep his anger in check. "That'd be a hard thing to make me do, considering I'd be dead. Maybe you'd want to cut something else off—a toe, maybe. Maybe even an arm—shit, a man can live without an arm. I've seen men with no legs that are still living to bitch about it. The heart though ..." He shook his head. "Nah, I don't think you've thought this through."

The man stepped forward, bringing the knife closer to Aaron, and Aaron noted that the man couldn't even keep his hand from shaking. "Think you're a funny man, do you fella?" the thug hissed. "Think you're a clever bastard? Well, I wonder how clever you'd be, if I cut out your fucking heart right now?"

"Not very," Aaron said dryly, "on account of I'd be dead."

"Ricky," the other thug—a big, thickly muscled man—said, "put that sticker away, will ya? Alder ain't gonna be happy he hears about you waving it at his customers and threatening 'em. Not before they've bought any ale, anyhow."

Ricky, if that was his name, didn't seem to hear his companion. "I could fuck you up right here, boy," he said, eyeing Aaron with that dumb meanness that was so common in criminals, "cut your fucking heart out."

"Yeah," Aaron said, the anger building in him as he stared at the knife point only a few inches from his nose, "you said that."

The man let out a growl, his arm going way behind him as if he was about to stab Aaron, and he wanted to make sure everybody in the city saw it coming. When he finally did lash out with the knife, Aaron pivoted, striking the inside of the man's wrist with the palm of his hand. The small man cried out in surprised pain, and the knife clattered to the street between them. The man crouched as if he'd go for it, holding his hurt wrist, and Aaron only stood there, watching him. "Don't. Your pride's hurt a little, that's all, but your day can get a whole lot worse, believe me. Now, all I want is a drink and a room—"

He noticed the man eyeing the knife where it lay on the cobbled street. "Hey," Aaron said, snapping his fingers, "look at me. I'm talking to you. Just leave it, and we can both be on with our nights. I'll have my drink, and you can take comfort in the fact that you'll be alive when the morning comes. Still an asshole but alive at least."

The man hesitated, knowing the wisdom in Aaron's words, but his pride not letting him heed them. His face twisted in anger, and he lunged down, meaning to scoop the knife up off the cobbles. He was slow and obvious, but the way he was bent put him in perfect position, and Aaron grabbed both his shoulders, jerking him down further still as his knee came up and buried itself in the man's gut.

The thug's breath exploded from him in a gasping wheeze, and he collapsed to the ground, rolling onto his back, his dirty hands pawing at his stomach and chest as if he could somehow force the breath back into them. Aaron stared down at him flopping there like a fish out of water, and he took a moment to gain control of his anger, the barrier he kept between him and it fraying dangerously. Once he thought he could control himself, he knelt down beside the gasping man. "Hey." The man didn't look at him quick enough, so Aaron reached out and slapped him in the face, hard. "Hey," he said, "look at me."

The thin man whimpered in pain, continuing to gasp for breath, but he did turn his wide, frightened eyes to Aaron. "Good," Aaron said, "now listen and listen closely because I'm particularly impatient just now, and at the best of times, I'm not a man known for his tolerance. I'm going to go into that tavern," he said, nodding his head toward its entrance. The other thug stood there with a confused expression on his face as if he was unable to decide whether he should help or not. "I'm going to have my drink," Aaron continued, "and I'm going to ask after a room. Do you have a problem with that?"

The man grunted and wheezed, shaking his head furiously as tears leaked from his eyes. "Good," Aaron said, "but here's the thing. That choking, suffocating sensation you're feeling is going to go away in a few minutes, and you're going to be alright again. A little sore, a little battered, but mostly like the same asshole you woke up as this morning. Once that happens, you're going to start to think that this could have gone a different way. That I was lucky or you were unlucky, that it was pure chance that allowed me to knock that pig sticker you got there out of your hands. You'll tell yourself that you are one mean son of a bitch, that nobody, *nobody* disrespects you like this and lives. You'll work yourself up to it, and I don't think that tree stump son of a bitch over there is going to talk you out of whatever it is you mean to do. Now, you work here, so it wouldn't be such a hard thing for you to figure out about the stranger that came in asking after a drink and a bed for the night, wouldn't be particularly difficult for you to discover which room that stranger rented."

He knelt down further and grabbed the thin man's throat in one hand, squeezing and ignoring the man's ineffectual pawing as he fought to break free, "Just let me warn you now, that I'm a light sleeper—there's dead men could tell you as much, if they had a voice to tell it with. I've no patience or mercy at all for some sneaky, conniving little bastard that thinks to break into a man's room and kill him while he's in bed. You getting me?"

The man nodded as best he could with Aaron's hand around his throat, hacking in what Aaron took for agreement. "Good," Aaron said, letting the man go and rising to his feet. The thug gasped and brought his hands to his throat as he sucked in air. "And stop telling people you're going to cut their hearts out. Do you have any idea how hard that is to do? If you're going to kill a man, you don't talk about it—you just do it. Though," he said, glancing at the short, crude blade lying on the cobbles, "I'd probably get a better blade. Unless you intend to pick his teeth for him first."

The man was still wheezing in rattling breaths when Aaron walked toward the tavern's entrance. "Sorry 'bout that," the big guard said, shaking his head, "Ricky's an alright sort, but he always seems to be spoilin' for a fight."

"If he was an alright sort," Aaron said, pausing beside the man and turning to meet his gaze, "then he wouldn't be flopping on the ground choking and lying in a puddle of his own piss. Now, you keep your fucking dog on a leash." Before the man could respond, Aaron pushed the door open and stepped inside the tavern.

The common room was crowded despite the fact that night was still a few hours; Aaron could feel himself getting sized up by the men and women inside as he made his way toward the dusty, dented bar, each of them trying to decide if he would be an easy mark. He met their eyes without fear as he walked, not because he cared about their games, but because it was the way it was done, that was all. Not meeting their eyes would have been worse, for the men and women inside the tavern were wolves—or at least thought they were—and if he appeared skittish or nervous, they'd be on him in moments, each of them trying to work their own particular brand of crime.

Finally, he came to the bar and knocked his fist against it, drawing the attention of the tall, fat barkeep whose back was to him as he laughed at some joke a man further down the bar had told. The man glanced over at Aaron, studying him. The man was big, and Aaron suspected he'd been some sort of street fighter in his youth. Judging by the fact that he was still alive, he'd obviously had some skill, but whatever muscle he had was now covered in a layer of fat. He apparently decided that Aaron was worth his attention, for he said something to the man he'd been speaking with then made his way over.

"What'll it be, stranger?"

"You got anything to drink that isn't going to taste like horse piss coming down and horse shit coming up?"

"Got an ale that some folks say is the finest in all of Baresh. Why, I've even had some noblemen come down from their pretty little mansions just to have a drink of it."

Sure you have, Aaron thought. Any nobleman that was fool enough to step into this tavern wouldn't ever be stepping out again, and that was certain. He tossed some coins on the counter. "I'll have one then, and this is for a room, too."

The tavern keeper grunted, "Sure thing, stranger. So, you don't mind me askin', what's brought you to Baresh?"

Aaron met the man's eyes, his anger still working on him from where the thin man had awoken it. "Actually, I do mind. An ale and a room is all I want. If I want to have a conversation, I'm pretty sure I can find a prettier face than yours to have it with."

The man's eyes narrowed at that, but he scooped the coins up and went to get the drink. Aaron looked around the room as he waited. Several men sat with hired women draped on their shoulders, too drunk to notice as the women's hands wondered into their tunics and trousers and robbed them of what little coin they possessed. Other men sat close together at several of the tables speaking in whispers, glancing from time to time around the room as if to make sure that no one was listening to what they were saying. *Darrell sure can pick them, I'll give him that,* Aaron thought. The place felt just like home—in all the worst ways.

Those in the tavern's common room eyed each other as if looking for one among them who would be an easy mark, and though that was a bit unusual, it wasn't exactly surprising. Wolves didn't generally eat wolves, preferring the taste of softer, easier meat, but a starving wolf cared only about filling the empty, gnawing hunger in its stomach. And these people *were* starving—there was no question of that. Aaron saw the tavern keeper coming out of the corner of his eye and turned back to the bar just as the big man slammed the mug of ale down on it. Ale spilled from the sides of the mug onto wood that looked as if it hadn't been cleaned in years, and Aaron nodded, grabbing the drink and rising. "Thanks."

The bar keep only grunted in response, and Aaron made his way through the common room to an empty table in the corner to wait for his friends. He sat quietly, drinking his ale and doing his best to ignore the stares as he replayed what the guard at the gate had told him.

He hadn't been sitting there long when he heard a commotion from the other side of the tavern, back by the bar, and he looked up to see a blonde-haired woman in a simple dress trying her best to extricate herself from the hands of a drunken fat man who'd pulled her down into his lap. The woman had a tray in her hands upon which sat several mugs of ale, and as the man pulled her close against him, he and the other men at the table laughing, one of the mugs toppled, spilling ale all over the woman. She cried out in surprise and fear as the drink soaked through her dress.

Her long mane of hair whipped around in her struggles, and Aaron was able to get a better look at her face. He frowned as he realized that the serving woman wasn't a woman at all but a girl that appeared to be no more than sixteen summers. *A lamb thrown in among wolves,* he thought. He started to get up from the table but hesitated. *It's none of your concern,* he told himself. *Remember why you're here. The last thing you need to do is attract attention.*

Still, he sat on the edge of his seat, his muscles tensed, until the girl finally managed to pull herself away from the man's pawing hands. The fat man made one last grab for her, missing the girl herself but catching hold of the flimsy material of her white dress. He gave it a drunken pull, still laughing, and the girl stumbled and fell to her hands and knees, dropping the tray and spilling ale onto the floor and the feet of the surrounding patrons as her dress ripped. She cried out again, her hand catching the torn fabric before it could reveal little more than the skin of a smooth, pale white shoulder and went about grabbing up the spilled glasses and tray.

You should help her, Co said in his mind, obviously angry at the girl's treatment.

Better if I don't. I wouldn't be doing her any favors, firefly, believe me. After all, it wasn't as if he could sit in this tavern every day and look out for her—sooner or later, she would have to learn how to fend for herself, how to protect herself. Aaron frowned, glancing around the room. There was a thug standing near the bar, no doubt another bouncer for the tavern, but Aaron watched him turn to the fat bar keep only to have the big man shake his head slowly, a disgusted look on his face.

No help from that quarter either, then. *Don't get involved, you damn fool,* he told himself, clenching his teeth together, *just leave it alone.* The girl was still trying to gather the spilled mugs, had just gotten hold of one, when the man who'd grabbed her reached out again, pulling her toward him. She yelled for him to stop, but he ignored her, yanking harder, and her dress ripped further exposing more pale skin. The girl screamed again and spun, swinging the thick glass stein she was holding. It struck the fat man in the face, and he cried out, tumbling out of his chair and falling on the floor, his hands going to his bloody face.

Good for you, girl, Aaron thought, but the men's friends didn't see it that way, and several of them rose and jerked the girl up. "You bitch," one of them growled, and he brought his hand back and slapped her hard across the face.

The girl cried out not just in fear but pain this time, and Aaron could see tears leaking from the corners of her eyes. "*Alder,*" she screamed. "Help!"

Everyone in the tavern turned to the bar keep including the thug who gave him a questioning glance. The fat man looked around the room, apparently enjoying his moment, then finally met the girl's eyes. "Not my problem, lass. Those are paying customers, and you've no right to hit on 'em so. You brought what's comin' on yourself."

By now, the man with the bloody face was up, and Aaron saw what he thought were pieces of glass sticking out of the man's cheek. Even from where he sat in the corner of the common room, Aaron could feel the power of the man's anger through his bond with Co. It was the kind of anger that wanted to hurt, the kind that wanted to kill. "*You'll pay for that, slut,*" he growled, and two of his friends held the struggling girl while he brought his fist back and sank it into her stomach. The girl's breath exploded in a wheeze, and she collapsed to her knees in a hacking, coughing fit, the sleeve of her torn dress hanging low.

"Didn't mean you no harm," the man said, his chest heaving as he looked down at her, "but I think now maybe I'll take what I want. I'll teach you how to treat a man right."

Don't get involved damnit, Aaron told himself, but he was already up and moving as the man fumbled with his trousers. He was still trying to get them down when Aaron's sword came to a rest barely an inch away from his crotch. "Whatever comes out of there won't be going back in, I can promise you that."

The man stared at the cold steel inches away from the place that did all of his thinking for him and swallowed hard, looking back at Aaron. "This ain't no concern of yours, mister. The girl hit me with a fuckin' ale mug—damn near shattered my face."

"I don't see that its hurt your looks any," Aaron said, "and as far as I'm concerned you had that coming—you've probably had it coming for a long time. Now," he continued, telling himself that he was being a damned fool and wanting only to get away from all of those staring eyes in the tavern, "you've had your fun, and she's had hers. How about we call it a day and maybe you find some different tavern to drink at?"

"How about," one of the man's friends said from behind Aaron, "We kick the shit out of you and then do what we want to the girl anyw—"

His words turned into a howl of pain as Aaron pivoted and brought his elbow back. The man's nose crunched under the force of the blow, and he stumbled backward. The fat man started forward but froze when Aaron turned and brought the blade back to its place once more. "Now then," he said, standing sideways and doing his best to keep both the man and his friends in his vision at the same time, "I've had my fun, too. So why don't you all leave before I start cutting?"

Aaron felt the power of the bond awaken, and he knew what one of the men was going to do even before he moved, so when the man rushed him from behind, Aaron stepped smoothly out of the way, and the man tackled his bloody-faced companion instead. The two slammed up against the table but before they could right themselves, Aaron grabbed the greasy black hair of the one that had rushed him and slammed the man's head down into the wooden table. The tables were built of thick, strong wood—why they were still standing after years of what had no doubt been significant punishment, judging by the tavern's customers—and when it met the man's face, the wood did not give. His face did, though, and the man rebounded off the hard wooden surface with a spray of blood, falling onto his back, unconscious.

Aaron felt something behind him and turned in time to knock aside a knife that had been aimed for his back. Every instinct begged him to bring the sword down, but he fought the urge, knowing that while the city guard might not take much interest in a tavern brawl, they'd definitely be more apt to if people wound up dead. So instead of using his sword, he grabbed the back of the man's head and jerked it down, bringing his knee up and driving it into the man's face. The man staggered, and Aaron struck him in the temple with the handle of his sword.

The man went down as if he'd been pole-axed and lay unmoving. Aaron's instincts warned him of someone behind him, and he spun in time to see one of the men charging at him. In time to see it, but not to dodge it. The man slammed into him, knocking him back against the hard wooden side of a table, and the sword slipped loose from Aaron's grip, clattering on the floor.

Growling in pain and anger, Aaron brought his elbow down on the man's back once, twice, three times, the man howling in pain all the while. On the third, the man rose back up and swung a meaty fist at the sellsword's face, but Aaron ducked under it, sending two rapid punches to his opponent's midsection. The man gasped, staggered, and Aaron's next punch caught him between the eyes.

The man cried out, stumbling backward, but Aaron followed after him. He grabbed the man by the front of his shirt and one of his arms and pivoted, slinging the big man over his shoulder to slam onto the top of the table in a shower of broken glass and ale. The man tried to rise, but Aaron kept one hand on his shirt and with the other he withdrew the knife from where he kept it at his side and slammed it into the table, inches from the man's face.

The big man froze at that, his eyes going wide, and Aaron glanced back toward the room. Three men were down now, and the fourth, the one the girl had hit, stood staring at him in something like shock. The expression was mirrored on the faces of those watching. Aaron looked at the bloody man for a moment, "Well? I thought you were leaving?"

The man didn't need any more encouragement than that and, in a moment, he was disappearing out of the front of the tavern, leaving his unconscious friends behind him. Aaron was suddenly overcome with a feeling of being watched, of being studied. And there was another feeling too, one of vague recognition, as if he'd caught a scent half-remembered from childhood. He glanced around the tavern trying to find the source of the feeling. The problem was that everyone in the damned tavern was watching him just then. The feeling was gone now but, he realized that the sense of recognition—gone as quickly as it had come—hadn't come from him but from Co. *Something up, firefly?* he asked, scanning the common room.

I...I'm not sure, Co said, *I thought, for a second, that I saw or felt someone that I recognize but...I must have imagined it.*

Aaron frowned, deciding that he didn't want to be in this tavern any longer, but he had one thing to do first. He jerked his blade out of the table top and started toward the fat tavern keeper. The man leaned back as he drew close as if expecting Aaron to attack him. An expectation that wasn't far at all from what Aaron wanted to do just then, for the anger had been awakened in full, and he was having a difficult time managing it. "Does she work for you?" he said, motioning to the girl who was just now getting herself up off the ground.

"Don't know what business it is of yours," the innkeeper said, his voice surly and scared at once.

"Let me hear of something like this happening again, and I'll show you exactly what business it is of mine," Aaron said. "What was it, exactly? You took her in off the street, figured maybe her pretty looks would help you sell more ale, is that it?"

Alder grunted, not acting angry or threatening, only pouty like a child who'd been called down for acting out. "She's lucky I took her in at all, the little whore. I wouldn't have if'n the last boy I had workin' here hadn't have walked off near two weeks ago with not so much as one word of thanks." He shook his head. "I found her on the street starvin', beggin' for food, so yeah I give her a clean place to sleep and a job, even pay her some coppers each day, and what's my thanks? Her spilling ale and smashing my mugs over the customers heads."

Aaron grabbed the back of the man's head and jerked it down, putting the knife up to his ample chin. "What did you call her?" he said. "Because it sounded to me like you called her a whore, and

I'm a sensitive guy—I don't think I could abide it, if that was the case."

Alder swallowed hard. "I...I ain't mean nothin' by it, mister. Just a word is all."

"And one you'll not use about her again," Aaron said, "not in my hearing and not in hers. As for clean," he laughed, "this shit heap of a tavern hasn't been clean since it was built; I think we both know that. I think we also both know that the girl was just defending herself. What the fuck do you hire those thugs for anyway, if not to stop trouble like that before it gets out of hand?"

"She spilled beer," the fat man said, as if it justified everything.

"And I'll spill your guts, if I feel there's a need," Aaron responded. "Now, I'm going to be living in Baresh for a long time—possibly forever—and I'll be stopping by here from time to time. After all," he said, giving the man a smile that never touched his eyes, "I like the company. And I think it's better to tell you now that the next time I stop by, I expect that girl to be being treated with respect, like a human being. If I come by and see that she's been hurt, or that she's not here, well," he said, leaning in forward and bringing the knife closer so that the tip of it pricked the man's fat chin and a bead of blood welled there, "then we'll have to have this conversation again, and I *really* hate repeating myself. Do you understand?"

"Y-yes, mister," Alder stammered, his eyes wide as they tried to take in the blade at his throat, "I understand."

"Good," Aaron said. He glanced back at the spilled ale in the floor and the girl still trying to clean it up. "Now, get over there and clean that mess up. It's fucking disgusting and, anyway, I think she could use a day off. Some new clothes while you're at it. Don't you?"

The man nodded, and Aaron pulled the knife back, watched as Alder made his way over to the girl and whispered a few words in her ear. In another moment, she was moving away and toward the stairs. As she passed him, she gave Aaron a quick, scared glance, then she was up the stairs and gone. He thought that was probably alright. The girl was right to be scared—she'd live longer.

Once she was gone, he sighed heavily as he noted all of the eyes watching him from around the common room. *Damnit,* he thought, *so much for keeping a low profile.*

It was a good thing you did, Aaron, the Virtue said. *You saved her.*

Maybe, Aaron thought back, *but, then, I might have just damned us and all of Perennia with us.* He was starting to head to the door when it opened and Wendell, Darrell, and Leomin entered, glancing around. Aaron winced and moved toward them. "Took you long enough," he said.

Wendell grunted, "Leomin here decided to make friends with one of the guards at the gate."

"He was actually quite an interesting fellow," the Parnen said. "You'd be surprised—"

"And then there was the tailor we passed in the street," Wendell offered.

"Some surprisingly fine quality clothes, too, for such a—"

"And the prostitute, though the gods alone know what she's doing working so early in the day."

Leomin cleared his throat. "Yes, well, she has to make a living just like anyone else, friend Wendell, and she seemed lonely. Anyway," he said, noting the looks of the three men, "we're here now, and that's what counts. I must confess that I am weary beyond belief and looking forward to spending the night in a bed for a change."

Aaron glanced behind him where the men were still lying on the ground unconscious, a few other of the tavern's customers trying to rouse them. "Yeah, well, I wouldn't get too excited. I think maybe we need to find another inn." *Besides,* he thought, *why do I keep getting the feeling that I'm being watched?* No, that wasn't right. After all, damned near everyone in the room was watching him. He felt as if he was being *studied.* As if someone or something was measuring his worth.

"And what, I wonder, happened here?" Darrell asked, pulling Aaron's attention back to the three men.

"I'll tell you about it later," Aaron said. "For now, let's just say there was ale involved and that we disagreed on a few matters."

Darrell nodded slowly. "Your subtlety never fails to amaze me, Aaron," the swordmaster said, giving him a small smile, "just like a chameleon, you are."

"Anyway," Aaron said, "I think it best if we left for now." Aaron followed them outside and as he went through the door, he nearly tripped on something lying on the ground. He looked and was surprised to find that it was the thin man who'd accosted him when he'd first come upon the tavern. The man was clearly unconscious and a fresh bruise had risen on his temple. "Huh," he said, glancing at the three men, "what happened here?"

It was Darrell's time to look embarrassed, "Yes, well...say that we disagreed on a few matters."

Aaron grunted a laugh. "Anyway, this doesn't solve our problem. We still need somewhere to lay our heads for the night."

"Oh, Mr. Envelar," Leomin said smiling, "I wouldn't worry overly much. I think I've got just the place."

***

The youth who'd been sitting to one side of the tavern's common room rose and started to follow the four strangers, but one of the men at the table reached out and grabbed his arm. "You said you'd pay us two gold coins a piece, and we've only seen the one. Now, I'll have the other one now, or I'll take it out of your skinny hide."

The youth frowned beneath the hood of his cloak, frowned but did not show fear. "That's not what we agreed on."

"Maybe not," the man said, tightening his grip on the boy's wrist, "but it's what's going to happen just the same. So why not be a good lad and give me my money—and double it for my trouble. If you do it quick enough, I might even decide to let you walk out of here without hurting you."

The youth sighed. "You're sure this is the way you want to do it?"

"You're damn right I'm sure."

"Alright," the youth said. He turned to a table beside the one at which he'd been sitting and nodded. The two big men seated there rose. The man holding his wrist frowned, starting to turn but not quick enough to avoid one of the men locking his thickly muscled forearm around his throat, while the other pulled his hand free from the youth's wrist.

The man's eyes went wide, as he struggled and failed to draw a breath. *"I-I don't....understand,"* he said, his voice coming out in little more than a croak.

"Don't you?" the youth said. "It's a simple enough thing really. You see, when hiring criminals, even for something as simple as sitting in a tavern with you so as to draw less attention to yourself, one must expect them to betray you. They're *criminals,* after all." The boy shrugged. "So I hired a few more."

He watched as the man's face turned a deep red, and he finally slumped, obviously unconscious. "Don't kill him, please," the youth said, "Just dump him somewhere." He reached into his pocket and withdrew a small sack of coins, passing it to the man whose hands were free. It was considerably more than he'd promised them, but then, he was surprised how easy gold was to come by when you knew how to get it. It was all about knowing.

"Good night, gentlemen," he said, bowing his head to each in turn and adjusting his hood so that it covered his face once more as he started toward the door of the tavern. Not that he needed to worry overly much about hiding his identity. Those few who had frequented the tavern for some time almost certainly wouldn't have recognized him anyway. Caleb had changed dramatically over the last few weeks and, in most ways, he was not the same boy he once had been. Not at all.

CHAPTER ELEVEN

"You've got to be kidding."

"I do not mean to, Mr. Envelar," Leomin said, "but I am not wrong in assuming we need a safe place, yes? A *friendly* place. And what place is friendlier than a place owned by friends? Friendly friends at that."

Aaron sighed. *Friendly to you anyway,* he thought, but he nodded. The truth was, it was a good choice and one that Aaron would have thought of himself if he hadn't been so distracted trying to get his anger back on its leash and trying to figure out why he felt as if he was being watched. "It was a good idea, Leomin."

The man beamed widely, and Aaron immediately regretted his words. He grunted, "Well, lead on then. This is your show."

"As you say, Mr. Envelar," Leomin said, and Aaron and the others followed him as he made his way into the inn.

They'd only just stepped inside—Wendell was closing the door behind them—when Aaron heard a surprised, ecstatic shout. *"Leomin! You're back!"* They'd barely turned to see who had spoken when the youth, Janum, Aaron believed his name was, came running up from behind the counter and pulled Leomin into a tight embrace. The boy was fifteen, possibly sixteen by now, yet his eyes shone like those of a child at the sight of the Parnen.

"Ah, friend Janum," Leomin said smiling, "it is very good to see you and be seen by you. Have you been good as we discussed?"

"Yes sir," the youth said, nodding his head so quickly Aaron thought it a miracle it didn't come flying off, "just as you said. I really have. And I tried those lines you told me on a girl I met but ..." He frowned slightly. "Maybe I said them wrong or something because I don't think she got it. The truth is," he said, his face coloring, "I'm not entirely sure I get them myself. For example, the one about the shepherd and his flo—"

"Yes, yes," Leomin interrupted, "we will most certainly discuss such things, friend Janum but, perhaps another time."

"You sure, Leomin?" Aaron said, unable to keep the grin from his face. "Because I think I'd like to hear about this shepherd and his...flock, was it?"

Leomin cleared his throat, and was about to say something when the youth suddenly stepped forward and gave Aaron a hug much the same way he had the Parnen. "I'm glad you're all okay," he said, and after a moment of shock, Aaron regained enough of his composure to hug the youth back.

Gods, but it's my day for getting hugs it seems.

Better that than someone trying to kill you, Co said, her tone amused.

Let me think about it, Aaron responded, but he found that he was smiling when the youth stepped away. "I did as you said, Mr. Envelar. I got a better blade—a *real* sword, this time."

Aaron felt the others studying him, and it was his turn to avoid their eyes, "That's good, Janum. Real good. But I hope you're careful with it—swords are weapons, not toys, and you wouldn't be the first to learn that lesson the hard way."

The boy's face took on a pouty, childlike expression, and Aaron wondered idly what had happened to the youth who had tracked him with the intention of killing him only months before. "No sir," Janum said in a depressed voice, "Uncle only lets me take it out to clean it and to knock the dust off as he says." He sighed forlornly as if such a thing was proof—were any needed—that the world was a cruel place. "Still," he said, brightening once more, "he found someone to help train me—an old friend of his who used to be a real castle guard under King Eladen. Swordmaster Lionel only lets me train with wooden swords right now, but he says that if I keep up at the rate I'm going, I'll be able to train with real swords soon."

Aaron smiled. "That's good, Janum. I'm glad you've found a teacher. I once had a swordmaster myself, though he's an old crotchety bastard now. Of course, he was an old crotchety bastard then too."

"So is swordmaster Lionel," the boy grumbled, "he says I've got the wits of a stone and the temper of a bull."

Aaron grunted a laugh. "Mine said much the same. I wouldn't worry about it, Janum. Just work hard and you'll get it—it's your swordmaster's job to be a pain in the ass that's all."

Janum grinned and Darrell gave Aaron a glance before stepping forward and offering the youth his hand. "A pleasure to meet you," he said wryly, "I'm the old crotchety pain in the ass. Darrell for short."

The youth's eyes went wide at that, but he took the hand and shook it, bowing his head slightly, "It's a pleasure, sir."

"Undoubtedly," Darrell said dryly, but he was smiling when he did.

"Speaking of your uncle," Aaron said, looking around the common room of the inn that was nearly empty, save for a man and a woman sitting in one corner, "where is he?"

"Oh, right," Janum said, "Uncle lets me watch the bar sometimes when he has to run to town, but he should be back soon."

"Watching the bar all by yourself," Leomin said, nodding in approval, "I am impressed, young Janum."

The youth colored at that, obviously pleased, then he slapped himself in the forehead, "Gods, but where is my brain. Come, and I'll get you all a drink. Uncle should be back any minute."

He led them to the bar and poured them each an ale. He poured Wendell's first, and by the time he'd finished pouring the last the sergeant's mug was empty, and Wendell was clearing his throat as if he'd been missed. Aaron stared at the man, shaking his head, but the youth grinned as he filled the mug again and gave it to the sergeant.

They sat quietly for a few minutes, each of them weary and content just to sit and think of the task ahead of them. It wasn't long before the door opened, and Janum turned with a smile, "Uncle!"

The big tavern keeper smiled and walked inside with a keg of ale on each shoulder as if they weighed nothing. He moved behind the bar, not yet noticing Aaron and his companions, and sat the kegs down. "I tell you, nephew," he said, his back to Aaron and the others as he situated the kegs behind the bar, "either the trip into town is getting longer, or I'm getting fatter. Next time, maybe I'll send you. Give you something to do besides sitting around here with your feet up."

Janum grinned. "I told you I'd be happy to go, Uncle."

"Aye, I'm sure ya would," Nathan agreed as he pushed the second keg beside the first, "and like as not you'd run off with my coin, join a troupe of actors or something just as foolish."

"Uncle," Janum said in mock-scolding, "I don't even like actors—you're the one that goes and sees every show that comes into town, not me."

The big man grunted as he rose, rubbing a hand over his lower back. "I can't help it. Sometimes a man has to see what it looks like for men and women to make their coin off of pretendin' to be somebody else. Shit, I know more than a few who do that often enough now, but the only coin they make is what they can sneak off their marks. Anyhow..." He turned, and froze as he took in Aaron and the others.

"Well shit," he said, grinning, "Leomin and Aaron." He barked a laugh and slapped first one and then the other on the shoulder with a big, meaty paw hard enough to nearly knock them from their stools. "By the gods, but I didn't think I'd see you all again. And you've made some friends too, have ya?"

"Maybe better to call them people I haven't got around to killing yet," Aaron said, but he was smiling when he said it, and the tavern keep barked a laugh.

"Aye, that'll do fine. Well," he said, shaking first Darrell's hand and then Wendell's, "it's a pleasure to meet ya both, I'm sure." He turned back to Aaron. "And where's that pretty thing you were in here with last time? Haven't gone and fucked that up, have ya?"

Aaron snorted. "Not yet, surprisingly enough. She wasn't able to make the trip this time."

"Well, that's too bad. The sight of her would have done much to lift an old man's spirits and that's a fact. Still..." He gave a shrug of his massive shoulders, leaning in close and speaking in a whisper, "probably better she didn't come. Things in Baresh have been...well. It's probably best she didn't come."

Aaron grunted, "That's the second time I've heard something about that. What are you talking about? What's been happening?"

A troubled look came over the tavern keeper's face, and he glanced at the couple sitting in the corner. They were bent in conversation, and they didn't appear to be the slightest bit interested in what Aaron or the others were saying, but Nathan shook his head. "Not here," he said, "later. I'll close early tonight, and we'll hash it out. At least as much as there is to be hashed out anyway which, truth be told, ain't much. But folks that talk too much about it seem to have a way of disappearin', if you catch my meanin'."

Aaron nodded, frowning and remembering the way he'd felt when he'd stared at the city from afar, the dark foreboding that had settled over him as soon as he'd entered its gates. "Alright," he said, "later."

***

Aaron and the others sat around one of the tables in the tavern's common room while Nathan walked to the door and locked it. "Alright, Janum," the tavern keeper said, "why don't you go on upstairs and get some sleep. The way I understand it, you've got an early morning with swordmaster Lionel."

"But Uncle," Janum said, "I want to stay."

Nathan patted the youth on the shoulder. "I know you do, boy, but you know as well as I that swordmaster Lionel doesn't tolerate tardiness. Besides, you don't need to hear what all we'll be talkin' about anyway."

Janum frowned. "I'm not a child anymore, Uncle. I'm sixteen next month and nearly a man. It's not like I don't know what's been going on in the city—people disappearing. That's all everybody's talkin' about. Anyway, Fenn's two months younger than me, and *his* dad talks to him about it." His frown grew deeper still. "Fenn's dad even lets him have some of his liquor sometimes, and you won't even let me have an ale!"

The big tavern keeper grunted. "I'd ask if Fenn's dad let him jump in front of horse carts for fun if you'd want to do that as well, but the gods know I'd be scared of what you'd say. Anyway, never mind what Fenn's dad will and won't let him do—that's his business, not yours. As for being a man, well lad, a man has responsibilities and your responsibility just now is getting some rest and meeting Lionel tomorrow. And don't you worry—there'll be time enough for drinkin' when you're older, and jawing on about whatever suits you. Now go on and get some rest."

The youth sighed, obviously defeated. "Goodnight, everyone."

They all said goodnight and watched as the youth slunk up the stairs to his room. When he was gone, Nathan shook his head. "That boy'll be the death of me, you wait and see."

"If you don't mind me saying so, friend Nathan," Leomin said, "the young Janum is much changed."

Nathan gave a doubtful look, but it quickly turned into a smile. "Yeah, and I 'spose I got you to thank for that." He turned to Aaron. "And you, of course. Not much that'll straighten a body out quicker than the fear of death."

Aaron cleared his throat as Darrell turned to him. "You threatened to kill the boy?"

"Oh, I wouldn't give him too much grief about it," the tavern keeper said, grinning, "I must have threatened him a thousand times myself, though he never seemed to care one way or the other. Anyhow, I got to admit that I'm surprised to see you all back so soon. And with companions as well. Come for the tournament, have ya?"

Aaron frowned, glancing at the others who shared his confusion. "Tournament?"

"Aye," Nathan said, "King Belgarin means to have a tournament the likes of which Telrear has never seen—or so the city criers assure me every time I so much as step outside the damned tavern. Surely, you must have heard them when you were comin' through the city."

Aaron shook his head slowly. The criers might have been there, but he'd been too distracted by his own thoughts to notice. A tournament. Only a couple of months ago, Belgarin was set on conquering the entire country, and now suddenly he was relaxing and holding tournaments? It didn't make any sense. Had Grinner or Hale been here, the crime lords would have probably claimed it was proof that the royal prince had given up his quest to rule all of

Telrear, and Aaron would have been forced to admit that it was a very strange thing to do for a man bent on conquering the country. Still, he didn't like it.

"A tournament?" Darrell asked. "Something's not right about this."

Wendell took a long drink of his ale, emptying the mug. He smacked his lips loudly and glanced at the others. "I ain't no genius, the gods know," he said, "but it seems to me that it's a little more than somethin' bein' not right. If I drink more than's good for me of a night, sometimes I put my left boot on my right foot and my right boot on my left foot the next mornin'. Spend some time stumblin' around before I figure out what's the matter." He nodded at that as if he'd made some grand pronouncement, but the others just stared at him.

Leomin blinked. "Sir Wendell, I am one who prides himself on hearing what is not spoken and seeing what is not there, but even I must admit as to some confusion about what you're trying to say."

He glanced to Aaron who only shrugged, grinning at the pleasure of seeing the Parnen being the one confused by another's speech for once. "Couldn't make any sense of it myself."

"Well, it's all pretty obvious, ain't it?" the sergeant asked. When they all just kept staring at him, he cleared his throat. "Alright, so it's like this. When I was a kid—nine or ten, no more than that—I used to try to sneak some of my parents' wine. They kept the few bottles they had locked up, you understand. Only brought 'em out for special occasions—marriages, or births or...well, I guess that was about all the special occasions we had. It was a small village, as I've told you. But my father wouldn't ever let me have any of the wine no matter how much I begged, tellin' me I was too young. But so far as I was concerned, I was nearly a man grown—not so unlike your Janum," he said, nodding his head to Nathan.

Wendell laughed as he remembered. "I reckon me and my friends must have tried to sneak one of those bottles a dozen times or more, but we never could get the lock my parents kept on the cellar open no matter how hard we tried. But every chance we got when my parents were away, we'd set to it, real careful, you understand, so that my parents wouldn't notice that the lock had been tampered with. Yeah," he said, grinning, "we figured ourselves clever, just a bunch of sneak thieves that were goin' to become men. Just as soon as we got into that cellar, anyhow."

He glanced around at the others and shrugged self-consciously. "Seems a bit foolish now, lookin' back."

"Just a bit?" Aaron asked.

The sergeant grinned and went on. "Anyhow, I reckon my ma and pa must have known somethin' was goin' on, and one day my friends and I came home from workin' the fields to find a full bottle of wine settin' on the table just as pretty as you please, and both my parents not due back for an hour or more. Well, we all figured this was our chance, and I guess we were just about as excited as could be. Excited enough that, when we opened the bottle, we didn't even take much note of the smell. Sure it stunk, and why not? That was the part of it got you drunk, we figured. If we hadn't been quite so excited, I suppose we might have noticed that the wine smelled like somethin' that had gone over and in a bad way. Which, of course, was exactly what it was.

"You see, my pa was the type of man believed that harsh lessons are the ones that take the best. So when he realized we'd been at the cellar lock, he decided one was due and filled up a whole wine bottle with spoiled goat's milk."

The other men at the table winced at that, and Wendell nodded. "Yeah. See, my friends and I, we'd been around goats and cows all our lives. Growin' up on a farm and woodland village you can't avoid it. But we were so excited at the thought of havin' some of that grown up wine that we didn't even take notice of a smell we'd known since before we could walk. 'Course, there's also the fact that my pa took it in his mind to add some crushed up peppers to the milk. For flavor, he told me later."

"Forgive me, Sir Wendell," Leomin said, "but I'm still not sure—"

"Ain't no sirs in my family, Leomin," the sergeant said. "Anyhow, the fact is that when I took the first sip of that 'wine' I knew somethin' was off. I'd never had wine before—never had spoiled goat's milk with peppers crushed up in it neither, mind—but I knew the moment that foul liquid touched my tongue that it wasn't right. My friends, they knew it, too."

Nathan, the barkeep, barked a laugh. "Aye, children can be foolish."

Wendell grinned. "That ain't what's foolish. What's foolish is we finished the whole damned bottle. I don't rightly recall if any of us got drunk, but I can tell you for a certainty that we *all* got sick. We spent the next day pukin' our guts out and sweatin' like somebody's just said they's executions to be had, and your name's first on the list."

"Wendell," Darrell said, smiling, "I still can't see how this is—"

Wendell held up a hand, forestalling the swordmaster. "Point is, we'd never had wine before, wouldn't have been able to tell you what it tasted like. The smell, maybe, for more than one of my parents' celebrations ended with folks spillin' wine and sometimes their dinners along with 'em, but not the taste. But we knew it for wrong when we tried it, just like we know this tournament for wrong. You ask yourself how wine could taste like that when so many folks are willin' to spend their last coin just for a sip of it. It can't, that's all. Now, you ask yourself why a man, a *prince,* who is known for being one mean son of a bitch, can bring himself to not just give it all up but to have a damned tournament. As if they was somethin' worth celebratin' in getting his army's ass kicked until it fled like a mongrel with its tail between its legs. He can't, that's all."

Aaron frowned. "What are you trying to say, Wendell?"

Just then, there was a knock at the door, but Nathan waved a meaty hand. "Leave it. We're closed, and they'll get the idea soon enough."

The knock came again, and Leomin smiled, "It seems to me that just such a one as you spoke of, dear Wendell—the man prepared to give up his last coin for a taste of wine or ale—stands outside in the night even now, knocking and mulling over his options."

"What did you mean," Aaron said, "that he can't be the same man?" A dark, terrible idea had taken root in his mind, a possibility that he didn't wish even to contemplate. Boyce Kevlane was a man capable of changing his appearance in a moment's notice—Aaron had seen him do it. Had he somehow...taken control from Belgarin? But no. It didn't make any sense. Belgarin had *wanted* to take over all of Telrear, had set himself against Aaron and his allies. If anything, the ancient wizard would have been thrilled with the man's ambitions.

Wendell shrugged. "Not sure what I mean, General, to tell you the truth. All I know is peppered, spoiled goat's milk ain't wine, and there ain't no amount of wishin' will make it so. Maybe the prince has been forced into a peace, somehow."

Leomin nodded slowly. "Or, perhaps, there is another possibility." They all turned to look at him then, and the Parnen gave a shrug of his own. "If Prince Belgarin has truly lost the urge for battle, if he has come to a place where he is prepared to give up a war he's fought for nearly half his life, then he is certainly not the same man as he was even half a year ago."

Aaron grunted. "I'm fairly sure that's what this ugly dog was just going on about." He nodded his head at Wendell, who grinned in response.

"Yes," Leomin said, nodding slowly, "but people are fickle things, Mr. Envelar. I think that you are in a place to know that better than most. A man's emotions—his wants, his desires might change, but only if a great change is first worked within him. Or on him. It seems to me that either Wendell is right, and somehow someone is forcing Belgarin to peace against his will, or that some event has taken place, some catalyst to create in Belgarin a new man with his own wants, his own desires.

"People can change, after all, though in my experience, it is a rare enough thing and it is rarer still for it to be a change for the better. You might meet a man from one day to the next, and though his outward appearance might be the same, it is only the mask he wears, only the window through which the world views him. This window is small and fogged over, and even a close study of it will reveal very little about the room behind it. Some vague shadows, some hinted outlines, but little more than that. Whatever else has happened, it is safe to say that the Prince Belgarin we once knew of is no more. In his place there is another prince, one who cares little for the ambitions of the old."

Aaron considered that then shook his head slowly. "No, that doesn't feel right. There's something here, Leomin. In this city. If Belgarin suddenly decided to become a priest, burning candles instead of villages, then why are all of his people walking around terrified, grown men too scared to venture out at night?"

Leomin frowned. "I have heard nothing of such things, Mr. Envelar." They all turned to Nathan, and the barkeep grunted.

"Yeah, I 'spose now's as good a time as any to jaw it out, but I'll warn ya that I don't know much, and what I do know I don't know for certain."

"There are no certainties, friend Nathan," Leomin said, "except, at least, that nothing is certain. Now, certainly, proceed."

Aaron sighed, but the innkeeper was nodding as if the Parnen had just said something profound. "Alright," he said. "Well, there's been some...disappearances lately."

Aaron grunted. "I grew up in a part of the city very much like here, Nathan, and I know enough to know that any place where people are desperate and poor will always have its disappearances."

The barkeep nodded grudgingly at that. "You're right, of course. But this here's different. Lots more folks than is normal have been vanishin' as if they never were. And not just from the poor district, neither. Why I've heard of at least a dozen cases of wealthy merchants and nobles up and disappearin'. Men of power and station. Men with enough gold to hire a dozen bodyguards, if that's what was needed. Men with pretty, trophy wives and big gaudy mansions.

"Sure, folks disappear, Aaron, but it's most always the ones that nobody misses when they're gone, the ones that don't leave hardly anythin' behind 'em. These men that are disappearin' now, lots of them got roots, you understand? Roots of gold, and connections that normally serve as a shield for the noble born and wealthy, but they're being snatched up and taken just the same. Right along with the rest."

Another knock sounded at the door, and Wendell and Leomin both jumped—the sergeant falling out of his chair, while the Parnen let out a squeak and brought both hands to his mouth like a child caught saying a bad word.

"Bastard's persistent, I'll give him that," the sergeant said as he climbed off the floor and sat down again, pointedly avoiding the grins of Darrell and Aaron.

"We're closed!" Nathan yelled, and they all waited a moment until the knocking finally stopped.

Aaron frowned at the door for a few moments before turning back to Nathan. "You're saying all of these people are being taken, but who's taking them?

The barkeep shook his head. "Nobody knows."

Aaron met the man's eyes. "Nobody knows. You mean to tell me that there aren't any rumors?"

"Oh, sure," the big man said, shifting uncomfortably, "plenty of rumors. There's talk that it's followers of the Death God needing people for their sacrifices. Others think there's a killer that has come to the city." He barked a laugh. "That's nobles mostly. The bastards seem too dumb to realize there's plenty enough killers here already. Shit, I know a dozen of them, some of them even pretty nice. Well," he grunted, "just so long as you don't piss them off."

Aaron frowned, considering the man's words. Darrell turned to him. "What are you thinking?"

"I'm not sure," the sellsword said, "but I don't like it."

The tavern keeper snorted. "What's to like? Folks disappearing off the streets like chickens when a wolf gets in the hen house, war with Isalla and Cardayum and the gods alone know who else, and these cloaked figures people keep talking about. Shit, much more, and I might think about mov—"

"Cloaked figures?" Aaron interrupted, leaning forward in his chair. "What are you talking about?"

The big man waved a hand dismissively. "Nothin' worth concernin' yourself over. Just more rumors in a sea of them—I wouldn't waste your time tellin' you about things that are just as likely the visions of men too drunk or high to see their hands in front of their face."

Aaron sighed. "I think you'd probably better."

"Fine," the tavern keeper said, "but I warned you." He hesitated as if unsure of how to begin. "Alright," he said finally, "well, it's like this—and I ain't sayin' I agree with any of it, mind. But ownin' a tavern, well, you get some interestin' folks walking through the doors; I can tell you that much. Folks as come in lookin' like murder's on their mind, and they're lookin' to do some right then, folks that treat the tavern like it's a sanctuary to save them from the night—which it is, I suppose to some of the poor bastards.

"Shit, you get women come in on account of they found out their husband's been cheatin' on them, or men come in because of their wives doin' the same. All kind of folks, really, but not too many normal ones, if there even is such a thing. In my experience, folks that frequent taverns, downin' ales like they got somethin' inside 'em they're tryin' to drown...well, they generally do. Still, I got to be honest as long as I been in this business, I'm startin' to think there ain't no normal, just different degrees of fucked up is all. I tell ya, I had a fella come in here the other day—"

"What about the people?" Aaron interrupted, feeling that he was getting close to understanding something, but he wasn't even sure what that something was.

The tavern keeper started. "Oh, right. Sorry about that one, Aaron. The older I get, the more often it seems that my mind tries to run away with me. Anyhow, what I'm tryin' to say is that a tavern gets all kinds: killers, thieves, whores, merchants down on their luck, farmers who've lost their crop to the weather. All kinds and all different. But all of these got one thing in common—they like to drink, and most like to drink a lot. And the thing about drunks is they like to talk. Put a man beside 'em, that man'll know their life's story in half an hour. Shit, most of 'em, I'm pretty sure you could stick 'em in a room by their self and before the night was over the walls'd know enough about 'em to write their life's story, if'n they had the hands to write it with."

Aaron forced himself to remain calm and keep his patience, but the tavern keeper had a way of saying a lot without really saying much at all—a thing he thought he'd grown accustomed to after having spent so much time with the Parnen. "What have they said?"

"Well, lots of things," Nathan said, and Aaron could have shook the man, "normally, men and women like that got a thousand stories to tell you, each one more unlikely than the last, if you'll stay there and listen. But lately..." He shook his head. "Gods, but I feel like a fool even sayin' it. Lately, the stories have been a lot darker than normal, and even I have to admit there's been some strange similarities in what they're sayin'. It's a funny thing, bein' an innkeeper. I reckon folks'll tell things to the man brings 'em a beer they wouldn't even think of tellin' to a priest or their wives. Anyhow," he said, apparently noting Aaron's impatient expression, "these ones been talkin' about figures in hooded cloaks. Some...shit on it, some are sayin' there's men up under them cloaks that are as much bigger than me as I am to Leomin here."

The Parnen sniffed at that. "A greater size, friend Nathan, only means that one takes up more space and, therefore, has more responsibility to justify said space."

Aaron waved his hand sharply. "Never mind that. What else?"

"Well," the tavern keeper said, his bushy eyebrows drawing down in thought, "I've heard some stories as say these fellas are bigger'n they have any right to be, bigger than a man *can* be. Eight, nine feet tall—shit, I've heard some say as tall as fourteen feet, but that fella was pretty deep in his cups, and I don't put much stock in it. One regular of mine even went so far as to say he was walkin' down the street over where all the blacksmiths work—Bertrand is a jeweler, but from what I understand, he ain't a very good one.

"Anyhow, he said he was walkin' by and he saw one of those fellas accompanied by a smaller man, an officious lookin' sort, the kind that'd scold you for spittin' on the ground then charge you for him to clean it up, you know? Thing is, Bertrand said that he saw ol' Odel the blacksmith talkin' to the two, lettin' em inside his shop but not like he wanted them there, you know? More like it was a chore he wanted to get over just as soon as he could."

He shook his head. "I'll tell ya, fellas, if you think I'm big, you ought to see Odel. That man's a monster and a half, and one I'd go out of my way not to cross. Used to have quite a reputation back in his day too, as the best street fighter Baresh has ever seen. Now, what was it they used to call him," he said, rubbing his thick chin in thought, "Steel Fist or Boulder hands. Some dumb shit like that, but I'll tell you, it wasn't as dumb as the folks he took issue with. The ones that lived don't say nothin' much anymore. Don't do a lot of thinkin' either, from what I gather. Bertrand said he was goin' on about his way, and he thought he heard shouts from the inside of the shop. Bertrand's a nervous man at the best of times, and this had him real shaken up. The bastard was cryin' when he told me, which I wouldn't think much of as lots of men cry when they're drunk, but Bertrand's never been one of them, not in my knowin'."

He laughed a loud, hearty laugh. "He told me it sounded like men were goin' to war in that shop, and he did the only thing he could think of—dove into a passing cart. Well, turned out the cart was full of chickens and by the time Bert felt safe enough to climb out, I guess those chickens had shit just about all over him. But before all of that, as the cart was drivin' away, Bertrand said he saw the big fella in the cloak and the small man come back out. Odel was with 'em too, only he wasn't walking. To hear Bert tell it, the big fella had Odel thrown over one shoulder like he didn't weigh no more than a sack of potatoes."

He grunted. "Crazy, of course. Odel is a good fella and a great blacksmith, but that bastard has to weigh damn near half again more than me, and I'm no small guy. I don't care how strong you are—there ain't a man in this world that could tote Odel over his shoulder and not show the strain of it, but that's exactly what Bert said he did. He said he got a look at the blacksmith's face, too, and it was all bloody and banged up like he'd been in a fight and got the worse part of the deal. He said he watched 'em walk down an alley and out of sight as if they didn't have a care in the world. Apparently, they didn't notice Bert and probably that's just as well. Bertrand is a talker, but I like him well enough. If even half of what he said is true, I'd hate to see him get mixed up in it."

Aaron met Leomin's eyes and saw his own troubled thoughts reflected in the Parnen's gaze. He turned back to Nathan. "Is that all of it?"

"Most of it, anyhow. I've heard a few more stories—folks as say they've seen kids runnin' around in cloaks, only the kids have arms that reach all the way down to their feet or damn near it." He shrugged. "Ridiculous, of course, but then people'll say just about anythin' comes to mind when they're deep enough in their drink."

Aaron frowned, his thoughts racing. *Kevlane. It has to be.*

Aaron, Co said, and he started at the sound of her voice in his head after she'd been silent for the entire conversation, *surely, you don't think that Kevlane...what? Started up his experiments again? My father told him to never do such things again, and he promised.*

Yeah, Aaron thought, *well, I don't know, firefly, not for sure. But what I do know is that three thousand years is a long time to keep a promise to a man that's been dead for just as long. And I think it's safe to say that Boyce Kevlane isn't the same man he was when your father was alive.*

"This Bertrand," Aaron said aloud to the barkeep, "you said he's a regular?"

"That's right." He frowned. "Though, now I think of it, it's been a while since I've seen Bert. Normally I guess he's here just about every night, but I haven't seen him in a few weeks now." He looked at Aaron. "You don't think…"

"I don't know," Aaron said, "but I think it'd be best if we check on him. Besides, I've got some questions I'd like to ask him. Do you know where he lives?"

"Sure," Nathan said, "Bert's got a place over in the merchant's district. Nice one it is, too. Still, do you think it's that important?"

"We won't know until we talk to him," Aaron said, meeting Leomin's eyes, "but yeah. Yeah, I think it is."

Nathan nodded. "Alright then," he said rising, "I'll show you where it's at."

"You won't find him there."

They all spun at the sound of the voice to see a cloaked figure standing inside the tavern's entrance, his hood obscuring his features.

Cloaked figures in the night, Aaron thought, remembering the innkeeper's words. He rose out of his chair, drawing his sword. "Who are you?"

"No one of any importance, sir," the cloaked figure said, "but you can put the sword away—I mean none of you any harm. Besides, judging by your stance and attitude, I calculate no more than a one in five chance that you'll attack me unprovoked."

Aaron laughed, but there was no humor in it. "I'm a sellsword, stranger. I've been in plenty of spots with a much less than one in five chance of surviving, but I've still come out the other side breathing."

The figure shrugged. "Then your math was wrong."

The big bartender grunted, taking a step toward the figure. "You the fella that was knockin' on the door?"

"I thought it best to be polite."

Nathan frowned at that, seemingly unsure of what to say. "Well…that is, we're closed. Why don't you come on back another time, friend? This ain't a group of men you want to fool around with, believe you me."

"Actually," the figure said, "this is *exactly* the group of men that I've been looking for. If, that is, you are looking into the disappearances in the city and the, for lack of a better term, 'figures' that are believed to have been seen prowling the streets."

Aaron frowned and reached out with his bond toward the stranger, trying to get some hint what he wanted. Had the figure been sent by Belgarin or, perhaps, Boyce Kevlane? Were they being surrounded, even now, while they listened to him? He reached further for the bond, drawing more on its power. At first, he picked up a snatch of emotions—fear chief among them—but suddenly, for the first time, he was rebuffed completely. It was as if a thousand-foot-high wall had suddenly appeared, blocking the path of whatever sense he used to quest into another's thoughts, a wall of flawless, pristine white, and he grunted in surprise, jarred by the abruptness of it. "You heard the man," he said, rubbing at a sharp pain in his temple. "The tavern's closed. Now, if you've nothing else—"

Suddenly, a blue orb blossomed to life in front of the cloaked figure and though Aaron had not seen this one before, he knew well enough what it was, and his eyes widened in surprise.

"Just how closed are you?" the cloaked figure asked, and if the fear Aaron had felt in the stranger was real, he did not hear it in his voice. "Forgive me," he said, bowing slightly to Aaron, "but as you perhaps know, the Seven act as guards against each other to a degree, and I thought it better that we got to know each other the old-fashioned way."

The figure threw back his hood, and the barkeep grunted. "A child." Aaron noted that the big man was right. The stranger appeared to be a young boy of no more than thirteen or fourteen years, but there was a sharpness, an intelligence in his eyes that was impossible to miss, one that spoke of someone far older and more experienced.

"I am, as you say, a child," the boy said, nodding his head to Nathan, "at least by the reckoning of our current culture."

"Child or not," Aaron said, staring at the floating blue orb and then back to the boy's face, "you're still here uninvited. How did you get in, anyway?"

The youth shrugged. "I used to…work at a tavern myself," he said, glancing around, "though, I hope you don't think it empty flattery when I say it was nowhere near as fine as this one. Alder, the tavern's owner, was a cruel master, yet even in such a state as I was in, I had the opportunity to learn much from those around me, though I did not know it at the time. You see, men rarely guard their tongues when they are in their drink, and even less around a dimwitted boy who is barely capable of coherent speech. One such man was a thief, and while I cleaned up an ale one of his friends had spilled, he busily recounted his most recent night's take, and the methods he'd used to gain entry into the house which he robbed. That was…four years ago, if I'm not mistaken."

Nathan snorted. "Well, you're right about men in their drink guarding their tongues, at any rate. But do you mean to tell me that you learned how to pick a lock from half listenin' to some thief four years ago? That would have made you, what? Eight, nine years old yourself?"

"Nine, actually," the youth agreed, "but I won't pretend that I learned it at the time—the man was quite drunk and despite his friends' questions, gave only a vague idea of how he had gained entry. Still, the knowledge stayed with me, and I was able to use it as a starting point to derive the best means of picking the lock to your fine tavern."

"The knowledge stayed with you," Aaron said flatly.

"Indeed," the youth said, smiling slightly, "as it almost always does. People, I find, often see and hear more than they realize at the time. But those facts, those experiences, stay with them for years, buried beneath thoughts of today and tomorrow, of how best to woo a woman or to get richer. Knowledge, then, *true* knowledge, is only knowing the location of things half-remembered, of taking a shovel, as it were, and digging them up and bringing them out into the light. It is knowing that they are buried in the first place."

"I don't know about all that, lad," Wendell said, rising and coming to stand beside Aaron, glancing suspiciously at the blue orb before looking back at the boy, "my ma used to tell me I didn't have enough sense to get out of the rain, and I reckon she was right. My question, though, is just who exactly you are, and why you felt the need to come here in the first place?"

"As for who I am…" The youth hesitated, glancing at Aaron. "I must first tell you who I was. Not long ago—weeks, no more than that—I was much like the girl who you saved in the tavern tonight."

Wendell glanced sourly at Aaron. "A girl. I should have known."

The youth smiled and, for a moment, the ancient light seemed to leave his eyes, and he was only a child. "I mean no disrespect to you sir," he said to Aaron, "in fact, quite the opposite. You see, I spent years as a slow-witted servant to Alder. I spent many nights getting ale dumped on my head or beaten when Alder had a mind to, and not in all that time did I ever see anyone stand up for me the way you stood up for that girl."

Aaron grunted, suddenly embarrassed. "Couldn't enjoy my beer with all that hollering, that's all. And anyway, that still doesn't explain why you felt the need to break in."

"Yes," the boy said, "well, enough to say I was at the tavern on my own business, with my own intentions. I had, in fact, been considering some sort of revenge—nothing serious, understand. But it had seemed to me then that I would have liked to have revisited some bit of the pain Alder and many of his regulars caused me over the years onto them. Strange, though, as the urge came upon me quite abruptly. Or, perhaps," he said, smiling, "not so strange. For it is true, is it not, that the Seven are attracted to one another, as if always seeking to become the One for which they were meant to be in Caltriss's time?"

"Alright just hold on a damned minute," Nathan demanded, pointing at the blue orb warily as if he thought it might attack him at any moment. "Just what in the fuck is that?"

"*That,*" came what sounded like the wizened voice of an old man, "dear barkeep, is Palendesh. Or, at least, I was. Now, I am less—and more—than the man I once was. I am one of the Seven, beings forged...well, I'm sure you've heard the stories."

Palendesh? Co said into his mind. *Can it truly be...?*

Aaron felt the Virtue's yearning. *Wait, firefly. Look, we don't know anything about this kid. For all we know*—But the Virtue was already moving and, in a moment, she appeared in front of Aaron, a bright, shining orb of magenta. "Palendesh," she said, "is it truly you?"

Nathan and Wendell both gave out shouts of surprise, stumbling away.

"It is I, Evelyn," the blue orb responded in a voice that sounded to Aaron like a kind grandfather speaking to his favorite granddaughter, "and it seems that the gods are not always cruel, for I hoped it was you."

"It has been so long," Co said, hovering closer to the orb until they were only inches apart.

"So it has, my dear," Palendesh responded, "too long. Tell me, how—"

Suddenly, Leomin's own Virtue appeared, hovering in front of him with a shout of girlish glee, and the yellow orb rushed across the room to float near with the other two. "Palendesh!"

"Ah, Aliandra," the blue orb said in an amused voice, "it is good to see you as well."

Aaron turned to the Parnen, who only shrugged, sighing. "Alright," Nathan said in a near whisper as he stared wide-eyed at the three Virtues, "somebody needs to explain just what in the name of the Fields is going on here."

"Co, why don't you and your friends run off somewhere and catch up." Aaron glanced at the other men gathered in the room, including the youth. "We've got some things to discuss ourselves."

In another moment the Virtues were gone, and Aaron and the others were once more seated at the table, Nathan with a worried, slightly crazed expression, and Wendell pouring ale down his throat as if there was a fire somewhere in his stomach he was looking to put out.

"Somebody gonna tell me just what all those things were?" Nathan asked.

"It's too much to go into now, Nathan," Aaron said, "it'd take too long to explain, and I don't think we have that kind of time. Whatever is going on in Baresh, I have to believe Boyce Kevlane is involved somehow."

The barkeep laughed at that but quickly sobered when he noticed the expressions on the others gathered at the table. "Wait a minute, you're serious. Boyce Kevlane as in *the* Boyce Kevlane, the ancient wizard from the stories, one that supposedly died a thousand years ago?"

"Thousands," Aaron corrected, "and he's no myth or tale for children—he's real. And very much alive. Now," he said, turning to the youth, "why don't you tell me what exactly you're doing here and why we shouldn't kill you?"

The kid smiled self-assuredly. "Kill me? Unlikely. Based on your pupil dilation and the timbre of your voice, I calculate—"

"Kid," Aaron said, "I've always been known for a bad temper, and I've got the Virtue of Compassion—one that makes me weep and fawn over small kittens. Now, if that isn't enough, it also makes me go into rages that I can barely control, let alone understand. So before you start telling me about my pupil dilation or whatever else is going on in that brain of yours, understand that *I* don't even know what I'm going to do from one minute to the next."

The kid's smug expression faded, and he swallowed hard. "As I said before, I mean you no harm. In fact, I mean to help you. You see, I have been doing my own investigation into what's been going on in the city. I've had to be very circumspect, mind you, but I have learned enough to support the claims that men and women of unique talents have been disappearing from the city for some time now. They have all left what valuables they have behind, vanishing as if into thin air."

"Wait a minute," Aaron said, "what do you mean 'unique talents'?"

The boy shook his head. "They vary from one person to the next. Odel, the blacksmith, was of course a man known for his prodigious physical strength, but there have been others, many others. Some known for speed or strength, others for ruthlessness or brutality. It seems that whatever force is seeking these men and women out, it is in search of people who embody some sort of extreme, not so very different from the Virtues themselves."

Aaron frowned. "So who is taking all of these people and what do they want with them?"

The youth sighed, "I'm afraid I don't know. I have had to be very careful, for it also seems true that those who happen to witness these abductions usually end up missing themselves, or are killed outright."

"So why did you say that we wouldn't find Bertrand at his home?"

"Because he isn't there," the boy said, a bit of the smugness returning to his voice. "I have already searched for him myself, meaning to ask some of the questions that you have just posed. It took me some time, but I believe I have discovered his whereabouts."

"Well?" Aaron said. "Did you go there? What did he say?"

The youth's cheeks colored, and he looked down at the table, unwilling to meet anyone's eyes. "I'm afraid I haven't gone there yet."

"Well," Aaron said, rising, "there's no time like the present." He grabbed his sheathed sword from where he'd draped it across the back of his chair and then slung it over his back, tying his cloak around him. "Darrell, you stay here with Nathan in case anything should happen. Wendell, Leomin, you're with me." They started toward the door, and Aaron turned back, glancing at the youth who was still seated at the table, pointedly not looking at Aaron and the others.

"Well, what is it boy? You've got to show us the way."

"My name's Caleb," the youth said, "and, anyway, it would probably be best if I didn't come. I could draw you a map—"

"No," Aaron said, "you're coming. If you're leading my friends and me into some kind of trap, I want you close enough so that I can have a quick word with you about it, do you understand? Oh," he said, smiling, an expression that held little humor and somehow seemed menacing, "and my name's Aaron. Nice to meet you."

The youth swallowed hard, his face paling. "I would say that it is my pleasure, Aaron, but given the circumstances…"

"Don't worry about it," Aaron said, "given the circumstances, we'll all probably be dead by breakfast."

He turned to where the three Virtues were at the far end of the room. "Come on, firefly. We're leaving."

CHAPTER TWELVE

Adina fought back a sigh of frustration as she dismounted, keeping hold of her horse's reins. She glanced up at the sun, low on the western horizon. Another hour, maybe two, and then it would be dark. She'd been hoping to make it to Stockton, a small village on the outskirts of her kingdom's borders by dark, but it was looking as if they were going to spend another night camped in the woods. In truth, she had thought they would already be in Galia by now and, had they been lucky, the issue of her rule might have been decided, one way or the other. She turned and looked behind her and this time she wasn't able to keep the sigh from escaping.

"I've got to be honest, Princess," May said as she also dismounted, "I've never seen a horse hate a man so much. I'm no expert on the creatures, but up to this point I would have said they were incapable of hate at all."

For a minute, Adina didn't respond. She was too engrossed in the spectacle playing out behind them—a spectacle that had been repeated half a dozen times since they'd left Perennia. Gryle's horse had bucked, sending him tumbling from the saddle, and the young giant, Bastion, was helping him back into the saddle.

The old woman, Beth, sat on her horse watching, smiling widely as she did each time the chamberlain was thrown. Adina had been reluctant to bring the old woman and the young soldier at first. In her mind, Beth would have been better served to stay in Isalla and watch over her grandson, and even without his uniform on, Bastion had the distinct look of a soldier—the kind of look that would draw attention they didn't need.

Still, they had both proven invaluable in the weeks since they'd left the city. After all, no one but the giant youth could have lifted Gryle back onto his horse, and the chamberlain—having no experience in horsemanship—seemed to become even clumsier than usual when he tried to climb up himself.

As for Beth, the old woman had proven herself in many ways, smashing up herbs and cooking them into teas to soothe an upset stomach Gryle had come down with shortly after leaving the city, or to help blunt the pain of Adina's own headaches. And she'd been a comfort in other ways too, her no-nonsense, gruff but somehow kind approach to conversation enlivening their talk around the campfire, and lifting Adina's spirits despite the dangerous errand on which they'd embarked.

"Oh, horses can feel hate," Adina said, nodding, "the question is why do they hate Gryle?" It was strange, that was true. Adina had ridden with Gryle before. The chamberlain had never been an expert rider, but horses were gentle beasts by nature, often showing far more patience for the lack of skill in their riders than any human ever would.

For all her talk, Adina had never seen a horse instantly dislike anyone as quickly as the animals did Gryle. Unlike humans, horses—and most animals in general—had reasons for their hate, most often because they had been mistreated or abused. The chamberlain, though, wouldn't so much as mistreat a fly, yet the horses bucked him when they could, even going so far as to bite at him, if he came within range. And it wasn't as if the chamberlain had just drawn a temperamental horse, either, for they had all tried switching their mounts with his, but it had made no difference. Whatever horse the chamberlain rode grew aggressive as soon as he drew close. As Adina watched, the horse snapped at Gryle, who had wandered dangerously close to its front, but Bastion slung out an arm, pushing the chamberlain out of harm's way.

"I've never seen a horse act like this around Gryle before," Adina said, shaking her head and doing her best to keep the annoyance out of her tone. She was frustrated by the amount of time they'd lost—the amount of time they still *would* lose—but she knew the chamberlain wasn't to blame. He'd volunteered to walk at least a dozen times but always Adina had said no, partially because she didn't want the man to have to walk while the others rode. Mostly, however, it was because even considering these intermittent stops, they were still making better time than they would if they were all forced to slow their pace so the chamberlain could keep up on foot.

"You think maybe it's because of the thing he carries?" May asked.

Adina frowned. "Perhaps. I remember Co—Aaron's Virtue—saying that Melan, the Virtue of Strength, was insane. Horses are smart creatures, smarter than most people give them credit for. It could be that they sense something about Gryle that they don't like."

May made a noise in her throat. "You say that horses are smart creatures, and I've no cause to disbelieve you, Princess. I'm a city girl, and I know little of such things. Still, I wonder, if the horse is worried...do you think we should be worried as well?"

Adina turned and met the club owner's eyes. "I hadn't thought of that."

May shrugged. "Something to consider, anyway. Don't get me wrong, I like Gryle as much as anyone can, but where we're going, it's going to be dangerous, and we need to know that we can count on those around us. I'd hate to think we were closing the barn door after one of the wolves already made it inside." She hesitated then. "Perhaps we could send him back."

She must have seen something in the princess's expression because she held up a hand forestalling her. "Believe me, I don't like the idea of it any more than you do, but it's a simple enough path back to your sister's kingdom. He should be able to make it without any problem. If you want, we can even send Bastion or Beth with him and wait for them in Galia. It might even be a good thing—people will be less suspicious than if we come in a large group."

Adina considered that, then finally she shook her head, "No." She glanced at May. "I know what you're thinking, and it isn't that I'm worried about Gryle—at least, it's mostly not that. Gryle might seem helpless, but he's got a way of surprising people. I'm sure Aster Kalen would tell you as much, if he could. It's more that, before it's through, I think there's a pretty good chance that we might need Gryle. Without him, I never would have made it out of the castle when the general and the nobles came for me. It was Gryle who learned of what they were planning, and it was Gryle who woke me up out of a dead sleep and led me out of the castle, managing to avoid all of the soldiers the nobles had sent for me. No," she said, shaking her head again, "Gryle stays with us."

"As you say, Princess," May said. "Besides, I'm not sure we could have convinced the chamberlain to leave your side anyway, so it's probably just as well. Either way," she continued, glancing back, "it looks like they're ready again." May swung into the saddle of her horse and turned to Adina. "What do you think, another few miles before dark?"

Adina smiled, feeling better after the decision had been made. However much time they lost, she thought it was the right one. "Another few miles?" she asked, mounting her own horse and glancing over at the club owner. "If we're lucky."

***

Gryle sighed heavily. "Do we really have to do this, ma'am?"

The old woman cackled, "Oh, come on now, you big baby. There's at least another fifteen, twenty minutes of light left, and I aim to make use of every one of them."

"It's just ..." He frowned. "Well, it's demeaning."

Beth snorted. "Demeaning is getting knocked from your horse and falling on your ass half a dozen times, chamberlain. This, well, this is just a game."

"Not a very fun one," Gryle muttered, but he took several steps away and prepared himself.

"Remember," Beth said, reaching into the basket and withdrawing two eggs, one in each hand, "you're not trying to squash it, only catch it. Soft hands, chamberlain. Soft hands."

Gryle frowned. She'd said much the same since they'd started this strange training, and he *wanted* to have soft hands, he did, but each time he caught the egg, it inevitably busted leaving him—and his clothes, the gods be good—covered in sticky yolk. "Soft hands," he muttered, "soft hands."

But he found that he wasn't thinking much of his hands or the eggs at all. Instead, his mind drifted to their time on the road so far, to the princess. She'd done her best to hide it, but Gryle had known her since she was little more than a child, and he could see the impatience in her gaze each time he struggled with his horse. And why *did* the animals hate him so, anyway? He'd never had such problems before. He'd considered that, perhaps, it had something to do with the Virtue he carried—a poor deal, if it were true. As far as he could tell, the only thing the Virtue was good for was making him break chairs and desks and, well, pretty much everything he touched, including what had been a near priceless vase in Queen Isabelle's castle.

Fresh horror washed over him at the thought of the vase, and he realized he'd let himself become distracted. He looked up and let out a squeak of surprise as he saw an egg sailing through the air toward him. He reached up on instinct and caught it, wincing and closing his eyes in expectation of the inevitable explosion of yolk and shell. It didn't explode though, and he slowly opened his eyes, peeking out as if still half expecting the shell to magically shatter in his hands. But the egg remained intact, and he couldn't help the stupid grin that rose on his face. "I did it, Beth! I caught it and it didn't break!" He was turning to look at her when something crunched against his forehead, and yolk began to run down his face in a slimy trickle.

Still, the grin didn't diminish from his face, and, for once in his life, he wasn't thinking about propriety or how foolish he must look. He wasn't even thinking about his clothes—another shirt that would have to be washed, and even then it might not be saved. He was only thinking of the egg in his hand, safe and unbroken.

"Sorry about that, Gryle!" Beth called, but he thought he detected laughter in her voice. "Great job catching the first one though."

"It's no problem," Gryle yelled back, "how many more do you have?"

"Enough to start a chicken city, if I've a mind to."

Gryle smiled and set his feet. "Alright then, throw me another one!"

CHAPTER THIRTEEN

The youth seemed to grow more and more anxious the further they got from Nathan's tavern, and Aaron watched him with a frown, his hand ready to clasp the handle of the sword at his back. The kid had given some decent reasons for why he'd come to the inn, but Aaron had lived around professional criminals for most of his life and knew better than to trust him just because he had a believable story.

As they made their way further into the city, he kept an eye on the dark alleyways around them, ready for the slightest indication that something was amiss. *But if the kid is setting us up*, he thought as he and the others followed him out of an alley and onto one of the city's main streets, *I'll make sure I don't show up in Salen's Fields alone. I'd hate for the god to make a trip just for me.*

Oh, I don't think he'd mind, the Virtue said, her voice sarcastic, *you've sent him enough clients over the years, after all.*

Aaron grunted, ignoring the looks the others gave him. *True enough, firefly.*

By the time Caleb finally stopped, Aaron's nerves were frayed and ragged, and he felt as if they'd been walking for hours. He glanced around them once more to ensure himself that no one shared the streets with them, then looked up at the building across the street. He was unable to keep the grin from his face as he turned to the kid. "You've got to be fucking kidding me."

The youth shifted uncomfortably. "I wish I were," he muttered.

Aaron laughed. "And here I thought you were setting us up, boy. All that talk of wanting to stay behind, I thought it was you being afraid of being caught up in whatever trap you'd set. I didn't realize you were scared of a brothel."

"I'm not *scared!*" Caleb protested, his face turning a bright, embarrassed red. In that moment he didn't sound like the bearer of a creature of myth and legend that had been around for thousands of years, a creature that had taken him from a self-admitted dim-witted child to the smartest man in the city, most likely in all of Telrear. Instead, he sounded like what he was—a thirteen-year-old boy with too much knowledge and too little experience.

Aaron raised an eyebrow at the youth's shout, and Caleb's eyes went wide, his face pale as he realized that he'd yelled. "Sorry. Only, it's not that I'm scared, it's just...I don't know. Thanks to Palendesh, I may be much smarter than I once was, but I'm still only thirteen, you know? Do you think maybe...I could stay here?" he asked, meeting Aaron's eyes with a hopeful gaze of his own.

"No," Aaron said, shaking his head, "I'm sorry but you can't."

The kid sighed. "You still don't trust me."

"Kid, I try to make it a habit of not trusting anybody, but there are several reasons why you're going in with us. First of all, if you really are trying to help stop whatever has been happening in Baresh, then I don't like the idea of leaving you out here in the poor district at night by yourself. Trust me, whatever dangers a brothel has for you, they are much kinder—and more entertaining—than the ones that could befall you out here. Secondly, we might need that brain of yours. There's no telling what Bertrand will say—if he's still alive at all, and I almost feel like that's hoping for too much—and it could be useful to have you around."

"So you're...actually doing this because you want to protect me and think that I could help?"

"Yes," Aaron said, surprising himself by ruffling the kid's hair. "Also, I don't trust you. Now, come on. The night's not getting any younger, and my father always told me that the sooner you start a thing the sooner it gets done." He looked to Wendell and Leomin and the two men nodded that they were ready.

Gods, it's a wonder that I've lived this long, Aaron thought, but he started toward the brothel anyway, his eyes still roaming the street around them. He could hear the laughter and feigned shouts of ecstasy of the women even before he opened the door, and he glanced back to see that Caleb had grown paler still, his eyes big and round as if he expected to find a horde of monsters waiting on the other side of the door. The thing of it was, Aaron had met quite a few prostitutes during his time in the Downs and, if Baresh was anything like Avarest, the kid wasn't far wrong.

"Alright then," he said to the others, "keep your eyes open and act natural—let's not get dead." With that, he opened the door and stepped inside. His nose was immediately accosted by a menagerie of smells, most unpleasant. There was the smell of ale, the smell of women's perfume—so strong and thick that it took some doing to keep himself from gagging—and beneath it all, the smell of sex.

The bottom floor of the brothel was similar to that of a tavern, the only major difference being a raised stage on one side of the room and the scantily clad woman that danced languidly upon it as half a dozen men looked on and cheered. The woman worked her way across the stage to each of the watching men, her body bending and shifting sinuously, giving them a look that said she could be theirs, that she could make their wildest dreams come true.

But no matter what her eyes and her body said, the woman was there to be seen, not touched, to give men their fantasies while keeping the reality they so desperately longed for out of their reach. The two thickly-muscled men standing on either side of the stage, clubs in their hands, made sure of that. Aaron was just about to turn when Wendell let out a whistle and stepped past him. "I'll guard down here," he said, "make sure nobody comes up on you fellas unawares."

Aaron sighed as the scarred sergeant hurried to one of the empty chairs and plopped down, already reaching into his pockets for coins. It wasn't a bad idea to leave a guard, but Aaron seriously doubted Wendell would notice anything even if a horde of monsters broke in and began to chew on the men seated around him. Still, there was no point in four of them finding Bertrand anyway.

Aaron turned back to the others and saw Leomin starting toward the stage. He caught the man by the back of his tunic. "Where do you think you're going?"

The Parnen looked back, a guilty expression on his face like a man caught in the middle of some terrible crime. "I...that is...I thought that perhaps Wendell would need some help. After all, there is poor lighting here, and he might very well miss—"

"Never mind what Wendell might miss," Aaron said, "what you're *going* to miss is a show. Now, come on. We didn't come here for this."

Leomin sighed heavily, shaking his head. "The sacrifices I make for the greater good are truly almost too much to bear. You make a martyr of me, Mr. Envelar."

"No," Aaron said, letting the man's collar go, "not a martyr. They die, after all, and you'll live. At least, you'll live just so long as you don't keep trying to creep over there as if I can't see your feet moving."

Leomin froze and, after a moment, his shoulders slumped. "Fine," he said heavily, "but she is good at her work."

"Yeah," Aaron agreed, leaning close, "maybe she is. Of course, even if she was bad, the worst that would happen would be that she left with fewer coins in her pocket. If we're bad at *ours* though, somebody—most likely *us*—will end up dead. Now, snap out of it and get your mind where it needs to be. I don't plan on dying because you can't go three weeks without a tumble in the sheets with some woman whose name you won't remember in the morning."

"*Three weeks?*" Leomin breathed. "Gods, has it truly been so long?"

Aaron frowned, narrowing his eyes. "*Leomin,*" he said warningly, and the Parnen held up his hands as if to defend himself from a blow.

"Very well, very well, Mr. Envelar. I only hope you can appreciate the degree of my affection for you, for were it not as strong as it is, I might very well be sitting in one of those chairs now."

"If it's any consolation, Leomin," Aaron said, "you never would have made it to the chairs. Now, come on."

"S-she doesn't hardly have any c-clothes on at all," the youth breathed, "s-she's taking them a-all off."

Aaron stared at the ceiling for a moment, barely suppressing a groan, then he turned to the boy. "Yeah. In case you ever want to start your own brothel, Caleb, here's a piece of advice for you: men generally pay better for women taking their clothes off than putting them on." He grinned as the boy visibly forced his gaze away from the woman. "To be honest," the sellsword said, "I'm a little surprised at your discomfort. Do you mean to tell me you have all of that knowledge and intelligence, and somehow you don't know what goes on in a brothel?"

"I knew it," Caleb said slowly, blinking as if awakening from a trance, "but now...now I *know* it."

Aaron grunted. "Come on." It didn't take them long to make their way to the bar. Other than the seats around the stage itself, the tables and other chairs of the brothel's common room sat almost completely empty, and that was no real surprise. People didn't come to brothels to sit around and chat or make friends. It was the upstairs where all of the real coin was made and where desperate men—and some women—got to live out their fantasies. Aaron had never been into whores personally, but he understood it well enough. A week of a man's pay could either be used on food and clothing, maybe to do some work on his house, or it could be used as a sort of key, a key that unlocked a room that otherwise would remain shut. A room in which all of the deepest, darkest desires of his heart could be made real, if only for a time.

Still, to Aaron it seemed a funny thing to do, to spend all of your coin for the time of your life when the only souvenir you might walk away with would be a rash that wouldn't go away, or weeping sores that made pissing an incredibly agonizing ordeal. Aaron had seen such men before, and during the few brief instances when he'd spoken with them, they had not spent their breath recounting the joys of that one, magical night, but instead cursing and moaning about the pain.

He didn't see anyone behind the bar, so he knocked on the hard wood of the counter and waited, ignoring the two other thickly-muscled men who stared challengingly at him from either end of the empty bar, as if looking for a fight. It wasn't long before a woman walked down the stairs, shaking her head in an astonished sort of way. In one hand she held a small, glass bottle of what appeared to be some sort of oil, and in the other a rag that was coated with the stuff. "Best go and fetch a healer, Eckard," she said, glancing at one of the big men at the bar. "Sticky Ricky will be wantin' one before long."

The man grunted, looking away from Aaron, a wide grin on his face. "What was it this time?"

The woman rolled her eyes. "You just never mind that and keep your smiles to yourself. I pay you for your arms, not your laughs or your questions. Ricky's one of our best-paying customers, and if the man has a particular kind of pleasure he's after, well, it's our job to provide it. Still," she said, shaking her head again, "the key to his house? I'm all for a good time but... never mind. Just go on and fetch the healer."

The big man nodded, frowning once more at Aaron before starting for the door. "Oh, and Eckard?" the woman said.

The big man turned. "Ma'am?"

She sighed. "Best tell the healer to bring a set of tongs, if he's got them. And let him know I'll pay him extra for the trouble."

The bounder bowed his head then turned and headed for the door. In another moment he was gone. "Remember," Aaron mumbled to Leomin and the youth whose skin had taken on a faint green color, "act natural."

The woman walked behind the bar, setting the oil and the rag down somewhere behind it and coming up with a clean rag, grimacing as she wiped her hands. Finally, she turned to look up at Aaron and the others. Judging by the way she moved and the face paint she wore, Aaron suspected the woman had been a dancer herself, in her time. But she was older now, her long black hair streaked with gray, and no amount of face paint could hide the wrinkles around her mouth and at the corners of her eyes.

"Well, strangers," she said, "what can I get for you? Not a key, I hope."

Aaron grinned. "No, not a key. I generally make it a point to wear trousers with pockets to avoid this exact kind of problem."

She grunted a laugh at that. "Yeah, well, the gods must have been drunk when they made Sticky Ricky, and that's a fact, but the man never hits or bites the girls, and his money is always good. A woman in my position can't afford to be too picky about the kind of people she accepts."

"And what position might that be?" Aaron asked.

The woman leaned forward and gave him an over-exaggerated wink. "On my back, if you want, stranger. My eyes aren't getting any better, and the gods know it's dark in here—better that way, as the men and women that come here generally don't want to look at one another anymore than they have to—but from what I can see, you'd be a fine tumble even if there wasn't any coin involved."

Aaron smiled. "I'm flattered, but I've actually come on another matter."

The woman grinned, apparently not done. "You follow me on upstairs honey, and you can come wherever you like."

Aaron cleared his throat, trying to think of what to say, but she saved him from making a fool of himself as she cackled a laugh and slapped him on the shoulder. "Oh, don't be so embarrassed, honey. A good-looking fella like you ought to be used to such comments. Anyway, I'm just playing with you, that's all." She smiled again. "Unless you say the word of course. And then I'll still be playing with you, but I've got a feeling we'll both enjoy it more."

"I'd uh...I'd love to," Aaron managed, "but unfortunately the business that brings me here really can't wait."

The woman sighed, shaking her head sadly. "Well, whoever she is, she's a lucky girl. As for your question, I'm the owner of this fine, sordid establishment you see before you. The owner and," she smirked, "the sometimes oiler when things grow slightly out of hand."

"And what about me, ma'am?" Leomin said, glancing at Aaron as if sizing him up before looking back at the woman. "I like to play games as well as anyone."

The woman stared him up and down and sniffed. "No, sorry friend. I'm sure you're kind enough—look like the type'd buy a girl flowers and a meal after, but you're too thin for my tastes. And shorter than I like too. The gods found it in them to grant me a need for tall, strong men but didn't give me sense enough to look for the nice ones." She shrugged. "A pity, but there it is."

Aaron heard a scream from upstairs, and while he'd been hearing them since even before they'd walked in, this one was different. Not a scream of ecstasy or pretended ecstasy, but a man's scream, and one of pain. His first thought was that something was happening to Bertrand, and he started to rise but the woman patted his hand. "Relax there, good-looking," she said, and Aaron noted Leomin frown in what looked like jealousy, "that's nothing but Sticky Ricky—I'd know that yell anywhere." She ran a hand through her hair. "I've heard it often enough to recognize it, the gods know," she muttered.

She leaned forward. "You see, we call him Sticky Ricky—"

"Because of the oil," Leomin said, blurting the words out like a child looking to be his tutor's favorite student, and Aaron frowned at him.

Natural, Aaron mouthed, and the Parnen cleared his throat.

The woman glanced between the two of them and shook her head slowly. "No, not because of the oil, I'm afraid, though that works, too. We call him that because his real name is Richard, and he's got a way of sticking things in places where they don't exactly belong." She seemed to consider for a moment and finally shrugged. "Well, the one place anyway."

Aaron heard a gagging noise beside him and turned to see Caleb with his hand over his mouth, his cheeks swelled up. The youth looked green in truth now. The woman sighed and brought out a metal bucket from behind the counter, handing it to him as if it was just another common chore of which she was not particularly fond. "In the bucket, hon. I really do hate mopping."

They waited awkwardly as the boy hacked and spat up the remnants of his last meal. Then, after what felt like an absurdly long time to Aaron, the boy lifted his head up out of the metal pail, wiping the sleeve of his tunic across his mouth. "T-thank you," he muttered, offering the woman the pail back.

She crinkled her nose and waved a hand. "Just sit it on the floor there, lad. I'll get one of the fellas to grab it in a bit. And say," she said, leaning forward and studying the youth, "aren't you a bit young for a place such as this?"

The youth glared at Aaron accusingly, but Aaron only smiled. "Well, Caleb here is my nephew," he said, slapping him on the back, "and much more mature than his years. You'd be surprised by how much. Sometimes, I think he's just about the smartest person ever to set foot on this country and, worse, he knows it too. Anyway,

I've been looking after him while my sister's out of town, and I didn't have anywhere to leave him when my business brought me here."

"There is that 'business' again," the woman said, frowning. "I'm a simple woman of simple pleasures, and I must say the word makes my skin want to break out in hives every time I hear it. Still, I guess it's best you let me know what it is you're after, so you can get the young lad out of here before I have to mop my floors. Unless, that is, you're wanting to find him a girl?"

She took in their incredulous expressions and laughed, shrugging. "He wouldn't be anywhere near the first young boy a family member's brought in with the intention of making him a man a bit earlier than most. Fathers mostly," she said, rolling her eyes. "It's as if somehow they're making themselves more of a man by thrusting manhood on their sons. Still," she said, holding up her hands, the rag still in one of them, "it's not my place to judge. I'm a woman who trades in pleasure, and I'm here at your pleasure, so if that's what you're looking for, I've got a few ladies who'll be willing to—"

"It's not that," Aaron interrupted, and Caleb breathed a heavy sigh of relief, "I've come on another matter. There's a man that comes here fairly often, name of Bertrand—short, sort of skittish? Type of man would take off running if someone looked at him wrong."

The woman's easy-going, pleasant expression vanished as she frowned. "Stranger, I may or may not have such a man that comes by the brothel to see the girls, but if you own a place like this for a few months, you learn that the discretion that comes along with it is just as important—if not more so—than the pleasure the visitors get when they come. After all, their coin pays for both, and I make it a point not to discuss my clients' affairs with others. You understand, of course?"

"I do," Aaron said, sighing, "and normally I wouldn't even think to ask. It's only …. Well, you see," he paused to wipe at his mouth as if hesitant to say what he was about to when, in truth, he had no idea what it would be until it was out of his mouth, "Bertrand is my cousin on my father's side. As for the boy," he glanced at Caleb who still looked as if he might vomit at any moment, "well, I might have lied to you a bit before. You see, he's not actually my nephew at all—he's Bertrand's."

"Is that right?" the woman asked, leaning over the bar and studying the boy. "Doesn't look much like him."

"We can hope," Aaron said, smiling. "Anyway, he's Bertrand's sister's boy. After her husband ran off and left her last year, well, she just hasn't been the same. Weeping all hours of the night, drinking more than is good for her and for the boy too." He shrugged. "Me and the rest of the family, we'd hoped it would get better—it almost even seemed to—but then one day she just up and disappeared. That was six months ago now, and we haven't heard a word from her since."

"A sad story," the woman said, nodding slowly, "and I'm sorry to hear it. So what, then, you've come to see if Bertrand will take the kid into his home?"

Aaron sighed as if in regret. "The thing is, I'm just not cut out to be a parent. It's the reason why I don't have any kids of my own. And I don't want you to think it's just selfish reasons that have me looking for Bertrand—though I'll admit there are a few of those—it's also because I think it's only fair to the boy to have his uncle take care of him. Bert's a funny guy, scares easy, but the boy would be a lot safer with him than he would with me—gods, I won't even get a dog for fear that I'll forget to feed it and the poor thing'll starve."

The woman nodded at that. "So you're just a good cousin trying to do right by the kid," she said, her voice doubtful.

"I'm sitting right here, you know?" Caleb said. "You don't have to talk about me like I'm not—" He abruptly grew silent as his cheeks bulged once more and he brought his hand to his mouth, grabbing the bucket with the other.

As the boy bent over the bucket and began hacking, Aaron turned back to the woman. "Look, I'm not going to sit here and pretend like I'm some priest, all dressed up in white so pure it'd blind you and shitting out rainbows wherever I go. But I think this would be the best solution for everyone involved, that's all."

The woman smiled slowly. "Shitting out rainbows. I like that. Still," she said, leaning back and frowning, tapping her chin with a long, thin finger in thought, "it is, as I said, generally against my policy to give away any information about my clients. I don't like to intrude on the privacy of others, and I truly believe that's one of the only reasons this place is still doing as well as it is. A woman has to be very careful crossing such a bridge as that."

"I understand," Aaron said, "but I don't mean Bert any harm, I swear, and I wouldn't even be asking this if I had any other choice."

The woman nodded, seeming to consider, and suddenly the power of the bond flared up unexpectedly. Though he didn't know the exact words the woman would use, Aaron found that he knew well enough what she was going to say.

"The thing is," the woman said, "Bertrand *is* a regular. Comes in here twice, sometimes three times a week just like clockwork. Mostly for the girls but not always. Sometimes, I think he comes in here just to drink and talk and be surrounded by pretty women—there are those that do that, more than a few in truth who'll pay just to be in their favorite gal's company and never so much as lay a finger on her. Bertrand is one of those, and when he's sitting surrounded by that beauty, sometimes he likes to talk, often to me, and as the man pays well and treats the girls better, I've always been inclined to listen."

Aaron glanced at Leomin warningly before looking back to the woman, "Ma'am, if you'll just—"

"The *thing* is," she repeated, "that in all the times I've listened to poor drunken, scared little Bert go on about his life and all the troubles he's forced to deal with, I've never once heard him mention having a sister or a nephew. Or a cousin for that matter."

"Well," Aaron said, trying and knowing it was useless even as he did, "we haven't been real close for a long time. Bertrand moved off from—"

"Haven't heard him say word one about any of his family at all, in fact," the woman went on as if he hadn't spoken. "A bit strange, that, now that I think of it. Anyway, I might not have heard him complain about any such thing while the ale or the wine had the better of him and loosened his tongue, but I *have* heard him complain about being an only child, sometimes blaming it on the life he's led." She met Aaron's eyes, and when she spoke again, her voice was hard, serious. "I don't know exactly what it is you think you're up to here, stranger, but I don't appreciate being lied to in my own place of business. It's impolite, and I *abhor* impoliteness.

Now," she said, motioning to the big man at the bar, "I think it's best you leave before one of us says or does something we might regret. Breaker here will show you out."

"Breaker?" Aaron asked, studying the thickly-muscled man as he stepped forward, doing his best to look intimidating.

"They call me that," the big man said, grinning widely to display a mouth in which several teeth were missing, "because I like to break things."

"Hmm," Aaron said nodding, "not bad, but what if I've got one better? How about 'walk-awayer?"

The big man's eyebrows furrowed up at that, and Aaron held up a hand, "Alright, fine. I'll admit it wasn't my best effort, but I can do better. What about, 'walk-awayer-while-you-canner?' No," he sighed, shaking his head, "too long. That's too damned long. Can you imagine having to sign it? Shit, if you tried to practice writing it—and by the looks of you, you'd need some practice—you'd run out of paper before you were anywhere near finished."

The big man's frown grew deeper, and his face took on a confused, unsure look. He glanced back at the woman who sighed wearily. "Just show him out, Breaker. Him and the other two as well."

The big man grunted. "Right, ma'am." The man walked to Aaron and slammed a thick hand on his shoulder. "It's time to go. Now, are you going to get up, or am I going to have to beat you up?"

Aaron turned and looked over his shoulder at the man. "I'm sure that last bit sounded better in your head. Anyway," he said, glancing at the hand on his shoulder, "I've got to be honest with you, big fella. I don't much like being grabbed or threatened." He glanced back at the woman behind the bar. "It's impolite. Now," he said, turning back to the man, "why don't you just go on back over there and concentrate on looking tough and not gnawing on your leash. Let me talk to your owner a little longer."

The big man was stupid, but not so stupid that he didn't understand when he was being mocked. He let out a growl of frustration and jerked Aaron up with surprising strength. He was faster than Aaron had given him credit for and when his fist lashed out Aaron wasn't fast enough to avoid the blow that struck him in the side. His ribs creaked painfully, and Aaron grunted, anger suddenly blazing up inside of him. The big man swung again, and Aaron leaned his head back, but still caught a glancing blow in the chin.

Suddenly, his mouth was filled with the coppery taste of blood, and Aaron growled as the dam that had been holding back his rage crumpled and shattered. The big man cocked his hand for another strike, and Aaron still couldn't break free of his crushing grip, so he slammed his head forward with all the strength he could muster. He felt the man's nose crumple against his forehead, felt the hot splash of blood and snot. The big man grunted in pain and surprise, stumbling backward, his grip on Aaron loosening.

The sellsword waded forward, throwing one punch and then another into the big man's midsection. It felt like he was hitting rock, but it didn't matter how big or how strong a man was—if he got hit in the floating ribs, he felt it just the same, and the big man staggered, curling his body inward in an attempt to block the blows. This had the added benefit of pushing the man's head forward, and Aaron had never been a man to pass on such an invitation as that. His first punch hit the man in his already broken nose and this time he didn't grunt—he howled. The second one took him in the temple, and the third, an upper cut that had all the momentum of Aaron's body behind it, struck him in the chin.

The big man staggered backwards and would have hit the floor if he hadn't fallen against a table. He was obviously dazed and shaky, but he was struggling up when Aaron charged forward striking his face, his sides, his stomach, anywhere that he wasn't able to cover. The big man managed to get a hand on Aaron's left arm, trapping his wrist, but Aaron was in the full grip of the rage now, and he barely felt it as his bones ground together. Instead, his left fist lashed out, striking the man in the pressure point on the inside of his elbow one, two, three times, and then the meaty hand opened and fell away.

Amazingly, the big man didn't fall, but he lurched off the table to unsteady legs, swinging a wide punch that Aaron easily avoided. The big man half-lunged, half-stumbled forward, reaching out his hands in an effort to get a hold of Aaron and bring his greater strength to bear. Aaron slid to the side and pivoted, kicking him hard in the side of the leg. The bone didn't break, but the big man screamed in pain and collapsed onto his knees, still refusing to go all the way down.

Aaron stood there panting out great, whooping breaths, watching in disbelief as the bouncer started to struggle to his feet. Before he could get all the way up, Aaron grabbed the back of his head in both hands and lunged forward, his knee leading. The blow took the man in the face, and he finally collapsed onto his back with a groan. Aaron thought that surely the man would be out of it then, but the bouncer was squirming on the ground, blinded by a mask of blood, no doubt in unbearable pain due to the broken nose, yet still trying to get to his feet.

"Fuck it," Aaron said, drawing his sword and letting the tip rest on the big man's throat, "stay down, you stubborn bastard.

"What's that?" Aaron glanced up at Wendell's voice and saw that the sergeant was staring at him and the semi-conscious bouncer in wide-eyed surprise as if he'd only just turned. The woman on stage and the rest of her audience were also staring in shock at the sudden violence that had intruded upon their evening. "Ah," the sergeant said, blinking. "By the gods, sir, it's like I can't take you anywhere." Then, reluctantly, "You need help?"

"I'm fine," Aaron managed with as much sarcasm as he could muster, considering the dull aches in his side and face where the man had struck him. "You just relax."

Either the sergeant didn't hear the sarcasm in Aaron's tone, or he didn't want to, because he turned around to the girl once more. "Well, you heard him, ma'am," he said, tossing another coin onto the stage, "let's keep this going."

Aaron was still staring at the back of the man's head in amusement mixed with anger when he felt the big man stir beneath him, and he brought the blade closer to his throat so that it drew a bright red bead of blood. "No, big fella. I think it's best for everybody involved if you stay just where you are. You didn't listen to me the last time, but I'd recommend you do it now. I'd rather not kill you, but I'll do it if I have to." The big man growled, trying to get to his feet anyway, and Aaron was forced to pull the sword away or let him impale himself. Despite his words, Aaron didn't let the blade have its way. Instead, he brought the handle down on the top of the bouncer's head. No matter how much muscle a man had, it didn't protect a place such as that, and the big man let out a wheeze as he crumpled to the ground unconscious.

Aaron spun then, leveling his sword in a line with the woman. "Now," he panted, his breathing labored, "I'll...be needing you to...show me where Bertrand is." Aaron felt movement behind him and glanced over his shoulder to see the other two bouncers that had flanked the stage coming forward. Aaron turned back to the woman, raising an eyebrow, and she held up a hand.

"Stop it, you fools," she said. "The last thing I need is for my damned brothel to turn into a blood bath."

Aaron watched the two men come to a reluctant stop, their faces twisted in anger, before turning back to the woman. "Sorry about your man," he said, offering her a bloody smile, "I know how you hate impoliteness."

She shook her head in disbelief. "He was said to be the best bouncer in Baresh. I paid a fortune for him."

Aaron shrugged one shoulder, forcing himself to hide a wince at the pain in his side—*The bastard must have hands made of fucking stones.* "If you would've let me know you were throwing away money, I would have come earlier, saved you a lot of trouble. Now, I'm going to need you to show me where Bertrand is, and I've got to be honest—I'm running a little low on patience."

"And what about him?" she asked, looking pointedly at the unconscious man on the ground, "Can I see to him first?"

Aaron shook his head. "You've got a healer coming already. Might as well make sure you get your money's worth." He glanced around at the floor, covered in blood and broken glass from several empty mugs of ale that had shattered when they'd been knocked from the table during the fight. "Sorry again," he said, looking back at her, "it looks like you'll be mopping, after all."

"And what makes you think I just won't leave and call the city guard right now? Or send one of my people to do it?" she said, nodding her head at the dancer, musician, and two bouncers near the stage. "I don't think you'd kill me, even if I did. It seems to me that you've gone through a lot of trouble not to kill anybody. After all, you could have drawn that sword a lot sooner and saved yourself some bruises."

Aaron gave her a wicked, bloody smile. "Lady, just because I'm stupid doesn't mean I'm kind, and you'd best understand that before you do something we'll both regret. As for going to a lot of trouble, well, it seems to me that's just about all I ever do. And in case you're wondering how I'll stop all of them if they all rush the door..." He shrugged. "Well, I probably wouldn't be able to. But, then, I didn't walk in here alone, did I?" He turned and glanced over his shoulder. "Wendell, if any of those make so much as a move toward the door, you cut them down where they stand, you hear me?"

"Sure, sure," the man said, waving a hand without turning as he stared at the dancer who was doing her best to perform, despite her obvious anxiety.

Aaron sighed, turning back to the woman. "As for you, well, I'm fairly certain I can get you without much trouble, if it comes to that. Do we understand each other?"

The woman frowned, considering. "And you don't mean Bertrand any harm?"

"Lady," Aaron said, "I didn't mean anybody any harm when I walked in here tonight. All I want to do is talk to the man. Now, why don't you just show me where he is? That way, you'll see the last of me, and you can go back to being a brothel owner who has to bring out her vial of oil from time to time, and we can all get on with our day."

The woman sighed heavily, then nodded. "Very well," she said. "But the other two stay here." She motioned to Leomin and Caleb.

"No," Aaron said, "they don't, and if I've somehow given you the mistaken impression that this is a negotiation, I apologize. If you make me, I'll tear apart this whole brothel to find him, and I don't believe either of us wants that."

She nodded, a sour expression on her face as if she'd expected as much. "Fine. This way."

She started toward the stairs, and Aaron motioned for Leomin and Caleb to follow him. "What happened to 'act natural'?" Leomin whispered as they started after the brothel owner.

"What? That?" Aaron said, glancing back at the unconscious man. "I'm a sellsword, Leomin. The only unnatural thing is that he's still breathing. Now, come on."

The woman led them up the stairs, past closed doors through which could be heard pleasured moans that rang just a touch false, and frantic grunts as the clientele did their best to get their money's worth. They must have passed at least a dozen rooms, maybe as many as twenty, the youth's face growing redder and redder by the moment. Finally, the woman stopped in front of a door and turned to Aaron. "This is the one. I trust you can get in yourself."

Aaron was going to stop her but before he could, she was walking down the hallway once more. He considered chasing after her, making her open the door but decided against it. He turned back to Leomin who shrugged, stepped forward, and knocked.

"Sorry," a woman's voice called from inside, "the room's occupied."

"Yes, ma'am," Leomin said, "but you see, I have a good friend, Bertrand, who is inside, and I would very much like to speak to him. It is about a matter of some...urgency I'm afraid."

"Go away!" a man's voice called, and though it tried for tough, Aaron could hear the quiver of fear in it. "We're busy."

"It's alright," Caleb said, stepping forward and bending down to examine the lock. "It appears to be a fairly rudimentary mechanism. With the right tools, I could have it open in a few minutes. Tell me," he said, turning to Aaron and Leomin, "do either of you have a needle?"

"Must have left it in my other pants," Aaron said dryly.

"There might be another way," Leomin said, meeting Aaron's eyes with a question.

Aaron sighed. "Fine," he said reluctantly, "but only because I don't think it wise that we stay around here any longer than we have to." The Parnen smiled, nodding before turning back to the door. "And Leomin?"

"Mr. Envelar?"

"A small one. The last thing we want is to bring the whole damned city down on ourselves, and if Kevlane is here somewhere—which seems to be growing likelier and likelier—we don't want to run into him and his cronies because you got careless."

"Of course, Mr. Envelar," Leomin said in what he must have taken for his most comforting voice, "I am known for nothing if not my subtlety."

The man's words did nothing to reassure Aaron, but in another moment he could feel the Parnen gathering the power of his Virtue, and it was too late to change his mind. "Bertrand," Leomin said, and as he spoke Aaron thought he could almost see invisible lines of power radiating out from him in the direction of the door, "my name is Leomin, and I am a friend. I would not tell you so, if it were not true. Now, will you not open the door and listen to what I have to say, for I would surely like to speak to you."

"I don't know a Leomin," the man's voice said from inside the room, but it didn't sound as scared or abrupt as before, only curious, "leastways, I don't think I do."

Leomin glanced at Aaron, and the sellsword gave a grudging nod. The Parnen closed his eyes, concentrating, and Aaron felt more power building. He was surprised that he could feel it at all—he'd never felt the other times he'd seen Leomin use his gift—but not too surprised. The power of his own bond seemed to grow stronger from day to day, and this was only proof of that—the same as how he'd known that the woman in the common room wasn't going to let him see Bertrand without a fight.

"Only more reason to open the door then, friend Bertrand," Leomin said, "for when one man is getting to know another, there should not be such walls and doors between them. Not, unless, they wish to know the door as well, I suppose. And a fine door it is, but I think it would look oh so much finer open. There is something final, something abrupt and a bit suffocating about a closed door, do you not agree?"

There was a hesitation—no doubt while the man inside the room tried to figure out just what the Parnen had actually said—then he spoke again. "My friends call me Bert."

"Very well, Bert," Leomin said. "Now, the door?"

They heard footsteps draw closer from inside the room and in another moment the door was easing open. The slowly widening crack revealed a thin, balding man with a slightly confused smile on his face as if someone had told a joke he wanted to be a part of, but that he couldn't seem to figure out. "Leomin?" the man asked.

"It is I, Bert," the Parnen said, "and these," he paused, motioning to Aaron and Caleb, "are my friends. Soon to be your friends too, I hope."

Bert licked his lips nervously, glancing at the kid before turning to Aaron where his gaze settled and took on a suspicious cast. "I assure you, friend," Leomin said, "he is not quite so dangerous as he appears."

"He's bleeding," Bert said in a voice that sounded as if he was talking in his sleep.

"Yes," Leomin agreed, smiling, "he usually is. May we come in, Bert?"

"O-of course," the little man stammered, "gods, where are my manners? I just had it locked in case any strangers came by. I would not shut my door to friends, never."

Leomin bowed his head in pleased agreement and soon he was following the small man inside. "That's amazing," Caleb breathed, staring after the Parnen with wide eyes.

"Yeah," Aaron said, rubbing at his temples as he moved toward the door, "amazing."

Once they were all inside, Aaron closed the door behind them. A woman sat on the bed in what appeared to be a silk robe, the bottom of which came to about halfway down her thigh. She was pretty, with long blonde hair and blue eyes, but there was a coldness to her gaze as was often present in women who sold their bodies for coin. She stared at the three newcomers warily, her arms folded over her ample chest. "I don't like this, Bert," she said, "you said not to let anybody in, not anyone. Now these three here show up, and you just open the door as if you've not a care in the world."

"But this is different, Carla," he said, turning to her, a smile on his face, "these are friends."

"The way you acted when you came by a week ago, it didn't seem like you had a friend in the world you'd trust," the woman said, unconvinced, "and these don't look like friends any sane person would want to have, you ask me. I mean, look, that one there's bleeding." She pointed a thin, painted fingernail at Aaron.

"He usually is," Caleb blurted, grinning widely as Leomin laughed.

"Trust me, Carla, it will be okay ... won't it?" he asked, turning to Leomin, a touch of uncertainty entering his eyes.

"You have nothing to fear from us, Bert," Leomin said, smiling reassuringly.

"You see?" Bert said to the woman. "Nothing to fear. You heard it out of his own mouth."

The woman scowled, "I've heard plenty of things out of plenty of men's mouths, Berty. That doesn't make them true. When I was younger, I had a man tell me about how he'd grown rich from the shipping industry, told me about all his nice and fancy things, then took me to bed. After that, I never heard from him again until I went searching and found that he lived in the poor district with his mother." She shook her head. "Just because a man says a thing doesn't mean it's true."

Leomin started to speak, but Aaron held up a hand, silencing him. "You're right, Carla," he said, "it doesn't. Men lie, and I won't pretend that I'm any different. But I would like to point out that if we *did* mean Bert any harm, the harm would have already been done. Men who come in the night to a man's room meaning him harm don't sit around and talk about it."

"Well," she said, "that makes sense at least, though I can't say as it's any comfort."

"The truth rarely is," Aaron agreed.

"Carla," Bert said, his voice taking on a wheedling tone, "why don't you go downstairs for a bit, maybe have a drink? I know you've probably got tired of being stuck in this room with me for the last week."

The woman shrugged, rising from the bed. "It's your coin and your affair, Bert," she said. She made her way to a closet in the corner of the room, stripping off her silk robe as she did and displaying the nakedness that had hidden underneath. She reached in and pulled out a dress that—from what Aaron could see as she slid it on—didn't cover much more than the robe had.

He turned and saw the youth, Caleb, watching her with eyes so wide it was a wonder he couldn't see the back of his own head. The youth didn't so much as blink, as if he was terrified of missing anything, and Aaron couldn't help but smile. "Anyway," the woman said, turning back and not showing the least surprise to see everyone in the room staring at her, "it's your life, Bert. I can't tell you how to spend it."

"I'll see you soon, Carla," the thin man said.

The woman gave a small shrug as she slipped on some shoes. Then she walked toward the door, opening it. "I hope so, Bert," she said, glancing back at him, "you were always one of the nice ones." Then she was gone, closing the door behind her.

The thin man looked at the three strangers, blinking as if seeing them for the first time, a tremor in his legs that made it seem as if they would give out at any moment. "H-how um...how can I help you, gentlemen?"

"Relax, Bert," Aaron said, motioning to the bed, "sit down before you fall down. We haven't come to hurt you—that was the truth. We just have some questions for you."

"A-alright," Bert said, walking over and sitting stiffly on the bed, trying to watch all three of them at once. "What um...what can I do for you?"

"A few weeks ago," Aaron said, "you were in a tavern and you told the barkeep, Nathan, a story about something you'd witnessed. Do you remember that?"

"M-maybe," the thin man said, swallowing hard, "b-but sometimes when I drink, I say things. I can't be sure of what I might have told him."

"Well, Bert, you told him that you saw the blacksmith, Odel, get attacked by two men. You said that you saw a big man in a cloak carry Odel away over his shoulder. Is that true?"

The man wiped a hand at his sweaty forehead and shook his head slowly. "No, I don't...Oh, you know what?" he said, giving a sickly smile. "It must have been a joke I told him, that's all. Just a way to try to mess with Nathan. I do that sometimes—tell jokes. I didn't see anything, I swear. I just made it up, you know, to get a laugh."

Sitting there sweating, his face as pale as a sheet of parchment, the man looked to Aaron like he'd never told a joke in his life. Or heard one for that matter. "Bert, we haven't come to hurt you, alright? We just want the truth, that's all. Once you tell us what you can, we'll leave, and you can go on about your night."

"Y-you swear?" the thin man said, meeting his eyes.

Aaron nodded, holding his gaze. "I swear."

"A-alright," Bert said, and he seemed to gain some bit of confidence, "well, I did see something, saw it just as I told Nathan, but he wouldn't believe me. The truth is, I've never *seen* a man as big as the one I saw carrying Odel. I liked Odel—we'd talk sometimes, when I was coming home from work, and he was getting ready to leave his shop for the day. He was nice. A lot of big guys usually aren't—I've had my fair share of experience with that, believe me, but he was. I didn't like seeing that," he said sadly, "the way the man was carrying him. And Odel was all bloody, as if he'd been in a fight."

"If that's true, Bert," Aaron said, "then why didn't you go to the city guard? Surely, they would have done something."

The thin man was shaking his head before Aaron was finished. "No way. I'm not the only one that's seen things, even known a man or two that did. *They* went to see the city guards, and no one has seen *them* since. No," he repeated, his head still moving from side to side, "not me. Whoever is out there, taking people, they also take people who *see* things. They come for them, snatching them out of their homes and their lives, and they're never seen again." He paused, his eyes welling with tears. "And I'm next. They're going to get me next."

"Relax, Bert," Aaron said. "They've not got you yet, and you were right to hide. But tell me, if you were so scared, why didn't you leave Baresh altogether?"

"I *wanted* to," the thin man said, "gods, how I wanted to. But, well, you may not believe this, but sometimes I've got a little bit of a reputation for...overreacting. For...being afraid."

Aaron had no problem at all believing it, but he only nodded. "Go on."

"Well," Bert said, "the thing is, I knew what I saw, and I even walked by Odel's shop the next few days—I figured that was safe enough as I always did when I came home from work—but I would always look for him. Normally around that time Odel would be getting ready to leave himself, in which case I'd often run into him coming out of his shop. Unless he was working late, in which case I'd still be able to see the smoke from the forge he uses, but I didn't see either for those days, and I knew that I hadn't imagined it, knew that it was true and he'd been taken."

"Yet you didn't leave," Leomin observed.

"No," Bert said in a voice that was almost a moan, "no, and I'm a gods-cursed fool for not doing it. It was just, I needed to be *sure*, you understand? I didn't want to think that, you know, maybe I'd just overreacted. I was hoping that if I could find some proof that people would believe me."

"So what did you do, Bert?" Aaron asked, his sense of urgency growing. The woman downstairs hadn't called the city guard yet—

those who lived in a city's poor district tended to avoid such things—but sooner or later she would decide that it would be better to have the guard poking their noses into her business than having Aaron and the others there, and they had to be gone before then.

"There's a guy I know," Bert said, "or, well, used to. He'd sometimes come into the office where I worked. A big man. Mean too," he said, frowning, "but, then, they usually are. Anyway," he shrugged, "he'd always come in with several guys with him—sailors they were, you could tell it by the way they talked and dressed, wearing sleeveless shirts and walking the way they often do, as if their legs are never really comfortable on land after so long at sea."

"Nathan, Odel the blacksmith, and now this other," Aaron said. "Bert, just how many freakishly big men do you know? What do you do, go looking for them?"

The thin man smiled, but there was little humor in it. "I know more than I'd like, sir. Many more. And when you're a small, thin man, prematurely balding, living in the poor district with a voice that sounds slightly feminine no matter what you do to change it, you don't have to go looking to find such men as that—more often than not, they find you. Usually in a tavern or when you're walking down the street alone. They like to make a big show of pushing you around, giving their friends something to laugh about. It's the reason I always went to Nathan's tavern—he was always kind, and he'd never let others harass me while I was there."

The thin man frowned. "That didn't stop them from waiting for me in the street, though. Why is it," he said, his voice both curious and hurt at the same time, "that the strong insist on targeting the weak? You would think they would like to match themselves against each other, to figure out who the best really is."

"Because the weak are easier," Aaron said, "that's all. Men like that, Bert, they don't want to be the best—they just want to think they are. Now, let's get back to your story."

"Fine," Bert said, taking a deep breath as if to steady himself, "anyway, Decker—that's the sailor—*was* strong, and it wasn't just a show. They have a fair here every year with a variety of games and prizes to win, and one of those games is a competition to see who can lift a barrel filled with the most bricks. Decker always competes and, for the last five years, he's always won. I needed proof and, besides, Odel had been a friend. So I thought..." He hesitated, shrugging, staring at his feet as if embarrassed.

"So you thought that if strong people really were being taken, you could wait and watch Decker and sooner or later whoever had taken Odel would come for him," Aaron finished.

Bert swallowed. "Yes."

Aaron stared at the man before him. A thin, frail-looking man with eyes that seemed unsteady in their sockets and a pale face that wore a perpetual grimace, as if he'd learned early on that life was a raw deal, and the world was always waiting for its chance to pull the rug out from under you. The type of man that looked as if he was always on the verge of running—more a rabbit than a man. Yet this same man had witnessed something terrible and, instead of fleeing as his instincts no doubt would have begged him to, he'd not just stayed, but put himself into a position where he might not only witness the same thing again, but also be taken himself. It had taken balls to do that, more than Aaron would have credited him with. Stupidity too, of course. But balls.

People, I have found, Co said in his mind, *are always much more complex than they may at first appear. You can never truly know them.*

It's more than that, firefly, Aaron thought back, *we can never really know ourselves.* "So what happened?"

Bert rubbed a hand across his mouth. "I took a week off from work. I haven't taken a day off in years, so my boss didn't give me too much trouble about it. You wouldn't think it from looking at me, but I rarely get sick. Anyway," he said hurriedly, apparently noting the impatience in Aaron's expression, "I went to the docks and found the boat that Decker worked on with his friends. And I...well, I followed him."

Aaron grunted. The man was surprising him more and more. "Then what happened?"

"Nothing at first," the thin man said, his face taking on a haunted look, "and I was just thinking that maybe I *was* crazy after all, planning to give it all up. But on the third night ..." He swallowed hard, his face growing visibly paler as if even the memory of what he had witnessed terrified him.

"Go on, Bert," Leomin said, putting a hand on the man's shoulder, "it's alright."

The thin man nodded, taking a slow, shuddering breath before continuing. "On the third night, Decker and some of his friends were in a tavern drinking. I stayed outside, figuring that whoever had been taking the men wouldn't come for him in a crowded tavern. And I was right," he said, closing his eyes and shaking his head, "but gods, how I wish I hadn't been. After a while, Decker left the tavern with his friends and one by one they split off to go to their homes or wherever they spend their nights, until finally I was following Decker and him only."

The man paused, grabbing a half-full glass of water from where it sat on the nightstand by the bed and downing it in one large gulp. "I followed him to his home, a small place close enough to the docks that he could walk to them without trouble." He paused, glancing up at the others. "I know you must think me a fool, following the very man who has been tormenting me for years and doing so at night in the poorest part of the city but, you see, I had to *know*. And...maybe it was more than that, too. For those three days following Decker, I didn't feel as weak and afraid as I always have. Oh, sure, I was still terrified. Terrified that Decker or one of his friends would see me, or that whoever—*what*ever—had taken Odel would come and take me if for no other reason than that I would be a witness to what had happened, but I also felt...it's hard to explain."

"You felt in control," Aaron said.

"Yes," Bert said, his head bobbing up and down quickly, "that's exactly it. It was as if, for once, I wasn't the one being targeted, being *hunted*. It was like..." He paused, shrugging. "Anyway, Decker had been inside for five minutes, no more than that, and I was just getting ready to go home myself, maybe get something to eat first. I don't guess any of you have done something like this before, but following someone is hard work, and I was always afraid to stop to eat for fear that I would lose him."

Bert waved a hand, shaking his head in frustration. "That doesn't matter. What matters is that I was just about to leave when I saw two figures walking down the street in front of Decker's house. At first, I thought that they were just some other sailors or men coming home from a long night at the tavern, but neither of them looked drunk. Instead, they seemed to be walking with a purpose, as if they were men who were out in the night on a very particular mission."

He swallowed hard. "It was a dark night, but the moon was up in full. I had hidden in a back alley, crouching behind a pile of trash that had been sitting there for the gods knew how long, the smell so strong that I nearly puked just sitting there. But then the men stepped out of the shadows and, by the moonlight, I noticed the impossible size of one of the two, at least as big, if not bigger, than the man I saw take Odel. He was cloaked, and I couldn't make out any of the features of his face, but no cloak could hide that kind of size, and they both paused in front of Decker's house, looking around as if to see if anyone shared the street with them. Smell or not," he said, a shamed look appearing on his face, "I burrowed down into that pile of trash as much as I could and as quietly as I could."

The man buried his face in his hands and, for a minute, the only sound was that of his quiet sobs. Leomin glanced at Aaron, a sad expression on his face, and started toward the thin man, but it was Caleb who got there first, sitting on the bed beside Bert and patting him on the shoulder. "It's okay, Mr. Bert," he said softly, "what you did was very brave."

Bert glanced up, his face covered in tears and a runner of snot hanging from one nostril. "Really?"

"Really," Caleb said, smiling. "I think that I would have peed my pants."

Bert smiled at that, the kid's innocent, kind face doing what the other men could not have, setting him at ease. "I won't say it wasn't close," he said, half-laughing as he wiped his face with the sleeve of his shirt.

"I'll bet," the youth said, his eyes wide. "What happened then? Did you run? I would have run."

"No," Bert said, "I didn't run. I just...waited. And watched. The two men walked up to Decker's door, and the one—the big one—he reached out. I thought at first that he meant to knock, but he didn't knock at all. Or, at least, not the way normal men knock. Instead, he reached out and laid one hand on the door, and it broke off the frame, falling into the house. I heard the crash from where I crouched in the alley, and the two men walked inside. A moment later, I heard Decker shout, angry, and there was another crash, and the shouting stopped." He paused, swallowing. "It all happened so fast," he said, shaking his head, "the men couldn't have been in his house for more than a minute, maybe two, and then they were walking out, the cloaked figure carrying Decker over his shoulder like he weighed nothing. Decker's shout had been pretty loud and, at first, I thought that someone would come out, that they would check on him." He shook his head sadly. "But either they didn't hear or they didn't want to help, because nobody came."

Oh, they heard alright, Aaron thought, *but hearing and acting on what you hear are two very different things.*

"Anyway," Bert said, staring at Caleb now as if the other two weren't even in the room, "I waited until they were further down the street and then I...I followed them."

Caleb's eyes went wider still. "You *followed* them? Uh uh, not me, Mr. Bert. You sure are brave."

Bert grunted, but he smiled as he did. "Not brave, lad, just stupid. Either way, I followed them, keeping my distance as they made their way through the back alleys of the city. I watched from as far away as I could be and still see them, when a man—drunk, I thought, judging by his walk—stumbled down the same alley they were walking down. The man froze, and the smaller of the two men motioned to the bigger one who started toward the stranger. Still, he was on the other side of the alley, and I thought that he would make it away." He paused taking a slow, deep breath. "But he'd made it no more than three steps before something flew out of the night, too fast to follow, and the next thing I knew his head was flying from his body and there was blood...gods, there was so much blood. In the moonlight," he said, finally turning to Aaron, "it looked almost black. I never knew that blood could look so black."

Aaron nodded, his face set. "Go on, Bert. Finish the rest of it. I think you need to tell it as much as we need to hear it."

The thin man nodded. "Whoever or whatever had done that to the man, they were gone in a blink, and I never even got a look at them. The two men just kept walking, striding by the corpse without even giving it so much as a glance. Anyway, long story short," he said, "I followed them through the city until they came to…" He shook his head. "No, you wouldn't believe me even if I told you."

"*Aaron!*" They all turned at the sound of his name. It was the sergeant's voice, and it was coming from downstairs.

"Shit," Aaron cursed, turning back to the thin man. "Where, Bert? Where did they go?"

"T-the castle," the thin man said, "they went into the castle."

The man's words hit Aaron like a lightning strike, but he also felt as if some half-hidden suspicion had been confirmed, as if, deep down, he'd been thinking that it had been the only possible answer, but that he hadn't wanted to believe it. He turned to Leomin, and met the Parnen's haunted, shocked gaze, no doubt a mirror to his own. An understanding passed between them, and Aaron turned back to the thin man. "Thanks for telling us all of this, Bert. I don't want to tell you your business, but I'm going to repay the favor with some advice. Get out of Baresh. Now. Don't wait until morning, don't try to get all of your affairs in order before you leave. Pack a bag tonight, take what coin you can get, and then get the fuck out of this city."

"B-but leaving Baresh?" Bert said, as if the thought was impossible, "I…I've always lived here. I was born here, raised in an orphanage not a mile from where we sit. How can I leave?" He met Aaron's eyes, his gaze desperate. "My life's here."

"From one orphan rat to another, Bert," Aaron said, "trust me and get out while you can. Your life might be here, but your death will be, too. The people you're dealing with don't like to leave witnesses, and it's only a matter of time before somebody talks a little too much, and the next knock on your door might not be a knock at all. Do you understand?"

"Yes," the thin man said, nodding slowly, "I understand."

"Do it, Bert," Aaron said. "Tonight. Whatever is going on in this city—it's going to get worse before it gets better. *If* it gets better."

The thin man sighed. "Very well," he said, "I will leave. T-thank you, Mister—I just realized I don't even know your full name."

"It's better that you don't," Aaron said, offering the thin man his hand. "Safe travels, Bert."

"And to you," the thin man said, taking it and giving it a shake that was surprisingly firm.

"Alright," Aaron said, turning back to Leomin, "we've got to go. Now."

They started for the door, but the youth paused, going back and giving the thin man a hug. After a stunned moment, Bert returned it, a small smile on his face. "Thank you, Mr. Bert," Caleb said, "you're the bravest man I know."

The man laughed at that, but he was smiling widely as Caleb walked up to stand beside the two staring men. "Well?" he asked. "Aren't we in a hurry?"

Aaron shook his head in wonder then turned and led them out the door. He had his blade drawn as they came down the stairs, ready for anything that might be waiting for them. So he was surprised when he found that the scene in the common room of the brothel was much like the one they had left. The woman stood behind the bar, her arms folded, a pouty expression on her face. Wendell still sat in the chair facing the dancer who was now naked from the waist up and performing in front of one of the other men who shouted in appreciation as he threw more coins onto the stage.

Aaron's gaze swept the common room as he stepped off the stairs. "Men and their swords," the bartender sneered, "you just can't resist waving that thing around, can you?"

Aaron frowned, not responding as he started toward the scarred sergeant. He noted, as he did, that a woman in a white robe was bent over the still prone figure of Breaker, ministering to him with a cloth and a vial of some liquid. Aaron passed her and knelt beside Wendell's chair. The sergeant didn't seem to notice.

"Well?" Aaron asked.

"What's that?" Wendell said, turning away from the show with obvious reluctance.

"You called my name," Aaron said, "what's happened? Have the guards come?"

The sergeant looked surprised, looking around the room as if seeing it for the first time. "Not that I'm aware of, sir." He started to turn back to the dancer, and Aaron clapped a hand on his shoulder, forcing him back around.

"Then *why* did you call my name?" Aaron tried again.

"Oh, that," the sergeant said, nodding. "I just was wantin' to see if you might have a few coins I could borrow, is all. It's a fine view here, but she's all the way on the other side of the stage." He frowned at the man who the woman was still dancing in front of. "That fucker's been hoggin' her for the last ten minutes. Bastard must have brought every coin he had." Wendell grunted. "Probably not gonna have enough to buy himself a decent meal later. Lucky bastard."

Aaron let out a growl and pulled the sergeant out of his chair. "We're leaving."

"Done already?" Wendell asked. "You sure there ain't nothin' else you'd like to ask that fella, sir? I mean..." He paused to glance back at the woman. "Cases like this, I reckon it's good to be thorough. My father always told me that a job done right is faster in the end on account of you didn't have to go back and fix none of the mistakes you made while you were tryin' to hurry."

"I'm sure," Aaron said dryly. "Now, are you going to come on, or am I going to have to drag you out of here?"

The sergeant held up his hands. "Easy, sir. I was just wantin' to make sure that we were all takin' the steps we needed to. Just concerned about the task at hand, is all."

"Yeah," Aaron said, "I'm sure that's what you were concerned about. Now let's go. We've pushed our luck here enough already."

Aaron scanned the city streets as they walked, his mind racing. *The castle. Why would they bring them to the castle unless...*

I don't like this, Aaron, Co said, *not at all. Only the strongest and fastest are being taken? That sounds much like Kevlane's work to me. And now Belgarin plans to hold a tournament where thousands of warriors, men and women who have trained their entire lives to be strong and fast, will show up to compete, creating the perfect opportunity for Kevlane?*

You're right, firefly, Aaron thought back, *it's not good. I think it's safe to say that Kevlane is here, in Baresh.*

And more than that, Co responded, her own voice troubled, *it would appear that there are only two realistic options. Either Belgarin and Boyce Kevlane are in league together, or Kevlane has found some means of manipulating or controlling Belgarin.*

You're leaving out a third option, firefly, Aaron thought.
Oh?
Maybe Belgarin isn't Belgarin at all. You know as well as I do that Kevlane can change his face whenever he wants. Besides, it

would explain Belgarin's erratic behavior lately, such as retreating with his army, only to have a tournament.

You mean that you believe Kevlane has taken over the throne of Baresh? That he is creating an army of his sick mutations?

I'm not sure, firefly, Aaron thought back, *but it fits the facts. Still, we need to be sure.*

And how can we do that? It's not as if we can walk up to the castle and say, "Oh, hey, how are you? By the way, I was wondering: do you feel like your king could possibly be a homicidal maniac that spends his spare time turning men and women into monsters?

I've always been a fan of the direct approach, Aaron thought, smiling without humor as he led the others back in the direction of Nathan's tavern. He glanced at Leomin. *That said, I think this time there might be another way.*

Aaron, Co said, *I like Leomin as much as anyone but surely you—*

She said something more, but Aaron wasn't listening, was too busy turning the idea over in his mind, looking for the weak points. Dangerous, sure, but then he couldn't remember the last decision he'd made that didn't have a very real possibility of winding up getting him killed.

Perhaps there's a lesson there, the Virtue said, her displeasure clear in her tone.

Maybe, Aaron thought back, *but I'll have time enough to learn it if we survive.*

He studied his three companions and saw the anxiety and worry he felt mirrored in their own expressions. The men looked like prisoners being marched to the gallows, dead already and knowing it. A thought struck him, and he found himself grinning as he looked at the youth, "Mr. Bert, huh?"

The kid glanced over, saw his smile, and seemed to tuck his neck further into his shoulders, looking away from Aaron's eyes. "I didn't know his last name. Anyway," he said, finally summoning the courage to meet Aaron's gaze, "it worked, didn't it?"

"Relax, kid," Aaron said, still grinning. "I'm not questioning your methods—the man had information we needed, and you got it out of him. It was a job well done."

The youth looked away again, but Aaron noted the pleased smile on his face as he did. "About that other bit though ..." Aaron went on, "the part about how you would have pissed yourself if you'd seen what the man had…"

"I was only saying what he needed to hear," Caleb said, avoiding the amused glances of the three men. "I didn't mean it."

"You sure? I only ask because I know kids sometimes have problems holding their water, and we've still got half an hour or more before we make it back to Nathan's. I'd hate for you to have an accident."

Wendell barked a laugh at that, and Leomin grinned. The kid frowned, but Aaron thought he could see amusement mixed with relief in his eyes. "I'm fine," he grumbled.

"If you're sure." They walked on in silence then, but one that felt less fraught than the one that had preceded it. It had not made their problems go away, of course, and it was all too likely that the doom he'd seen before in each of their expressions would come upon them before long; but, the way Aaron figured it, if a man was going to die, he might as well do it smiling.

CHAPTER FOURTEEN

During their journey to Galia, Adina's thoughts had been focused on getting to the city as quickly as possible and worrying about Aaron and the others. She had felt an urgency building in her with each passing night and, with it, the irrational belief that if she were able to win back her kingdom, then Aaron and the others would be okay, would *have* to be okay. Now, though, standing in line to enter the city—what had once been *her* city—the urgency had fled and in its face was a deep, abiding fear.

As they waited their turn at the gate, a thousand different scenarios—all bad—played through Adina's mind. What if the guards recognized her and swept her and the others off the street and into the dungeons before anyone could do anything about it? She was covered in road dust, wearing a simple tunic and trousers, and Beth had crushed up some plant Adina hadn't recognized and stained Adina's hair so that it was a red close to May's own, but her heart hammered in her chest anyway. She was their *queen*, after all. How could the guards at the gate not recognize her? She felt like a fool, like a child that had been so focused on getting what she wanted that she hadn't paid attention to the dangers not just to herself, but to her friends as well.

She was so lost in her thoughts that she didn't realize that her feet had carried her to the gate until one of the guards spoke.

"Ma'am?"

Adina looked up, her heart pounding even harder in her chest. "S-sir?" *We could run,* she thought, preparing herself for it, *they couldn't catch us, not all of us. We have the horses. They're tired from the journey, but surely if we put enough distance—*

"I said what business brings you to Galia?"

Adina felt hope flood through her. No shouts of alarm then, no yell for more guards. "I—that is—"

"Pleasure brings us, soldier," May said from beside her, smiling and giving him a wink, "it is what drives the world, after all. That and, admittedly, we are looking for jobs. Still, I've heard that the men of Galia are the finest in the entirety of the world. So far, at least," she said, smiling seductively, "I cannot say that I disagree."

The man blushed at that, but he cleared his throat. "And you, ma'am?" he said to Adina.

Adina tried to answer, but the words wouldn't seem to come, and the club owner smiled, chuckling softly. "You must forgive my sister, sir. She is very shy, I'm afraid, particularly when in the presence of such a handsome man. Still," she said, winking once more, "she is not so shy in bed, or so I hear."

Adina felt her face heat, and in her anger at the club owner speaking of her in such a way, some bit of her fear vanished, and she was able to find her voice once more. "You must forgive *my* sister, sir," she said to the guard, "she has a tendency to flaunt what she has and, if she's not doing that, then she's flaunting what someone else has. We are simple women come to see if we can find work, that's all."

The guard grunted, studying Adina up and down in a way that made her face heat further. "Very well," he said, "welcome to Galia, ladies." He gave a slight bow, directed at Adina, then stepped to the side, holding his arm out in invitation. "I hope that you find the work you're looking for."

"Thank you, kind sir," Adina said, bowing her own head in return as she started into the city, the club owner beside her.

"And just what was *that*?" she whispered harshly once they were away from the guard.

"That, *sister*," May said, "was me getting us inside of the ci—"

"Ma'am, stop please!"

Adina froze, her breath catching in her throat as the soldier jogged toward them. She watched in surprise as he bowed to her again. "Forgive me, ma'am," he said, "I'm usually not so forward, I swear, but I find myself unable to keep from asking...would you like to perhaps get a drink later? There's a tavern on God's Row, the Toppling Tankard, it's called. You'd make my week, if you were able to come."

Adina gave the man a smile. "Thank you for the invitation, but I'm afraid—"

"She'd be happy to come," May interrupted, and Adina gave the club owner a sharp look before turning back to the guard.

"I'm sorry," Adina tried again, "but I've already got someo—"

"What time?" May said, not giving Adina a chance to finish.

The guard looked between the two of them uncertainly. "Um...my shift's over in two hours so...three hours from now?"

"And the Toppling Tankard, you called it?"

"That's right," he said to May, his voice unsure. He turned back to Adina, an apologetic expression on his face. "It really is quite a nice tavern, and all I ask is a drink, I swear. It would be my pleasure, and I expect no more than that."

Adina opened her mouth to respond, but found that her anger at the club owner was such that she couldn't seem to find the words.

"Nor should you," May said in a slightly scolding tone. "My sister is no harlot or street walker to be purchased for the price of a glass of wine."

The man's young face grew red. "I...that is, I didn't mean—"

"Never mind what you meant," May said, folding her arms, "you've got your wish, and my sister will have her drink. Perhaps it's best that you don't linger any longer."

The guard cleared his throat. "Yes, of course, I—" He hesitated, as if unsure of what to say. "That is, I'll see you tonight," he said, bowing low to Adina once more, and Adina watched dumbly as he walked back to the gate.

"May," she said, her voice cold, "would you care to explain to me what it is you think you're doing?"

"Tell me, Princess," May said, raising an eyebrow, "how many rebellions have you waged in your time? For make no mistake, it is a rebellion you intend to wage here, and I myself have some bit of experience in such matters."

"It's not a *rebellion*," Adina hissed, angrier than she had been in a long time, "it's *my* kingdom."

"Ah, I see," May said, "and are you currently in power here?"

"Well, no," Adina said, flabbergasted, "you know that. I told you—"

"And do you intend to wrest power from those who currently have it?"

Adina sighed, frustrated. "Yes, but that's only because—"

"And to do so would you be prepared to do things that they would no doubt deem illegal, going so far as to break the laws that they have set?"

"Yes," Adina hissed through gritted teeth.

The club owner smiled, shrugging. "Sounds a lot like a rebellion to me."

"Rebellion or not," Adina said, grabbing the woman by the arm and leading her to the side of the street, "you had no right to tell that guard I would see him tonight. I didn't come here to find a man—I already have one, if you hadn't noticed. I came here to win back my kingdom, and I *thought* you had come here to help me."

"Ah," May said, nodding as if she understood, "I see. Well, I apologize, Princess. I had thought you were serious about taking your kingdom back."

"Damnit, May," Adina said, incredulous, "I *am* serious; have I not shown you that already? I won't let that bastard Ridell and the nobles sit in power for one moment longer than they already have. They are selfish men and women who care nothing for the people, only their own ambitions."

"Uh-huh," May said, "so then you have some plan to speak to this loyal captain of yours this...what was his name again?"

"Captain Oliver," Adina hissed, "and no, I don't have a plan yet, you know that. I needed to see what the city was like first, to see what opportunities there might be to meet with Captain Oliver privately."

"And this Captain Oliver," May said, "would he be in charge of the city guards?"

Adina blinked. "Yes...yes he is. Technically, so is General Ridell, but Captain Oliver runs the day to day. Why?"

May ignored the question. "So, if Captain Oliver is in charge of the city guards, then it stands to reason that our amorous city guardsman there," she said, nodding her head the guard who was now back at his position at the gate, "might very well know him?"

Adina huffed. "Of course he'll know him, but I don't see wha—" She cut off, her eyes going wide in realization. "Gods, how did I not think of that?"

May smiled and patted Adina's hand. "I wouldn't worry overly much about it, sister. After all, it's not every day that a woman gets to practice leading a rebellion now is it?"

Adina shook her head angrily. "Gods, I'm a fool. If Aaron were here, he wouldn't have missed such a—"

"If Aaron were here," May interrupted, "we would no doubt have corpses at our feet and angry city guardsmen all around us. Never mind what Silent would do—the man's the best killer I've ever seen, but his people skills are...well...he doesn't exactly have what you might call people skills, and subtlety is as beyond him as flying is beyond a fish."

"Maybe," Adina said, suddenly self-conscious, "but he wouldn't have to go on a date to have a chance at taking back his kingdom either."

May laughed, clapping the princess on the back. "Let Silent have his weapons—you have your own. And don't look so worried. It's not as if you've been promised to the man. Besides, it will give us an excuse to go shopping—if you're anything like me, you're sick of wearing the same clothes and sleeping on hard ground. It'll do you good to brush the nettles out of your hair and get dolled up for a change."

Adina shrugged. She didn't care anything about shopping—growing up, it had seemed to her that shopping was all the other noblewomen had ever wanted to do, and she'd found it boring beyond belief. Still, a warm bed sounded good. Very good. "Fine," Adina said, "but a drink and no more than that, May. If that's not enough then we'll just have to find another way to get to Oliver."

"Don't decide so soon," May said, "he was a handsome enough man, and he seemed nice. Who knows," she said, grinning, "might just be you'll enjoy yourself."

"*May,*" Adina scolded, "enough. I love Aaron, you know that."

"Who said anything about love?" May asked. "I was just talking about cleaning the rust off the—"

"Well now, that was fun." Adina, grateful for the interruption, turned to see Beth, Bastion, and Gryle walking up. The old woman was grinning, and both men were studying their feet, rubbing at their ears.

Adina frowned. "What happened to you all?"

"Oh, nothing important," Beth said. "I just told the nice fella over there that these un's here were my son and grandson, draggin' me all the way to Galia because they want me to pay for 'em to start up a tavern, as if the world don't already have enough of those. It ain't good, don't ya know, to be draggin' around a woman at my age. Plum selfish." She said as she gave the two men a mock-frown.

"You didn't have to pinch our ears so hard," Gryle muttered.

"I can't feel mine at all," Bastion grumbled.

"Well now, that's just like my layabout son and grandson to be complainin' about a little pain in their ears while my poor old self aches from head to toe from following them on some mad dream to start up a tavern so as to make sure they don't drink up all their coin."

The two men looked up at Adina as if hoping for her to come to their rescue, but she only smiled, glad that they were all safe within the city. "We should get off the street and find an inn." She took in the dirt-stained forms of her companions and nodded. "A warm bath would do us all good, I think."

"And a healer, maybe," Bastion grunted, still rubbing at his ear. "I'm half sure my ear's getting ready to fall off."

"Listen to you," Beth said, shaking her head, the smile still on her face, "a giant like yourself, and here you are complaining about a little ear ache. Everybody gets them, you know."

"Well," May said, turning to Adina, "where would you like to go, sister? After all, we don't have long to prepare you for your date."

"Date?" Gryle said, his eyes going wide.

Adina turned and glared at May. "Never mind, Gryle," she said, "I'll tell you about it, but not now—right now, we need to get off of the streets. No one's recognized me yet, thank the gods, but that doesn't mean they won't if we push our luck. As for where we're going..." she smiled, turning to them. "Follow me."

CHAPTER FIFTEEN

Once the messenger was gone, Maladine Caulia, representative of the Golden Oars Bank, stared down at the letter of summons in her hand with something like trepidation. There had been only two such summons of the council since King Belgarin had come back from his battle with Isalla, and both had left her disturbed. A thing that was worrying in itself as Maladine had always prided herself on not being disturbed by anything.

She had been born to a poor family in a poor town and had promised herself at a young age—after seeing her father imprisoned for debts he couldn't pay—that she would become wealthy enough that she would never have to worry about such a thing again. What people born into riches never seemed to understand was that gold acted as a shield against the world, a wall between a person and the cruelties that could and *would* be visited upon a person. Particularly a young girl already displaying much of the beauty she would grow into in time, one who was desperate to find something to eat, anything to stop the gnawing of hunger in her belly.

The rich knew nothing of such problems, nothing of the pains a woman, or a young girl, might go through to ensure that she would never go hungry again. She spoke with nobles often—in her role as the bank's representative it was inevitable—and she knew that they coveted her and her body, could see it in their eyes, even on the rare occasions when they did not speak their desires. Men such as that often did, for they were used to wanting things and even more used to getting the things they wanted. Never *needing* things though. No, need was something they never really understood. They used the word as if it had no real meaning of its own, as if it were only a substitute for "want."

But Maladine knew the difference. She had seen the difference visited upon her, and she hated them for their ignorance, their blind, blissful ignorance. They wanted her, believed they needed her, yet they knew nothing of those tortures she'd had visited upon her. Tortures which, should she give them their desires, should she unclothe herself before them, would be all too visible to their hungry gazes. They knew nothing of what she had endured, or of what she had made others endure to get where she was.

Maladine Caulia was not a woman easily disturbed. Yet she found that as she reread the summons once more, that was *exactly* what she was. The last two council meetings had been painful, tense affairs, and for the first time since she'd taken on the role of representative of the Golden Oars Bank and began interacting with the king, she had felt afraid, felt as if her very life might be in danger.

Belgarin, before the battle at Perennia, had been like a noble child: rich, powerful, angry but, for the most part at least, no true danger as long as you patted his head from time to time and told him what a clever, handsome boy he was. She'd even gone so far, many months ago, to sleep with him, a pathetic episode that had left her feeling like she needed to wash for days, but, in doing so, had gained herself some favor. Another connection that she could exploit when necessary. Never overtly, of course, but even the worst of men generally felt some tenderness to the women they took to their beds—that was another truth that Maladine's life had taught her.

Belgarin had been willful and stupid and vain, but before the battle at Perennia was lost, and he was forced to retreat with his troops, he had been manageable, a horse that would allow itself to be guided just so long as it was blind to the reins wrapped about it. Since returning from Isalla, though, the king was a different man entirely. His voice was calmer, his demeanor too, and he did not shout or scream or beat his fists as he once had. Instead, he spoke softly, sometimes almost too soft to hear, but in a voice, a *tone* that expected unflinching obedience, and Maladine knew that she was not the only member of the council who had noticed the change. The others rarely spoke during the meetings now, and never unless asked a direct question by the king.

Even Caldwell himself acted different. She'd had some dealings with the man in times past, times when he'd paid her in coin for her support on one decision or another, and she had always been more than happy to oblige. Words meant little, opinions meant little, but coin meant everything. Coin was the difference between life and death, between crying your battered, broken body to sleep as you lay on some flea-ridden excuse for a mattress, and lying down to rest in a feathered bed with silk sheets so soft you felt as if you were reclining on a cloud.

The advisor had not visited her once since the king's arrival back in Baresh, however, and he, too, spoke little during the meetings and only when spoken to by the king. No longer did the advisor attempt to guide events. Instead, he seemed content to sit back in the relative safety his silence afforded him and leave the king to lead unhindered or guided. Yet even that was not the most noticeable change in his demeanor, the one that had made Maladine aware that she was not the only one who had noticed the differences in the king. It wasn't even that Caldwell seemed to respect the king, a thing she had never seen from him before. It was something deep in the advisor's gaze, so well hidden that you might miss it, if you didn't look close enough. It was in the way he spoke and the way he bowed, and it had taken Maladine some time to realize what it was. Fear.

The advisor—a man who had manipulated the king for years in small matters and had shown nothing but disdain for him when given the opportunity to do so—was afraid of the man Belgarin had become. That, if nothing else, would have been enough to cause Maladine worry.

For a brief moment, she entertained the idea of sending another in her stead—one of her employees, perhaps—but she quickly dismissed the thought. No, she would go, of course. She was quite sure the king would not look kindly upon her sending someone in her place. Better to feel like one's life hangs by a thread than to cut the thread yourself and know the truth of it.

She read the letter once more, ensuring that she had the correct time then glanced out the window of her second story office at Baresh's branch of the Golden Oars. The sun was low in the sky and soon night would settle upon the city.

The meeting was set for early the following day, and she knew the wisest thing would be to spend the remainder of her day preparing for any questions the king may have, and getting to bed early to ensure that she was well-rested. The wisest thing maybe, but she found that, just then, what she wanted more than rest or preparation was a drink. A drink to steady nerves that were so rarely unsteadied. Yes, that would do perfectly.

She rose from her desk, folding the letter and sliding it inside of one of the drawers. She took a moment to grab the key that hung about her neck from a silver chain and lock the drawer before throwing a scarf about her shoulders. She had lived in Baresh for many years, yet she had grown up in a much warmer town, and her body had never become adjusted to the cooler climate of the city. She glanced at the drawer, considered reading the letter again, as if she might divine from its contents some clue to the drastic change that had overcome the king, then, frowning, she forced herself to turn and walk out of the office.

"Ma'am?" Her secretary, a competent if plain girl, asked from her seat behind her desk, "Is there something I can help you with?"

"No, thank you," Maladine said, "but it is kind of you to ask." The woman smiled wide at that, opening her mouth as if to speak, but Maladine spoke first. "Enjoy your night, Brigitte. I will not be back in the office until tomorrow."

"Of course, ma'am," the woman said, and Maladine thought she detected a hint of disappointment that whatever words she had been about to say had gone unsaid.

And that was alright. Maladine was always kind to those under her not because she cared a whit for their thoughts or opinions but because, should anything happen and they somehow gained a position above her, she wanted to be sure that they thought well of her. Always kind but never friendly. Friends, after all, were nothing but one more weight dragging a person down. "Good night, Brigitte," she said, heading for the door.

"Good night, ma'am."

Outside, the sun had not yet set, but the air was cool against her skin, and she pulled the scarf tighter about herself as she stepped out into the street. With some day still left, she knew that the streets of the poorer districts would be crowded with men and women going about their lives, working hard to provide food and shelter for their families. But here, in the heart of the noble quarter, the streets were nearly empty, save for one well-dressed couple she saw in the distance, strolling casually down the street as if the approaching night held no concern for them.

And why should it? Sure, there had been rumors of disappearances in the city of late, but such men and women as this, born to privilege and power—and the safety both provided—would no doubt think the rumors exaggerated if, that was, they were true at all. It was hard to believe that the shadows of night hid monsters when so much of your life had been spent under the sun. Maladine could have told them the truth of things, had she wished to, but she did not. After all, if the disappearances continued as they had been, she suspected they would learn it soon enough.

She considered going back inside and calling for Brigitte to send for one of her body guards—men who were almost always with her when she made her way through the city. Though the nobles might not have learned it, Maladine's past had taught her the lesson well that the quiet peace of the night was no more than an illusion, easily shattered. Still, she knew that it would take time for the man to arrive, and she did not want to wait, felt that she needed a drink now, a drink to bring her perspective back into focus, to help her find some means of turning even this strange situation with the king to her advantage.

And with that thought, Maladine Caulia did something she made it a point never to do—she ventured forth with nothing but her hope—a hope that everything would be okay—to guard her. As she walked, she got the distinct feeling that she was being watched, but she looked around herself multiple times, searching for the not-quite normal shadows that she knew often presaged a shattering of the night's illusion. None were in sight, and when she stopped to listen the only sound she heard was that of her own breath in her lungs. *Just your nerves, woman, nothing else.*

Still, the feeling of being watched, of being followed, did not leave her, and she increased her pace the slightest bit, not a casual walk but a purposeful one, the walk of a woman who had important business to attend to—which she did. She did not run, never that, for running was a sign of weakness, a trait displayed by prey, and where there was prey there were, inevitably, predators.

She made her way toward a nearby tavern called the *The King's Own*. It wasn't, of course—one of the many benefits of being a king is that you had people to bring and pour your ale for you. But the tavern was a nice, clean place, much finer than those filthy, rowdy taverns that she had come to know—always to her detriment—in her youth.

There was a man waiting outside in a well-made, expensive shirt, and trousers that did little to hide the bulk of muscle underneath. He bowed low as she approached. "Madam Caulia," he said, "it is a pleasure to see you once more."

Maladine didn't answer—the man was a simple bouncer after all, never mind what he wore—and being kind had its limits. Instead, she walked to the door. The man opened it for her, and she stepped inside with the slightest nod of her head.

She took a moment to survey the room. Several noblemen and noblewomen she recognized sat in the high-backed, cushioned booths, but they were minor nobles and of no real concern. After all, most of them she knew from their visits to the Golden Oars when they came requiring—never asking or begging, not nobles— a loan of funds for some venture of theirs. Despite their frilly words and false talk, such ventures usually amounted to little more than young noblemen and women borrowing money to purchase new dresses or trousers for some ball or other while they waited on their parents to give them their allowances.

In her role working for the *Golden Oars* bank, Maladine had loaned coin to more than a few of them, but when they glanced to the door and saw her, they looked away as if not noticing her and that was as was expected. She, after all, was not of noble blood no matter how much coin she had. And that was fine with Maladine. The coin was all she wanted, and that she had in abundance, more than any two or three of the nobles and their families combined, for her masters paid well as long as she got her job done. But the nobles, of course, did not know it.

Maladine allowed herself a small smile as she sauntered to the bar. "Ah, Mrs. Caulia," the barkeep said, bowing his head low, "I hope the day sees you well." Alec was a handsome man with a shock of blond hair that fell to the length of his chin, and she could

A Sellsword's Valor

see the muscles of his arms even as he finished cleaning a glass mug and set it back down. He was the type of man that many women would have swooned over—and many did, noblewomen included—during their visits to the tavern. Maladine, however, was not one of them, for she had little interest in men or women either beyond how they might benefit her in reaching her goals.

"Alec," she said.

"I must be blessed by the gods themselves to have you visit me again so soon," he said, smiling a smile that had no doubt undressed many maidens in its time.

"Rather," Maladine said, not taken in by the smile in the slightest, "that I visit wine, and you happen to be here as well."

The blond man laughed, not put off by her words and why would he be? After all, there were a lot of women in the city, and Maladine—who made it her business to collect information as well as coin—knew for a certainty that Alec had bedded at least two of the women here, who even now giggled and fawned over their husbands.

"Would you like for me to prepare you a seat at your usual booth, mistress?"

Maladine glanced to the booth at which she normally sat, considering. It was a comfortable seat, comfortable and isolated, protected from the world on both sides by the high backed chairs...but just then it seemed somehow suffocating to her, and she felt a hint of claustrophobia at the thought of it. "I will take my drink at the bar tonight, Alec," she said.

"Of course, madam," he said, "and what would you like to drink on this fine evening?"

"The usual, Alec," she said, sitting on one of the bar stools.

"Very well, ma'am." The blond barkeep stepped away and returned a few moments later with a glass of red wine. Maladine placed a coin on the table and slid it to him.

"Thank you, Alec."

"Of course, mistress. If you need anything else, just let me know."

How about a look alike to go to a meeting with a king that scares me? Do you have one of those lying around? But she only nodded as the barkeep turned and went to check on another customer.

Maladine watched him leave and saw a man further down the bar staring at her, eyeing her up and down as if she were some horse he was considering purchasing. She pretended not to notice, taking a sip of her wine. The very last thing she wanted just then was to find herself in a conversation with a fool who thought a woman enjoyed being ogled like a piece of meat.

She took another sip of wine as she thought about the coming council meeting. She wondered if it would have anything to do with the people who had come up missing over the last few months, or if Belgarin intended to amass troops for another campaign against Isalla. The first didn't concern her much, as she knew people always disappeared in the poor districts of large cities. The second though…the second could be quite interesting and, if she played her cards right, beneficial as well. After all, wars cost money—money that the king would need to borrow and when looking to borrow coin, where better than the richest bank in all of Telrear, the Golden Oars?

She risked a glance up. The man at the end of the bar was still eyeing her, but he didn't whistle or shout, and that was something at least. Such things were not tolerated in the tavern as it catered almost exclusively to nobility. Not that noble women didn't have affairs—Maladine had dealt with enough to know that it was one of their favorite pastimes—but even such pampered fools as they were, they still understood the importance of discretion in some matters. At least, most of them did. Still, shouting or not, the man's steady, unflinching gaze made his intentions—and his wishes—clear enough. Maladine felt a flash of irritation at the man's boldness, was considering saying something, when the door of the tavern opened behind her, and she turned to look, grateful for the distraction.

She expected to see some pompous lord or preening lady, so she was surprised to find that the man who entered didn't look like any noble she'd ever seen, and she'd seen more than enough to last a lifetime. In fact, all in all, Maladine decided that the newcomer was, without a doubt, the strangest-looking man she'd ever seen in a life filled with strange men.

His dark skin marked him as one of the Parnen, the race of quiet, conservative people to Telrear's south. The Parnen were known to be almost impossibly subdued, particularly around strangers, and in large part, kept to their own country and their own people. Seeing one here, in the north of Telrear and so far from his own country, would have been enough of a reason for the whispers of the nobles upon his entrance, but the fact that the man was Parnen was not the oddest thing about him.

His long, dark hair hung past his shoulders and things were intertwined within it. It took Maladine a moment of curious consideration to realize that they were in fact bells, bells that rang and jangled with each step the Parnen took toward the bar. He wore an outlandish motley of various shades and hues, each of them nice, fashionable pieces of attire on their own, but when put together, they had the effect of making the man look like some strange, strutting rainbow, and Maladine found herself unable to look away from the garish display. The man was smiling as if he hadn't a care in the world, ignorant or unconcerned by the stares that followed him as he made his way to the bar.

The barkeep, Alec, at least, didn't seem disturbed in the slightest by the man's appearance, and he bowed his head in a recognition that was further proven by the smile that rose on his face. "Ah, Mr. Leomin. It is quite a pleasure to see you again, sir."

The Parnen grinned displaying a set of very straight, very white teeth. "Ah, master Alec," he said, sitting down at one of the stools at the bar, "the pleasure is all mine, I assure you, though it is kind of you to say so."

"Please, Mr. Leomin," Alec said, "you do me too much honor. Still, I seem to recall telling you that just 'Alec' would do fine."

"Yes," the Parnen said, as Alec placed a mug of ale in front of him, "and I seem to recall telling you that Leomin would do. My father is mister, my mother miss, and I, for better or worse, am simply Leomin."

The bartender nodded. "Very well, sir. I confess that I am surprised—though pleased—to see you again. I had thought your business was taking you out of Baresh."

"And so had I, alas," Leomin nodded, "but there has been some small matter with my finances, I'm afraid."

"Oh?" Alec asked. "Nothing serious, I hope."

The Parnen shrugged as if it mattered little. "There are those who would tell you, friend Alec, that any matter of finance is serious, but I am not one of them. My mother and father would no doubt tell you as much, were they here to do so." He leaned in conspiratorially, and Maladine found herself sitting forward to hear the strange man's words. "I'm afraid they think me quite irresponsible. Both fiscally and physically," he said, winking.

Maladine was intrigued by the Parnen despite herself, but she did her best to affect disinterest as she took a drink of her wine and forced her eyes on the bar in front of her.

Alec laughed. "That, Leomin, is perhaps a trait we both share."

"No," the Parnen breathed, his eyes wide, "say it isn't so, friend Alec. After all, you own this wonderful tavern, as fine an eating and drinking establishment as I have ever had the pleasure of patronizing. Truly, you strike me as a man my esteemed father would love to call son." He let out a small sigh, grinning. "If you've any plans on visiting my home country, I do believe he is taking applications for the position even now."

Alec chuckled, but then his expression grew sober. "Wait, is that the problem? Forgive me for prying, but if they've cut you off, surely—"

"Oh, no," the Parnen said, waving a hand that glimmered with stones of various shades and hues, a match for the eccentric attire he wore, "it is nothing so serious as that, I assure you. My father would never allow one of the Blood to travel into the world a pauper, not even his wayward son." He winked again. "It would reflect badly on him, you understand? No, it is only that the baggage train that was carrying my supplies and allowance has been somewhat delayed." He sighed heavily. "On the morrow, I will be forced to travel into one of the lending houses in this fine city of yours and make some inquiries as to what monies might be forwarded to me in the meantime. After all," he laughed, "I have a certain wayward, irresponsible lifestyle to uphold, do I not?"

Alec grinned, snapping his fingers as if an idea had just struck him. "But Leomin, it might very well have been the providence of the gods themselves that brought you in tonight." He glanced at Maladine. "I hope I'm not speaking out of turn when I say that Miss Caulia here is, in fact, the representative of the Golden Oars bank. Perhaps she could help you with your temporary problem."

Maladine started, surprised to find herself the center of the conversation. "Um...well..." she said, hesitating. She studied the man's clothes and the jewelry that bedecked both hands and his neck, a variety of precious—and very expensive—stones, never mind how they clashed. "Perhaps, I might be of some service to you."

The Parnen seemed to consider for a moment then shook his head slowly. "It is very kind of you both," he said, "but as is often the case, I have not come for business, but pleasure. It is, my father would tell you, one of my many failings. Besides, I would not want to bother..." He paused, turning his eyes on Maladine, and she found to her surprise that her heart sped up in her chest. "Miss Caulia, wasn't it?"

Maladine was having difficulty speaking under that gaze, but she finally managed to get the words out. "Um...yes," she said, "it is."

He smiled then, and Maladine felt an unfamiliar thrill run through her at the sight of it. "No," he said, turning to Alec, "I thank you for the attempt, kind Alec, but I do not wish to bother Mrs. Caulia anymore. People come to taverns, after all, to drink—that much I have learned and not from the mouths of my father's tutors either. Now," he said, bowing his head to each of them in turn, "I'm quite sure that you are both busy, and I have intruded upon your time as much as I dare. I will retire to one of your fine booths, but I wish you both a merry and," he glanced at Caulia, "eventful or uneventful night, depending upon which it is that you seek."

With that, the Parnen rose, grabbing his glass of ale and made his way to one of the booths. As he did, a man who Maladine had not noticed moved toward the booth, withdrawing a white cloth from the pocket of his trousers and wiping down the cushioned chair before the Parnen finally sat. The man had a jagged scar across his face, and he wore nice clothes, though nothing so fine—or outlandish—as the Parnen himself. By the way he bowed low to the dusky-skinned Parnen as he sat, it was clear that he was a servant of some kind.

Maladine watched them for a minute, then turned back to the blond-headed barkeep only to see that he was watching them as well, a small smile on his face. "Alec?"

The barkeep blinked and turned to her. "Forgive me, Miss Caulia, what may I help you with?"

"Well," Maladine said, "you can start by refilling my glass—the same as the last. And next, you can tell me about that man there."

"Mr. Leomin do you mean?" the barkeep asked as he poured her some more wine. "There's not very much to tell, I suppose. Mr. Leomin has visited us a few times now, and it is always a treat." Maladine was surprised to see the man smiling even as he spoke of it. "Have you ever met a man quite so interesting, Mrs. Caulia?"

"I'd say he's interesting," Maladine said, glancing at the man once more, "the clothes themselves are enough to give any tailor the fits."

Alec laughed at that. "Mr. Leomin always comes dressed so. I asked him about it the first time—perhaps a week ago now?—and he told me that our country is full of such wonderful fashions that he could not choose one and decided that he didn't have to."

Maladine nodded slowly at that, thinking. The Parnen was interesting, that was certain, and she found herself being attracted to his strangeness for reasons she didn't understand and couldn't have explained if asked. Still, whatever magnetism the dark-skinned man had—and there was no denying that he did—it was not the only thing which drew her eye. The man was obviously rich. The rings on his fingers alone were worth a small fortune. "Is he truly so wealthy?" Maladine asked. "Or is it just some show he contrives?"

The barkeep grinned. "I suppose that if you asked Mr. Leomin, he would claim that everyone is always contriving to put on a show, only that some are better at it than others. Still, he's here on business from the Parnen capital. He is a visiting dignitary to Telrear and, as I understand it, he is of royal blood. He told me that his parents sent him to Telrear in the hopes that witnessing our country's, let me see, how did he put it? Oh yes, 'manic boisterousness' I believe he said, would somehow calm him down. Apparently," he said with an amused shake of his head, "it hasn't worked."

Maladine nodded, but she was hardly listening, thinking of the man's words. A rich man but not just rich, a royal of the Parnen blood-line. Such a man as that would have connections any bank's representative would dream of making not to mention the wealth his family no doubt commanded. She said a quick thanks to the gods that she had been moved to get a drink. Opportunities such as this rarely came along, and Maladine had learned long ago never to let them pass when they did. "Thank you, Alec."

"Of course, ma'am," the barkeep said, then he excused himself to help another customer.

When he was gone, Maladine turned and studied the Parnen, trying to figure out what it was about him that was so captivating. Finally, she rose and started toward the man's table almost before she knew she'd made the decision to do so. As she walked to the table, the Parnen looked up at her from where he'd been studying the ale in his mug as if intending to divine some secrets within. The servant took a step forward, putting himself between the Parnen and Maladine as if to protect him should she attempt anything.

"F-forgive me," Maladine said, surprised, "I hadn't meant any offense."

"Oh, do relax, won't you, Servant?" the Parnen said in a tone that was both weary and amused. "The kind lady does not mean me any harm, surely."

The scarred man frowned at her, but he took a step back so that he was no longer between the two of them. "You must forgive Servant," the Parnen said, sighing, "my parents found him on the borders of our lands when he was but a child. His family had been set upon by bandits, and he was the only one left alive, though, I'm afraid he did not escape without some souvenirs from the encounter." He nodded at the man's scarred face. "Still," the Parnen said, smiling, "Servant may not be pretty to look upon, lady, but I assure you that he will do you no harm so long as I tell him. He is nothing if not loyal."

"I'm sorry," Maladine said, "but...the way you say it...is his name 'Servant'?"

The Parnen shrugged. "It does as well as any other, does it not? I'm sure that he had another, once upon a time, but all those who knew it are dead. Except him, of course, but Servant has not spoken since he was found so many years ago. Now," he said, waving his hand dismissively, "I do not wish to bore you with such trifling matters. Tell me, what can I do for you?"

Maladine cleared her throat, feeling out of her element for the first time she could remember. She took a slow, deep breath in an attempt to gather herself. "I...actually, Mr. Leomin, I came to speak with you about something that I might be able to do for you."

"Oh?" the dusky-skinned man asked. "Well, in that case, please do have a seat," he said, waving at the chair across from him in invitation.

Maladine felt an unexpected thrill of pleasure run through her, but she pushed it down and concentrated on finding her equilibrium once more as she sat. "Yes, well, forgive me, but I couldn't help overhearing some of your conversation with the barkeep."

"Alec," the Parnen said, nodding with a smile, "a truly gracious host. There are those in my father's country who would do well to learn from such as him."

"Yes," Maladine said, "well, I heard you mention some issue with your baggage train being delayed."

"Ah, that," the Parnen said, frowning, "yes, a most embarrassing predicament to find oneself in, particularly when one is accustomed to…" He shrugged. "Well, a particular life-style."

"As you say," Maladine said, pushing her hair back with one hand, "though I thought that, perhaps, I might be of some small help with your…predicament, as you call it."

"Is that so, Miss Caulia?" the Parnen said. His eyes met hers, and she felt as if some invisible power lurched in her chest, making her heart race and a sweet ache form in her as she looked at him. Gods, but the man was beautiful. Never mind the mismatched clothes or the bells that dangled from his hair, there was something about him that she found herself immensely attracted to. An unusual occurrence, as she had not found herself attracted to any man since she'd been a young girl, but there it was. Under the man's dark gaze, she found all of the lessons she'd taught herself over a lifetime—lessons of manipulation, of using whatever means she had to gain advantage—vanishing in an instant. Even thoughts of the gold she could make seemed trivial and unimportant beside the power which now gripped her.

"Tell me, Miss Caulia," he said, and Maladine found herself watching his lips as he spoke, her body feeling flushed and hot, "is business the only thing I have to thank for such a beautiful companion as yourself?"

Maladine swallowed, feeling as if some force had taken over her body. "I…that is…no. I wanted to talk to you."

"And yet you do not any longer?" the man asked, leaning closer, and Maladine found herself leaning across the table toward him, so that she could feel the heat of his breath on her face, could smell some minty herb or clove on it that gave her a fresh rush of pleasure.

"Yes," she managed, "yes."

The Parnen smiled. "Ah, then it is good between us, Miss Caulia, but it will be better still before the night is done. Good is good, after all, but great..." He paused, shrugging. "Well, let us find out together, shall we?"

"Yes," Maladine said, surprised to hear the excitement in her own voice.

"Would you like to hear my single, overriding philosophy on life, Miss Caulia?" the Parnen said, his voice soft and strong at once.

She nodded, not trusting herself to speak as she leaned in even closer so that their mouths were only inches apart.

"Very well," the Parnen said. "It is that, in any matter great or small, a wise man will always put pleasure before business. For it is why we exist, is it not?"

Maladine grinned, her face flushing. "Yes."

The Parnen smiled wide. "And so I have told you my secret, the guiding principle of my life, yet the words do not do it justice, not truly. Come," he said, offering her his hand, "let me show you."

***

You really should relax, Aaron. Nathan won't thank you for wearing a hole in his floor from all your pacing.

Aaron sighed, walking back to the table where Darrell and Caleb waited and sat in one of the empty chairs. "They will be alright," Darrell said. "Leomin strikes me as a clever man, and Wendell is not without his own...resources."

Aaron grunted. "Well, they'd better be, Darrell. We've spent nearly two weeks in this damned city, and we've got nothing to show for it. Another week, two at the most, and then we've got to start heading back to Isalla either way. Those bastards Grinner and Hale won't wait around forever. If this doesn't work..." He finished with a shrug. They all knew well enough what would happen if the plan failed, so there was no use saying it. Without proof to show to the leaders of the alliance, the armies would leave and there would be little hope left for the people of Telrear. Anyway, it had been his plan and, if it failed, it would be his failure. The thing about failures, though, was that it was rarely only the men who failed that suffered for them.

"It is a good plan," Darrell said as if he knew what Aaron had been thinking, "it will work."

The youth, Caleb, nodded. "Based on what factors we understand, I calculate a one in four chance of success."

They both turned and looked at him then, and the youth ducked his head low, clearing his throat. "That's um...actually quite good. Under the circumstances."

Aaron was not a man used to waiting, to not being in control. For the majority of his life, he had kept others at a distance, relying only on himself. Since then, he'd learned the importance of friendship, of having people who you would die for and who would die for you. But some habits were hard to let go, and it was all he could do to keep from rushing out into the night himself to make sure that Leomin and Wendell were alright.

Aaron, you're pacing again.

Aaron looked down and was surprised to find that the Virtue was right, though he didn't even remember rising from his chair. He was just about to sit once more when he heard a key turn in the tavern's door, and the two men walked inside, Leomin with a wide smile on his face, Wendell looking tired and irritable.

Aaron hurried to the two men and for all their talk and feigned calm, Darrell and Caleb were close behind him. "Well?" he said. "How'd it go?"

"Wouldn't be askin' that if you had to listen to all the screamin'," Wendell muttered, clearly annoyed.

"Friend Wendell," Leomin said, turning to him, "we've gone over this. During the act of lovemaking, passions run high, and it is not so unusual to hear such 'screams' as you call them." He smiled as if remembering. "Though I myself find them to be more of some grand masterpiece, a music all their own."

"It ain't screamin' in general that I mind," the sergeant said, "it's just that I'm used to hearin' it mostly out of the woman. And what need did I have to stand right on the other side of the damned door, anyway?"

Leomin cleared his throat. "The Lady Maladine was quite...vigorous, and they were not screams, dear Wendell. Manly roars of passion perhaps but no more than that."

Aaron frowned and opened his mouth to speak, but the sergeant beat him to it.

"Sure sounded like screams to me. And that still don't explain why I had to stand by the door, folks walkin' down the hall lookin' at me like they done found a fly in their beer and I'm it. All the while me standin' there not knowin' whether to grin or look serious, or which'd make me look less like a man needs the city guard called on 'em."

Leomin sighed, "A servant would not abandon his master's company and would be sure to stay within shouting distance, in case he was needed."

"Speakin' of that," Wendell said, his expression darkening, "what was all that callin' me 'Servant,' anyway? You get to drink, get laid, and I don't even have a gods-cursed name?"

"Yes, that," Leomin said, suddenly looking embarrassed, "well, I thought that it would give our story a touch of...verisimilitude."

Wendell frowned in confusion. "Veri-what? Never mind, I'll tell you very. I'm very pissed off about the fact that while you gallivanted and screamed like a girl woken from a nightmare, I didn't even get so much as a drink."

Leomin cocked his head. "If you had wanted a drink, friend Wendell, you needed only to ask. I would have been happy to have ordered one for you."

"Yeah, well, that'd be a trick wouldn't it," Wendell growled, "considerin' as not only do I not have a name, but I haven't spoken a word since I was a gods-cursed child."

"Ah, right," Leomin said, "well, surely a bit of embellishment was called for to—"

"Enough," Aaron said, holding up a hand, "gods, enough already. Just tell me how it went. What happened?"

They all sat around the common room of the tavern as Leomin recounted the evening's events in precise—and often painful—detail, with Wendell jumping in from time to time, usually with a muttered curse. By the time the Parnen was done telling his story, sunrise was only a few hours away, and they all looked exhausted. "Alright," Aaron said, nodding, "so you got her attention. That's good."

"I'll say he did," Wendell muttered, "about three or four times. Not that I was counting."

Darrel raised an eyebrow at the scarred sergeant. "Forgive me, Sergeant, but it seems as if you were counting."

The sergeant shrugged. "Not much else to do, standing outside that damn door half the night."

Aaron couldn't help but grin as he spoke. "And did she say anything useful to us? Does she know anything about what's going on?"

"Don't think there was much talkin' going on, you ask me," Wendell said. "Some screaming—Leomin, that—and that was about it."

Leomin scowled at Wendell before turning to Aaron, his expression sobering. "Maladine did not know any specifics, of course, for whatever is transpiring in the castle she is not a part of it, of that much I can assure you. Still," he said, hesitating, "she said some things that I think you will not like."

Aaron raised an eyebrow, waiting, and the Parnen nodded. "During the times between our...bouts," he said, clearing his throat, "Maladine confided that the king has not been acting like his normal self of late. She explained that he was once given to tantrums and would shout angrily at his counselors, lashing out when any subject arose for which he found distaste. Even his advisor, Caldwell, she claims often talked of him as if he were a fool behind his back. But since arriving back from his battle with Isalla, Maladine says that the king's demeanor has...changed."

Aaron leaned forward, feeling that he knew what was coming but needing to hear it anyway. "Changed how?"

"Boyce Kevlane," Caleb breathed, and they all turned to look at him curiously. The boy seemed to shrink under the attention before finally shrugging his shoulders. "Palendesh told me about him. He's not a nice man at all."

"No, Caleb," Leomin agreed, "he is not a nice man and, I'm afraid that your thoughts mirror my own. Maladine doesn't know of Boyce Kevlane, of course, at least not as anything more than a children's story, but she told me that since he's been back, the king has been acting differently. No longer does he seem like an ill-tempered child determined to get his way, but a man of utter confidence, one who speaks and expects nothing but to be obeyed."

"I see," Aaron said.

The Parnen sighed. "The truth is, it's more than that. It wasn't just what she told me, but the way she told me—Maladine was afraid, Aaron. I grew to know her some small bit in the time that I was with her, and I do not think she is one to frighten easily. But Belgarin—or, at least, the man posing as Belgarin—scares her very much indeed."

"It's Kevlane," Aaron said, knowing it was true even as he said it. "it has to be."

The youth, Caleb, nodded. "Yes, Palendesh agrees that there is a nine in ten chance that the man ruling in Baresh is no longer King Belgarin."

"But if that's the case," Darrell said, frowning, "then what has happened to the real Belgarin?"

Aaron sighed, sitting back in his chair. "It seems clear enough, doesn't it?" He glanced around the table at the confused expressions of the other men then turned to see the youth nodding to him. "Look at what we know," he said, turning back to the three men, "we know that Boyce Kevlane would do anything to cause more pain and suffering, to have as many killed as possible."

"You especially, I imagine," Wendell said, "on account of you throwin' him out that window."

"It was a balcony," Aaron corrected, "but never mind. You're right enough. Even in the fight for Perennia, when it looked as if Belgarin's army might be pushed back, Kevlane—still injured from his fall from the balcony—showed up and jammed the gate in an attempt to ensure Perennia was conquered."

"Ah, right," Darrell said, a small smile on his face, "and this, as I recall, is the treachery that prompted the idiotic heroics that you took part in, is it not? Charging out of a defensible position and a natural funnel into an army of thousands?"

"Right," Aaron said, scowling at the swordmaster, "but you're missing the point. Despite Kevlane's efforts, the walls held and Belgarin's army retreated. Knowing what you know of Kevlane, how do you think he felt about that?"

Darell's smile faded, and his eyes grew wide. "But why? Why would Belgarin retreat in the first place?"

Aaron shrugged. "We don't know. We may never know, and it doesn't really matter in any case. What matters is that he did. I can't imagine Kevlane was too pleased about that, and it certainly wasn't in his plan. So he had to improvise. Not that much trouble, I'm sure, for a man who can wear any face he wants."

"Wait a minute," Wendell said, frowning in concentration, "are you saying that this ancient wizard, what, exactly? That he took Belgarin's place? And you ain't never said what happened to the real prince. What is he squirreled away in some closet somewhere?"

"No, Wendell," Aaron said, "I don't believe so. I believe that, on our return to Perennia, I will have to let Adina know that she has lost another brother."

"Damn," the sergeant said, "but I wouldn't want to be a royal right now. Bastards are dyin' left and right."

They lapsed into a brief silence then, each of them nursing their own thoughts, their own worries, until finally Leomin spoke. "So what do we do now, Aaron?"

They all turned to look at him, and Aaron felt a flash of irritation. Why him? He'd only ever wanted to be a sellsword, that was all. To make a little coin and be left alone. Why was all of this suddenly his responsibility? Why did they look to him for answers as if he had any to give?

My father often asked himself the same question, Co said into his mind.

And what answer did he come up with, firefly? Aaron thought, *because I'm out of them.*

He never found one, the Virtue said, her voice musing.

Aaron grunted. *Thanks for that, lightning bug. You're a big help as always.*

I believe you're missing the point, Aaron. It was not important whether or not my father was able to convince himself. Others were convinced for him. Sometimes, a man does not choose his path, but the world chooses it for him. In such times, with such men, the only thing to do is walk the path before you, wherever it may lead.

And sometimes, Aaron thought back, the world doesn't choose a man's path any more than he does himself. Sometimes, it's a fucking glowing ball of light.

Yes, Co said, amused, sometimes.

Aaron sighed, meeting the eyes of the waiting men and boy. "Our goals haven't changed. Now, more than ever, we have to make it back to Isalla with proof of what's happening." He frowned, considering. "We will need all the help we can find, in the days to come."

"There's still somethin' I'm not getting," Wendell said, scratching his head in a confused way that would have been comical under other circumstances. "If all that you say is true and Boyce Kevlane has really taken Belgarin's place, then why hold a tournament? Seems to me that the man would be concerned with marchin' his army back toward Perennia not sittin' on his ass and eatin' pastries while fools play at war. Not exactly the actions of a man whose whole goal is to conquer the world."

"You're wrong, Wendell," Aaron said, dreading what he had to say next, "they're exactly the actions such a man might take."

"The disappearances." They turned to see the youth, Caleb, sitting with his hands clenched into fists on the tabletop, his eyes wide. "Gods, but I should have seen it sooner."

"Wait a damned minute," Wendell said, "what disappearances, the ones in the city? What's that got to do with anything?"

"Go on, kid," Aaron said, "tell them."

The kid shook his head, his face going pale. "Those men and women that were disappearing, they weren't just leaving or being murdered in some back-alley squabbles or crimes. They were being taken on purpose. Gods," he said again, "Bert as much as told us. Only the strong, he said, only the fast. Men and women in prime physical condition. Men and women," he said, turning to Aaron, "who would make the best test subjects."

"Yes," Aaron said, "whatever may have happened in the past, whatever promise Kevlane made to Aaron Caltriss, it is clear that he's broken it. He has begun his experiments once again. The tournament is nothing but a ruse to draw in candidates for his experiments."

"Aaron," Darrell began, "if this is true..."

"Not if, Darrell," Aaron said, "it is true."

"Very well," the swordmaster said, nodding his head again, "but this is no normal tournament, Aaron. From what Nathan said, the purse is several times larger than any that has ever been offered before." His expression grew troubled. "For such a fortune, men and women will travel from all over the country."

"Yes," Aaron said, "and that's exactly what Kevlane is hoping for."

"Well shit," Wendell said. "It doesn't seem to me..."

A strange feeling of something being suddenly, terribly wrong overcame Aaron, and though the sergeant continued to speak, his voice seemed to come in an indecipherable whisper. *Co*, Aaron thought, his heart speeding up in his chest, *what is it?*

*I don't...*the Virtue began, her own voice confused and afraid, but she trailed off into silence.

The others were saying something else, but Aaron might as well have been alone in the room for all the notice he took of them. His mind was on that feeling of strangeness, of wrongness that had come over him so abruptly. He reached down into himself, gathering up the power of the bond and, not knowing how he did it, he sent tendrils of power questing out around him in all directions. Where they touched the others, he felt their emotions, their worries and their fears. Then he reached further, the tendrils of power, visible in his mind's eye as thousands of extending strands of magenta light, stretching past the men, past the tavern itself and out into the city.

At first, there was nothing, and he thought that perhaps he had imagined it after all. Not wholly convinced, he dug deeper into the power, gritting his teeth as he strained against its invisible force, closing his eyes and bending over the table as he did. For several moments, he still felt nothing. There was only the darkness around them, a city draped in fear, its citizens lying in their beds afraid that they or someone they loved would be the next ones taken. He moved past those hundreds of worries, hundreds of fears, and searched further, bending his will in the direction from which he felt the disturbance had come.

Nothing. Only darkness and emptiness until—there. He felt something, felt it and, in that instant, knew it for what it was. Not an emptiness, not exactly. It was as the feeling of something half-formed, something incomplete. A creature that had once been a man but was no longer, one who'd had that which made a man taken from him, ripped from him as he screamed his tortured agony, his voice falling only on the ears of those who did not care about its pleas or its pain.

"Aaron."

Aaron jerked back in his seat, gasping for breath, his eyes snapping open. "What?" he said, momentarily disoriented as he turned to the scarred sergeant.

"I said, is everything okay, sir?" Wendell asked.

Aaron, it's comi—

"Run," Aaron croaked, his eyes wide, and the others only stared at him as if he was possessed by some spirit of madness.

"Aaron," Darrell said, "what is—"

"Run, damn you!" he bellowed, rising from his chair so fast that it fell backward. It was then that the door to the tavern gave a warning creak and exploded inward in a shower of splinters and shattered wood.

CHAPTER SIXTEEN

"I still think this is a bad idea," Adina said.

"Look at you," May said as if she hadn't heard, standing behind Adina in the tailor's looking glass, a pleased expression on her face as if she were some proud mother shopping with her favored daughter. Adina wondered if any of the criminals May spent her life dealing with would have recognized her during the last hour that she'd spent clucking and tutting like a mother hen over the dresses Adina tried on.

"Finally," May said, turning to the tailor—a thin, gaunt-looking man with gray hair who was smiling wearily. The club owner gave one firm nod. "It's about time you brought us something to match my sister's beauty. Better than those rags you showed us before."

"Which rags were those, May?" Adina asked dryly. "Were they in the first batch of one hundred or the second? I'm afraid I've lost count."

"Just stunning," May said, turning back and examining Adina in the mirror once more, "Fields, but if you're not careful men will take you for a goddess come to visit the city when you're walking the streets. I'd be surprised if you don't have priests following you around before long asking to swear oaths to you," she said, winking, "or forsake those they've already taken, if that's more of what you'd like."

Adina sighed. "May, honestly, I think there has to be a better way than this. And this dress is so tight I can barely breathe."

"It's perfect, dear," May said distractedly, then turned to the tailor. "Now, how much do you aim to set us back to buy this dress, and the shoes along with it? And I warn you," she said, somehow looming over the thin older man despite the fact that he stood several feet away, and she hadn't moved any closer, "we are no country bumpkins to be taken advantage of. I know a fair price when I hear it, and I won't be swindled by the likes of you."

The man blinked, a nervous look on his face as if he'd just woken to find himself holding the cub of a very large, very angry she-bear. Which, of course, wasn't that far from the truth. "I...madam, I'm sure that we can come to some arrangement, and I would never think of 'swindling' anyone, I assure you. I run an honest business and—"

May snorted. "In my experience, thieves don't advertise their occupation to those they intend to rob, mister."

"Honestly, May," Adina said, "the man is just doing his job, that's all. And I feel like you're not even listening to me."

"Now," May said, not listening to her, "why don't you tell me how much you'll charge for the dress and the shoes—and some pretty bauble for her to wear. One that will set off her eyes—my but they are lovely—and be quick about it. I won't sit here while you come up with some extra charge to steal what little money we might have. Tell me your number, and I'll tell you just how much of a thief you are."

It was another half an hour before Adina and May stepped out of the tailor's and into the street. Adina took a deep breath of the cool air, grateful to finally be out of the shop and done trying on dresses. She wondered idly if a person could spontaneously become claustrophobic. If the club owner noticed the princess's sigh of relief, she gave no sign. Instead she grunted in satisfaction, closing her coin purse and sliding it into a dress she had somehow picked out during the interminable length of time it had taken for Adina to try on all the dresses May had wanted her to. "That'll teach that old swindler. I wasn't born yesterday, and I won't be giving up my coins just because a man says 'silk.'"

"May," Adina tried one final time, "do you really think this is the best way? I mean, I was thinking about it, and there are some other options we might pursu—"

The club owner clucked, waving a hand dismissively, "Oh never mind that, dearie. This will work you have my word. Why, once he sees you in that dress, that guard would abandon his post, his family, and anything else he had, if that's what it took to have a drink with you. Now, stop worrying so much. Do try to have a good time." She grabbed Adina by the shoulders and held her out at arm's length. "Relax, dear, you're not exactly marching to your own execution, are you?"

That was true, at least, but Adina thought that if she'd been forced to try on any more dresses, the execution would have been preferable.

The club owner studied Adina, looking her up and down as if she was a child examining her favorite doll. "My, my, my," she said, shaking her head as if in wonder, "That dress is truly remarkable."

Adina rolled her eyes. "I guess you'd know considering the fact that you seem to have purchased some for yourself as well," she said, motioning to the bag of clothes in the other woman's hand.

"What, these?" May asked innocently. "Well, dear, I don't expect you to understand, but plain, simple women like myself well, we have to have our fun too, don't we?"

Adina snorted. "You're a lot of things, May, but plain and simple aren't among them. As for having fun..." She smiled. "I wonder what Thom would think."

May turned her nose up with disdain. "That old fool can think whatever he likes, I'm sure, just so long as he keeps it to himself." She frowned. "It isn't as if we're married, after all. That old stubborn bastard wouldn't know how to find a wife, if he pulled one up in his fishing net."

Adina's smile slowly faded. "Is everything alright with Thom, May?"

The club owner waved a hand. "Oh, it's fine. Don't you worry about your old, May. I've conquered harder opponents than some gray-haired first mate, I can promise you that."

Adina gave the woman a smile. "If it makes you feel any better," she said, glancing back at the tailor's shop, "I'm all but certain that poor tailor is feeling conquered at the moment."

May smiled back. "It's sweet of you to say so, dear. Now, we had better hurry—we don't want you to be late for your big date."

No, Adina thought, *not late. We want me to miss it completely.* But she followed the club owner as she started down the street, if somewhat reluctantly.

***

Adina was all too aware of the stares that followed her as she entered the tavern in her new dress and shoes, her hair prepared and fixed at May's insistence, the necklace the tailor had sold her glittering in the lamplight. She forced herself to avoid fidgeting as she walked toward the bar. She was, of course, accustomed to wearing such fine clothes from her time in her father's court as well as her own castle, but they did not seem to fit the same as they had before. She felt as if she were being somehow pretentious, as if even being a princess, she did not deserve to wear such finery while others in the world struggled to find enough food to feed their families.

A dress like the one she now wore—not to mention the shoes and necklace—would sell for enough to feed such a family for a week or more. *Unless, of course,* she thought wryly, remembering the harried, frightened-looking tailor, *the seller is unlucky enough to find May as his buyer. In that case, he'll be lucky if he makes it away with the clothes on his own back.* The thought did little to distract herself from the sense of being an imposter, though, or from the anxiety she was feeling. She wondered what Aaron would say if he saw her meeting some guard she didn't even know for a drink, and decided it would be better if he never found out about it at all.

As she weaved around tables toward the bar, she inwardly cursed May for picking the tightest dress the tailor had shown them. Any tighter, and Adina would have passed out before making it a dozen steps. The woman behind the bar looked up from where she'd been wiping down the already spotless counter and smiled. "Hello, how may I help you?"

"I'm…" Adina cleared her throat and tried again. "That is, I'm meeting someone."

"Looking like that," the older woman said with a kind smile, "I do not doubt it. Is there a particular lucky gentleman that you're after, or would you like for me to just give a shout? I'm certain that there are a dozen men at least that would be happy enough to fill the role."

Adina felt her face heat, glancing around the tavern self-consciously. Some of the men watching had the grace to look away when she turned but most did not, and she felt her face heat more, focusing on the inside of the tavern in an effort to distract herself. Whatever else the guard had said, he had not lied. The tavern was a fine establishment. Instead of the bellowing, drunken laughter and angry shouts that usually filled the places she'd gone with Aaron and the others recently, there was only a low murmur of subdued voices here as people spoke quietly in conversation.

There was a stage in the back of the tavern and while the places she'd visited of late would have had a scantily-clad woman shifting her body in ways that made Adina hurt just to watch, this stage held only a single harpist, a woman. She was little more than a girl really, in a fine if simple dress, who strummed lightly on the strings of her instrument creating a soft, melodious sound that filled the room.

Adina was surprised to find herself missing the loud boisterousness of the taverns in Avarest and the Downs. True, there had been dangers in those places. Perhaps there had been angry men, but there had also been happy ones and whichever they were, they had owned it completely with a passion that bordered on desperation. A very different approach to drinking than the one she saw in the reserved faces of those sitting at the tables of the tavern, whispering in quiet voices, their expressions neither angry nor sad—nor happy for that matter—instead appearing only bored.

"Miss? Did I lose you?"

"Ah, forgive me," Adina said, turning back to the barkeep with a nervous laugh, "I'm afraid that, for a moment, I might have lost myself. And no, thank you for your offer, but I am meeting a particular person."

The woman smiled, nodding her head politely, "Of course, miss. And this lucky man's name?"

Adina opened her mouth to answer and realized with embarrassment that she didn't remember the guards name—if that was, he'd ever told her. "I..." She hesitated, not knowing what to say, and she felt her face flush once more at her own foolishness. *I'm going to kill May,* she thought.

"Oh, never got around to exchanging names, I suppose?" the woman asked, grinning. "Well, the gods only know I had such difficulties in my youth as well. Tell me, sweet one, can you describe what this man of yours looks like for me? Perhaps, I'll be able to help you find him."

Adina started to answer and realized that she couldn't remember a single defining feature about the man. He'd been wearing a helmet, of course, and the uniform of a guard, but she couldn't recall anything else, and she already felt foolish enough without telling the woman she was looking for a man in a guard's uniform. She opened her mouth, not sure what she was going to say, but was saved by a voice behind her.

"I can't believe you actually came."

She turned to see a man standing behind her, a smile on his face. It didn't take her long to realize it was the guard from the gate as he still wore his uniform, though without his sword and helmet, at least. "If you don't mind my saying so," he said, "you look lovely."

Adina glanced down at her own dress, feeling ridiculously overdressed next to the uniformed guard. "My sister's idea," she said, "she can be quite...forceful."

He laughed, and Adina had to admit that the man wasn't terrible looking, and he seemed kind enough. Things she would most definitely not share with Aaron even should she somehow tell him the rest. "I'd noticed that," he said. "Anyway, let me first apologize again for accosting you at the gate as I did. After you left, I realized I must have sounded like a fool or some cretin who uses his role as a guard to flirt with women. I swear neither is true."

"No?" Adina said, reminding herself that she needed to win the guard over. "And here, you seemed so good at it."

He laughed at that, a deep, melodious sound that was not altogether unpleasant. "You mock me, but that's alright. I deserve it and more besides, I don't doubt."

"Do you mean to tell me," the woman behind the bar said, "that this is the man you were wishing to meet?"

"Yes ma'am, this is him. Although, I'm afraid," she said, turning back to the guard, "I never got your name."

It was the guard's turn to blush, and he ran a hand through his curly blond hair, "Ah, yes. I really am a fool. Forgive me, it's Raste."

"Oh, go on," the woman behind the bar said, "nobody's called you Raste in years, and you know it." She winked. "Why don't you tell this fine woman what your friends call you?"

The guard winced, obviously uncomfortable. "Ah, I'd rather not. She already thinks I'm fool enough."

"Oh come on now," Adina said, smiling, "it is the very least you could do after you, how did you put it? Oh yes, accosted me at the gate and used your position as a guard to flirt with me." As soon as the words were out of her mouth, she felt an unexplainable sense of guilt. Gods, it wasn't as if she were actually *interested* in the man. She was here on a quest to win back her kingdom, that was all, and he was the best way of doing that.

No matter her justifications, the guilt lingered but the man, at least, didn't' seem to notice. He sighed heavily. "Right. Well, my name *is* Raste," he said, giving the barkeep a mock frown before turning back to Adina, "but most people around the city, they just call me 'one-pint band.'"

Adina raised her eyebrows. "That's a mouthful."

"That's what I tried to tell them," he said ruefully, "but the basta—err, the guys, well, once they get a hold of something, they don't tend to let it go."

"And may I ask," Adina said, amused despite herself at the man's obvious discomfort, "where such a name came from?"

"Very well," the man said, sighing heavily and running his hand through his hair once more. He really did have fine hair, she was forced to admit, soft and a golden tone of blond that most women would kill for. "But it's a story best told over a drink, if it's all the same to you."

"That would be alright," Adina said. She wasn't interested in the guard of course, but now that she was here, with him, she wasn't as nervous as she had been. He was nice, if in a bumbling, almost childish sort of way.

Smiling, he led her to one of the empty tables against the wall and waited for her to sit before taking his own seat. "Now then," he said, "where were we?"

She offered him a small smile. "I believe you were preparing to make a fool of yourself, if I'm not mistaken."

He cleared his throat. "Right, that. Well, the thing is, I've sort of got a thing about drinking."

Adina raised an eyebrow. "Let me guess—you do it too much."

The guard laughed. "No, no but I wish that was it. In fact," he said, pausing to take what was an almost dainty sip of his ale, "this is the first drink that I've had in no less than two months."

"And now I feel guilty for driving you to drink."

"What?" He blushed. "Oh, no that's not what I mean, not at all. You see, my problem isn't with drinking too much but drinking...well, poorly."

"You drink poorly," Adina said dryly.

The guard winced. "Right. Anyway, as for the reason why they call me 'one-pint band.' I can't swear to any of this as...well, I don't remember much of that night. But a few years ago, me and some friends of mine went out for drinks and...well, I had too many."

Adina nodded slowly. "How many did you have?"

"Well...two."

Adina raised her eyebrows. "Two drinks?"

"Yeah," he said defensively, "but they were abnormally large drinks."

"Aaah, were they then?"

He ran a hand through his blond hair once more, giving out a little laugh. "To be honest, I don't remember. Like I said, I don't remember much of that night. But according to what my friends told me, I apparently decided that it would be a good idea to jump up on the stage in front of the tavern's singer and, well...perform."

Adina found herself laughing. There was something about the man's bumbling demeanor that made her want to trust him. After the things she'd seen in the last months, the people she'd dealt with, his innocence was refreshing. "You sang, then."

He coughed. "And danced."

"Well, were you good at least?"

"Terrible," he admitted with a laugh, "and I somehow managed to fall off the stage onto a table. It wasn't a particularly strong table either, and it broke beneath my weight. I went around the next day to pay the tavern keeper for the damages, of course," he finished hurriedly.

"That was kind of you," Adina said.

"He didn't seem to think so," the man said, sighing, "threatened to fine me for the loss of business if I showed my face there again."

He shook his head regretfully and took a drink of his ale. Adina eyed the glass. "Should I be worried, then? If there is going to be a free show, I'd at least like to be warned. It will give me time to step away from any nearby tables."

The man laughed good-naturedly at that. "Oh, I won't finish it," he said, eyeing the glass of ale almost sadly. "I never do. Anyway, now you know the story, and I've thoroughly embarrassed myself. And come underdressed too," he said, glancing down at his plain uniform. "In truth, I hadn't expected you to show at all. You must think me a complete fool."

Adina saw a chance to steer the conversation to the topic she really cared about and she took it. "Oh, your uniform is fine with me, I promise. My father was a guard many years ago. In fact, he actually spent some time in the Galian city guard."

"Is that right?" the man said, sounding surprised.

"It is," Adina said, nodding, and reminding herself to take it one step at a time. It wouldn't do to seem too eager or too curious. "So you've nothing to worry about with the uniform you wear. I saw my father's old one many times growing up in a trunk he kept in his room, along with his old sword and armor. I have found, over the years, that I've a special place in my heart for guards—and fools alike."

The guard grinned at that. "Well, I cover those two, at least. Anyone who knows me could tell you that. About your father though, that's interesting. I haven't seen you in the city before."

"Nor would you have," Adina said, "I haven't been to Galia in many years. My father was injured during a practice bout. Nothing life threatening thankfully, but enough to keep him from being able to perform his duties as a city guardsman. It wasn't long after that realization that he took my mother, my sister, and me—I was little more than a baby at the time and know this only because my mother has told me—to a small village to the north and tried his hand at farming."

"Farming is no easy work," the man said, "I've a cousin who's a farmer."

"No," Adina agreed, "it is not easy work. But, then, neither is being a city guardsman."

The man blushed at that as if embarrassed. "Well, it's not so bad. They make sure that we're well fed, anyway. About your father, I wonder if I haven't heard of him. If you don't mind my asking, what was his name?"

"Marcus," Adina said before she could think better of it, and she inwardly cursed herself for a fool.

"Ah," the man said, nodding, "named after the late king. A worthy name for what sounds like a worthy man."

Adina managed a smile past the sudden lump in her throat. "That is kind of you to say," she said, scolding herself to be more careful. It was no great slip—Marcus was a common enough name as once many of the citizens of Telrear had named their children after their favored ruler—but it *was* a slip. *Gods, protect me from my own foolishness.* Still, there was more to be done, so she forced down her fear and took another chance. "My father once spoke highly of a man who served with him in the city guard." She paused as if trying to remember. "Oh yes," she said after a moment, "Oliver was his name. My father said that this Oliver was like a brother to him and, if I were ever in Galia, I should stop by and see him."

The man's eyes went wide. "Do you mean Captain Oliver?"

It was Adina's turn to look surprised. "Captain, is it? I...don't know. The man my father told me of served as a guard with him but then that was years ago."

The man nodded thoughtfully. "Did your father tell you anything else about this man?"

"Only that he was short," she said, pretending a grin, "my father said he was the shortest man he'd ever seen and that he and the other guards had always given him grief about it." Not a complete lie, as the captain *was* short, an inch or two shorter, in fact, than Adina was herself. Not that anyone who'd spent time in a practice ring with him would risk saying it to his face—short he might be, but even in his relative old age, Oliver was known for his skill with a blade and his fierceness in combat. "Oh and there's one other thing," she said as if only just remembering it, "my father mentioned that this Oliver had a quiet way about him, rarely speaking and then only when he had to." She shrugged. "It seems a strange enough trait for a captain, but then I am far from an expert on such things."

The guard grinned. "Oh, you're talking about Captain Oliver alright. The man is shorter than most women," he paused, glancing around as if he expected the captain to appear out of nowhere. "Not that I would ever tell him so," he went on in a near-whisper. "The captain may be short, but take my word for it, there's not a man in the city that would like to find himself on his bad side." He shrugged. "Not that anyone would really know if they were on his bad side considering the fact that, as your father told you, the captain speaks very little."

"Really?" Adina said. "Well, that is quite a coincidence, me happening to meet someone the very moment I arrived in the city that knows the man my father told me stories about when I was a child."

"Not a bad coincidence, I hope?"

"Are you kidding?" Adina said, not having to feign her excitement. "This is *wonderful.* I'll confess that I had no idea how I would go about finding him. The gods themselves must have been smiling on me when I entered the city."

"Smiling on us both."

Adina nodded excitedly, pretending not to notice the intended flirtation in the man's words. "Tell me...no," she said, shaking her head slowly, "that would be too much to ask of you. Too much by far."

"What is it?" the man said, leaning forward, his hand finding hers. Adina's initial reaction was to jerk her hand away, but she stopped herself. The man was friendly enough now, willing enough to help, but he might not be so if he felt his advances were being spurned, so instead she smiled.

"Oh, I don't want to sound selfish," she said, "only...I was wondering if you might, I don't know, arrange a meeting with me and this captain of yours." She looked down at the table as if nervous. "I am sure that I could go to the guards' barracks and find him, but he does not know me, you see, and I would not want to embarrass him. Or myself," she added.

"Is that all?" The man laughed, sitting back, and Adina felt a sense of relief as his hand—slimy with sweat—came away from hers. "Gods, but the way you were acting, I thought you were going to ask me to kill somebody or something."

Adina gave the man a scowl. "I'll ask you to sing if you're not careful."

"Please don't," he said, grinning. "I like it here, and I'd rather not be kicked out for life. Anyway, I'd be happy to introduce you to the captain. We can do it tomorrow, if you'd like."

"Really? I mean, you truly wouldn't mind?"

"Why would I?" the guard said. "It's a favor I can do for a beautiful lady, not to mention the fact that my captain will, I'm sure, be thrilled to meet the daughter of an old friend of his. Why, the man might even go so far as to force the word 'thanks' out of his mouth, but I won't dare to hope for too much."

The smile that came to Adina's lips was genuine, and she felt a heady sense of satisfaction and excitement at her own success. "That would be wonderful," she said, "thank you."

"If you really want to thank me," he said, staring at her wineglass, and Adina noticed with surprise that it was empty, "you'll stay for another drink."

She rolled her eyes. "Oh, very well, if you insist," she said. "Just so long as *you* don't have another."

CHAPTER SEVENTEEN

Adina sighed heavily as she unlocked the door and let herself into her room. She was tired from a day of traveling and a night spent pretending to be someone she wasn't and wanted nothing more than to lie down and sleep. Yawning, she closed the door behind her and bent to slip the shoes off of her aching feet.

"It's about time," a voice said, "I was beginning to think you weren't going to come back to your room at all tonight."

Adina let out a squeak of surprise and nearly tripped, falling back against the door instead. "Who's there?"

There was a burst of flame in the darkness and a candle came to life, outlining the forms of May, Gryle, and Bastion. The two men sat at the small table in one corner of the room while the club owner lay reclined in Adina's bed holding the burning candle.

"Gods, you all nearly made me die of fright!" Adina snapped, "What are you doing sitting in here with the lights off—trying to scare me out of my wits?"

"Of course not, dear," May said in a humoring sort of way as if she regularly let herself into people's rooms without their knowledge and didn't understand what all the fuss was about. Which, for all Adina knew, might very well be the case. "We were only waiting to hear how your night went. A quite boring, quite *long* wait, if I do say so myself...though perhaps not for some of us," she said, giving Adina a wink.

Adina let her breath out in a huff. "Nothing happened, May, don't be ridiculous. I only went because of *you*, if you'll recall. And anyway, all of you wanting to know if I learned anything doesn't explain why you've been sitting in my room without even a candle to see by. What if I had screamed and one of the tavern's bouncers had come running?"

"Then I'm sure you would have done a marvelous job of convincing the man that you'd had a bad dream," the club owner said as if it was obvious. "In that dress, I imagine you could convince a man of pretty much anything you wanted to. As for why we're sitting here without a light, well, we didn't want the innkeeper to wonder why there was a light on in your room while you were gone, come inside, and find us. We wouldn't want him thinking we were waiting in here to ambush you now would we?"

Which is, if I'm not completely wrong, Adina thought, *exactly what you were doing.* But instead of saying so, she merely sighed and finished taking her shoes off before sitting down in the bed beside the club owner. "And where is Beth?" Adina asked. "Am I going to find her hiding under the bed, ready to jump out like some bogeyman?"

May sighed in a long-suffering way. "Of course not. Beth is sleeping, that's all."

"Mistress," Gryle said to Adina, "I do not mean to be prudish or to step outside of my bounds, but it is not normally customary for a queen, or a princess for that matter, to go on a secret rendezvous with a suitor. Especially without someone—her chamberlain, for example—to act as a chaperone and a shield against the man's possible intentions." Adina detected a hint of hurt and scolding mixed into the chamberlain's voice. Or, at least, as scolding as he ever got.

"It *wasn't* a secret rendezvous, Gryle," she said, turning to scowl at May, "and this man was *not* a suitor. As for what is customary, it's not normally customary for a queen's nobles to turn against her and steal her throne either, but that didn't stop it from happening."

The chamberlain recoiled as if he'd been slapped. "Forgive me, Princess, I did not mean to—"

"No, Gryle," Adina said, waving her hand, "I am the one that should be asking for forgiveness. It is late, and I am tired from weeks on the road and a night spent acting as if I'm some sort of spy—and not a very good one, I might add."

"It didn't go well then?" Bastion asked, the young soldier shrugging his massive shoulders as if he'd expected as much. "Well, it was a long shot. We can find some other way to get to this captain of yours."

"Actually," Adina said, "it went quite well. Raste agreed to set up a meeting with Captain Oliver and myself tomorrow."

"*What?*" May said, her eyes going wide. "Why didn't you say that in the first place? Here you had us thinking that our plan had failed, and we were back at square one."

Adina gave the woman a smile. "And here I was thinking that I was going to come back to my room and get to relax after a long, tiring day. It seems that both of us have suffered our own surprises."

The club owner stared at her for a moment as if she was seeing her for the first time, then let out a loud, warm laugh, shaking her head slowly. "Gods, Princess, but I think it for the best you didn't have too good of a time with that guard, and never mind how handsome he was. You and Silent were made for each other, and that's a fact."

Adina nodded her head primly. "I'll take that as a compliment. Now," she said, taking in all three of them with her gaze, "we had best talk about tomorrow and how it's going to go. If we do this right, we'll have several thousand more troops to stand against whatever my brother sends at us." *And there's the little issue that, should we do it wrong,* she thought, *we'll all be dead by tomorrow night.* "So let's figure out what we're going to do and let's do it quickly. I wasn't lying before—I'm exhausted."

CHAPTER EIGHTEEN

Aaron's career as a sellsword had brought him in contact with some of the biggest, meanest bastards in the world, but as the hulking figure stepped inside the common room—bending nearly double to keep from knocking his head on the top of the door frame—he felt his eyes widening in shock. The man—if man it was—moved to the side of the door, saying nothing, and Aaron tried and failed to get a glimpse of his features beneath the dark, hooded cloak he wore.

A second man stepped in behind the first, picking his way past the shattered remains of the door and this one, at least, was of normal size, though Aaron didn't miss the sword sheathed at his waist. "General Aaron Envelar," the man said smiling, "the one some call the Silent Blade. I have heard much of you."

"Well," Aaron said, "I haven't heard a fucking word about you, and I'd just as soon keep it that way. Why don't you and your pet ox turn around and go back out what's left of the door?"

A twitch of anger came across the man's face but it was gone in an instant, and he was smiling again as he ran a finger along first one of his eyebrows and then the other, "And just as pleasant as they say. I wonder, what of your skill with the blade? Is that true too or only an exaggeration?"

"Keep on talking," Aaron said, "you're likely to find out."

The man nodded slowly as if he'd expected as much. "My name is Captain Savrin, leader of King Belgarin's household guard and the best swordsman Baresh has ever seen."

"And I'm a flying horse and a golden halo," Aaron said.

The man frowned at that, raising an eyebrow in question, and the sellsword shrugged. "Turns out, saying a thing doesn't make it true, stranger. But I'll tell you this much, and you'll never hear truer words—turn around and walk out that door now, or your day is going to get a whole lot worse."

"Oh, I'm afraid that's just not possible, General," the man said, his smile widening.

They all looked up at the sound of heavy footsteps upstairs. The door to the stairway flew open and Nathan, the innkeeper, peered down into the common room. "Just what in the name of the gods is all this racket?" he demanded. "Here I am tryin' to catch what little sleep I may, and—"

"Go back to your room, Nathan," Aaron said then considered. "Where's your nephew?"

"Asleep," Nathan said, "just like I was before—gods curse it, is that my *door* lyin' there?"

"What's left of it," Wendell muttered, his eyes studying the hulking, cloaked figure.

"Nathan," Aaron said again, his own gaze never leaving the two men, "go get your nephew and get out of here as quick as you can. Is there another way out of this place?"

"Sure there is," Nathan said, "right behind the bar there, but what diff—"

"Damnit," Aaron said. The bar was in between his own group and the two strangers, and he had the feeling that the two men wouldn't sit around and wait for him and the others to escape.

Not men, Co said in his mind, and he could feel as much as hear the fear in the Virtue's voice, *at least not both of them. Don't you feel it, Aaron? There's something wrong with the other.*

I feel it, firefly, he thought back, *but right now, I'm more concerned with not feeling a sword skewer me anytime soon.* "Doesn't matter," he said finally. "You get your nephew and you both climb out of a damned window if you have to—I've had to do it before myself. Just get out, Nathan. Now."

"Look, Aaron," the barkeep said, "I got respect for you and what you're doin', but ain't nobody gonna come in my tavern and—"

"*Do you want your nephew to die?*" Aaron shouted, finally turning to look at the man who recoiled as if he'd been struck. "Then get the fuck out of here, Nathan. While you still can."

The innkeeper disappeared up the stairs again, and Aaron turned back to see that the stranger was still smiling. "There's really no point in all of that," he said. "I'll find them again after I'm done here. Of course, they will have to be made an example of, to show people what happens to traitors to their king."

"Somebody might find them," Aaron agreed, "but it won't be you. Dead men have their own worries and an innkeeper and a boy aren't among them."

"Aaron," Darrell said as he came to stand beside him, his steel in his hand, "how do you want to handle this?"

"I was thinking maybe we'd try to get out alive," Aaron said. "Start there."

"Wendell!" he yelled.

"Sir?"

"Find us another way out of this place."

"Yes sir."

The stranger sighed as if bored. "Are you done now?"

"One of us is," Aaron said, moving toward the man. "Darrell, Leomin, take the big guy. This bastard's mine."

"A-are you sure you wouldn't like to trade?" Leomin asked, but Aaron was barely paying attention. As so often happened when his life hung in the balance, the rest of the world seemed to fade until it was only him and the man in front of him, only the blades in their hands and the blood in their veins.

"Well? You wanted to see if the stories you heard were true or not. Now's your chance."

The man let out a sound somewhere between a growl and a hiss and rushed forward, his blade flashing out of its sheath like a bolt of lightning aimed for Aaron's neck. He was fast but so was Aaron, and his own sword rose to meet it, knocking the stranger's blade aside. He countered, lunging forward—careful of his footing among the shattered pieces of wood littering the common room's floor—but the man parried the strike almost contemptuously.

The stranger stepped back, his sword held at the ready and smiled. "I had heard you were faster than that."

Aaron shrugged, his own blade held in front of him. "I'd say the same, but then, I haven't heard anything about you at all."

The man's face twisted in anger at that, and he sprang forward again, his sword leading, whistling through the air. Aaron managed to parry the strike and the follow up, launching an attack of his own, and a deadly web of steel weaved itself between the two men almost too fast to see. Suddenly, their blades met with powerful force and both of them went wide. The stranger's free hand lashed out, catching Aaron in the face as Aaron's foot caught the man in the stomach, and they both stumbled backward with grunts of surprise.

"*Gods be good!*" Leomin shouted, and Aaron risked a glance to see that the hulking figure had picked up two of the inn's solid oak tables, one in each hand as if they weighed nothing at all. He was moving toward Darrell, the old man waiting with his sword extended down at an angle in front of him, his face a mask of serenity while Leomin stood beside him, his eyes wide, his own sword in a shaky hand.

"How's that back way coming, Wendell?" Aaron yelled, not daring to look completely behind him to see how the sergeant was faring.

"Working on it!"

Too much longer, Aaron thought as he faced his opponent once more, *and it won't matter one way or the other.* He wanted to help the others with the monster they faced, but knew that if he turned his back on the man in front of him he'd be of no help to anyone. Corpses never were. Except to the worms, that was, and they weren't known for being particular.

"You're bleeding," the man said, nodding at Aaron, a grin on his face.

"And you're ugly," Aaron said, wiping an arm across his mouth, "now, are we going to do this, or are you going to stand around running your fucking mouth all night?"

The man growled at that, and Aaron smiled. An angry bastard, this one. The man rushed him with a shout, his sword a blur, and Aaron barely managed to get his own blade up in time to meet it. Then they were at it again, steel striking steel and creating a melody of what would almost certainly be the last song one of them ever heard.

When they both stepped back, they were panting for air, and Aaron sported a cut on his arm, his opponent one across his left thigh, but neither deep enough to make any real difference. Suddenly, a *crash* erupted in the common room, so powerful to shake the floor beneath Aaron's feet. It was followed a moment later by another, and he turned to see that the hulking figure was swinging the tables at Darrell as if they were clubs—but the swordmaster danced and weaved away from strikes that were surprisingly fast. The swordmaster hadn't been touched—if he had, Aaron supposed the people the king sent to clean up the mess would have been better off bringing sacks than a coffin—but Aaron noted that the mask of serenity on the swordmaster's face had cracked a fraction, displaying a slight strain that was rare in the normally composed man.

Darrell tried to move forward for an attack of his own, but the hulking figure brought one of the tables flailing up, and the swordmaster had to jump back to avoid being sent through the ceiling by the blow. Leomin moved forward on the creature's other side, but the other table went sailing toward him, and he stumbled backward, tripping and narrowly avoiding the strike by what appeared to be luck more than skill. *Damnit,* Aaron thought. He thought that the swordmaster would be able to keep the thing busy, at least for another minute, perhaps two, but that was all. Weave as he might, his old master couldn't get close to the creature, and he would tire soon.

"*Wendell!*" Aaron shouted. "Back door!"

"Trying!" the scarred sergeant shouted back.

Aaron felt movement near him, though whether by instinct or the power of the bond, he didn't know, and he threw his sword up in defense as he spun back, and saw that it had caught the man's blade inches away from his own throat. Growling, Aaron forced it away, and they strained against each other, each looking to overpower the other. The man was fast, but he was also strong, and for a time the two blades seemed locked in place. They hissed and gritted their teeth with the effort of keeping the other's sword at bay like two opposing knights painted on some castle fresco.

But Aaron was no knight—just about as far as a man could get from one, in fact—so he allowed the sword to slip a little, then a little more. The man grinned as he saw the change, felt Aaron's strength weakening beneath his. Then, just when the man's confidence was fully clear on his face, Aaron allowed his sword to be pushed away as he stepped to the side, scooping up a long piece of wood that had, until recently, been a part of the door, then swung it with all the strength he could summon at the man's face. His opponent's sword was out of position, and he didn't react in time, was unable to avoid the thick piece of wood that smashed into his face. He cried out in surprise and pain as he stumbled, tripping over a piece of the shattered door and falling.

There was another ear-shattering crash to Aaron's side, and he spun to see that the cloaked creature had apparently grown angry at the swordmaster's ducking and dodging, and had decided to throw one of the tables instead. The thick oak wood, swung by the thing's impossible strength, had struck the wall and gone through it, tearing a hole into the side of the tavern. "Sir," Wendell said, turning to look at Aaron, his eyes wide and wild, "I think I found that back door you were looking for."

"Well, don't just stare at me," Aaron shouted, "run, damn you!"

None of the men needed to be told twice, and for all the creature's strength, its pursuit was slow and plodding as they all dashed through the newly-made hole in the tavern's wall. Out in the street, Aaron shot a quick glance around them at the shadows, searching for the other troops that would have no doubt been stationed outside. He saw nothing but took little comfort in it. He had seen enough dead men with knives in their backs to know that it was most often the blade you didn't see that took you, in the end.

"*Aaron Envelar!*" came a shout from the inside of the tavern, and Aaron peered through the hole to see that the swordsman had risen shakily to his feet, his jaw already beginning to swell. *"I will kill you!"* the man yelled, stumbling drunkenly toward the hole through which Aaron and the others had made their escape.

"You'll have to get in line," Aaron muttered as he glanced up at the sky. Another hour before sunrise, maybe more, and no telling what surprises the night held. Still, there was no hope for it. "We've got to go. Now."

The others nodded, and Aaron followed them down the street a few steps before he realized the youth was missing. He turned back to see Caleb staring at the hole in the wall as if it were some puzzle he was trying to figure out. "Caleb, come on! They'll be out here in a second!"

"Seven, by my estimation," the boy murmured as if he wasn't really paying attention, and Aaron gaped.

"What? Boy, get the fu—"

The youth suddenly reached down and picked up a piece of the broken brick that had once made up the tavern's wall. He used it to strike one of the stones in what was left of the wall, almost daintily. There was a creaking, shifting sound and the youth took a step back as the remaining part of the wall and roof collapsed with a thundering sound of breaking wood and falling rock, blocking the hole.

Caleb turned to Aaron and the others who stared at him as if they'd just witnessed magic. The youth looked away from their eyes, shrugging embarrassedly. "The structural integrity of the tavern had been compromised, that's all."

"Well, alright then," Aaron said, staring at the pile of rubble in disbelief. "Anyway, come on before your living integrity is compromised. It's time to move."

This time, the boy nodded and hurried along after them as they made their way into the streets, cutting through back alleys at random in an effort to throw off their pursuers. It would have taken a crew of men the better part of an hour or two to clear away the rubble of the roof's collapse, but from what he'd seen of the cloaked creature's strength, Aaron didn't think it would hold them for long.

Aaron, Co said in his mind as he led the others at a sprint down the streets, *there are others. Can you—*

I know, he thought back, his breath coming in gasps as he ran, leading himself and the others further into the city. He didn't need the Virtue to warn him. Now that he knew what to look for, Aaron could feel others like the hulking figure, others who had been warped and twisted by Kevlane, throughout the city. Dozens of them, maybe more. And if each of them was as dangerous as the creature...*Well,* he thought, *at least Adina's safe.*

CHAPTER NINETEEN

Adina did not feel safe. The sun was still two hours away from rising, and what few people she passed in the street seemed to study her more than she liked. When the others had asked her what time she was to meet Raste, she'd lied and had snuck out of the inn while they were all still sleeping. At the time, it had seemed like the right thing to do. The smart thing. She would be less conspicuous traveling alone, not to mention the fact that there was no need to risk their lives along with hers. After all, if something went wrong they'd have the entire city after them and even May's cleverness, Beth's speed, and Gryle and Bastion's strength would mean little against an army of trained soldiers. She'd realized on her walk back from her night out with the guard that she could not, *would* not risk her friends' lives without good reason.

Besides, it would have to be her. Captain Oliver was a good man, but he was also a notoriously suspicious one. He would not agree to any coup without seeing Adina in person, she knew. They were good reasons, wise ones. At least, they had seemed like it when she'd reached her decision the night before. Now though, faced with the reality of walking into an unknown location with a man she knew nothing about, her reasons didn't seem wise at all but foolish, not compassionate but careless. *Never mind that,* she told herself, *it's too late now. You've made your choice, and it was the right one so stop worrying so much. You're not a child to be taken care of, you're a princess of the royal blood, and it's time you started acting like one.*

By the time she reached the place Raste had told her of, the sun had only just peeked over the horizon, bathing the streets in pale, early morning light. As she drew closer, she saw the guard waiting with his back propped against the outside of a tavern. He smiled when he noticed her approach and there was enough guileless innocence in that smile to set some small part of the tempest of worry and fear roiling through her at ease. "There you are," he said, "and here I was beginning to think you weren't going to show."

She smiled back. "I am right on time as I said I would be. To be honest, I'd half expected to find myself alone here—thought that maybe the one ale you had would have left you too hung over for arranging meetings and accompanying a lady to them."

He shook his head ruefully at that. "Remind me never to tell you anymore embarrassing stories about me."

"Oh?" Adina asked, coming to stand beside him. "There are more?"

He sighed heavily. "Many, I'm afraid, but I'll have to tell you about them another time. The captain waits."

He offered her his arm, and she hesitated for a moment before finally taking it. He gave her that innocent smile again, then began leading her down the street, whistling as he did, and a little more of the trepidation Adina had been feeling slid away. The morning was cool, close to chilly but not quite, and she could smell bread baking in a nearby shop, the baker preparing for the day's business. She noted buildings she had not seen in months and had not thought to see again as she passed them, and soon there was a smile on her face as she took in the sights, smells, and sounds of the city. *Her* city.

She was so lost in the pleasantness of it, the feeling of the warm sun on her skin and the cool breeze, of the sounds of doors beginning to be unlatched as shopkeepers prepared for the new day ahead. She turned and opened her mouth to tell Aaron she was glad he'd finally been able to see her home only to remember that it wasn't Aaron whose arm she held at all, but a stranger's. A handsome, kind stranger but a stranger just the same.

The warm, comforting feeling she'd been experiencing left her at that, blown away as if by a cold wind, and she told herself to focus on the task at hand. There would be time to appreciate her city, her home, later. If, of course, she didn't mess up and get herself killed; if, of course, there *was* a later.

They walked for nearly an hour. Adina was just about to ask Raste where he was taking her when he stopped in front of a church. A statue of an old, wizened figure in flowing robes stood in front of it marking it as a church dedicated to the worship of Nalesh, Father of the Gods.

"Only our second outing," Adina said, turning away from the church's closed doors that seemed somehow menacing to her and trying a smile that felt unnatural on her face, "and you intend to take me to a church?"

The man grinned, and if he noticed her discomfort at all, he didn't show it. "No fear, my lady. I've no intention of tricking you into marriage. Not yet, at least."

Adina glanced around the deserted street. Unlike the others they'd traversed, the road was empty save for the two of them, and she turned back to Raste. "Where is everyone?"

The man shrugged. "I could not say, my lady. Still, it is early yet and many will not rise from their beds to start their day for another hour or more. And if it is brigands or sneak-thieves you're worried about," he said, pausing to give her that innocent smile once more, "then I would merely seek to remind you that you are in the company of a city guard, and I will allow no harm to come to you." He winked. "Now, are you ready to meet the captain?"

Adina frowned. Perhaps her discomfort wasn't justified. As Raste had said, it *was* early, and the street they were on held few shops, mostly churches dedicated to one god or the other. What services they held would not start until later in the morning. "Yes," she said, wanting nothing more than to get the subterfuge over with, to meet with Captain Oliver and have it done. May and the others would be angry when she told them—Gryle, of course, would be hurt—but she thought they would understand the necessity of what she'd done, given time. She glanced around the empty street once more then nodded. "Let's go."

The inside of the church was dark, the only illumination coming from the pale, weak light that managed to seep in through the windows past the heavy curtains that hung upon them. No worshippers here to celebrate the Father of the Gods, no priests to guide them on their holy journey. "Where is everyone?" she said again. Even if the official church services hadn't started yet, Adina knew that the priests would have normally already arrived, making themselves available for guidance to those who came with questions or problems, intermediaries working on behalf of the Father of the Gods.

"Nalesh is not worshipped much, anymore," Raste said dismissively, staring around the empty church as if its state didn't bother him in the slightest. He ran a finger along one dust-covered pew then blew on it. "People prefer to worship gods they understand, gods closer to their own lives, their own problems, than some aloof old geezer in a silly robe."

Adina frowned at that, bothered by Raste's dismissive tone and sacrilegious words. It was true that Nalesh, the Father of the Gods, was not worshipped as much as he once had been, but that was no cause to disrespect him. "Without Nalesh," Adina pointed out, "none of the other gods would exist. He created them, after all. We owe him respect."

The guard shrugged as if he cared little either way, "My dad created me, and he's a right bastard. Making something doesn't make you worthy of it."

Adina stared at the man, shocked at the difference in his temperament and behavior compared to the bumbling, buffoonish guard she'd met the night before. She took a step away from him, pulling her arm back and, for a moment, it seemed to her that he held it intentionally, as if to show her he could, before letting it go. "Where's the captain?" she said, making her way down the center aisle and examining the pews without really expecting to see him. The light through the windows might have been poor, but she thought that it would have been enough to have seen the captain if he were there.

"Perhaps Oliver has not yet arrived," the man said from behind her, and Adina spun at that.

"You mean Captain Oliver, of course."

He smiled a humoring smile. "Of course. Captain Oliver."

A sense of foreboding rose in Adina, and she turned and started hurrying down the aisle, casting her gaze almost frantically to the left and right until she reached the end and still there was nothing. She looked behind the altar and saw a door leading further back into the church. *"Captain Oliver,"* she called, "where are you?"

"I don't think he's going to hear you, my Queen."

Adina's breath caught in her throat, and she turned to see Raste pulling his sword from the scabbard at his side as he walked toward her. Gone was the kind, slightly foolish expression he'd worn. Instead, the eyes that met hers were calculating, devious and, worst of all, amused. "After all," he said, bringing the sword up to point it at her, the tip resting in the air no more than a foot away from her throat, "the dungeons are a long way from here."

"Why?" she whispered, her throat unaccountably dry.

There was no innocence in his smile, not this time. "For the money, of course. Why else?" He must have registered some look of surprise on Adina's face because he let out a soft laugh. "Surely, you didn't think they would just let you walk back into the city and take control from them, did you?"

"But..." Adina said, "everyone in the city thinks I'm dead. They were told a horse—"

"Trampled you and killed you, yes I know," the man said, rolling his eyes. "Personally, I think they could have come up with something better than that, but then, it was not my decision to make. Still, the fool commoners seem to have bought it, so I'll give them that.

"It's funny, you know. At first, the general and the nobles thought they'd seen the last of you, thought that you'd run off somewhere to cower and hide. Of course, they still sent spies out to all of the major cities, men and women put in place to keep an eye out for any sign of the princess and, if possible, to finish what they had started. It was then that these spies started sending back very interesting reports. Reports of a woman claiming to be Princess Adina, daughter to the late King Marcus, wrapped up in some conspiracy with a sellsword and some others.

"When news of your presence in Perennia reached the council, they thought it best to prepare just in case. After all, Isalla is not so very far away, is it?" He smiled. "And a good thing they did, for I was there when you walked through the gate and now here you are. Trapped."

Adina threw the cloak she was wearing over one shoulder and reached behind her, drawing the slim sword that she had secreted there, a precaution she'd purchased during the shopping trip with May. She took a step back, getting into a defensive stance as Captain Gant had shown her, but Raste only grinned wider, nodding his head as if in appreciation.

"A pretty thing," he said, eyeing the slender blade then looking pointedly at his own wider, longer sword, "tell me, what's it for? To pick my teeth with after a meal? Or perhaps to butter my bread. Yes," he said, nodding, "I believe it would work quite well."

"Say what you want," Adina said, her face turning red with anger, "but its steel is sharp, and it will cut you quick enough, if you make me use it. Now, get out of the way and let me pass."

The guard cocked his head to the side, studying her. "Forgive me, my Queen, but that is one order that I'm afraid I must decline. You see, I have plans for that reward money—oh yes, they told the few of us they recruited about a significant reward should we find and apprehend you—big plans. And unless you've got a few sacks of gold hidden away in that dress somewhere? No," he said, "I thought not. Now, put that toy away. They will pay me the same whether you're dead or alive, but I'd really rather not hurt you, if I can help it."

"The only way I'll put this sword down is if you kill me," Adina hissed through gritted teeth.

"My, but you are beautiful, even angry," he said. Then he let out a long sigh. "Very well, if you insist."

In a moment, he was on her, swinging his sword in a wide arc meant to overpower her, but Adina remembered Captain Gant's words. *Use your strengths. You're fast so be fast.* Instead of meeting Raste's blade with her own, Adina hopped back, lashing out with her thinner, lighter blade, and Raste cried out as her sword cut a bloody line down his sword arm. He did not drop his own blade, as she had hoped, but he growled in pain, taking a step back as his free hand went to the wound on his arm. "You bitch," he said, "I'll kill you for that."

"And what of the tavern owner?" Adina said. "She claimed she knew you—or was she in on it too?"

"Of course she was," the man growled, "not that it'll matter to you soon."

He rushed her then, his sword leading and between her anger and her fear, Adina felt as if all of the techniques and maneuvers that Brandon Gant had taught her flew from her mind. Yet, when the man's sword came slicing at her, her body acted on its own, her feet stepping to the side, her blade flying up to parry the blow. The impact nearly sent the sword flying from her hands, but she managed to hold on, spinning and lashing out with her blade again before the man could recover and cutting a horizontal line across his chest, the blade slicing cleanly through his shirt.

The cut was not deep, but Raste cried out in pain and staggered back, studying the bloody cut in surprise. "Just let me go, Raste," Adina said, nearly pleaded. "Ridell and the others don't have to know about any of this, okay? We can both go on about our lives and that can be the end of it."

The man stared at her blankly for a moment, then his expression twisted with rage. He charged her, bellowing in fury and swinging his sword in with a two-handed grip, a horizontal slash that would have cut her nearly in half if it had hit. It didn't, of course, as Adina ducked beneath it. The man shouted again, his sword coming in great, sweeping blows, but after hours spent with Aaron and training with Captain Gant, the guard seemed impossibly slow, almost clumsily so, and his footwork was adequate at best.

Adina dodged the blows when she could and parried them when she needed to until the man grew tired and the strikes came even slower, fewer and farther between each, and he was panting and covered in sweat as if he'd just run a race. "*Bitch,*" he growled, swinging his sword again and, this time, Adina evaded the blow and lunged forward just the way the captain had drilled her on so many times in Baresh.

The blade went into the guard's chest easily, *too* easily, and Adina imagined she could feel the blade sliding into her own heart. They stood there for a second, both of them frozen, the captain looking at the sword piercing his chest with shock as his own blade clattered to the church floor beside him, and Adina staring wide-eyed. Then Raste let out a wheezing groan, and Adina pulled her sword free before he toppled to the ground and lay still.

Adina stood in shock, having a difficult time comprehending the finality of what she'd done. It sometimes took husbands and wives years to conceive a child only for the woman to endure nine difficult months of carrying it before it was finally born. So much time, so much difficulty in creating a life, and she had just ended one in no longer than it took to draw a breath. She looked at her hands and saw that they were shaking.

She knelt, her eyes blurry with tears, and wiped the blood from her blade on the dead man's shirt. Brandon had told her never to put the sword away unclean, and so she made sure she'd removed all the blood she could before sliding it back into the sheath at her back, her eyes never leaving the dead man before her.

He had been a traitor, but he had also been a man, somebody's son, somebody's brother, perhaps. She took a slow, deep breath in a failing effort to gather her composure, then wiped her arm across her eyes before starting for the church door. She paused at the threshold and glanced back at the dead man. Not a man any longer though, for whatever had made him such was gone, and what was left was only an empty shell, devoid of hope or meaning.

Then, her heart aching as if she had been the one pierced with a blade, feeling both terribly cold and impossibly hot at the same time, Adina turned away and opened the church doors, stepping into the street.

Two dozen men in the uniform of the city guard waited for her, crossbows trained on her and Adina froze. She did not scream or cry out in surprise, for she was far too numb to feel something as mundane as that. Instead, she only stared at the guards, at the crossbows in their hands, until two of them stepped to the side and allowed a man to walk through.

He was tall and thin, a dark beard covering what Adina knew was a weak chin, his eyes appearing beady and shifty beneath thick eyebrows. "Princess Adina," General Ridell said smiling. His hands were clasped behind his back as if he were at some military function instead of preparing to commit murder and treason in the streets of the city he was sworn to protect. "How good it is to see you."

"*Queen* Adina to you, *worm*," Adina hissed as rage, bright and hot and sudden, engulfed her, and she took a step toward him.

The general held up a finger. "Easy, Princess," he said, smiling as if he didn't have a care in the world as he gestured to the two dozen men arrayed in the street. "I do not think you would make it far, do you? And tell me," he said, peering at the church doors as if he could somehow see through them, "where is Raste?"

"Dead," Adina said, "by my hand." There was no satisfaction in the words, no boasting; only a cold truth that she could not deny no matter how much she might have wished to.

The general frowned at that for a moment then finally he shrugged. "Saves us having to give him the reward, then. You really shouldn't have come back here, you know."

"Dark times indeed when a queen is not welcome in her own city," Adina said.

"Not dark for all," the general said, motioning to the soldiers. "Good bye, Queen."

Adina closed her eyes, heard the snap of the crossbows' release and waited for death to claim her. When a moment passed, then another and she still felt no pain she slowly opened her eyes and stared in shock. A small, old woman stood between her and the men, her back to Adina. The old woman heaved in great, gasping breaths. She held several long, slender pieces of wood in both hands at her side, and it took Adina a moment to realize with shock that they were crossbow bolts. The general and the soldiers with him also stared in wide-eyed shock as the woman let the crossbow bolts fall to the ground.

"Impossible," General Ridell breathed, "that's impossible."

"Impossible?" said the old woman in a familiar voice. "Nah, not that. Impossible is the fact that you're still alive with a heart as black as the one you carry in your chest." Beth glanced back at Adina and gave her a smile, shaking her head. "You shouldn't have tried to leave without us, Princess."

Adina was just about to respond when she heard the sound of footsteps off to her left and looked to see May, Gryle, and Bastion emerging from beside the church and running toward her. "May, I don't—"

"You didn't honestly think that we'd let you go alone did you?" the club owner asked, panting for breath. "Gods, Princess, I work with criminals for a living—I know when I'm being lied to. Now, we'll talk about how foolish you've been later, if we survive this. For now, let's get into the church before those boys get their crossbows reloaded."

Adina felt stunned, but she let the red-haired woman lead her to the door. Gryle and Bastion were close behind, but Beth was still standing and watching the men even as they reloaded their crossbows. "What about Beth?" Adina asked.

"Never mind her," May said, pushing Adina toward the door, "get inside."

The moment they were inside, Gryle and Bastion were closing the doors, and she thought that they meant to leave the old woman outside with the soldiers, but there was a blur of movement and a *pop* in the air, and the next thing she knew Beth was beside her. The old woman collapsed on a pew with her elbows on her knees, gasping for air. "Close it!" May yelled, and the two men slammed the doors shut.

No sooner had they closed them than there was a rapid *thump, thump, thump* as crossbow bolts embedded themselves in the wood of the door, several sticking through only inches from Bastion and Gryle. Adina turned to the club owner, "May, I'm sorry I left. I thought—"

"I know well and good what you thought," the club owner said, "and I know the reasons you'd give for doing what you did. It was foolish, and I'll lecture you on it later, but right now we've got more pressing concerns." She cast her eyes around the dim church. "Is there a back door out of this place?"

Adina's heart was still racing from the last few minutes, her mind trying to catch up with her unexpected salvation. "I...I don't—"

"*Mistress!*" Gryle ran clumsily toward her, examining her as if he expected a crossbow bolt to be sticking out of her somewhere. "Are you alright?"

"I'm okay, Gryle," she said, giving the man a small smile, "For now. But...but I think I've been a fool."

May snorted at that, but Gryle stepped forward, studying the princess's clothes. "I'm so sorry, Princess, but I think the shirt is ruined. There's...is that *blood*? Are you bleeding?"

"It's not mine, Gryle," Adina said, waving away the man's attentions. She indicated Raste's corpse a little way further into the church. "It's his."

The chamberlain stared with wide eyes at the dead man, his face turning a slight shade of green as he took in the blood pooling around him. "This, Princess," he said in a prim, disapproving voice, "is why it is important that a lady of your station have a chaperone."

Adina found herself laughing unexpectedly at that, but soon her laughing devolved into tears at what she'd done, at what she'd dragged her friends into, and she was shocked when Gryle stepped forward and embraced her in a hug. Suddenly feeling wrung out and weak, Adina buried her head in the man's shoulder and cried. "It's alright, Princess," he said in the soft, soothing voice one might use with a child or a frightened animal.

"I've been a fool, Gryle," she said, "and you're all going to die for my failure."

"It is not our failures that define us, Princess," the chamberlain said, "but what we do after that matters. Your father told me that once."

Adina stepped back, looking up at the man's eyes, seeing the compassion and understanding there. "Oh, Gryle," she said, "what would I do without you?"

The chamberlain smiled and despite the men outside the church, men looking to kill them all, the expression was so genuine, so true, that Adina found herself smiling with him, "Well," he said, "it is a chamberlain's duty to see to his mistress's needs, Princess."

"You are not my chamberlain, Gryle," Adina said. "You're my friend."

He smiled widely at that, his eyes twinkling. "Thank you, Pr—"

"*Gryle, I need you!*"

They both looked to see the giant soldier, Bastion, with his hands pressed against the door, the muscles of his back and arms straining. Even as they watched, the door bucked inward, and he was pushed back a step before resetting his feet, growling with the effort.

"I'll be right back, Princess," Gryle promised, and then he hesitated, grabbing her shirt sleeve and examining the blood stains, shaking his head sadly. "As soon as we're out of here, we'll see what we can do about those clothes."

"*Gryle!*" Bastion bellowed, and the chamberlain let out a squeak as he hurried toward the door.

"Beth?" Adina said, moving to crouch beside the old woman. "Are you alright?"

"I'm...fine," the woman panted, "just...tired is all. You might...not think it. But catching a...few dozen crossbow bolts in flight is...a little draining."

"You saved my life," Adina said, putting her hand on one of the woman's own, "thank you. Is there anything I can do?"

"Yeah," the woman said, pausing to swallow, "you can...find us a way out of here. I'd rather...not die in a church. Feels sacrilegious."

Adina nodded and rose, moving to May. "Sometimes churches will have a separate door behind the altar for the priest's quarters and for them to enter and exit without disturbing the parishioners."

"And does this one have such a door?" the club owner asked, hopeful.

"There's only one way to find out," Adina said, hurrying toward the door she'd seen behind the altar when Raste had attacked her, and throwing it open. Inside was a small hallway which she followed to the priest's quarters. In some of the churches dedicated to the younger gods, the priest's quarters were so opulent as to almost belong in some noble's manse or castle, but here the accoutrements were austere and simple. Several plain beds sat within a small room along with a separate altar for the priests to take devotion with their god. Adina went around the room searching for a door, her heart hammering in her chest as she listened to the soldiers trying to batter their way into the church.

"Anything?"

Adina turned to see that the club owner had followed her inside and now stood in the doorway. Hurriedly, Adina went around the outside of the room once more, checking behind the altar and the beds, searching for any sign of some hidden door then she cursed, turning back to May. "There's no door. This church must have been built before they started adding them."

May opened her mouth to respond but suddenly there was a deafening *crash*, and both women's eyes went wide. Adina rushed out into the church, expecting to find the great doors collapsed inside. And sure enough the doors *were* broken down, but Adina realized with surprise that they had broken outward, not inward, and she could just make out several pairs of legs sticking out from underneath the thick oak doors.

"What happened?"

Bastion stared slack-jawed at Gryle. For his part, the chamberlain was staring at the floor and rubbing his hands together, clearly embarrassed. "I...that is...I didn't mean to. I had only meant to hold it, but I must have pushed too hard and—"

"Gryle, watch out!" May shouted, and Adina looked up to see two of the soldiers rushing the doorway, swords in their hands.

Bastion drew his own sword, but Gryle let out a squeak of fear, picking up one of the long, solid oak pews that sat nearby as if it weighed nothing. He stepped outside the opening and swung it at the approaching men. Adina had enough time to see the shock on the two soldiers' faces before the pew struck them, and they went soaring through the air as if they'd been hurled from a catapult, screaming as they flew into the distance. Then, there was crash from far away, followed by a stunned silence as everyone, friend and foe alike, stared at the chamberlain. "*Sorry,*" Gryle called after the two men.

Beth was the first to recover, and the old woman let out a weary cackle as she used the pew to lever herself to her feet. "Those eggs are cracked and no mistake," she said, grinning as she took several steps toward the door before turning back to May and Adina. "Well? You all comin' or are you just gonna sit there with your mouths hangin' open, see if maybe you can't catch a bug?"

"Right," Adina managed, swallowing hard, "let's go."

She and the others rushed outside to stand beside the chamberlain who was holding the church pew over one shoulder as if it was a club. If hefting it strained him, he gave no sign. Adina drew her sword, along with Bastion, and May produced two knives, though from where Adina couldn't have guessed. Beth only stood, staring at the soldiers across the street as if they were wayward grandchildren who needed to be punished.

The general and what remained of his soldiers stared wide-eyed at the troops that had been crushed beneath the door, and at the chamberlain himself, still holding the pew. "This...this is impossible," Ridell breathed. "You're...you're monsters."

"No, Ridell," Adina said, shaking her head, "we are not the monsters. The monsters are men like you who care only for their own ambitions and nothing about the lives they leave broken and shattered in their wake. Monsters who would throw away the lives of their soldiers," she said, motioning to the men with him, "only to satisfy their own lust for power."

The general sneered at that. "Oh, it is rich for you to talk of monsters while you and your royal siblings have killed thousands with your years of warring for who gets to sit on a throne."

The man's words stabbed Adina sharper than any blade might have. The man was right. The people *had* suffered because of her and her siblings' war against Belgarin. How many wives left without husbands? How many children without fathers?

"Don't be any dumber than you have to be, General," May said from beside Adina. "A man—or a woman—must fight evil where he finds it and what losses result are not to be laid at such a man or woman's feet, but at the feet of the evil itself. It is those like you who create such evil while Princess Adina and those like her do what they can to stop it."

Adina stared at the club owner as if seeing her for the first time, and she felt the woman's words resonate within her, felt her back straighten once more as her resolve returned. "Lay down your arms, General. You soldiers as well. There are greater threats in the world than this, and there is little time to prepare. What you have seen today is nothing compared to what is out there."

The soldiers glanced uncertainly at each other, but Ridell sneered. "To the Fields with this. Kill them, kill all of them!"

The men hesitated as if unsure, and Ridell's face turned bright red. *"Kill them damn you!"* he screamed, but still the men did not attack. They all turned to look at Adina, and one soldier dropped to his knees, bowing his head to his queen, then another, and another until all of the soldiers were all kneeling.

"This, this is *insane,"* Ridell screamed, "this is *treason!"*

"No, Ridell," Adina said, "this is not treason. This is setting things right." She nodded to Bastion. "Take him."

The giant youth started forward, and the general's eyes widened. Then he turned and ran, sprinting down the street. Bastion set out after him but there was another blur of motion and suddenly Ridell was pitching forward, crashing to the ground, and finally rolling to a stop up against the side of a building. Beth, who now stood in the street, turned to them and shrugged, "Tried to catch 'em, I swear."

"Well," May said, staring at the unconscious form of the general, "that'll do pretty well for him, I think."

"Yes," Adina said, "but we're not done yet. Rise, soldiers of Galia." And slowly, they did, watching her expectantly. "I have one more task for you."

"What do you have in mind, Princess?"

Adina glanced through the city to where she could see the castle in the distance, rising up over the buildings around it. "I think I'd like to visit my castle."

CHAPTER TWENTY

Aaron led the others through the city's twisting alleyways, not knowing where he was going only looking to put some distance between them and any pursuers. The streets were deserted, though whether the denizens of the city had elected to stay indoors because of the fight at the tavern or because of the recent disappearances, he could not have said for sure, and it didn't matter in any case.

What mattered were the men chasing them—and they *were* chasing them, of that he had no doubts. The only surprise for Aaron was that the entire city and all of its soldiers hadn't descended upon them seeking blood and death. For if Boyce Kevlane really had taken over the city—which seemed apparent—the man would stop at nothing to see Aaron and his friends dead.

Aaron expected to find soldiers waiting on them around every corner but, so far at least, no one had tried to bar their path. He'd only just had the thought when he was struck by the same feeling of wrongness as before, of something that was not quite complete coming closer, and he held up a hand, signaling the others to stop.

"Thank the gods for that," Wendell groaned, leaning over with his hands on his knees, "a belly full of ale doesn't do a man any favors he ends up having to run for his life."

"What is it, Aaron?" Darrell asked. "What do you feel?"

Aaron shook his head, closing his eyes, and concentrating on that feeling. It was similar to the other he'd had, but it was not the same. There was something different about this wrongness, yet he felt it coming closer all the same, felt it moving at an incredible speed and—"*Down!*" he shouted.

The men hit the ground almost before the word was out of his mouth but the youth, Caleb, seemed frozen with fear. Aaron dashed forward, knocking him aside and throwing his sword up by instinct as the power of his bond surged through him. There was a blur of motion in front of him, and a sword seemed to materialize out of the darkness, striking his own with enough momentum and force to send the blade back into Aaron's shoulder. He grunted in pain as it cut him, though not too deep. At least, he hoped not, but there was no time to be sure as he felt it—whatever *it* was—turning and coming back at him.

He couldn't see the blade coming—it was much too fast for that—but the power of his bond let him know what shape the attack would take. Instead of throwing his sword up this time, he ducked underneath the strike and even knowing that it was coming, he was almost too slow, and he felt the wind of its passage just over him. He spun, peering into the darkness of the street and could just make out a figure standing all the way at the mouth of the alley. *How in the fuck did the bastard get there already?* He'd never seen a man so fast.

This is no man, Aaron, no person at all. Not anymore.

The creature wore a long robe, the sleeves nearly twice as long as normal, and Aaron could see its thin, slender left hand coming out of its sleeve, hanging at its calf. The other hand held the sword it carried up at an angle behind it as it moved closer. Even though it walked and moved slowly, its whole body shifted and swayed with each step, as if it had difficulty moving at such a pace.

"Aaron!"

Aaron risked a glance back to see four city guardsmen at the other end of the alley. "Shit." He looked at the creature coming toward him. Whatever danger the four guards posed, the others would have to deal with them. He didn't dare turn his back on the creature for long. What was worse, he knew more soldiers would be coming. If he and the others didn't make it out of this alley soon, they wouldn't make it out at all. *Well, say one good thing for it,* he thought as he watched the freakish figure move closer, *whatever happens, at least it'll happen quickly.*

He'd no sooner had the thought than the creature sped forward in a blur of movement bringing the long, slender sword up at an angle. Aaron's bond warned him of the attack, and he lunged out of the way. He managed to avoid the blade, barely, but in his haste he hadn't been thinking of the alley wall, and he grunted as he slammed into it. Not wasting any time, he spun back around, searching for his opponent.

It stood in the alley with the sword at an angle down and behind it now, watching him with its head cocked as if trying to figure out why he wasn't dead already. The truth was, Aaron wasn't sure himself. Feeling a sense of urgency building within him, knowing that they were wasting time they didn't have, he followed some advice Darrell had given him once, long ago. "In fights for your life," the swordmaster had said, "there can be no half measures. When you decide a battle must be fought, attack at once and without hesitation, for it is most often the man who strikes first who walks away in the end." And so Aaron did. He was tired from his fight with the swordsman and their run through the city, but he forced his body forward with as much speed as he could muster, swinging his blade at the slender creature's neck.

The creature did not change its stance, yet its arm flashed up, independent of the rest of its body, and Aaron's sword met its blade with a ringing chime that filled the alley. Growling, Aaron pressed the attack, swinging as fast as he could as he waded forwarded, forcing the creature back, yet no matter how fast he was, the creature was faster, and he thought he saw something like amusement in its dark gaze, the only thing he could make out in the shadow of its hood.

Finally, he backed away, his breath coming hard in his lungs, and stared at the creature. It stood much as it had before, its head still cocked to the side, and while Aaron gasped for breath, the creature seemed unaffected by the exchange. Aaron reached out with his bond, trying to gain some understanding of the thing's thoughts. If most people's minds were as clear as a mountain lake, their thoughts there if a man only bent down and looked, then the mind of the thing before him was more like a bog of mud and mist. In that place of confusion and mystery, Aaron could make out no specifics, but could hear tortured screams coming from somewhere off in the distance. He jerked the power away, feeling tainted somehow.

"What are you?" he breathed, and the thing cocked its head the other way as if trying to understand. Aaron could hear the sounds of fighting further down the alley and wanted to turn and see if the others were alright, but he didn't dare. They either would be okay, or they wouldn't be, and there was nothing he could do about it now. *Handle the problem in front of you before borrowing troubles from tomorrow.* His father's words, spoken to him as a child, words that had stayed with him when so much else had faded and been lost from memory. He had always done his best to follow them—not that it was all that difficult. A life spent in the Downs around men and women that would just as soon stab you as look at you taught a man that today had plenty enough problems of its own. There was no need to go looking for them. Problems like the one staring him in the face now, with its not-quite-empty gaze, a thing worse than if it had been completely vacant, for Aaron thought he could see a sliver of the person the creature had been.

Suddenly, the thing burst into motion, lunging forward, its unnaturally long arm swinging the slender blade at Aaron's throat. The thing didn't have good technique—its footwork barely existed at all, and it swung the blade like a man out chopping wood. The problem, of course, was that being faster than a galloping horse with a reach twice as long as your opponent's went a long way toward making up for any lack of technical knowledge.

Aaron pivoted, bringing his sword up to parry and caught the blade only inches from his throat. Their blades locked only for a moment, but it was enough for him to realize that he could push the creature's sword away easily enough. Not strong then, weaker than pretty much any man he'd fought, but fast enough to make up for it. Even as he thought it, the creature demonstrated its speed as it spun in a full circle, too fast for his eye to follow, and brought the blade back around at throat-level on Aaron's other side. Turning your back on your opponent was never a wise choice in a swordfight, and so Aaron had not been expecting the move and nearly lost his head because of it, only just managing to bring his blade around to knock the attack away.

What followed from the creature was a flurry of frantic, blurring attacks that Aaron did his best to parry, calling on years spent training with the sword and fighting for his life—but in the end, it was only the power of the bond that kept him alive in those panicked moments. It could have went on for a minute or an hour, Aaron's mind had no time to consider, as he desperately tried to keep the blurring sword at bay, then finally managed to retreat a step. The creature did not follow and push the attack, and Aaron stood there gasping for air.

Despite his best efforts, Aaron noted idly that he was bleeding from a shallow cut on his forearm and another on his side, where the thing's blade had scored him before he'd gotten his own sword around to parry. Neither of the cuts were deep, but they were distractions, ones he could ill-afford. *Can't keep this up,* he thought.

He knew it, and the creature seemed to know it, too. It stepped forward slowly, almost casually, and Aaron retreated a step as it did, continuing to do so as the creature walked at him in its confident, leisurely pace. Suddenly, it burst forward again, but this time Aaron was waiting on it, calling on all the power his bond afforded him to know where the strike was coming. He gripped his sword in both hands, swinging it against the incoming blade not to parry but to hit it as hard as he could. A loud ringing filled the air as the two blades met, and Aaron knocked the creature's attack wide. He took the brief opportunity this afforded him and lunged forward, his sword leading.

He half-expected the creature to somehow dodge out of the way, but all the speed in the world couldn't help you if you were-off balance, and thanks to his strike, the creature was. It tried to move, but stumbled as its feet twisted beneath it, and in another moment Aaron's blade plunged into its chest, ripping out of the other side. The creature tried to bring its long blade down, but Aaron was inside its reach now, and he felt only the dull thud of the handle of its sword as it struck his back.

The creature did not scream or cry out at the mortal wound, not even when Aaron turned the blade and ripped it free, taking a hurried step back from it. The cloaked figure seemed to regard him from beneath the hood it wore for several seconds, before it crumpled to the ground without a sound. Aaron stared at it, his blade at the ready, his breath wheezing in his throat. When it still did not move, he eased forward, crouching and pulling the hood back to reveal the creature's face. Aaron grunted in surprise and disgust as he took in the thing's features, shame and repulsion welling up in him.

Oh gods, Aaron, Co said into his mind, *oh gods be good.*

Aaron only knelt and stared at the creature's face, his own expression hard while, inside of him, a storm of emotions raged. There were deep, fresh scars covering the creature's face and shaved head, and its expression was twisted in one of agony. It was as if whatever horrors it had endured to be made into a monster had been so terrible as to stamp themselves permanently onto its features. All of this was bad, but the worst thing about the face was that, judging by what was left of the delicate features, the creature had once been a woman. *No,* he thought, *not a woman at all but a girl. No more than seventeen years old if she was a day. A child.*

Not a child anymore, Aaron, Co said. *You have to remember that. Whatever it was, whatever she was, she was not what she had once been. You had no choice.*

"I've heard that a lot lately," Aaron said, his voice dry and without emotion as he stared down at the corpse. "Tell me, firefly, if a man never has a choice in the things he does, then how is he a man at all? What good can such a one as that do for anyone?"

*Aaron...*the Virtue began, but then she grew silent and it seemed that she had nothing to say. Nothing she *could* say.

Aaron felt guilt settling on him, felt his shoulders slump under the weight of it. *No,* a part of him said. Rage—the mirror of the compassion the bond granted him—began to well up inside him. *You won't take credit for this. You can't. You can bury your head in your hands and weep later if you have to, but for now there are people who are counting on you. Not just Leomin and the others but thousands of people back in Perennia. Now. Get. Up.*

At first, his body didn't want to obey his commands, and it seemed impossible to pull his eyes away from the dead girl lying in the street, but finally he was standing and turning to check on his friends. Two of the soldiers still faced off against Darrell. Wendell was crouched on top of another that was obviously unconscious or dead, beating him in the head—with a boot of all things, and Aaron had a moment of confusion, wondering where the sergeant had gotten it, until he noticed that one of Wendell's feet was bare. Leomin was standing back with Caleb, the two of them watching the swordmaster. A deep cut on the Parnen's arm bled blood that looked black in the moonlight.

Aaron turned back to look at Darrell and saw that his breathing was labored, and he was trying to keep both of the men in sight as they attempted to get on either side of him. Watching it, Aaron felt the rage that was always so close to the surface blaze to life, slipping loose the chains with which he had bound it. At that moment, he did not feel his own exhaustion or his own wounds, and even his remorse about killing the child was a distant, unimportant thing.

In that moment, he forgot about everything else, every*one* else. It was only him and the soldiers—even Boyce Kevlane didn't reckon into it. These men. *These* men were the ones responsible. If they had their way, more children would be taken, more lives would end in torture and agony. There would be no guilt, no shame in the killing of them, not these. The rage was a blazing fire inside of him now. Some men were better off dead, that was all, and the world a better place when it had moved on and forgotten them.

He was running before he knew it. The night was suddenly filled with a bestial roar of rage but that, too, was beyond his thoughts. For him there was nothing but the men and the sword in his hand, slick with a child's blood. He was on them in an instant, knocking the weary swordmaster aside and parrying a strike that had been aimed at Darrell's neck. He waded into the two men with a flurry of vicious blows, giving no thought for his own safety or even the safety of his companions. His only thought was for blood and his need for it. They were well-trained and fought in unison, watching each other's backs, and that was good. That was alright, for the blood would come—he knew that as certainly as he knew anything—and, when it did, it would be all the better for the wait.

They tried to counter attack, and Aaron stepped out of the way of the blades only enough to ensure they were not fatal, that they would not keep him from fulfilling the demand of the song roaring in his head, a song of pain and death whose promise had to be kept. Their blades scored him glancing blows on his arm, his shoulder, his chest, but he did not concern himself with them, was glad in fact, for the song cared little from whence the blood came, only so long as it *did* come. He beat at their swords, a mad grin etched into his face, a low, steady growl issuing from his throat. He watched their faces, their eyes, and saw the moment when they realized he would not stop, would not *be* stopped.

He struck at one of them with his blade, hissing with his need, but the man retreated, throwing up a clumsy parry that managed to keep the questing steel at bay. Aaron felt the next man's attack coming, a lunging stab that would skewer him. He shifted to the side enough to keep the strike from penetrating, but not enough to keep it from slicing a ragged tear in his side. The soldier shouted in what might have been triumph or fear, but Aaron had used the opportunity to step past the man's blade and swing his sword in a wide, two-handed arc. The steel tore a jagged, bloody swath into the man's neck but got stuck halfway through.

Aaron laughed as the man collapsed to the ground in a crimson shower. He gave his blade a jerk, trying to loosen it, but it was stuck fast. He was still trying to pull it free when the man's companion rushed into him from behind. Aaron stumbled forward then took a few more purposeful steps, just enough to get out of reach of the man's follow-up attack, and he spun, grinning as the blade cut the air in front of his throat, missing it by inches. Aaron went to raise his own sword and realized to his surprise that he'd dropped it when the man struck him.

The soldier backed up one step, his sword in front of him, but Aaron could see the confidence building in the man's face; he now fought an unarmed foe. "You don't understand," Aaron rasped, his voice barely human at all, "the song isn't in the sword or the steel. It never was." He grinned, baring his teeth. "It's in me. It always has been." He lunged forward, striking the flat of the soldier's blade with his wrist and knocking it aside as he leapt onto his opponent, his feet striking the man in the waist, his hands gripping the back of his head and digging into his eyes.

The soldier screamed as he tumbled onto his back and tried to push Aaron free, but the anger would not be pushed aside so easily, and the sellsword wrapped his legs around the man's waist even as he continued to dig his thumbs deeper and deeper into his eyes. The soldier screamed again, louder this time, and something *popped*. Warm fluid spilled over Aaron's thumbs, but he wasn't finished, and he jerked the man's head up and slammed it into the cobblestones of the alleyway again and again. By the time he came to a panting, satisfied halt, the back of the man's head had lost all semblance of the shape it once had held, and his struggles had long since ceased. Aaron pulled his thumbs free and jerked himself upward, spinning. There were others here, other blood to shed, and the song was not yet finished.

Three men and a youth stared at him with wide eyes, and he grinned as he stalked to where his sword lay, still stuck in the dead man. He grunted as he bent and ripped it free. The steel might not carry the song, but it made its notes ring clearer. "Alright then," he rasped, turning back to the others, "who's next?"

The man closest to him, an older man with white hair said something, but he might as well have spoken in a different language for all that Aaron understood him. Aaron started forward, raising his sword to cut the man down. Once that was done, he would finish the others. Four would not be enough for the song, not nearly, but he could feel the thousands in the city around him, feel their hopes and their dreams and their worries. He could have told them to let them all go, for once he was finished here, they, too, would become a part of the song.

The old man held a sword, but he did not raise it as Aaron approached, instead holding up a hand as if to ward him away. Aaron and the rage inside of him thought to tell the old man that the song could not be stopped, but didn't bother. He would know soon enough. He was just about to strike when a voice spoke behind him.

"Aaron, stop."

Aaron's arm froze of its own accord, and he felt like he was moving in slow motion as he turned to see the Parnen man staring at him. The man's brow was furrowed as if in concentration and sweat coated his forehead.

Aaron growled in frustration, trying to bring his blade around to deal with this new threat. But it was as if the sword in his hand weighed a ton. He hissed and strained, spitting with fury, and finally the blade *did* move. Inch by agonizing inch, he brought it closer to the Parnen. The man did not move but his hands clenched into fists at his sides, and he began to shake. "*Aaron, no!*" The words resounded in Aaron's head like a thunderclap, and he howled in pain and anger.

He bared his teeth, grabbing the blade with both hands and pushing it through air that felt as thick and impenetrable as a stone wall. His muscles screamed in protest, but the blade moved another inch. Then another. "Aaron," the man said, the words echoing in Aaron's mind, "we are your friends. You do not want to hurt us. Remember, Aaron. I am Leomin. Remember me."

The name tickled a memory in the back of Aaron's thoughts, buried deep beneath the sea of rage that roiled through him, and he hesitated, uncertainty creeping into his thoughts. "*Leomin?*" he rasped.

"Yes," the Parnen said, nodding slowly, "I am your friend. Remember me, Aaron. Remember why we are here."

And suddenly, Aaron did. The rage vanished in an instant, leaving in its wake exhaustion and searing pain from his wounds, and he stumbled and collapsed to his knees, letting the sword fall on the cobbles. "Gods, Leomin," he said, his voice weak and full of fear and shame at what he had almost done. "I'm ... I'm so sorry. He stared at his hands, coated with blood, and they felt as if they belonged to someone else. A stranger's hands. A monster's hands. "I'm so sorry."

"He alright?" another voice asked, and Aaron turned to see Wendell moving closer, holding the boot over his head as if he'd intended to brain Aaron with it.

"Yes..." Leomin panted, "I believe he is." Then he stumbled and would have fallen if Darrell hadn't stepped forward and caught him.

"Well," Wendell said, "in that case, I wouldn't worry overly much about wantin' to kill Leomin, sir. It'd be my guess that most of his friends have considered doin' the same thing at one time or another." He knelt, offering Aaron his hand.

"*No,*" Aaron rasped, "don't touch me, Wendell." His eyes glanced back at his hands, stained with blood. "It doesn't wash off. It never washes off."

"Eh ... are you alright, sir?"

"I have to be," Aaron said, mostly to himself. Then, grunting with the effort, he rose unsteadily to his feet.

The sergeant shot an uncertain, worried look at Leomin before turning back to Aaron. "Now then, sir," Wendell said, "I ain't tryin' to be contrary, but I wonder if, maybe next time, you wouldn't give us a warnin' before you go all crazy, eh? If I wanted to get surprised with crazy every day, I would've gotten married a long time ago."

Despite the shame he felt, Aaron found himself giving the man a weary grin. Then, his thoughts returned to the child lying dead only a few feet away, and he sobered. "Children," he said, turning to meet Darrell's eyes, "they're using children, Darrell."

"I know," the man said sadly, "I saw."

"What's the plan, sir?" Wendell asked.

Aaron glanced at the Parnen. "How much did you have to use on me, Leomin?"

The Parnen captain was still breathing hard, and he took a minute to swallow before shaking his head regretfully. "I think I told you once before, Aaron, the bond of a man with a Virtue acts as a sort of buffer between him and the others. It can be overcome, but..." He shook his head again.

"How much, Leomin?"

The Parnen met his eyes. "All of it," he said, "all of it and more, Mr. Envelar. I have never carried so much of the power at once—I felt as if my body was going to be ripped apart from it."

"Which means that if Kevlane *is* in the city, he knows we're here now whether he did before or not."

"Yes," Leomin said, "I'm sorry, Aaron."

"It's not your fault, Leomin," he said, shaking his head as he struggled to get his breathing under control. "It's mine."

"So I ain't tryin' to rush you fellas or nothin'," Wendell said, "but if that's the case...shouldn't we ought to be runnin' about now?"

"I might know a place we can go," the youth offered, and Aaron noted that he stood behind Darrell, eyeing Aaron as if he were a rabid animal that might attack without warning. The sight of it wounded Aaron more than he would have thought, but there was no time to worry about such things now.

"No," Aaron said, shaking his head, "there's no time. We have to get out of the city now." Even as he spoke, Aaron bent and tore a strip of cloth from the shirt of one of the dead guards and began wrapping his wounds.

"But, sir," Wendell said, "and don't get me wrong—there's just about nothin' I want more than to get out of this city with my parts all in their right places, but what about the proof we come here lookin' for?"

Aaron glanced at the dead girl lying in the street. Bringing her would be proof enough, but their chances of making it out of the city were already slim without being weighed down by a corpse. No, taking her wasn't an option, and he found himself glad of that. "We'll tell them what we've seen here."

"And what if they don't believe us?" Leomin asked.

Aaron met the man's eyes. "Then we'll make them believe."

CHAPTER TWENTY-ONE

The man screamed and begged, but Kevlane barely noticed. After all, they always did and the work still had to be completed despite that. "It hurts, doesn't it?" he asked in a voice that was not unkind as his fingers dug into the latest wound the knife had made.

The man screamed louder, most likely too far gone in his agony to hear Kevlane at all. "It wasn't always this way, you know," the ancient mage said in a regretful tone as he paused to roll up the already bloody sleeves of his robes. "Once, long ago, long before your parents' parents met," he said, giving the bloody, screaming man a wink, "the Art was always waiting there. All I—or those like me—had to do was reach out and grab it, to use what knowledge we had to shape it to our wishes, our desires."

He considered for a moment, then gave a shrug, before bringing the knife back down and starting to carve the man's flesh once more. "But the world moved on—it always does. Still..." He paused, grunting with the effort, trying to remove the short blade that was stuck in the man's side. He'd had it sharpened only this morning, but it had been a long, busy day, as he sought to finish with those specimens he was holding before the tournament began. Then, he knew, the work would start in earnest.

"Anyway," he said, "there's no use mourning what was lost. All things eventually are, and the Art is no exception. Most think it dead but it is not—at least, not completely. A skilled man might still draw upon it—though, admittedly, he will receive only a trickle where once there was a river—if he but knows the means of doing so."

He glanced at the man's face to see if he understood. His eyes were wild, and he thrashed against his bonds, heedless of where the steel manacles dug deep furrows into his wrists and ankles. He paid the mage no attention. Kevlane sighed. "With the use of great emotions as a conduit, such a man might draw on what Art is left, and out of all the emotions that exist—lust, love, hate—there is none greater than that despair caused by pain. This was true many years ago, when I first began my experiments, and it is even truer now."

The man's only answer was a scream, but that was alright. He didn't need to understand Kevlane's words, for soon his body would stand testament to the truth. If, that was, he survived. Kevlane was pulling the knife out, just about to start another cut when he froze, his eyes going impossibly wide, the wildness in them a match for the insanity lurking in the manacled man's gaze.

"*It can't be,*" he breathed. "They wouldn't dare." Even as he said it, a burst of power came again, stronger than before. It was as if he was standing on a dark shore and somewhere, across the water, someone had set to light a bonfire whose flames reached into the clouds themselves. There was no denying it. They were here. In the city.

He cocked his head, pushing away his sudden fury and disbelief as he focused on trying to determine where that burst of power came from—where it was *still* coming from. The man on the table continued to scream, his wailing, tortured cries making it difficult for Kevlane to concentrate. "Shut *up,*" he hissed.

But the man continued screaming, and with a growl of frustration Kevlane buried the knife in his throat. He stared down at his latest experiment, watched as the man breathed his last breaths through a mask of blood, listened as his screams turn to gurgling, choking gasps, then stopped altogether. The light of life faded from the man's eyes, but Kevlane didn't notice, for he wasn't seeing the man at all but that bonfire on the distant horizon, was busily tracing its sparks and smoke back to the source.

"Master?" Caldwell asked, and Kevlane barely managed to suppress the suddenly powerful urge to rip the blade free from the corpse lying on the table and use it on the man. "Is everything alright?"

"They're here," Kevlane said, still having difficulty believing it. "Evelyn and Aliandra."

"Sir?" Caldwell asked, his voice uncertain.

"The Virtues, you fool," Kevlane hissed, "Aaron Envelar is in Baresh as we speak!"

CHAPTER TWENTY-TWO

On the outside, the castle was the same as Adina remembered it, but the inside had not escaped the rebellion unscathed. The portraits and tapestries of her and her family that had once hung on the wall had been replaced with portraits of the inner council members and their families. They passed a portrait of the general himself in his military dress uniform, his chin high, a nobility to him that shared few similarities with the man that shuffled along behind Adina and the others. Ridell had been knocked unconscious when Beth tripped him, and when he'd woken he'd tried to fight his way free. Bastion had managed to dissuade the man of thinking he could get away, but the general's broken nose was a testament to the fact that the young soldier hadn't been particularly kind in doing so. Not that Adina had minded. The man had tried to kill her after all, not once, but twice.

As they made their way through the castle, startled serving men and women that Adina didn't recognize stared at the bared steel Bastion now held at the general's back with unveiled fear. Adina had no doubt that once she and her friends passed the servants would go running to the nearest guards to warn them, but she had other concerns on her mind just then.

She'd stopped and asked one frightened serving girl where the members of the inner council were, and had been thrilled to learn that they were even now in session. She shot a glance behind her and saw Ridell scowling, the side of his face covered in blood. "Oh, don't look so down, General," Adina said, "these are your friends we're visiting, after all."

The two guards standing outside of the council chambers drew their swords as they saw Adina and the others approach. Adina recognized one of them and she found herself smiling. Apparently, the noblemen and the general had neglected to completely change the castle staff. "Hello, Franklin," she said, pushing back the hood of her cloak, "how are you?"

The guard frowned for a moment, clearly confused, then his eyes went wide with realization. "Q-queen Adina?" he stammered. "But…but I thought you were dead."

"It seems," Adina said, glancing back at the general, "there was a bit of a misunderstanding. One which I have come to rectify."

The guard nodded and dropped to one knee, bowing his head. After a moment, he glanced over and saw that the younger guard who stood with him was still holding his own sword up uncertainly. "Drop the blade you damned fool!" he hissed. "That's the queen!"

The young guard let the blade fall to the floor and followed after it, kneeling. "Forgive me, Majesty," he said, "I didn't know."

"There is no forgiveness necessary," Adina said. "Please, rise. Both of you." She motioned to the closed door, "Are all of my counselors inside?"

"Yes, Majesty," Franklin said, "they've all arrived for the meeting."

"Perfect," Adina said, she started forward, then paused, turning back to the older guard. "Tell me, how is Esmerelda? And your daughter, Constance, wasn't it?"

The man beamed at that. "Yes ma'am. Thank you for remembering. They're both great—the little one's a handful just like her mother."

"And her father too, no doubt," Adina said, smiling.

The guard grinned. "As you say, Majesty. Eh, Majesty," he said, his face twisting into a scowl as he stared at the general, "would you like for us to come in with you?"

"Oh, that's quite alright, Franklin. Thank you though, and we'll speak again soon."

"It would be my honor, Queen," he said, bowing his head.

"Oh, and Franklin?" She said as she pulled the hood of her cloak over her head once more.

"Yes, Majesty?"

She winked. "I'd like to surprise them, if it's all the same to you."

He nodded then he motioned to his companion and in another moment they were swinging the doors open.

"What is the meaning of this, guard?" a familiar voice said from inside, its tone somehow angry and whiny at the same time. "We explicitly told you that meetings of the High Council are not to be interrupted under any circumstances."

Franklin glanced back into the hallway at Adina. "I believe they're ready for you, Majesty," he whispered.

Adina nodded and led the others inside. "I *demand* to know the meaning of this," the man said.

Adina heard a noise behind her and turned to see Gryle trying to fit the pew through the doorway. He couldn't seem to get the angle right, and he gave a grunt as he pulled it through, tearing a gaping, pew-sized hole in the doorframe and wall. He winced, his body tensing, and glanced back at Adina, his eyes wide. Adina only laughed, and Bastion grunted, shaking his head. "Told you to leave that damn thing," the youth said.

Adina laughed again then stepped into the room, glancing at the five counselors seated in the chambers. All men and women she knew, men and women she had *trusted,* up until they had done their level best to have her murdered and steal her kingdom.

"Who are you to *dare* to enter the chambers of the High Council?" A woman's voice, and Adina turned to look at the heavy-set gray-haired noblewoman who'd spoken. She would have looked like a kindly grandmother if not for all of the face paint she wore, and the sparkling, gem-encrusted dress with a low neckline that would have looked out of place on someone twenty years younger. "*Guards,*" the woman snapped, "take these ruffians away."

"Ruffians is it?" Adina said, sliding her hood back, "and what, I wonder, Lady Aversham, is all this talk of a 'High Council'?" She shrugged. "But, then, I suppose vanity is the least of your crimes, wouldn't you say?"

A Sellsword's Valor

The old woman's face went pale, and her mouth worked for several seconds without making any sound. "I-it can't be. But how did you—?"

"Make it back into the city and the castle itself?" Adina asked. "Oh, it wasn't so difficult to get in here. The general was kind enough to provide an escort," she said, nodding at the wounded man behind her.

"You fool," a man's voice said, and Adina turned to the other side of the room to see Lord Marion rise from his seat behind the table. He was no more than thirty-five years old and wore ostentatious clothes he'd clearly spent more time and money on than any woman she knew. Not that he didn't have it. Marion was his father's only son and when the old man—a kind, gentle soul, a retired soldier who had been one of Adina's closest confidants and also had just so happened to be the richest man in all of Galia—had died, his son had inherited his fortune, as well as his position on the council. This man, at least, Adina had never cared for.

"Do you really think you can just walk back in here and take over a kingdom?" he said, his voice incredulous as he motioned to her friends. "With whom, exactly? A fat woman in a dress, that useless chamberlain Gryle, an old woman, and some farm boy that's grown freakishly large from a life spent hauling shit and cleaning out slop?" He laughed, a high-pitched, grating laugh that Adina remembered all too well. "I only see one sword between you. And do not think you might call on the guards, for they are spread throughout the castle and the barracks, and even if they wanted to help you—which they don't—they would not arrive in time. The city has moved on, *Queen*," he said, drawing his sword and motioning to the two other men on the council who rose and drew their own, "and we'll be doing its people a favor to kill you now."

"*Fat woman?*" May said, her tone shocked and angry at the same time. She started forward, but Adina held out a hand, stopping her.

"Only one sword, you say, Lord Mary?" Adina said, and the man's face flushed with anger at the use of the nickname many used behind his back, one brought on by his name, and his decidedly feminine interest in clothes and perfumes. "And as for the guards..." She shrugged. "I'm afraid you're wrong. You see, it has been so long since I've visited the people of Galia that, well, I may have made a few stops before coming here." She smiled as, on cue, over two dozen armored soldiers poured through the door, fanning out to either side of the room.

The other two councilmen dropped their swords immediately, holding up their hands in surrender, but Lord Marion did not let his own go so easy. He sneered, but Adina could see the sweat on his upper lip and the way his hand shook on the sword's handle. "How do we know you won't just have us killed as soon as we lay down our weapons?" he asked, doing his best for bravado but managing only barely-contained terror.

"You don't," Adina said, shrugging. "It's up to you, Marion. I'd rather you put the blade down—I'd hate to cause the serving women any extra work if I can help it—but either way, this farce ends now."

The young noble seemed to consider, then finally, he let the blade drop as Adina had known he would. The man might have inherited his father's fortune, but he'd certainly not gotten any of his courage. "Very well," he said, his voice sounding as if he was on the verge of tears. Once the blade was down Adina motioned for the soldiers, who moved forward and clamped irons on each of the five council members.

"What would you like us to do with them, my Queen?" one of them asked once the prisoners were secured.

"Take them to the dungeons for now," Adina said, "I'm sure I'll think of something."

"Of course, Majesty."

Adina watched the council members being dragged from the room until it was only her friends and the general remaining. "Do you know," she said, "I've imagined this moment a thousand times, imagined the satisfaction I'd get from it. But I find that, now the thing's done, I only feel tired."

The club owner nodded knowingly. "Such is the way with revenge, Princess—or should I say, Queen. People seem to believe that taking away another's happiness will somehow add to their own, but it never works like that."

"Did you see the faces on those fools?" Beth cackled, shaking her head as she wiped a tear from her eye. "They looked like the old dog Salen himself appeared out of the ground and was leadin' 'em to the Fields personally."

Gryle, who'd been holding the pew like a club once more at the threat of Marion's attack, now sat it down awkwardly before glancing around and easing down to sit into it. Adina found herself smiling despite the trials of the last few days. Some things, at least, never changed. May stared at him, shaking her head in bemused wonder before turning to Adina. "Well. What now?"

Adina's expression sobered, and she met each of their eyes in turn. "Now, our real work begins. General," she said, looking at the wretched, bloody figure who seemed to have aged twenty years in the last few hours, "show me to my troops."

CHAPTER TWENTY-THREE

"Get out of the fucking way!" Aaron shouted as he gave his horse's reins a jerk, narrowly avoiding a fat, well-dressed man who stumbled out of his path.

The sun had only just risen, but there were a surprising amount of people already on the streets, opening their shops and preparing to start their days. He risked a glance behind him and saw the others following, Darrell and Wendell closest, then Leomin and the youth in the back. Intelligence Virtue or not, it was clearly the first time the boy had ridden a horse and anyone watching would have guessed it was the Parnen's first time as well the way he bounced roughly along, looking as if he would be thrown at any moment.

They'd stolen the horses from a stable they'd passed less than an hour ago. They were good, strong animals, no doubt worth a small fortune. Aaron hadn't felt great about stealing them and, judging by the looks that had been on the faces of the others, neither had they, but he consoled himself with the fact that he'd get over the shame of the theft better than the kiss of a headman's axe. Besides, worth a small fortune they might be, but he had a feeling the horses wouldn't be fast enough if a few more of those creatures—*children, gods they were children*—decided to run them down.

He'd been expecting just such an occurrence with each minute that passed but, so far at least, none had shown. He didn't know what to make of that, for he knew that Kevlane would do anything to see them dead if he knew they were nearby—but he would take what luck he could get. The chances of them making it out of the gate of the city were small enough even without more of those *things* showing up.

Aaron took a moment to concentrate on his bond, calling on its power, and detected a pursuit coming from behind them, no more than fifteen minutes away. A dozen men, maybe more. "Come on!" he yelled at the others. As they drew closer to the gate, the street became more and more crowded and, for a time, his thoughts were only on dodging around men and women who seemed to have all decided to commit suicide by jumping in front of a galloping horse.

Finally, they rounded a turn in the street, and Aaron was relieved to see Baresh's western gate in the distance. His relief was short-lived though when he drew close enough to make out the people standing at the gate. Four guards, their swords drawn, and in front of them two figures Aaron recognized. One was the swordsman he'd fought at Nathan's tavern, and despite the fact that even from this distance, Aaron could see that the man was covered in dust and bloody scrapes, he stood confidently enough. Beside him, seeming somehow even more grotesque in the daylight, stood the hulking, cloaked monstrosity.

Aaron pulled his horse to a stop and waited for the others to come up beside him. "Well, shit on it," Wendell said, pausing to spit into the road, "what do you want to do now, sir?"

"We have to go through them," Aaron said, eyeing the distant soldiers, "there's no time for anything else."

Darrell nodded. "How do you want to handle it?"

Aaron considered. "I'll take the swordsman."

"Very well," Darrell said, "I will handle the four guards."

Wendell grunted, glancing at Leomin and Caleb. "I guess that leaves us the big fucker. Unless, that is, you fellas want to run the other way, in which case I reckon I'd be honor-bound to come along. As protection, you understand."

"Mr. Envelar is right," Caleb said, his voice calm despite the fear that showed in his pale face, "there's no time."

Wendell sighed. "What about you?" he asked the Parnen. "You feeling as suicidal as the rest of this lot?"

Leomin stared at the figures and, for the first time Aaron had ever seen, he did not speak, only drew the sword at his side instead. The sergeant spat again, "Ah, fuck it then. There's worse ways to die." He turned and looked at the hulking figure in the distance and sighed. "None come to mind, understand, but I'm willin' to believe they're out there."

"Alright then," Aaron said. "But remember, we have to do this fast."

Wendell snorted, still eyeing the giant creature, "Oh, no worries there, sir. I'm fairly well convinced that whatever happens is goin' to happen faster than we'd like."

Aaron bared his teeth in a grim smile, then he gave his horse's sides a kick. The beast whinnied, charging forward toward the gate and whatever fate awaited them there. The swordsman he'd fought before stood with a smug look on his face, and he began speaking, shouting to be heard over the thunder of the horses as they came closer. "It was only too obvious that—"

Aaron didn't slow as he drew closer to the waiting men, and the swordsman, Savrin, he'd said his name was, cut off as Aaron leapt from the saddle, his blade flashing forward the instant his feet hit the ground. Savrin hissed in surprise, his own sword leaping up with impressive speed and parrying the strike, but Aaron wasn't done. He growled as he waded forward, his sword moving in a blur and, for several moments, Savrin was able to do nothing but mount a desperate defense, his smug expression gone as he strained to keep pace with the rapid attacks.

Aaron was exhausted, and the only reason he was able to keep going was the understanding of what would happen should they fail to make it out of the city. Yet even with such motivation, he knew that he couldn't continue at such a pace for long...and then he realized something. The man he fought was without a doubt an exceptional swordsman—he himself had claimed that he was the best in Baresh, a matter that Aaron didn't particularly doubt. A man like that, a man obviously so confident in his own abilities, would not expect to lose, would expect to be better than any man he fought.

Aaron's life on the streets had not always been kind or easy—never had been, in fact—but it *had* taught him a few things. One of those things was that no matter how strong a man thought he was, there was always someone stronger, and overconfidence got men killed faster than almost anything else. The man expected Aaron to be a worse fighter, so Aaron gave him what he expected. He still pushed forward, still gave every bit of speed and strength he could to each strike, but he allowed his attacks to become predictable, following a pattern.

The strain slowly started to ease from the swordsman's face as he settled into blocking the pattern of the sellsword's blows. As he fought, Aaron reached out with the power of the bond, touching his opponent's mind. In an instant, he was flooded with the man's thoughts, his fears and desires. He knew of the man's sister and his nephew. He knew, too, without a doubt, that Kevlane had taken over Belgarin's place as king. But more importantly at the moment was that he could feel the man's confidence returning, feel him settling into the predictable rhythm of Aaron's attacks.

He gave it what time he could—not long, considering the fact that he felt as if he would collapse at any moment—then he started the pattern once again. A low strike on the man's right, followed by a lunge that he batted aside almost before it was even there. But instead of bringing the sword around from his opponent's left, as Savrin expected, Aaron lunged forward. Fooled or not, overconfident or not, the swordsman was fast, and his blade lashed back toward Aaron, cutting the sellsword across the shoulder even as Aaron's fist lashed out, smashing the swordsman's nose.

Aaron hissed in pain but didn't relent, following the stumbling swordsman and punching him again and again in the face and the stomach with his free hand as his sword blocked the man's panicked, uncoordinated strikes.

Under that battering fist, the man lost his composure and dropped his sword, throwing his arms up to protect his face. Aaron immediately changed tactics, sweeping his leg out and knocking his opponent's feet out from under him. Savrin fell backward, striking the ground hard, and before he could rise, Aaron brought the tip of his blade to rest inches from the man's throat.

"—ou *cheated*," Savrin squeaked, cradling his broken nose in one hand in a futile effort to stop the stream of blood pouring from it.

"I won," Aaron said, "and because of that I get to live. We are not knights, and this is no tournament. There is no purse full of gold as a prize, no judge to call whether a strike was foul or good.

In real life, in real fights, the only prize you stand to win is to keep breathing for a little while longer." The man didn't respond, meeting Aaron's eyes, and the sellsword knew he was waiting, showing what courage he could as he prepared for the blade to slide home, to finish it.

Aaron knew that he should, that it would be the smart thing. An enemy you leave behind you is in all the better position to stab you in the back and a man with such skill as the swordsman possessed wasn't the type of enemy you wanted to leave breathing, if you could help it. Only a fool would do such a thing, take such a risk, yet despite knowing it was the right thing, Aaron found himself unable to drive the blade the few inches forward that would be necessary to finish it. His sword felt heavy in his grip, impossibly so, and he hissed a curse as he realized that he couldn't do it. There had been so much killing already with more to come, and the thought of taking this man's life sickened him. After all, in that moment when he'd touched him with the bond, Aaron had come to know the man, know him, in some ways, better even than Savrin knew himself.

Shaking his head at his own stupidity, Aaron crouched down, bringing the blade so that the sharp edge of it rested no more than an inch from the man's throat, and met the swordsman's eyes. "Finish it," the man said, his voice hoarse with pain and fear.

Aaron considered that. "Listen to me," he said. "I should kill you—the gods know I'm a fool not to do so—but I won't. If I run into you again, though, I won't hesitate. Do you understand me?"

The man nodded his head a fraction, all that he was capable of with the sword's blade so close. "Good," Aaron said. He sighed. "Why don't you leave this place, Savrin?" he said, waving his hand at the city. "Your new master cares nothing for you. You know that, don't you? He cares nothing for anyone. As for Pella and little Larn, do you really think you can keep them safe from half way across the world?"

The man's eyes went wide at that. "But how...you can't know about them."

"Never mind that. Yes, I know of your sister and your nephew and plenty more besides. There's a doubt in you, isn't there? That you're not good enough—that you never have been. A doubt that's been growing in you since you were a child. Since you took your beatings and listened to your old man tell you how worthless you were, how pathetic a son."

The man's eyes grew wider still and looked as if they would pop out of his head, and his mouth worked in silence. "You couldn't protect your sister from him then, Savrin, and so you think yourself incapable now. You challenge yourself to be the best, to beat any that come against you because you think you've got something to prove." Aaron leaned in closer to the man. "Well, you're not a child anymore, Savrin. You're a damn good blade—one of the best I've seen. You can protect them, but not here. As for your father, fuck him. He's just one bastard among many—the world's full of them. You're better than he ever was. Even as a child you were better and he knew it. It's why he beat you. Now, go and be with the people that matter, Savrin. Go while there's still time."

"W-what are you?" the man breathed.

Aaron grunted, rising. "A dead man, if I don't get out of this city. Now, will you do what I've asked?"

"I...I'll think on it," the man said, "truly."

Aaron shrugged. "Fair enough. But don't think too long—the graveyard's full of men who spent too much time thinking and not enough acting. Oh, and sorry about this."

"S-sorry?" the man asked. "About wha—?"

Aaron brought the handle of his sword down into the man's temple, knocking him unconscious. He stared down at the man for a second, hoping that he would listen and would get out of the city before it was too late. Then he turned to see how the others were faring. Darrell had one man left standing in front of him; the other three lay on the ground bleeding, though whether dead or unconscious Aaron couldn't tell. Leomin was facing off against the hulking creature, the blood on his blade letting Aaron know he'd at least gotten in a glancing blow, but the creature seemed unaffected.

Wendell stood a short distance behind the creature. He held a handful of rocks, and he was shouting curses as he threw them at the back of the thing's hooded head, but it didn't even seem to notice. *It's as if the bastard forgets he has a sword every time he gets in a fight,* Aaron thought. The kid, Caleb, stood behind the sergeant, his eyes scanning the street as if looking for something.

Aaron turned at a shout from Leomin, and saw the Parnen backpedaling away from the swings of the creature's mighty fists. He saw, too, that in another few seconds the Parnen was going to be trapped against the gatehouse with nowhere to run.

Aaron forced his weary body into a sprint, coming at the creature from the side just as it jerked the Parnen up off the ground by the front of his tunic. He slammed into it with all the strength and momentum he could muster. It was like striking a wall of solid brick, and his teeth smashed together, cutting his tongue, and the warm, coppery taste of blood flooded his mouth. He rebounded off the thing, falling to the ground, and it barely even staggered a step, but it was enough for it to relax its hold on the Parnen. The creature growled and started toward Aaron with long, deceptively fast strides. "Caleb!" Aaron shouted, as he stumbled groggily to his feet and backed away. "Get the horses!"

He didn't have time to look and see if the boy was listening as the creature was swinging an arm with enough power that it could knock Aaron's head from his shoulders. He ducked under the blow, striking it on the pressure point on the inside of the under-arm, but it didn't seem to notice. It swung again, and this time Aaron stepped to the side, bringing out his sword and ramming it into the creature's stomach.

It let out a growl that sounded more like annoyance than pain, and back-handing Aaron in the shoulder. Aaron's sword ripped free of the creature as he went flying through the air, his entire arm abruptly numb. He struck the city wall with a crash that made his bones ache and collapsed to one knee, hissing in agony. Pain, white-hot and terrible, lanced through his shoulder as he tried to rise, and he faltered. He risked a glance up, saw that the creature was moving toward him, saw that the sergeant had finally drawn his own blade and was moving in behind it. "No!" Aaron growled, remembering how useless his sword had been against the creature. "Help the boy get the horses, Sergeant!"

Wendell hesitated, as if unsure. "That's an order, you ugly bastard!" Aaron yelled. Then he leaned back against the wall and used his good arm to lever himself up, grunting in pain as he did, his entire body feeling as if he'd been trampled by a horse. He'd only just made it to his feet when the creature was there, grabbing for him. Aaron stumbled away, barely avoiding the thing's grasp.

He saw his sword lying on the cobbles a few feet away and began limping toward it. A shout from down the street drew his attention, and he looked up to see at least two dozen soldiers rushing toward the gate from the other end of the street.

"*Shit.*" He spun and saw that Wendell was leading the horses out of the gate and that Darrell and Leomin were helping, the swordmaster apparently having finished his last man. "We've got to go!" Aaron yelled. "Where's the kid?"

The three men looked around, obviously clueless themselves. "Damnit," Aaron said, shuffling toward where his sword lay. He bent down and scooped it up with his good arm, turning back to see the creature walking slowly toward him, implacable and unafraid.

Aaron backed toward the gate's entrance, but the creature took two long, lumbering steps and was on him. He tried to dodge its grab, but his injured body was slow to respond, and it caught the front of his tunic, lifting him up much as it had the Parnen. Aaron hissed and ran his sword through the creature's chest, but it didn't even flinch as the steel sank in. It wrapped its other, massive hand around his throat and began to squeeze. Aaron struggled and failed to draw a breath as he kicked his legs out in a vain effort to break the thing's hold.

"*Aaron, move!*" He turned at the shout to see the kid, Caleb, sprinting out of the gatehouse toward Wendell and the others. Frowning, he followed the kid's wide-eyed gaze up to see the gate falling down and realized that he and the giant creature were standing right in the path of the metal spikes underneath it.

Knowing he had only a moment, Aaron stopped struggling against the creature's grip for long enough to rip his sword free of it and to swing it at the thing's wrist, as hard as his awkward position would allow. Unbelievable strength and an incredible tolerance for pain were all well and good, but a man's body was still connected by muscles and ligaments, tendon and bone, and the blade bit deep into a wrist as thick as most people's thighs. The creature let out a roar so loud that it seemed to shake Aaron's chest, but its grip loosened. Aaron planted both feet on the creature's stomach and, with a shout, he kicked off as hard as he could, sailing through the air to land hard on his back, rolling end over end until he finally came to a stop in an exhausted, agonized heap.

A *crash* split the air, and Aaron lifted his weary head, blinking away the spots that had formed in his vision and gasping air into his starved lungs. The spikes of the bottom of the gate had impaled the creature through its back, but it still stood, its thick muscles straining against the heavy metal. Its hood had flown back at some point, and Aaron stared into the twisted, scarred face of a thing out of nightmare, a face that could express nothing but rage and hate. He watched as the gate slowly, inexorably, forced the creature further down until it fell onto one knee with enough force to shake the ground. Aaron glanced past the creature and saw that the soldiers were halfway to the gate, then he started to struggle to his feet.

He gasped from the pain of trying to move his battered body and, in a moment, Darrell and Leomin were on either side of him, helping him up. "Can you ride?" Darrell asked, eyeing Aaron with a troubled expression on his face.

Aaron hacked and coughed before he was able to speak. "I damned sure…better be able," he panted. "Just help me to get on a horse."

They led him to his horse, and lifted him into the saddle. Aaron swayed uncertainly for a moment, dark spots dancing in his vision, but he managed to keep his seat. His left arm was still numb and hung useless at his side. He glanced over, his head bobbing dangerously, to see that the kid had already mounted. "Won't they just open the gate?"

The youth gave a vicious smile. "Eventually, but they won't have an easy time of it. The gate operates with a two-part counterweight system neither of which, I'm afraid, is still connected."

"How long?"

The youth's smile faded, and he shrugged uncertainly. "There's no way to know for sure. A few hours, perhaps a little longer."

Aaron nodded. The men might ride around to one of the other gates, but they would lose time doing it just the same. "Alright, you heard the kid," he said to the men, "let's go."

***

They rode on through the forest for the rest of the day, stopping from time to time to walk the horses and give them a break. They spoke little, as it was all any of them could do to not fall out of their saddles in exhaustion. A thing Aaron thought was just as well since the quiet would give them a better chance of hearing any pursuers. *Unless it's one of those fast bastards,* he thought, *then we'll all be dead before we hear anything at all.*

It wasn't a comforting thought, but then there wasn't much to find comfort in given their current situation. They were being hunted by creatures that most people wouldn't believe existed, they were battered and bruised, not broken but nearly so, and even if they somehow managed to make it to back to Perennia, they had no proof to offer the armies of Avarest, no evidence to show them. Only words, and after a life spent in the Downs, Aaron knew well the worth of words, had seen their uselessness in the empty promises of whores, and the vows of men hired to be bodyguards only to turn on their masters as soon as they saw an advantage in doing so.

They will believe you, Co said, *they have to.*

I wouldn't get my hopes up, firefly. Aaron thought back as he dismounted his horse and starting leading it down the path, the others following his example in silence. *Men have a tendency not to believe anything they don't want to unless the undeniable proof is before their eyes—sometimes even then. And we're going to go back and tell them that Belgarin isn't really Belgarin at all but an ancient wizard from thousands of years ago who is creating an army of monsters to take over the world?* He grunted. *Might as well tell them that the dead have risen from their graves and are marching on the city. They still wouldn't believe it, but at least it would get a laugh.*

So what do you intend to do?

Aaron sighed, rubbing at his grainy eyes as he focused on putting one foot in front of the other, *I intend to try, firefly. It's the most that any of us can do.*

They led the horses on in silence, the minutes stretching on and on. Several times, he or one of the others slipped and fell. The first few times, they helped each other up, asking if they were okay, but in the face of their overwhelming exhaustion, soon even those niceties vanished, and they would all merely wait, silent, as the one who had fallen dragged himself to his feet. They kept going until the sun set and darkness took over the world in full. Aaron intended to keep walking, but after the kid fell for the third time within no more than a fifteen minute span, he decided that they had to stop. "We've got to make camp." None of them had spoken in several hours, and his voice sounded strange to his own ears, an intruder in the darkness of the forest.

"You...sure, sir?" Wendell asked, his own voice raspy from disuse. "The soldiers..."

"I know," Aaron said. "But either they'll catch us or they won't. At least this way, maybe we'll have some rest when they do. Besides, they show up now, I don't trust myself to fight very hard, as death is starting to seem more and more like an opportunity to rest."

No one else objected, but Aaron expected that was more due to their own exhaustion than agreement. Still, they followed him as he led them off the path and into the cover of the forest. They tied their horses to a nearby tree and made camp, if it could be called that. They lit no fires, nor did they even take the time to take out their bedrolls or remove their boots. Instead, they all lay down in a ragged circle, the others asleep almost instantly. Aaron lay awake, gazing at the night's sky and listening to the sound of his companions' ragged snoring. For him, sleep was not so easy in coming. His wounds pained him, but at least he was beginning to get the feeling back in his arm from where the creature had struck him.

He lay there, staring between the boughs of the trees overhead at the moon hanging distant in the sky, his eyelids growing heavy. *Should really set someone to watch,* he thought, even went so far as opening his mouth to say so when sleep lunged forward, a beast that had been waiting for its chance to strike, and took him down, down, down into the darkness.

***

Aaron awoke to someone nudging him in the side with the toe of a boot. He opened one eye, glancing up to see that the moon was still high in the sky, and rolled over. "Not yet," he grunted. "Get some rest."

The offending boot prodded him once more, hard enough to hurt, and Aaron growled, lurching to a sitting position. "Look, we've got a long couple of weeks ahead of us and—" He went silent at the sight of the man standing over him, a drawn blade in his hand. Aaron didn't waste time on words—he'd seen plenty of men do just that when he was the one with the naked steel, and they the ones roused from sleep. Most were dead now. Instead, he lunged from his seated position—his wounds crying out in protest as he did—and tackled the man at the knees. The stranger, whoever he was, cried out in surprise, and Aaron punched him twice in the face. He saw movement out of the corner of his eye, a shadow gliding closer out of the darkness, and he rolled off of the man, toward where he'd left his sword lying on the ground.

He searched frantically for the blade, but the only thing beneath his questing fingers was dirt, grass, and the dead leaves that littered the forest floor.

"You won't find it," a feminine voice said from somewhere in the darkness, "and it wouldn't matter if you did. Even you, Mr. Envelar, for all your skill, could not, I think, dodge two dozen crossbow bolts."

Aaron searched for another moment then grunted with pain as he rose to his feet, peering into the darkness. He couldn't make out much, but what little moonlight there was allowed him to see shadows surrounding him and the others, shadows that held what very well could have been crossbows. "What do you want?" he said, gazing in the direction from which the voice had come, a voice that struck him as vaguely familiar.

"It is not about what I *want*, Mr. Envelar. It is about what the world *needs*."

Aaron grunted in recognition. "Damn but I knew I'd heard that voice before. You know, lady, you really need a new line. That shit about what the world needs is getting pretty old. Now, what are you doing out here? Little bit of a change from that cave you live in."

Tianya, the leader of the Tenders, stepped out of the shadows so that he could vaguely make her out in the streaks of moonlight that found their way in through the branches of the trees. "I am doing what I must, Mr. Envelar. What you have forced me to do."

Aaron didn't like the sound of that, not at all. "Look, Tianya," he said, moving toward her, "I don't know what you're talking about, but I don't have time for your games right now. We only stopped to get a few hours of sleep. There are people a—"

The woman motioned with her hand, and Aaron grunted in surprise as something struck him in the side of the head. He fell to his hands and knees from the force of the blow and looked up, his head spinning, to see a soldier standing over him holding a sword, the handle of it bloody in the moonlight.

"Yes, Mr. Envelar," Tianya said, moving closer so that she stared down at him, "there *are* people. People who will all suffer and die terrible deaths if Kevlane gets his hands on the other Virtues. And yet you and the Parnen traipse across the countryside as if you're on some sort of holiday while you carry the fate of the world with you."

"*Holiday?*" Aaron rasped, pausing to spit out a mouthful of blood. "Damnit, you don't have any idea what you're talking about. Tianya, listen to me, there are things—" He had just started to look up at her when a boot connected solidly with his jaw, knocking him onto his back.

"No," the woman said, her voice stern as if speaking to some wayward child, "the time for talking is past, Mr. Envelar. I tried to make you understand, to make you see reason, but if you will not flee, will not do what needs to be done to protect the world from this threat, then there are other ways." She turned to one of the men beside her. "Rouse the others and bind them."

Grunting, Aaron pushed himself to a sitting position, all too aware of the crossbows pointed at him as he rubbed at his jaw where she'd kicked him. "What do you think you're going to do, Tianya? Throw us in a cage and ship us away to some far-off land? Wherever you put us, we'll break out. Surely, you're not so stupid you don't realize that."

In the shaft of moonlight, he saw the woman's slow, sad smile. "The thought had come to my mind as well, Mr. Envelar," she said, her tone regretful, "we would take precautions, of course, but a man of your talents and skills...well, I do not think it would be long before you managed to break out of whatever prison we put you in, even if it was for your own protection that you were placed there."

Aaron shook his head in an effort to clear his blurry vision. "Then why the fuck are you out here?"

The leader of the Tenders sighed. "Unfortunately for you, Mr. Envelar, there is another way to ensure that the Virtue is kept well away from Kevlane and those who serve him. By giving it to someone who will listen, who will see reason and allow himself to be protected, we will ensure not just his safety, but the safety of the world itself."

"Wait," Aaron said, realization settling in him. "I didn't think there was any way to take a Virtue from another person. What are you talking about?"

"There's not," the woman agreed, "at least, that is, while the Virtue's bondmate is alive."

Aaron opened his mouth to speak but several soldiers, their blades drawn, led Wendell, Leomin, and Caleb forward. The youth rubbed at his eyes, glancing around himself as if confused about what was happening. "I told you to bind them," Tianya said.

"Of course, ma'am," one of the soldiers said, bowing his head in acquiescence, "only, there's something I thought you should know."

"Well?"

"Darrell's not here, ma'am. We found some of his things, but as for him..."

Tianya let out a hiss of frustration at that, and turned back to Aaron. "Where is Darrell?"

Aaron frowned, seeming to consider. "Darrell...I know that name seems familiar. Can you describe him?"

The woman's face grew hard, and she motioned to the soldier standing beside Aaron. Something struck him a powerful blow in the head again, and the next thing he knew he was lying on his back staring up at the trees overhead, their branches like grasping hands in the darkness. The soldier who'd struck him stood over him, a small grin on his face. Aaron put his hand to his head and felt it come away wet with blood then stared up at the soldier. "You'll pay for that."

The man's grin only widened further. "I have little patience for your mockery just now, Mr. Envelar." Tianya said, looking down at him in disgust. "In order to protect the world and its people, I have no choice but to sacrifice you, to take back the gift which you have been given so that it might be safeguarded from Kevlane and those like him. You must die, either way, but if you tell me where Darrell is, you need not suffer."

"Lady," Aaron said, spitting out another mouthful of blood, "I grew up as an orphan in one of the meanest places a man can find. Suffering is how I know I'm alive."

"Wait," the woman said, holding up a hand, her head tilted to the side as if she could hear something. Suddenly, her eyes went wide. "Behi—" She hadn't got the word out before a sword was suddenly at her throat.

"Hello, Tianya," Darrell said, grabbing her and moving her so that she stood in front of him, his blade within inches of her neck.

Several of the soldiers started forward, and Darrell brought his blade closer, "Tell them to drop their crossbows. They might take me but not before I kill you."

"Darrell, Darrell," Tianya said, "do you really not know me better than that after all this time? Kill them all," she said to her soldiers, "and take the Virtues away from here."

The men hesitated as if unsure, and Aaron rose laboriously to his feet. He glanced around him, reaching out to the soldiers with his bond, and felt the uncertainty in them. She was their leader, after all, and they dared not risk her life, yet the Virtues had to be protected. Aaron smiled, turning back to Tianya. "Well shit, lady. It seems to me that maybe not everybody is as willing to kill to get what they want as you are."

"It's not about what I want, you fool!" she screeched. "It's about the world!"

"Yeah," Aaron said, nodding and immediately regretting the motion as pain shot through his neck and throbbing head, "and if you believe that," he said, turning to look at the soldiers scattered among the shadows of the trees, "then I've got a potion I'll sell you. Tastes like water, but it'll make your dick grow five inches." The men didn't laugh, but then he hadn't really expected them to. For all of their indecision, these men had dedicated their lives to protecting the Virtues, to doing what their leader told them.

"Listen to me, Tenders," Tianya yelled, her voice filling the clearing, and Aaron noted by her pained expression what it cost her to speak so loudly while having the Virtue of Perception, "what we do is not about one man or woman but about the world itself. Now, fulfill your oaths and do what has to be done!"

Through his bond, Aaron felt the minds of the soldiers shift at her words, felt each of them making the decision to follow their leader's orders.

"You don't have to do this," Darrell said, but Aaron knew, even as the swordmaster spoke, that it was too late. The men had made their decision, had jumped from a precipice from which there was no coming back.

The man beside him began to raise his sword, but Aaron felt the attack coming, and he was faster. His blow struck the man's throat, and he felt something crush beneath his fist.

The man stumbled backward, dropping his sword as he fell, and Aaron scooped it up off the ground, spinning. A crossbow bolt flashed out of the darkness and sunk into the swordmaster's shoulder, its tip coming out only inches from Tianya's face. Darrell cried out in shock and pain, releasing the leader of the Tenders as he spun toward the soldier who'd fired.

There was a frozen instant of confused silence as Aaron and his companions stared at the soldiers surrounding them, and the soldiers stared back. Then, suddenly, the night was filled with a thundering roar louder than anything Aaron had ever heard, and Tianya screamed in agony, falling to her knees, her hands clasped over her ears. Something massive charged out of the night, slamming into the nearest warrior. There was a loud snapping sound as the man's bones broke on impact, and he went flying through the air, dead before he slammed into the thick trunk of a tree.

The soldiers had been ready to murder, had been willing to even give their own lives for their duty, but that didn't stop them from shouting in shock and fear at the sight of the impossibly big, lumbering figure. It stepped into a bit of moonlight, and Aaron noted that there were several large bloody holes in its chest, and one of its hands hung uselessly from its wrist, nearly completely severed. "Son of a bitch," he said. *It's the same one we fought. But the gate collapsed on it, I saw it. How is that even possible? That fucker should be dead.*

In his experiments while under my father, Co said, *Kevlane also learned how to make those he twisted with the Art take great wounds without dying.*

Something you maybe could have mentioned earlier, firefly, Aaron thought. "Darrell!" he shouted. He hoped that the swordmaster would hear him over the tumult of battle as the massive creature waded into the soldiers, flinging them left and right like broken dolls, and seemingly unaffected by the dozen crossbow bolts sticking out of him. The swordmaster turned to look. "Horses!" Aaron yelled. "Get the horses!"

Darrell gave a nod and vanished into the darkness. Aaron turned to see Wendell struggling with one of the soldiers that had apparently decided to follow his leader's orders, and never mind the hulking monstrosity killing his friends. Thinking of Tianya, Aaron glanced around and realized that she was gone. "So much for the greater good," he muttered.

He half-stumbled, half-ran to where the soldier had knocked Wendell onto his back and was preparing to strike. Aaron didn't hesitate, sweeping his sword out and taking the man's head off at the neck in a shower of blood.

Wendell sputtered, gagging as the blood flew into his face, before he managed to push the man off. "Gods, sir, but you could have warned me first." He hacked and spat as he rose to his feet. "Damn, but it's in my mouth."

"Sorry," Aaron said dryly, "next time, I'll try to let you know before I save your life."

"Good," the sergeant said, nodding, "that'll be fine."

"You two okay?" Aaron asked, turning to look at Leomin and Caleb.

"F-f-fine," Caleb managed, and the Parnen nodded.

Aaron risked another glance back into the chaos, and saw that the Tenders were now working in unison. They got in several good strikes, but the creature didn't seem to mind, and anyone it laid a hand on was left a battered, broken corpse. There were only a half a dozen of the soldiers left, and the thing showed no signs of slowing. "Alright then," Aaron said, "time to go."

He led them to where he'd seen Darrell vanish into the trees, and they'd only just arrived when the swordmaster returned leading five horses. They maneuvered them out of the thick trees and toward the forest trail, the sounds of men fighting and dying echoing behind them in the darkness.

On the trail, they mounted their horses. Aaron listened and realized that he no longer heard the sounds of fighting from within the forest. "Shit. Let's go." They started down the path at a gallop, Aaron in the lead, Wendell bringing up the rear. They'd been moving for no more than thirty seconds when Aaron heard a loud *crack* and a massive tree tipped over, crashing down in front of them. He shouted in surprise, jerking on his horse's reins, and they skidded to stop just in time to avoid charging head first into it.

Aaron scanned the forest around them, and wasn't surprised when the creature stepped out onto the trail. Away from the cover of the trees, the moonlight illuminated the path enough that Aaron could see the hulking figure as it walked toward them. Its cloak had been torn off at some point, and its naked chest and back were crisscrossed with old scars and long, jagged cuts that leaked blood, proof of its recent battle with the Tenders. It was bloody and it was hurt, but it was coming just the same.

Aaron slid from his horse, his wounds still paining him, and pulled his sword, watching the creature approach. "*Get back to Perennia,*" he yelled to the others. "I'll hold him for as long as I can. Someone has to make it back, otherwise this has all be—" He cut off at the sound of a shout, and turned to see Wendell atop his horse, charging straight at the creature, the horse's hooves striking the ground with a sound like thunder. Aaron dove out of the way of the onrushing beast, hitting the ground and spinning to look back. The horse struck the creature with incredible force, and unnatural twisted strength or not, the creature went down beneath its kicking, trampling hooves as Wendell was thrown from the saddle. Aaron stared as the horse brought its legs down again and again on the creature's chest and face, smashing what was left of the thing's nose and, by the sound of it, breaking several ribs.

I'm really going to have to send that stableman some gold, Aaron thought. He was just starting to think the horse would do the creature in, when the monstrosity suddenly reached out with a hand twice the size of a normal man's and grabbed hold of the horse's throat. The animal let out a cry, struggling to get away, but the creature strained its massive arms, and the horse flew through the air, striking a tree with a terrible crash. It collapsed to the ground where it lay unmoving.

Aaron was still staring at the thing lying on its back, stunned, when the sergeant limped toward him, his left leg dragging. His face was twisted in pain but when he came to stand in front of Aaron and speak, his voice was calm enough. "If you don't mind, sir," he said, reaching for the sword Aaron still held in his hand, and Aaron let him take it.

Sword in hand, the sergeant limped toward the creature who was even now trying to rise, but failing due to one of its legs having been crushed by the horse's hooves. When Wendell halted, standing over it, the creature's fingers moved sluggishly as if it was trying to reach for him. But apparently, throwing the horse had taken the last of whatever strength it had left, and it only watched him with eyes that, to Aaron at least, seemed all too aware.

Wendell didn't hesitate, driving the sword into the creature's chest. "Die, you fucker," he said, but the creature's remaining hand still stirred toward the sergeant. He stepped out of the way of the slow grab, driving the blade into the creature's chest and stomach again and again. "Die, you fucker!" he yelled. "Die!"

The sergeant kept at it, and Aaron only watched, saw the moment when the creature finally grew still and the light of life left its eyes, but Wendell didn't stop, panting as he brought the sword down with all of his strength, over and over again. Aaron heard someone approach and turned to see Leomin moving to stand beside him. "Mr. Envelar," he said, his tone worried, "perhaps we should let friend Wendell know that it—whatever it was—is dead."

"It's not though," Aaron said, his eyes going back to the sergeant as he went about his grizzly task, "not to him, anyway. Sometimes, Leomin, defeating the thing that scares us isn't enough. Sometimes, we need to see it chopped up into little pieces in front of us, to see the pieces burned to ash and scattered on the wind. Trust me on this."

The Parnen nodded slowly. "As you say, Mr. Envelar."

After a moment, Darrell and Caleb came to stand beside the two of them, bringing the horses with them, and the four of them watched as the sergeant continued driving the blade in. Oblivious—or uncaring—of the blood that splashed onto his tunic and trousers, he began to swing the sword in wide, two-handed arcs like a man chopping wood for his fire. Five minutes later, Wendell stumbled and half-sat, half-collapsed on the ground, his breath coming in ragged gasps.

"Are you finished, Sergeant?" Aaron asked.

"Yes...sir," Wendell panted, "just...wanted to make sure is all."

"Well," Aaron said, "if you're satisfied, how about we get out of here?" He glanced back down the path leading to Baresh. "That one might be dead but, unless I miss my guess, there's plenty more left to get the job done, if we hang around long enough."

"Sounds good," Wendell said, nodding as he wiped his arm across his forehead to clean off the blood. The problem, of course, was that he was soaked from head to toe in the stuff. He seemed to strain for a minute, his face twisting with effort, then grunted. "Think I might need a little bit of help here."

Darrell and Leomin hurried forward, pulling the sergeant to his feet. The swordmaster was saying something to the sergeant, congratulating him for his quick thinking, Aaron thought, but he was barely listening. He was too busy staring at the dead creature lying in the road, an idea forming in his mind. "Hurry, if you can," Aaron said, "we're going to be making worse time on the way back as we'll be riding two to a horse."

Leomin looked up from where he and the swordmaster were helping the sergeant to his own horse. "Double, Mr. Envelar? Then...who gets the extra horse?"

Aaron gave the man a grim smile, pointing his finger at the massive corpse. "He does."

CHAPTER TWENTY-FOUR

Savrin woke to a world of pain. His entire body hurt, and he looked down to see that he was lying in a bed. He tried to sit up but groaned, falling back against the mattress.

"Ah, you're awake."

He turned at the sound of the voice to find the king's advisor sitting in a chair beside the bed, watching him. The thin man had a slight smile on his face, but there was nothing reassuring about it.

"Where...where am I?" His words came out in a dry rasp.

"A healer's tent," Caldwell said. "A good thing too. From what I saw while you slept, you needed it." The advisor studied him, shaking his head slowly. "You must tell me, Savrin, what possessed you to go after Aaron Envelar and his companions by yourself. A foolish mistake, that."

Savrin watched the thin man studying him with eyes that somehow reminded him of a vulture's, and he forced what strength he could into his voice. "Wasn't...alone."

"Ah, I see," the king's advisor said, nodding slowly, "you speak of the experiment, do you not?"

"Yes," Savrin managed, "they were hurt, nearly done in. I'm sure it must have taken them after—"

"It is dead," the advisor said flatly.

"Dead?" Savrin said, disbelieving. From what he'd seen, the creatures were almost impossible to kill.

Caldwell shrugged as if it made little difference. "It hasn't returned at any rate, and it would have by now, had it been able. I must tell you, Captain," the advisor said, leaning forward, "the master is not pleased. No," he said, shaking his head, "he is not pleased at all. Not only did you cause a scene in the city with one of the experiments—experiments the master wishes to keep hidden as long as he is able—but you also learned of the presence of the master's worst enemies, and chose to take it upon yourself and one other to attack them."

"I...I thought—"

"Oh, never mind what you thought," the thin man said. "I know that well enough, I believe. You wished to capture them yourself, did you not? Thought that, perhaps, if you should deliver unto the master his worst enemies, then you might be allowed to absent yourself from his service. Might even be able to go to your sister Pella. Isn't that right?"

Savrin felt a rush of fear at hearing the cruel man voice his sister's name, but he did his best to hide it. "There...wasn't any time," he said. "They could have left the city or..." he shrugged, unable to think of anything else to say.

"Captain, Captain," Caldwell said, shaking his head disapprovingly, "surely, you can do better than that, can't you?"

Savrin swallowed hard. "There was another, though. One of the fast ones. It—"

"Dead," the advisor interrupted, "found by some sailor out for a late-night drink." He waved a hand at the alarm on Savrin's face. "I wouldn't worry about him—he was silenced, as were those who were present near the western gate when the fugitives made their escape. No, were I you, Captain, I would have some very different concerns. The master is not a man—a *god*—known for his patience or his mercy, and after the trouble you caused him two nights ago, he is even less inclined to either than usual. In fact, he has asked me to make his disapproval clear to you."

Suddenly, Savrin's mouth was terribly dry. "I can fix this," he said. He strained once more to sit up, but his body would not obey his commands, and he finally collapsed back to the bed covered in sweat, his breathing ragged. "I can fix it," he said again, "just...if you'll just give me time."

"Time?" Caldwell asked, as if he'd never heard the word before, "Oh, I'm afraid we are out of *time*, Captain. You see, Aaron Envelar and his companions have made good their escape, taking—thanks to you—more than a little knowledge of what they will face and, as a result, taking whatever time you might have had."

"But...it's not too late," Savrin said, "the fast ones—"

"The 'fast ones,' as you call them, are not made to travel long distances, Captain. Envelar and his followers are on horse with a two-day lead. They would not catch them, not before they reached the walls of Perennia."

"I'll take a horse then," Savrin said, hating the desperation he heard in his own voice. "I'll handle them myself. If you'll just let me try to—"

"Handle them yourself?" the advisor asked, his voice almost kind. "The same way that you handled them at the gate? The same way that wound up with them escaping and you lying in a healer's bed, too hurt to move?" He shook his head. "No, Captain. The time for such things has passed and, even if you were to catch them, you would not be able to take them. Not as you now are."

Savrin felt hopelessness rise in him and, with it, anger. "Well, if you've come to kill me," he said, "then just get it done with. I won't beg, not for you or for *him*."

"*Kill* you?" Caldwell asked, his voice shocked. "Why, Captain, we aren't going to kill you. A man with such martial prowess as yourself? No, that would be a foolish waste, and my master does not believe in waste." The advisor paused, his grin widening, and there was something about the expression that sent a shiver of fear down Savrin's back. "We will not kill you, Captain. But we *will* make you better. So that, next time, you will not be defeated so easily."

Savrin's eyes went wide. "No," he said, "you can't mean..."

"But I do," Caldwell said, "and do not look so frightened, Captain. You have always wanted to be the best fighter in the world, have you not? Well, you will not believe the things of which you will be capable, once my master has finished with you."

"You...you mean to make me a monster," Savrin said, his voice low and weak.

Caldwell rolled his eyes, "*Monster*, you say. You are to be made to serve, Captain, that's all. It is an honor. But, alas, as for your belief that you will not beg...I'm afraid that is one promise that you will break. You see," he said, leaning closer so that Savrin could feel the warmth of his breath on his face, "big or small, strong or weak, they always beg, Captain. Always."

"No," Savrin growled, struggling again to rise. His fear lent him strength, and he managed to jerk himself to a sitting position, but he was forced to pause there for a moment to catch his breath. "I won't let you do that to me."

Caldwell sighed. "Oh, Captain," he said, "after all that you have witnessed, you still think that you have a choice?" The advisor rose and walked to the door, swinging it open and stepping to the side.

One of the massive cloaked creatures walked into the small room, having to bend nearly double to make it through the door frame.

"No!" Savrin yelled, real panic setting in now. He threw his legs over the side of the bed and rose on uncertain feet. "No, gods, please..."

"Gods?" Caldwell asked, looking back at him from the doorway, "there are no gods here, Savrin. As for *our* god, well, you should be grateful. He has given you a second chance."

Savrin screamed, charging for the man, but the massive creature scooped him up easily. Savrin called on what little strength he had and struck the creature in the face as hard as he could. Its head didn't even so much as rock back, and it reached out a hand, almost casually, and grabbed his wrist. It twisted with apparently no effort and all, and sudden pain, hot and bright, shot through Savrin. He screamed again, but this time it was not in anger but in unbelievable agony and shock as he stared at his twisted wrist, his hand dangling at an impossible angle.

"If he continues to scream," the advisor said, his voice calm, "rip out his tongue."

Savrin struggled against the pain, his breath coming in ragged gasps. "I will kill you," he said, meeting the thin man's gaze.

Caldwell smiled, "Oh, Savrin," he said, shaking his head, "once our master is done with you, you won't even remember me." He turned to the creature once more. "Let's go. It would not do to keep the master waiting. And take care of the healer on the way out—there cannot be any witnesses."

The creature hefted Savrin over one shoulder, not even seeming to notice his weak, useless struggles. *Pella*, he thought, *I'm sorry. Gods, but I'm sorry.* They were his last thoughts before the pain washed over him in a towering tidal wave, burying him, and his consciousness, beneath it.

CHAPTER TWENTY-FIVE

Aaron stumbled out of the last of the forest and breathed a heavy sigh of relief as he looked on the white stone walls of Perennia in the distance. The trip through the forest had been a long, hard one. They had done what they could to bind each other's wounds, but they were no healers, and the exhaustion and pain they'd experienced had long since etched itself onto the faces of him and his companions. The journey had been made worse by the fact that they had regularly been forced to stop and switch the corpse to another horse as the animals could not bear the weight for long. The creature weighed far more than any normal man and that, coupled with their injuries, had made moving it from one horse to another almost an impossible task. Several times, Aaron had considered leaving the damned thing and never mind Grinner and Hale and their "proof."

Now though, gazing at the walls of the city, he was glad that they hadn't. So close to the city, the trials they'd experienced over the last several weeks did not seem as bad, and he was surprised to find a small smile on his face. The coming danger was still very real, but he felt better than he had in a very long time.

The others, clearly sharing his relief, moved to stand beside him. "Ah, thank the gods," Leomin said, "I would really love to take a bath."

"Yeah," Aaron said, glancing at the man and raising his eyebrow, "and maybe see a healer."

"And a whore."

They all turned to look at Wendell, and the sergeant shrugged, clearly unashamed, "You've got your ways, and I've got mine."

Aaron shook his head slowly. "Come on," he said, "let's get this walk over with."

***

Everyone was already in the audience hall when Aaron and the others shuffled in, their bodies covered in bandages nearly from head to toe, and the foul taste of the healer's drink still thick in Aaron's throat. Queen Isabelle sat on her raised dais in between the two tables. On the left table sat Adina, Gryle, May, Beth, Bastion, Captain Brandon Gant, and an older man that Aaron didn't recognize. On the right sat Grinner, his thickly muscled bodyguard standing behind him, Hale, and General Yallek.

They all looked up as Aaron and the others made their way inside, their faces stricken with surprise. "*Aaron?*" Adina said, then she was up and running to him, throwing herself against him. Despite the dull ache of his wounds, Aaron was glad for the embrace, for the feel of her against him.

"Thank the gods you're okay. But..." She paused, looking him up and down. "What happened to you? Are you alright?"

"I'm fine, Adina," Aaron said, giving her a smile.

"I'm good too," Wendell muttered, "in case anyone was wonderin'."

Several people laughed at that, including Aaron. The princess stepped forward and gave the sergeant a hug before kissing him on the cheek. "I'm very glad you're okay, Wendell." The sergeant's face turned a bright shade of red, and he grinned so widely that Aaron thought the man would be sore in the morning.

Adina went to Leomin and Darrell next, hugging each of the men in turn. She made it to the youth, Caleb, who looked shy and uncertain. "Hello," the princess said with a smile, "my name's Adina."

"M-my n-names, Caleb," the youth managed, swallowing hard.

"Normally," Aaron said dryly, "he doesn't stutter so much. Still, without him we never would have made it out of Baresh alive."

The youth shot a frown at Aaron, but Adina only laughed, offering him her hand. The kid blushed as if she'd just kissed him on the mouth and took her hand. "It's a pleasure to meet you, Caleb," Adina said, winking. "And thank you for keeping this one safe," she said, motioning to Aaron, "I know it isn't an easy job."

The kid nodded solemnly at that and soon the others were rising, even Isabelle herself, and moving toward Aaron and the others. "I knew you'd make it back," Captain Gant said, grinning. "Some bastards are just too stubborn to die."

"Got to admit, Silent," Hale said, the big man clapping Aaron on the back, "I didn't expect I'd see you again, not alive anyway. Still, I 'spose it ought to be a comfort, knowin' I ain't the only one has a hard time killin' you."

Aaron grunted. "Well, just so long as you're comforted, Hale. Next, maybe I'll read you a bedtime story."

The big man laughed his loud, bellowing laugh at that, and Grinner stepped forward, his bodyguard hovering behind him. "Yes," the older man said, "so you have returned. Still, I cannot help but notice that I do not see anything on you that might show us Belgarin's intentions. Are we to assume, then, that you failed at your task?"

The others looked at Aaron and his companions with the same question in their eyes, and Aaron turned to Wendell. "You may as well get it now."

The sergeant nodded, shuffling toward the doors, his leg still not fully healed. He gave the doors a rap, and soon the two guards stationed on the other side opened them wide. Aaron noted that their faces looked pale and sickly beneath their helmets. As pale as they looked though, they appeared considerably better than the eight men who carried a large, wrapped bundle, clearly straining under the weight of it.

"Where would you like for us to put it, sir?" one of the men asked, sounding out of breath.

"Just there will do fine," Aaron said, motioning in front of Grinner's feet, and the old crime boss gave him a suspicious frown, his bodyguard moving closer as the guards laid the bundle at Grinner's feet.

Aaron knelt, wincing as his wounds pulled, and glanced up at everyone who watched him, their expressions sober. "You wanted your proof," he said to Grinner, "well, here it is." They'd wrapped the body in blankets to try to keep the elements away as much as they could, but the smell of decomposition struck Aaron like a fist as he pulled the blankets free, exposing the creature. The days spent in the forest had not been kind, and its body was bloated with noxious gas, but its form and features could still be made out well enough, judging by the shouts of surprise as the others recoiled. The crime boss, Grinner, let out a squeak, stepping back and putting a hand over his mouth, and even Hale grunted in a mixture of surprise and disgust.

"Gods protect us," the queen said, her eyes wide, her complexion parchment-white. "What...what is it?"

"It used to be a man," Aaron said, "that much I can tell you. As for what it is now..." He glanced at the youth, Caleb, who looked slightly green despite the fact that he'd spent the better part of two weeks riding beside the creature.

"An abomination," the youth said, "created by Boyce Kevlane's use of the Art, his twisting of it."

Adina swallowed hard, coming to stand beside Aaron and leaning into him as if she'd fall without support. "It...are there more?"

"Many," Aaron said, "and this is not the only kind. Princess," he said, turning and holding her arms gently, "your brother, Belgarin...Kevlane has taken his place as king and used his powers to convince the city that he is their rightful king still."

Adina's eyes went wide at that and a flurry of emotions passed across her face. "Belgarin...he's dead then?"

"Yes, or so I believe."

She nodded, taking a slow breath, and Grinner grunted, "I'm sure this is all shocking enough—you should consider putting on a show in the street. I'm quite certain the poor commoners would be throwing their coppers at you for a chance to look at it. But are you trying to tell me that this," he said, and for all his talk, Aaron noted that he took another step back when he gazed at the corpse, "is the work of some wizard from thousands of years ago?"

"Yes."

"That's *ridiculous*," Grinner said, "everyone knows that Boyce Kevlane was just a myth. There is no truth—"

"Ah, shut the fuck up, Grinner," Hale said, pointing a thick finger at the corpse, "lay off it. Your proof is right there, plain enough to see if old age hasn't robbed you of your sight along with your wits."

The two men glared at each other, like animals preparing to go for one another's throats, but Brandon Gant stepped between them. "That's enough of all that," the captain said. "We've got more important things to worry about than your egos. Now," he said, turning to Aaron, "you said there were more of them?"

Aaron nodded. "If I'm not mistaken, a lot more. And there'll be more still before Kevlane's done."

The captain shook his head slowly, his eyes on the creature. "Gods preserve us. Was he as strong as he looks?"

"Stronger," Wendell said. "Fucker got impaled by a castle gate fallin' on 'em and had enough left to chase after us."

General Yallek moved forward, eyeing the corpse as if he thought it might rise and attack them at any moment. "This...Mr. Envelar, this changes everything."

"Aye," Hale said, "well, I 'spose we'll be needin' those troops from Galia sooner than we thought, aye, Princess?"

Aaron frowned at that, turning to look at Adina who had a slightly embarrassed expression on her face like that of a child who'd been caught doing something she shouldn't. She cleared her throat and met Aaron's gaze. "Aaron," she said, "I would like to introduce you to Captain Oliver." She indicated the man standing behind her. He was short but muscled, and the way he stood, light on his feet, made Aaron sure that the man was a skilled fighter.

Aaron nodded his head, and the short man nodded his in turn, his expression grim. "Captain Oliver," Adina said, "that is...*General* Oliver, is the commander of Galia's army." She met Aaron's gaze once more. "*My* army."

Aaron frowned. "Galia? But your kingdom was taken..."

"Yes," May said, coming to stand beside Adina and putting a hand on her shoulder, "but the princess here took it back. Or *queen*, I should say," she said, giving Adina a wink.

"You...went to Galia?" Aaron said, disbelieving. "Adina, the dangers..."

"Are no greater than what you four—sorry," she said, smiling at Caleb, "*five* faced. In fact," she said, looking meaningfully at their bandaged limbs, "I'd say they were less."

Aaron winced at that, but he finally nodded.

"Funny thing, sir," Wendell said. "You come back with a corpse, and she comes back with a kingdom."

May laughed, and Aaron turned to scowl at the sergeant. "Just whose side are you on, Sergeant?"

"The woman's, of course, sir," Wendell said as if it was obvious. "It's always the safest thing."

"This is some trick, that's all," Grinner said, shaking his head, refusing to believe it, "there is no way—"

Aaron, tiring of the man's blather, held out his hand, palm to the ceiling, and in a moment, Co appeared above it, a magenta ball filled with twisting, shifting light.

Grinner and several of the others gasped, retreating several steps back, as Leomin and Caleb followed suit, summoning their own Virtues. Aaron glanced at Gryle, and the man looked sheepishly around him before reaching out his own pudgy hand, a grimace on his face, as if he was preparing himself for pain. Then his, too, appeared, floating next to the other three.

Grinner stared at them wide-eyed. "What...that is...how—?"

"The Virtues, Grinner," Aaron said. "Everybody knows they're myths, but here they are anyway."

The room lapsed into silence then, the people unable to decide whether to keep their eyes on the Virtues or the corpse at their feet. Captain Gant was the first to recover. "So...what do we do?" he asked.

Aaron glanced at those standing around him before meeting Brandon's eyes. "What we can, Captain. We do what we can."

***

Boyce Kevlane stood gazing at the tournament grounds, his hands clasped behind his back. He watched as laborers went about preparing the fields for the coming contest. A contest in which the best warriors in all of Telrear would compete in feats of arms, of strength and speed where only the greatest of their number might triumph, winning gold that they would never have a chance to spend. *After all,* Kevlane thought, *wars must have soldiers.* "How long?" he asked.

"The workers assure me that it will be no longer than a week, Master," Caldwell said. "Nearly all of the inns in the city are already packed with men and women come for the contest, and more flood in every day."

"Good," Kevlane said, nodding, "that is very good. You have done well, Caldwell."

The advisor bowed his head. "Thank you, My Lord."

"And Captain Savrin?"

"We have him, as you requested, Master. He awaits your attention in the dungeons. If you'd like, I can have him put into a cell until you are ready for him."

Kevlane shook his head. "No, Caldwell. That will not be necessary. I had best see to Captain Savrin immediately. If he is as good of a swordsman as I have heard, then we might create something very special, he and I. Besides," he said, glancing once more at the tournament grounds, "before long, I will have more than enough work to keep me busy."

***

Aaron stood on the castle's balcony staring out at the city below, its building and people cloaked in a blanket of night. He'd spent most of the day since he and the others had returned listening to Leomin recount the events that had occurred in Baresh. Then Adina had described what had taken place in Galia. After that, they had spent the next several hours deliberating on their best course of action, the two crime bosses arguing and disagreeing with each other at every opportunity.

He was exhausted, not just physically but mentally as well. Yet the thought of going to sleep, of closing his eyes on the world while Kevlane and those who served him prepared an army greater—and more terrible—than any Telrear had ever seen gave him a panicked feeling. *Gods, but it's too much,* he thought.

You will do no one any favors by killing yourself with worry, Aaron, Co said.

No, I won't, he agreed. *Besides, there are plenty of people out there who'd feel cheated if I did.*

Once, long ago, when my father possessed little more than a band of a hundred soldiers, I snuck into his and my mother's room. I heard the same sort of doubt in his voice then as I hear in yours now. He was a man whose hopes for the world were matched only by his fears for it. Yet with those hundred men he was able to create a kingdom where people could live their lives in peace, protected from those who would break into their houses and murder them for no other purpose than the enjoyment of it.

Your father was a great man, firefly.

Yes. He was. And so are you.

Aaron snorted. *I'd have to disagree with you there, firefly. Anyway, you're forgetting one thing,* he thought, doing what he could to convey compassion in his thoughts, *your father died, in the end. He was conquered, his city brought low, and those people he had sworn to protect all murdered along with him.*

Yes, the Virtue said, and then they settled into silence. After a few minutes, Aaron heard the door open behind him and turned to see Adina walking outside to him, and despite all of his worries, his fears, he could not help but admire her beauty in the moonlight. "I thought I'd find you out here," she said, coming to stand beside him at the balcony's railing.

"Everything seems so small from up here," he said, turning to look back out at the city, "all the problems we face, the enemies who want to see us destroyed...nothing but tiny little specks, no bigger than grains of sand." He grunted. "And no less numerous."

"Perhaps our enemies are numerous," Adina said, putting her hand on his shoulder, "but so, too, are our friends, Aaron."

Aaron sighed. "Grinner and Hale, do you mean? If we somehow managed to defeat Kevlane, Adina, one of those crazy bastards would be next in line for my head."

She smiled, running a hand across his face. "And such a pretty head it is, too. Anyway, you don't have to worry. I'll protect you."

Aaron barked a laugh. "That so?"

"You would be surprised what I can do, if I have to," she said. "Only ask Captain Gant. He has been training me, after all."

"A real warrior then, are you?" Aaron asked, smiling.

She grinned too, slapping him on the arm, then suddenly her face sobered, her expression growing dark, and Aaron didn't have to use the power of the bond to know what she was thinking. She had, after all, told them of how she'd been forced to kill the man, Raste. "It wasn't your fault, Adina," he said softly, turning her to face him, "you did what you had to. That's as much as any man or woman *can* do."

She wiped at the tears gathering in her eyes, nodding. "I know," she said, "I did what I had to." She pulled him into a tight embrace, her breath warm on his neck. "And so will you, Aaron. So will Grinner and Hale, for that matter. We all know what is at stake now." She stepped back, meeting his eyes. "Tell me, truly, do you think we can beat Kevlane?"

Aaron considered, wishing he could lie to her but knowing she'd see it in his face. "No," he said finally.

"Oh, Aaron," she said, pulling him close once more, "then what do you aim to do?"

Aaron held her tight, feeling her warmth against him. "I aim to fight," he said, turning and looking once more in the direction of Baresh, at the dark fields and forest that were all that stood between them and an insane, ancient evil that sought their destruction. "It's as much as any man or woman can do."

**THE END
OF
BOOK FOUR
OF
THE SEVEN VIRTUES**

BY JACOB PEPPERS

To stay up to date on the next release and hear about other awesome promotions and free giveaways, sign up to my mailing list. For a limited time, you will also receive a FREE copy of *The Silent Blade,* the prequel to The Seven Virtues, when you sign up!

Go to JacobPeppersAuthor.com to claim your rewards now!

Thank you for taking the time to read *A Sellsword's Valor*. I hope you enjoyed reading it as much as I enjoyed writing it. If you're ready to continue your adventures with Aaron and the others, you can pick up your copy of *A Sellsword's Will*, the fifth book in The Seven Virtues, today!

If you enjoyed the book, I'd really appreciate you taking a moment to leave an honest review—as any author can tell you, they are a big help.

If you want to reach out, you can email me at JacobPeppersauthor@gmail.com or visit jacobpeppersauthor.com. You can also follow me at Facebook or on Twitter.

I can't wait to hear from you!

Note from the Author

And so we've come to the end of A Sellsword's Valor, the fourth book in The Seven Virtues series. This one was a blast to write, and I hope you enjoyed visiting with Aaron and the others once again as much as I did. We have come far into the darkness now, dear reader, where enemies abound and the true battle fast approaches. I will not tell you not to be afraid, for there is much to fear waiting further along the path we travel, and I worry that not all those who we have come to love will survive what's coming.

I cannot promise you safety where we go, nor can I promise that all will work out as we might hope, but know that wherever the path leads us, I will go there with you. And not only me but many others, a veritable army travels this ground with us, so many in number that their boots might shake the earth for miles in any direction. If, that was, they wore boots. Still, before the battle begins, I think that it is only decent of us to acknowledge them and their sacrifice, so I shall do so now.

Thank you, as always, to my wife for keeping the lights on while I venture into these worlds of shadow and sunlight. Thank you to my family for always standing at the ready, brandishing their weapons at the approaching hordes, and if sometimes they "accidentally" hit me in the back of the head with those weapons, well, I cannot fault them for that as the journey, and the book, always end up being better for it.

Thank you to those beta readers who have taken the time to journey into my world—they are the trailblazers, those who venture forth into the wilderness without home or hope and no idea of what they might find waiting for them.

Lastly, thanks to you, dear reader. Perhaps, you are not the first to arrive in this place, but you are no less necessary for all that, for without you, the battle cannot be fought at all. Now, this leg of the journey is done, but there is so much more waiting, good and evil both, I'll wager. I cannot swear I know where the path ends myself, nor what waits for us along it—I have a vague vision but no more than that, and it twists and shifts like shadows in the darkness. So keep your torch handy and your sword steady. We will be needing them before long.

Yours in battle,
Jacob Peppers

About the Author

Jacob Peppers lives in Georgia with his wife, his son, Gabriel, and three dogs. He is an avid reader and writer and when he's not exploring the worlds of others, he's creating his own. His short fiction has been published in various markets, and his short story, "The Lies of Autumn," was a finalist for the 2013 Eric Hoffer Award for Short Prose.

Printed in Great Britain
by Amazon